The
Teleportation
Of an
American Teenager

~ A Novel for All Ages ~

By
Andrew J. Rodriguez

Outskirts Press, Inc.
Denver, Colorado

The Teleportation of an American Teenager
A Novel for All Ages

Outskirts Press
http://www.outskirtspress.com

ISBN-10: 1-932672-79-6
ISBN-13: 978-1-932672-79-4

Library of Congress Control Number: 2005921069

Outskirts Press and the "OP" logo are trademarks belonging to
Outskirts Press, Inc.

Printed in the United States of America

Contents

Dedication

TO: My Grandchildren, Rachel, Jack, Alexia and Risa

Part One

CHAPTER *One*

THE WISDOM OF THE AGES

"Those who cannot remember the past are condemned to repeat it." *Jorge Santayana*

An eighteen year old from Yonkers, New York, crosses the boundaries of time to ensure spiritual enlightenment and everlasting peace to future generations of humans.

How did he do it?

I shall tell you:

By reaching the souls of the dead, ancestor worshippers of primeval Europe claimed to have found a way to capture the *"wisdom of the ages"* – a truism known to these prehistoric wizards as *"the incorruptible truths of history."*

To secure this incontestable power, Druid priests taught their Celtic clans the occult practice of dream teleportation, a surreptitious mode of traveling to the past by way of the subliminal.

In the 1920s, the spirit of a Druid high priest from ancient Ireland vests upon Ivan McKinley, an Irish-American teenager the gift of traveling back in time.

1

The condition; Ivan must help his mentor develop a universal order rooted in historical wisdom.

As a preamble to this incredible story, it is essential to disclose the unusual set of circumstances leading to the upcoming chain of events. Please bear with me for the next few pages as I try to legitimize Ivan's narratives thus adding a sense of virtue to a truly amazing story.

Some time plus or minus 5000 years B.C., mysterious events appear to have taken place in many parts of Europe, mainly from the area south of Gaul all the way north to the British Isles.

Stones cut in various shapes and sizes, some weighing up to thirty-five tons have been discovered from this period. Puzzling to the eyes of the modern observer, these systematically arranged megaliths seem to have been set, among other reasons, for a given tribe to worship and honor their ancestors, as observatories where primeval people studied the movement of the stars, sun and moon, and according to some scholars, as sacred places to reflect over incomprehensible events such as the alignment of the planets, giving us the impression that these ancient people were already familiar with various disciplines including astronomy.

Circular monuments such as the one found at Stonehenge, England, apparently were used as temples where worshippers would ask their ancestors for the fertility of the tribe, a successful hunt, and for their blessings.

Among the many shapes and sizes of these stones, those standing with a flat face, known as dolmens, were usually aligned with a conspicuous spot on the horizon to mark the extreme points of sunrise and sunset at different times of the year - in this way the tribe's astronomers could figure out the exact moment when a solar or lunar eclipse would occur, as well as determine with remarkable accuracy the exact dates when the changes of season would take place.

Tribal rituals were closely tied to these celestial wonders and it was important for the priests to know the exact moment to schedule their celebrations. We can also see from the precise alignment of these monuments that those erecting them were no

2

primitive food gatherers, but clever men of discipline, familiar with mathematical calculations, distance and space, and that they were expert geometrists and astronomers. Few places on earth have generated as much interest and controversy as the assembled megaliths of Stonehenge. As a person travels through the Salisbury Plains, finding this awesome and unusual monument provokes much wonder, as well as feelings of awe and insignificance brought about by its imposing presence. According to current archaeological theory, the monument must have been built 3000 years ago. A complex question remains however: How were these stones transported from quarries two hundred miles away?

Among the different hypotheses as to who built these mystifying monuments and why, most anthropologists attribute their existence to the Druids.

Recent speculation indicates that Stonehenge was not merely aligned to follow and record solar and lunar cycles, but for more complex and profound events taking place on Earth relative to outer dimensions.

Assumptions such as these recently paved the way for a group of speculators to assert that supernatural beings somehow intervened in its construction and reason to exist. In addition, some philosophers agree that the purpose for erecting the monument was to allow for harmonious interaction between Earth and the Otherworld. The stones were mysteriously chosen for their magnetic qualities perhaps because they were compatible with the magnetic grids believed to surround our planet.

According to another theory, some megaliths were placed in spots of solar and lunar concurrence, based on the builder's beliefs that planetary alignment must exist for divine interaction to occur -- the final communion between the living and the dead.

Most visitors feel its impact goes beyond understanding. Others contend it is a revelation from the past encrypted in stone for the benefit of the future.

Druids, besides being familiar with the arts of magic, telepathy, and telekinetics, also had a highly developed level of perception, as well as profound awareness of a universally consecrated plan. Recognizing the existence of humanity as an intrinsic part of a divine scheme, they respected and worshipped creation along with its spiritual abstractions. Unfortunately, their presence in world history did not endure long enough for humanity to appreciate their everlasting hunger for wisdom and truth.

Followed by setbacks inflicted upon Druid society by Saint Patrick, and then by the Romans, an enormous and complex infrastructure of knowledge and spirituality was totally destroyed. It wouldn't be an exaggeration to say that they were almost annihilated.

Patrick who referred to the Druids as "snakes", once attempted to starve and destroy their culture, and even though their desire was to compromise, the saint did not accept a dialogue or a resolution to their differences. In fact he resented their claim to access divine intercession through dreams for which they were renowned. Crying for their annihilation, Patrick accused them of heresy and witchcraft.

Though the Christians destroyed the Druid culture, the few who survived were able to maintain their beliefs and traditions by secretly passing them down to future generations.

The ancient Celtic society was broken into classes and social groups made up mainly of warriors and Druids, or priests, the latter also known as magicians and psychics. Celtic cultural values were equally based in spiritual beliefs and natural law. Their clans held democracy and responsibility as an intrinsic part of their value system, claiming that since all of creation originated from an omnipotent spiritual energy, everything in the universe, regardless of its reason to exist, shall be considered divine.

Most Celtic cultures worshipped their ancestors, and many of their early legends focused on defining how those relatives made their journeys into the Otherworld realms, from where they would become guides and shelter for future generations of their kin.

The Otherworld existed and exists for reasons

4

incomprehensible to the living. Yet, according to mythical accounts it is ever-present and all encompassing. Therefore, if we try to interpret ancient Irish beliefs with an open mind, we conclude that such realms indeed existed in their midst. They attributed the phenomena of dreams to profound spiritual energies arising from the Otherworld that would enable the living to tap the wisdom of their ancestors.

Let me take this opportunity to assure the reader that this story is not intended to stand as a recounting of ancient history or as a philosophical dissertation on Druidism; yet it is downright important to lay a solid and credible base to what will become an unusual journey into the Otherworlds of our past.

In fact, let's take a detour for a moment and talk about dreams. Every time we awaken to real life, we seldom recall the images that went through our minds the night before. Yet we experience dreams or nightmares almost every single time we sleep. In this light, shouldn't we consider them a fundamental part of our existence? Let's face it; the fact we can't remember them in the morning doesn't alter this underlying issue.

As another example, how many times do we awaken to chest palpitations in the middle of the night following a nightmare, and then feel suddenly relieved after realizing it was just a bad dream? Yet, what makes us feel so certain it all took place in our head? Is it because we feel safer accepting the scientific community's notion that dreams are nothing but brain waves? Or is it because some nightmares are so horrifying that we prefer to live in denial?

Regretfully, the significance of dreams has been so largely underestimated by our materialistic society that perhaps their impact should be re-evaluated to keep us from overlooking something in life we were never supposed to miss.

Modern technology has produced incredible scientific achievements, and yet we have totally forgotten the mystical realms that reign over creation and within ourselves.

The people of antiquity interpreted dreams purely as metaphysical experiences; therefore every dream encounter meant to them another form of reality impossible to elucidate, yet as real as the firmament above their heads. We must conclude that to these primitive societies, real life was mostly a combination of daily physical and metaphysical experiences in contrast to today's simplistic and elusive perception of the latter. It would take a profound philosophical and anthropological discussion to attain a consensus on all these issues. In the interest of brevity, I therefore propose we take a detour from these reflections and enter instead a less vague and more objective course, in the hope that by now the reader should feel more receptive and open-minded to viewing as reality what otherwise would have been interpreted as a series of impossibilities.

With this in mind I shall turn to the arrival of Grandfather McKinley to our real world.

George McKinley saw the light of day for the first time during the year 1840 at his parents' cottage near the small town of Newbridge in County Kildare, Ireland.

The son of potato farmers, he lived most of his younger years in the barren countryside with very little knowledge of the world. Introspective, analytical, and a good observer, George spent most of his free time analyzing the universe around him and searching for answers to the purpose of life. As a result of his efforts, he became versed in ancient Irish history, particularly the role played by Druid and Celtic cultures in the historical and cultural development of his people.

Arriving at his own conclusions, George vehemently claimed to be a direct descendant of the Druids of the past, to the point where he observed ceremonies, celebrated days of significance, and spent most of his life teaching others Druid concepts and values. Once a year he visited Stonehenge with the hope of someday establishing contact and dialogue with his ancestors. He talked to them every night but never received an answer; yet he was certain they listened to him.

A hard-working man, George provided sustenance to his wife Maureen and son Finn by growing potatoes and selling them in the open market. He worked like a slave for meager rewards, while his wife consumed endless hours crocheting

Kenmare lace on the edges of white linen scarves. This was the only remunerative employment available to women during those days and her way of contributing a small share of financial assistance.

Slowly but steadily their economic situation worsened, due to a vicious and destructive blight attacking the potato crops, which left every piece of Irish farmland useless and contaminated. Consequently, small Irish farmers found their food supplies rotting, and the potatoes harvested to pay the rent to their British landlords completely spoiled.

Hungry families who ate tainted produce got sick; thus entire villages became decimated by cholera and typhoid fever. Furthermore, since overworked parish priests were saving money on coffins in order to help the living, the dead either went unburied or were interred in common graves.

Hundreds of thousands of peasants, evicted by their landlords, crowded every warehouse and train depot in the country. The most compassionate landowners paid for their tenants to emigrate to the United States, as well as other English-speaking countries.

More often than not, ship owners crowded thousands of frantic passengers in dilapidated vessels ironically known as "coffin ships", and in many instances, due to disease, cold, and hunger, the old tubs reached their port of destination with less than a third of the passengers originally on board.

The Irish famine, along with disease, cold, and hunger, decimated a population of eight million down to a total of five.

According to George, due to the merciful intervention of his Druid ancestors on his family's behalf, the three survived the worst of the famine.

Their debts grew less and less manageable every day. As Maureen continued to sell her crochet pieces in different markets, her husband took temporary employment in a cutlery business while he waited for the rot to dissipate.

Ireland's scenario was pathetic, and hopes of a rapid recovery were at least dim. On the positive side of the tragedy, hundreds of years of archaic agricultural practices were eliminated by ending the division of family estates into tiny lots incapable of sustaining a family with one potato crop. And if Irish nationalism was dormant during the first half of the nineteenth century, the famine convinced leaders and politicians of the urgent need for social and economic change.

All in all, the McKinleys were caught in the midst of political, social, and economic turmoil, making their survival even more difficult, if not impossible, farther down in time.

In the middle of the disaster, Maureen, a diabetic from birth, died one morning of complications from an infected wound in her left foot caused by an injury.

Finn and his father were then on their own. George could not possibly provide for his son and be a caregiver at the same time, so they went to live with his older sister Charlotte, a spinster, while George tried in vain to support his son and banish their debts.

Approximately seven years after the famine "officially ended", the older McKinley continued to carry out his desperate struggle to provide sustenance.

Years later in total despair, he decided to visit Stonehenge in another attempt to communicate with his Druid ancestors hoping to obtain advice as to the most prudent course of action to be taken with their lives.

As it always happened, his relatives and particularly the aunt who took care of Finn resisted the idea of passing to the young boy his father's "superstitions." Being a staunch Catholic, bordering on fanaticism, her daily admonition to Finn's father was: "You will finish up in the bowels of hell for being such an irreconcilable heretic."

Unconcerned with the opposing views of others, "even if they came from the archbishop of Ireland," George was absolutely convinced that one day he would be able to communicate with his ancestors. Until then no one on earth was powerful enough to change his mind. One misty morning after packing his personal belongings, he took off in a horse-drawn carriage toward the eastern coast of Ireland, from where he planned to catch a ride to the Salisbury Plains and visit the megalith. Following several days of muddy travel, George McKinley was finally crossing the Salisbury plains. After providing transportation by land and sea, an old friend left him in the outer reaches of the monument: alone, before sundown, and very frightened.

Carrying his duffel bag over his shoulder, George began to trudge cautiously in the direction of the sacred stones. Once there, he intended to recite the same invocation passed down through generations, or as he said, "From the beginning of time". There was no one in sight. A few students of anthropology who were visiting the megalith that morning had disappeared, giving the monument a timeless presence, and a truly mystifying and foreboding appearance.

Stonehenge is completely encircled by a five-foot deep ditch. It measures 340 feet in diameter. In its center there is a bank with fifty-six pits or holes. At the northeast end a break in the ditch affords access to an avenue bordered by trenches that extends in the general direction of the east Avon River. The avenue is seventy-five feet wide and two miles long.

Drawing closer to the monument, George strange feelings of depersonalization and anxious anticipation took him over. Sensing some sort of strange affliction invading his body, he began to wonder if he was better off running away before something terribly traumatic happened. "After traveling all the way from Newbridge, this is not the time to quit!" he said aloud, trying to convince his wits that everything was fine.

With unsteady legs, and drops of cold sweat running off his brow, George McKinley finally arrived at the altar stone. After laying his staff and duffel bag on the ground, he sat leaning against the megalith in a state of apprehension and confusion.

For an instant, the faithful pilgrim lost complete notion of his identity, where he was, and what was he doing there. Following this hypnotic state, George's mind went blank as he lost all control of his will. Staring at the dim rays of the setting sun, McKinley gradually closed his eyes, falling into a deep sleep.

Moments later Brigitt, the Celtic goddess, disguised as a swan revealed herself to George in a dream. She was the daughter of the Dagda, the deity of the Tuatha de Danann, who was one of the most ancient peoples of Northern Europe. "Listen to me George!" she decreed with an authoritative voice. "Listen very carefully to what I am about to say. I have been selected by your Druid ancestor, the Grand Priest of Ulster, to intercede between his Illustrious Eminence and you, for the purpose of delivering a message in his own words and through my lips just as it was conveyed to me."

At this point her voice dropped to a rumble.

"'An indebtedness of sincere gratitude dwells within my soul from the time you, dear brother George, faithfully accepted the rules of Druid moral law, followed our ceremonies, celebrated sacred rituals, and pledged from deep inside your conscience resolute allegiance to our values and ideals, which, as you know, emerged from the truths and wisdom of the ages. You believe, just as I had, from the time we declared Earth to be our temple to the time of our virtual annihilation by the Romans, that humanity shall never survive itself unless it faithfully and truthfully learns to respect and obey the wisdom of its ancestors.

"'Humankind lives just long enough to acquire a minute amount of insight through individual experiences. Then they die, carrying along every word of wisdom to the grave. Consequently, succeeding generations repeat the cycle over and over ad infinitum, since in your stone-blind societies, older persons are considered archaic, useless, inferior to the young, and with an instinctive dislike for change. In Druid culture, such an attitude would be considered an abomination, a shameful waste of human worth and knowledge that could only be attained by experiencing life over the years.

Where it otherwise George, would have been what creation first intended it to be, and not an infinite and purposeless circle where mankind measures its human growth and divine mission in direct proportion to material conveniences and scientific achievements." The goddess continued, "Humanity remains hampered by the predicaments of its past. Human beings have not grown any wiser, nor know dignified behavior any better, or for that matter, know no meaningful and everlasting purpose to

10

life at all. The reasoning to explain and justify their own existence and therefore its continuity until the end of time, was and continues to be directly tied to the fear of death and extermination, the unknown, and mankind's own inability to understand the real meaning of divine purpose.

Humanity finds no ethical reason for accountability, unless threatened by penalties. Given the same set of circumstances contemplated by the barbarians, today's human being will act in kind. A tribe of animals, living by habits and thinking in symbols; nothing has changed. The vicious cycle continues.

As you know, dear George, in our Druid culture the greatest responsibility vested in every person consisted of taking good care and becoming individually and collectively responsible for our Earth and each other. We were not motivated by fearing superstitions or cruel reprisals, but by our deepest convictions that only through personal inner growth and spiritual awareness, would the natural, primitive, and animalistic instincts imbedded in our beings from the time of creation be eventually replaced by wisdom, common sense, and compassion. We should also understand that everything that exists and lives in the material world since its conception is not the result of accidental conditions and random occurrences, but a perfectly planned path toward immortality. Sadly enough humanity refuses to accept responsibility for the development and completion of its divine mission, thus living eternally condemned to a state of petrification. We were criticized, ostracized and virtually exterminated by earthly powers that refused to acknowledge and accept the significance of moral continuity by, as they said, 'worshiping our ancestors.' They unjustly classified our divine role as a mirror reflection of evil and our customs as invalid, rooted in demoniacal superstitions inspired by so-called negative and destructive satanic forces.

As you know, George, nothing could be further from the truth. We worshipped the wisdom of our ancestors, and not their persons as individuals, and by carefully listening to them in our dreams, our inner selves became, through the years, exponentially purified, thus increasing the validity and noble

11

purpose of our existence.

I wish to reward your faithfulness to Druidism by favoring your descendants with the 'wisdom of the ages' with the condition that your kin accepts and practices our dogma as faithfully as you have.

I will empower you with a supernatural capacity to influence time and space regression in your descendants, for as long as they believe in our values as you have, hence improving their quality of life through inner enlightment. Remember George; only in them I shall bestow this power.

In the event of a transgression, the spell shall be dissolved and reclaimed forever by me, the Grand Priest of Ulster. You shall be instructed on how to exercise such power at precisely the time by I selected, not before and not after, and to a particular individual of my choice.

Your son Finn has lived under his aunt's dark influence for too long. Therefore I shall forewarn you: He is not a suitable candidate for dream teleportation. However, he will give you a grandson who will be able after age eighteen, and it shall be entirely up to him to pass the wisdom acquired to future generations - If he demonstrates he has inherited your courage and sufficient nerve to stand in support of our Druid concepts and beliefs. I shall then assign this privilege unto him in due time. And if he does not have the integrity and honesty of purpose that you have shown in this regard, or negates or relinquishes his obligation and commitment to share his experiences with others, I shall immediately deprive him of all privileges.

Dear George--do you understand? Please answer to me immediately and without hesitation."

George, rapt with wonder, nodded affirmatively.

"My next command: For your son's sake and yours, leave Ireland and go to America. You will never regret it!

I shall entrust you this golden ring as symbol of our mutual loyalty and solidarity. This ring shall be passed down to your grandson in due time. Then he shall pass it to his kin, and from generation to generation thereafter, so long as its bearer meets the conditions previously set forth. Otherwise, I shall reclaim it forever."

After a moment of silence, the image of the swan slowly vanished as George began to awaken from his deep sleep, finding himself totally perplexed.

Was it a dream? He wondered. *Or was it real? And what's the difference, anyway? It really happened! I have established contact with my ancestors!*

George resolved he would bear testimony to the world regardless of everyone else's reaction. If they laughed at him, well... let them laugh! He'd been ridiculed in the past, so what would be new in life?

"Now, the swan mentioned a ring. Where is that ring?" George exclaimed in frustration. "If there is no ring, then there was no truth in the encounter!"

He searched the ground before him even as he realized that the significance of the ring was not its intrinsic worth, but its symbolic value to prove the legitimacy of the meeting. If the ring could not be found, the dream was just that, and nothing else.

Frantically he searched the ground of the monument, the grass, and the altar stone: Nothing.

George extended his arms toward the heavens, wailing aloud and with teary eyes, "Oh God, please don't let this happen to me! Please have mercy. It's not that I don't believe in you. I do! I do! And you know it, contrary to my sister-in-law's distorted accusations of heresy. Please, God. Please let me find it!"

He covered his face with his hands, praying silently and fervently. As he raised his hands a second time, George saw the golden ring on his right ring finger. He had looked for it everywhere except in himself. And there it was, shining in the soft light of dawn as a symbol of a new beginning. Then he knelt and thanked his Creator for such a wonderful revelation.

"We are definitely part of one, and one is part of all!" George exclaimed at length as he rose to his feet.

Returning home, George did not utter a word to anyone

regarding the supernatural encounter - Not because he refused to share the experience, but because he was so absorbed by the event. He returned entirely guided by instincts, while his mind wandered in a state of shock.

As he arrived at his sister's cottage to pick up Finn, she asked him point blank, "Why in God's name do you go to Stonehenge every time life gets difficult or you feel a vacuum inside? Where's your faith, George? Why don't you search your spiritual life and realize its emptiness?"

Staring at her, George replied, "Be fully convinced that what I am about to say is the truth, the only truth I know. I have just spoken to Brigitt the Celtic goddess. See this ring? My Druid ancestor offered it to me. Just because my ideas are different than yours, doesn't mean mine are flawed. I shall continue to visit Stonehenge and communicate with my ancestors as I wish. Please stop wasting time trying to instill in me a fear you call faith. There is an abyss of difference between the two.

I know there is a God in the universe and I have faith in His power. Whether or not you believe my experience to be real is irrelevant as far as I am concerned."

Outraged at George's audacious remarks, Charlotte's eyeballs seemed to be about to pop out their sockets.

"I've had enough of your heresy, George. You help us financially, I take care of Finn and that's all I care to talk about from now on. You understand?"

A bitter and resentful woman throughout her life, Charlotte found in the church a refuge that provided a sanctimonious sense of security, and if someone dared to disagree with her ideology, the spinster would become irrational and warlike, as if her very life were endangered. To her, taking fresh bread every morning to the parish priest equaled a full atonement for a day's transgressions.

In spite of her paranoid disposition, and in recognition of their mutual need for each other, she invariably made peace with George following every argument.

After listening to his Stonehenge experience, which she thought was a result of Satanic intervention, the woman instituted a holy war against George by intimidating Finn with threats of going to hell if he ever paid any attention to his father's stories.

Inspired by his Druid ancestor, George began working extra time at the cutlery, saving enough money to finance their emigration to the United States as soon as possible. He could hardly bear his sister's conceit and arrogance any longer, especially when Finn began to show signs of defiance against his *Satanic superstitions.*

On the fall of 1870, after saving enough money to pay for a one-way trip to America, George and Finn boarded the ship *Bridgewater* en route to the port of New York.

The money he had saved through sweat and hardship and an invitation from a distant relative living in Yonkers, N.Y., were their only hopes for immediate survival during the painful transition. George had learned enough of the cutlery trade to feel confident he would find a similar job after arriving at his newly adopted country.

The crossing lasted a little over fifteen days, and rough seas due to a dying tropical storm that spawned south of Bermuda made their journey a nightmare. The *Bridgewater* was an old freighter that carried passengers for much less money than passenger ships; but it had much less stability and no creature comforts whatsoever. Its tired heating system was faulty, since the boiler did not work all the time. Hot water was almost non-existent. Damp, leaks, and cold were the prevailing conditions inside their floating coffin. Finn spent most of the trip a ghostly pale from seasickness. George did not feel the effects of the huge swells that much.

Food was consistently cold and tasteless, with an unappetizing, ugly look, and if a person paid enough attention to the surroundings, rodent droppings were easily spotted almost everywhere. Their berths stunk of dry old sweat and urine, which made both wonder whether their yellowish sheets had ever been washed.

The ship was a single-funnel steamer that bellowed black smoke incessantly, staining passengers' faces with thick black soot. Its acrid odor irritated their throats and sinuses, especially children who for ten days and nights had to remain inside cramped quarters, crying, sneezing, coughing, and vomiting.

Could this be a mirror image of Dante's inferno, a preamble to the Great Tribulation, or was it God's retribution for his failure to follow his sister's religious beliefs? These and other doubts almost drove George to the verge of insanity. His prayers did not resemble her religious recitations, but they were honest and spontaneous.

On November 26th the miserable crossing came to an end as the *Bridgewater*, listing slightly on its port side, finally arrived at her designated dock in New York. George's second cousin Chad anxiously awaited their arrival.

The next day they strolled through the city's wide avenues and boulevards, watching produce and flower stands add color to an otherwise gloomy afternoon. As they listened to the sounds of horse drawn carriages, and of boys wearing gray berets shouting the headline news, both immigrants shared the same sense of awe any visitor would upon witnessing the pulse and vitality of a great metropolis like the city of New York.

Thanks to his cousin's financial help, George and his son settled in the town of Yonkers, where he was able to start a cutlery business, selling, repairing, and reconditioning all cutting edges from table knives to butcher's axes. Intensely motivated by a longing to find purpose in the human experience, he consumed books like a termite, reading about any subject relevant to his former country's history and mythology.

Not a single day passed without George reminiscing at least once over his extraordinary encounter at Stonehenge. The idea of sharing a supernatural experience with a future grandson overwhelmed him to no end. In fact, he wished the goddess had offered more information instead of presenting only a fraction of the story and leaving the rest to his wild imagination.

If faith alone took him to Stonehenge, and the Grand Priest's reward resulted from George's unbreakable trust, an attempt to know more only to satisfy his curiosity would contradict the intent of the reward itself.

He soon gave up worrying. Unless he learned to accept his improbable situation on faith alone, George would waste years of energy distressed about an event over which he had absolutely no control.

The Irishman was entirely dedicated to the business and Finn to his education. At age twenty-seven the young man married a beautiful American girl named Clare, his serious sweetheart from college.

George, of middle age by then, remained single. More obsessed as time wore on with the couple's likelihood of having children, if there were to be any, for neither one wanted a family until later in their marriage. That will make him an old geezer by the time his grandson had reached his eighteenth birthday.

Faith will reach a point where a person begins to question his or her own judgement. An individual as tenacious and persistent as George, however, didn't even consider the slightest deviation from his lifelong commitments. Nonetheless, after ten years, he couldn't wait much longer to see the prophecy fulfilled.

At the beginning of the century Finn and Clara welcomed their first child, Ivan, a beautiful boy with blonde hair and blue eyes. George became ecstatic and somewhat overwhelmed with the news. He didn't know whether to celebrate or feel scared. Predetermined events seemed to fall in place in so timely a fashion he couldn't help but feel some degree of apprehension.

Clare and Finn never truly believed the truthfulness of George's encounter at Stonehenge. They took his stories with a grain of salt and a tad of gentle humor.

George was experiencing the same rejection felt by religious believers when they share with more pragmatic people a personal spiritual event, or for that matter an unusually mysterious occurrence that was perceived only by them. The Irishman felt secure of his mission, but very much alone. However, an inexhaustible store of patience was George's most valuable asset in life.

He prayed to God every night, followed by a request to his ancestors for wisdom and also for a signal as to when and how they intended to make his 'reward' a reality.

Through the years George tried his best to become a trusted friend and confidant to Ivan in order to develop and nourish a mutual bond. He knew beforehand the importance of sharing his convictions with the boy, thus inducing him to believe in the veracity of his supernatural encounter at Stonehenge without disturbing his Catholic traditions.

Ivan was only a young and handsome lad when his grandfather decided to visit the monument once again, this time looking forward to receiving instructions as to how and when he would be accepting the promised gift.

Again, George visited the site at sunset, but now he went on his own, as the friend who took him before had by then passed away.

The same feelings of depersonalization and anxiety he had experienced during his previous visit to the site arose once again.

Leaning against the same stone, George began to lose perspective of reality as his mind went totally blank. Again he fell into a deep sleep.

The swan appeared, and he heard a rumble:

"Listen to me George. Listen carefully.

You have been faithful to our code of ethics. We are also aware of the many stories you have related to your grandson Ivan since he was a toddler, as well as the bond established between the two of you. Therefore, pay close attention to my instructions on how and when to execute your supernatural powers.

Somewhere in Ivan's mind rests a deep conviction that your stories, including that of our encounter over thirty years ago, are legitimate. Fortunately, the boy has inherited an inquisitive personality as well as an open mind to meet our guidelines, and therefore can become your trusted partner while traveling through time and space. Hence, contingent upon the conditions previously set forth, you must follow this procedure every time the two of you decide to choose a destination:

Since you have become quite a cultivated man in matters of the Earth, its natural and human history, its fascinating places, and in the successes and failures of man as he travels through time and space without compass or direction, your obligation to us shall lie strictly in the quality and purpose of your selections. When Ivan reaches the age of eighteen, and at a time mutually selected, you shall induce him into a deep slumber that shall last several hours as he travels in his dreams to a time and place previously determined by both of you.

Even though his sleeping time shall only last one night, the teleportation of his soul could last, days, months, and even years. It will be very difficult for you to understand the time warp through which he will be moving, since time and space can be easily manipulated by our encompassing powers.

Upon reaching his destination, Ivan's soul shall become embodied into a person also mentally predetermined by the two of you. This individual will be the result of your own imagination and design, and he shall live for as long as Ivan's soul dwells in him, instantly disintegrating upon his awakening.

I shall reveal myself in his dreams when appropriate. Thus forewarn him to be watchful and open-minded at all times during his teleportation experiences.

The trip shall be concluded upon Ivan's command while he remains incarnated. Then, back in his own realm, he shall disclose the whole episode to you, who shall remain by his bedside until he awakens in the morning. Ivan's solemn duty shall be, as I said before, to reveal his experiences to the world, in the most efficient way or form. Otherwise his privileges shall be forfeited forever.

The wisdom gathered as a result of each teleportation experience shall lie at the center of his exhortations, and nothing shall hinder in any way or form his contractual obligation to share his discoveries with others.

Touch his forehead with the golden ring while both of you concentrate in the trip's intent. Ivan will know exactly who he is at all times, and shall be very cautious in deciding whether to reveal his true identity or the purpose of his transitory existence to anyone as he travels through the past.

Before reaching a very old age, you shall pass him the ring. By that time, he should be well aware of our intentions and principles towards its wise use, as he shall also understand my prerogative to recall its magical powers without given notice.

Ideally you, and hopefully the rest of the world, will have the opportunity to save future generations from repeating the same historical mistakes over and over, and it shall be entirely up to humankind to pay special attention to the morals and lessons ingrained in his exhortations.

George: You shall now return to your family. No more instructions will be given. No second chances allowed. Good luck to you both."

As the last words were spoken, the mystifying swan slowly vanished, and George McKinley awoke back into the real world.

In Yonkers, anxious and overjoyed, Ivan listened attentively to his grandfather's experience.

"When should I tell my parents?" He posed as a first question.

"Remember, you must be eighteen before the first experiment, so don't worry; we still have time."

"I wish I was eighteen now. I can hardly wait for something so awesome and exciting to occur."

"Ivan, Listen to me carefully: Patience, besides being a virtue, is the most important word of wisdom in the dictionary. You must train yourself to follow this belief and stop wanting everything immediately. This, you must never forget."

Months later, the long awaited birthday finally arrived, and immediately following the celebration, Grandfather McKinley told Ivan to meet him the next evening just before bedtime.

In his room that night, George asked his grandson if he thought he was mentally ready for the first teleportation experiment. Ivan replied excitedly:

"Of course I am! Am I leaving tonight? Do you know where I'm going?

"Don't get so excited! Remember what I've told you about being patient." George replied. "First, let me brief you about the time and place of your coming journey, since I have been considering a mission for some time. Then, before we act hastily, you should fill your mind with the knowledge necessary to survive all of the circumstances surrounding your destination. You will be speaking and writing the language of your target area fluently. It is also essential for your first teleportation experience to educate yourself regarding customs, traditions, and all the particulars concerning the time period in question. Spend several weeks at the library searching for information, and wait until you feel competent enough before embarking on such an unpredictable trial, and for Christ's sake, it is in your best interest to take your time.

Remember, you'll always be aware of who you are. However, your features, demeanor, mannerisms, and even your personality will change in order to blend in. Also keep in mind that you'll always be in full control of your return. I also want to mention that certain subjects, such as the newly learned languages, will be erased from your mind upon return, as well as some of the details concerning the experience."

"I understand, Grandpa. Please tell me some more. This is so overwhelming! Lisa would never believe it, much less my friends."

Ivan was known in school as a young man who never allowed an attractive girl to squeeze by unnoticed. With his good looks he was seldom rejected for a date, and Lisa a striking brunette was Ivan's most recent girl friend.

"Don't tell your sweetheart yet. You see, many of mankind's most intriguing and fascinating episodes took place during the Middle Ages, resulting from the trade between China, Central Asia, and Europe. I am sure you have learned in school about what is historically known as the Silk Road, an ancient trade route that linked Asia with the West. Travelers carried goods and ideas between the civilizations of Rome and China. Silk came westward, while wool, gold, and silver went east. Religions such as India's Buddhism and Nestorian Christianity arrived in China via the Silk Road.

Originating in Xian, the seven thousand mile road, which was nothing more than a caravan track, followed the Great Wall of China to the northwest, the perimeter of the Taklamakan desert, climbed the Pamir Mountains, crossed Afghanistan, and went on to the Levant. From there, goods were shipped across the Mediterranean Sea. Few merchants traveled the entire route; therefore middlemen transported most commodities over a period of time in a staggered succession.

With the gradual loss of Roman territory in Asia and the rise of Saracen power in the Levant, the Silk Road became increasingly unsafe and less traveled. The route was revived under the Mongols during the thirteenth and fourteenth centuries, at which time Marco Polo used it to travel into Cathay (China)."

"I learned in school that the Route did not exist solely for those reasons," said Ivan, "but for the trading of ivory, plants, exotic animals, precious stones, and more, and in the opposite direction furs, ceramics, jade, bronze, lacquer, and iron. Many of those goods were bartered along the way, and objects often changed hands several times before reaching their final destination.

I've also learned that bandits plundered these caravans, forcing most merchants to carry along their own defenses in order to survive the journey."

"The Silk Route took the caravans to the farthest corners of the Han Empire," Grandpa continued, "and policing it became a problem that was partially solved by building forts and defensive walls along the road. Sections of the Great Wall were built for this purpose as well.

The region separating China from Europe and western Asia was not the most hospitable, since much of it is taken by the Taklamakan Desert, one of the most abominable and inhumane environments on earth. There is virtually no vegetation and no rainfall. Furious sandstorms are common, and they have claimed the lives of thousands of people. The locals have a great respect for this 'Land of Death,' and few travelers had anything good to say about it. Its climate is harsh: During the summer, temperatures reach one hundred and thirty degrees Fah. at daytime and twenty-five degrees during the night.

The different Routes that made the Silk Road, went around this deadly desert - To go across was suicidal at best."

"Which one is the largest, the Taklamakan or the Sahara?"

"This one is the largest on Earth, and it extends six hundred miles from west to east and two hundred and sixty from north to south. According to Marco Polo, the most famous western traveler of the Silk Route, it would take him at least a year to cross it from one end to the other provided he survived.

Among the inhabitants of these remote areas, the Tartars were the most historically significant. They were nomadic herders living off their cattle who were also tributary to their first emperor - Genghis Khan.

Genghis'grandson, the famous Kublai Khan, governed most of that region from 1260 to 1294, thus establishing the Yuang dynasty in China.

Let us use the rest of tonight and tomorrow to consider questions that may arise. Then, take the necessary time to search for more information. In the end, and because of possible encounters with historical figures, your destination will be the Oasis of Dunhuang, in the province of Tangut in northern China, right across from the Taklamakan Desert, some time during the year 1266 AD.

You will emerge somewhere over the northeastern section of the Silk Route. Walk a few miles until you find a group of nomadic Tartars in their felt-covered tents. Your features will resemble a vague mixture of Mongol and Caucasian, with naturally tanned skin, brown eyes, and flaccid dark hair. You will be approximately nineteen years of age, and fluent in the Mongol, Tartar, and Chinese tongues, as well as the Italian language. You will be carrying a leather pouch filled with an extensive stock of precious stones, gold, and jewels, to be used exclusively toward the achievement of your mission, which would be to learn from the trials and tribulations of people living in that era."

"Why would I speak Italian in such a remote area of the world, and why did you choose the Silk Road and the Oasis of Dunhuang?"

"First, to communicate with European merchants traveling the route, and second, I've chosen your destination following a series of dream revelations."

Being late into the night, George decided to stop the conversation and let Ivan go to bed so he could continue doing more research the following morning.

Ivan spent the night restlessly staring at the alarm clock... He woke early the next morning all stressed out. He ate two cold doughnuts and drank a glass of milk, then ran to his grandpa's bedroom for more talk and excitement. His outgoing personality and positive attitude made him a perfect candidate for the long awaited experiment.

That same day both decided to avoid as much contact with Finn and Clare as possible, in order to continue their plan without interference.

Two weeks later they met again. This time they only had one purpose in mind: The teleportation of Ivan's soul to the "ends of the Earth."

On the night of June 10, 1926, while everyone slept, George carefully followed his ancestor's instructions by placing his gold ring on Ivan's forehead, and after invoking the name of Brigitt the Celtic Goddess twice, he watched him fade away slowly into a deep sleep.

"What happens if his parents call, or if the house catches on fire, or an emergency arises and Ivan's soul is not back yet? George thought. We didn't think about that possibility.

If she suspects that something weird is going on, Clare might decide to enter and wake him up? What if he can't feel her touch or hear her voice? Would she call the ambulance or the police for help! Oh my God, What have I done?

Good Heavens; we should tell his parents everything as soon as he returns!"

CHAPTER *Two*

THE TELEPORTATION OF IVAN
TO THE SILK ROAD

In Xanadu did Kubla Khan
a stately pleasure dome decree
where Alph, the sacred river ran
through caverns measureless to man
down to a sunless sea.
So twice five miles of fertile ground
with walls and towers were girdled round
And there were gardens bright with sinuous rills
where blossom many an incense-bearing tree,
and here were forests ancient as the hills
enfolding sunny spots of greenery.

Samuel Taylor Coleridge, 1796

A moment after Ivan McKinley felt his grandfather tap his forehead with the golden ring, sending him into a deep sleep; he opened his eyes to a time almost eight hundred years before him. He blinked and rubbed his eyes. He found himself surrounded by an almost invisible landscape at the northeastern edge of the Taklamakan desert in the midst of a raging windstorm that blew sand and dust at a rate of 50 mph or better.

He was wearing heavy leather boots, and a fur-lined dress common to all ages and sexes of Mongols, clasped by shiny brass buttons on his left side, and belted with a sash. He also wore a violet funnel-shaped hat. He realized he understood his new culture; he also had a new name: Sikin.

According to Grandpa, I am supposed to walk not too far down this rocky path. But how can I walk straight? Or walk at all?

Feeling the fine sand blowing into his mouth, he continued his thoughts in silence, squeezing his eyes shut against the particles that pelted him like tiny sharp pins. *I must cover my eyes, or they'll be severely damaged. I can feel the dust drying my sinuses already, but if I breathe through my mouth, I will be chewing and swallowing sand for as long as the wind lasts. This is terrible! How can humans endure this? Perhaps I should take cover behind a rock — but first I have to find one.* He ventured a peek, but could see nothing but endless, swirling sand. The only way he could tell earth from sky was by stamping his boots.

Lacking alternatives, Sikin chose to lie face down on the hard ground with both arms crossed behind his neck. He stayed in the same position for what seemed like an eternity, waiting for the wind to diminish, until he began to feel weighted down. He lifted his head and noticed that over two inches of sand had already accumulated on his back.

Remaining motionless for several hours, Sikin rolled over frequently to shed the collected sand. His mouth was as dry as the chalky dust beneath him, and his mind, due to the incessant craving for water, had entered a state of confusion. In his lucid moments he worried he might be losing his sanity.

Suddenly and unexpectedly, Sikin noticed he had also lost his sense of direction. It was shortly past mid-day, and it seemed as if dense fog had covered every point of reference. As the wind force increased and the temperature began to drop, he felt every grain of cold sand blasting his exposed face and hands, thus spending the rest of the day trying to survive the blowing assault.

Ultimately, Sikin came upon the idea of canceling his trip and returning to his peaceful life in America. What if in his maddening thirst and the freezing darkness he forgot who he was?

What if he died of exposure? He wasn't sure of the implications, if any, that would result from the physical death of his new body. Would his soul rejoin Ivan's or end up in oblivion?

As more frightening possibilities came to mind, Sikin realized how careless they had been by not allowing enough time to prepare for such an experiment. Ivan and his grandfather had completely ignored factors such as climate, time of year, topography, and adaptation to the harsh surroundings.

During spring, he recalled reading, as surface sands warm up and ascending currents of strong northeasterly winds develop, hurricane force windstorms fill the atmosphere with dust to altitudes exceeding thirteen thousand feet. Winds from other directions also raise clouds of fine sand into the air, thus shrouding the Taklamakan in a dusty mist almost year round.

If grandpa had spent over forty years of his life ruminating, anticipating, and worrying about this moment, why hadn't he dedicated more time to planning for life threatening situations such as the one I'm facing? Sikin thought in frustration.

"This must be my first lesson in wisdom!" he exclaimed, realizing the inevitability of failure in any undertaking where, despite potential dangers, one jumps unprepared into the action, merely to satisfy curiosity, or a need to stimulate a false sense of immortality. He continued to grumble aloud in anger and self pity, blaming others for his own impetuous judgment, until out of nowhere, he heard the grainy voice of a man asking in the Mongol tongue, "Is beine? Ou su?"

Sikin easily understood the questions: "Who are you, water?"

The man's words sounded so kind, that he turned around to identify the Good Samaritan's face.

The stranger had typical Mongol features — squat of figure, round of head, sunburned face. His eyebrows were so thick;

Sikin would have said it was evolution's way of protecting his eyes from the blowing sand.

After curiously examining the stranded traveler, the Mongol handed Sikin a goatskin full of mare's milk, from which he took a few short sips.

Aware that in the Mongol tongue there were no words to express gratitude, Sikin did not acknowledge the man's generosity with words of appreciation. He recalled an ancient Buddhist proverb: *Only accomplish moral deeds and expect nothing in return.* This seemed to be the man's only motive for assisting a traveler in need.

The nomad pulled back the fur-lined cuffs protecting his bare hands almost all the way to the elbows. After stretching out both arms, he offered their symbolic sign of welcome by asking Sikin to lay his hands on top.

Barely able to stand up against the blowing sands, the nomad tied a silk scarf over Sikin's face and eyes and laid him on the back of a four-wheeled cart that was pulled by two black asses.

The Mongol rescuer, who went by the name of Amur, walked in front and alongside his camel, apparently the only creature among the five who still had some sense of direction left.

After a brief journey through the impenetrable surroundings, Amur brought the Bactrian beast to a sudden stop by piercing his upper lip with the sharpened point of a saltwort twig.

Gee, how did I know that? Sikin wondered.

With the scarf still covering his nose and mouth and his torso sharply bent forward, he clambered off the cart and closely followed Amur's footprints. Before them Sikin could see Amur's yurt or tent-like hut easily identified by its dark silhouette against the ominous sky, and by the aroma of food and smoke.

Growling and barking ferociously, two indigenous dogs rapidly approached the visitor to sniff his boots. In an instant, Amur called them off by uttering an unusual guttural sound. "Noho! Noho!" the Mongol yelled repeatedly as they got closer to the yurt. Still, smothered by the violent windstorm, the sounds were barely audible. The two entered through a relatively small cut in the felt wall, which seemed to Sikin more like crawling into a bottle through its narrow neck than visiting the living quarters of a prolific Tartar clan.

Consistent with the golden rule of nomad hospitality, Amur welcomed his guest into the families' quarter, which was firmly established in the center of the yurt. Inside, Sikin saw no visible evidence of a chimney or stack that would allow the smoke from the brazier to escape outdoors. He could make out a three-foot hole atop the shelter through which the smoke was supposed to rise but didn't because of the wind pressure. Therefore, its thickest layers tended to float slightly above his neck.

Choking desperately, physically exhausted, suffering a painful sore throat, his nostrils plugged, and his eyes severely irritated, Sikin laid on his back on the dirt floor saying, "Sein Oh! Sein Oh!" in greeting.

Once he'd recovered a bit, Sikin introduced himself as a camel driver who had accidentally lost his caravan due to the lack of visibility.

One of Amur's four wives, whose age was impossible to determine because of her sooty face, offered Sikin a cup of horsemeat stew, a piece of bread harder than the sole of his boots, and warm mare's milk, which he graciously accepted, since any moisture traveling through his throat produced at least some degree of relief.

A young child, scared by the presence of a stranger, ran naked from under cozy goatskins and woolen blankets to the arms of a woman in search of protection.

Sikin realized in amazement that the chubby toddler was totally impervious to the cold temperatures and asphyxiating smoke.

The following morning, on opening his irritated eyes, Sikin noticed the captivating figure of a young woman in her late teens or early twenties. She was of uncommonly exotic beauty – lightly tanned skin, large and revealing blue eyes sharply contrasting with her long black hair, full red lips, and delicate facial features, perhaps resulting from a blend of Hindu

European, Mongol, and Caucasian strains.

With her bare hands, she was preparing a mixture of millet, mare's milk and horse's blood, shaping the pasty looking dough into little balls. The blood, Sikin knew, had been siphoned from an incision made days, or perhaps weeks before, in the vein of a horse. The resealable cut would also provide sustenance to the horse's rider while traveling through the desert.

Another man, whose features resembled those of Amur, entered the hut via the same slit, carrying several rabbit-like rodents known as Pharaoh's mice. About his waist he wore a sash holding jingling knives and pouches. The man was Amur's oldest brother and head of another family, who had just returned from a short falconing trip. Mongols were known for owning the best hunting falcons in the world, Sikin remembered.

As a sign of welcome, the man produced a small porcelain snuff-bottle that Sikin was supposed to accept in the palm of his right hand followed by a bow - A protocol the young man carried out to perfection. If the herder happened to be out of snuff, the bottle was offered all the same, and the other person must pretend to take a pinch of its non-existing sneezing powder.

The nomads hardly ever remained fixed. Depending on the season, they migrated from one area to another in pursuit of greener pastures and fresh water for their herds. Their yurts were made of felt, supported by wooden rods. The tents were completely round and almost airtight on all sides. The yurts could be neatly assembled and disassembled, the pieces gathered into bundles, and carried along in their migrations, usually atop a four wheeled-cart.

In addition to the awkward four wheelers, they also had a much better version of a two-wheeled cart, which was pulled by scrawny looking oxen and covered with a felt tarp for the protection of those traveling inside.

Their food consisted of mare's milk, as well as meats from horses, camels, dogs, or whatever their hunt produced.

The women took care of the needs of husbands and families by trading, buying, and selling wares, while men devoted their time to hawking, hunting, and matters of war.

First wives were considered the most legitimate, and the men were allowed to have as many as they wished, as long as the required dowry was paid in advance. Consequently, the family offspring was incredibly large.

Upon the death of a father, the oldest son could marry his widows, except for his own mother or sisters. Upon the death of their brothers, they could marry their sisters-in-law, and every marriage, regardless of how many wives the man already had, was carried with the greatest pomposity.

Sikin didn't want to overextend his welcome unnecessarily, so during that evening, as the men sat to chat around the brazier and children slept on a grass covered slab that served as a bed for the father and his first wife, he decided to ask the brothers for help.

While they shared the hot tea recently brewed by the attractive young woman, Sikin presented his request, reassuring them he had plenty of riches to pay for all expenses.

Following an intensive bargaining session, it was mutually agreed that for two ounces of gold, the brothers would furnish a healthy horse, a camel, scimitars, daggers, plenty of dried horse meat, three skins filled with melted snow and one with mare's milk, plus enough dry dung to feed the fires. Finally, for an additional ounce they offered him the company of the young woman.

According to Amur and his brother, she knew the route to Dunhuang, with all its dangers and peculiarities, like few people around.

The proposal threw Sikin momentarily off balance.

What would I do with her? He wondered.

Did this offer mean marriage? What would her fate be like after his return? But then – she was so beautiful and her smile was so sweet.

Assuming they became close friends or intimate with each other, it just wouldn't be fair to her. Yet, she could very well become a great asset to the mission, either as a traveling companion or as a knowledgeable scout with whom to share local knowledge, survival issues, and so on. If the girl happened to be trustworthy, she could very well become an advisor in other matters as well.

Amur, anxious to hear Sikin's comments, interrupted his concentration asking for answers. "I'll be worried about her fate after I leave Dunhuang." Sikin replied.

"That woman is strong as a yak, has a lot in her head, and knows the route like the palm of her hand. In fact she could make the difference between life and death to you, my friend" Amur winked and smiled confidently.

"Don't look so puzzled!" his brother growled. "If down the road you find her boring, well...all you have to do is sell her to another master!"

"Is she related to anyone in your family? I don't suppose she is your daughter. Is she? Or you wouldn't be..."

"Oh no! Not my daughter, not my brother's daughter either. After Tiblina became an orphan during the massacre of Mongku Khan's funeral procession, we took her into our family."

"How did that happen?"

"It occurred they carried the body of the Great Khan for burial atop the Holy Mountain, the sacred place where all Khans are taken for interment. It is our custom during the procession, for the escort to kill as many persons as they wish, as long as they yelled admonitions, such as 'Depart this life to enter the Otherworld, and there serve upon your deceased master!'

The ones so honored will become the Great Khan's servants in the afterlife. Likewise, they slaughter the best horses, so he can use them in the coming kingdom. When the body of Mongku was taken to this mountain, the horsemen accompanying it, slew upwards of twenty-thousand persons, including Tiblina's father who was one of our cousins, and his wife."

Amur looked at his brother, who nodded, then continued.

"As a result, we kept their property and his daughter, since none of the local men wanted to marry or adopt the girl."

"Why not?"

"For fear her obscure fate and bad luck might be transmittable. Being such a lovely young woman, most men believed her parents were killed by mistake – That she was supposed to be the one offered to the Khan for his pleasure instead. For that reason, men feared her unique beauty might become a curse to those sharing her life. As you can see, the girl has been part of our clan for several years and nothing bad has happened to us ever since."

"Wouldn't she be scared to travel with a stranger? Suppose I abuse her? Don't you think a person is worth more than an ounce of gold?"

At this the women giggled, while Amur and his brother laughed so loud at his concern that Sikin couldn't help to ask what was so funny about giving away a defenseless woman to a man they did not know.

"Young man, where did you come from?" Amur asked jovially.

"Haven't you heard of Mongol hospitality? It has been a centuries-old tradition to offer our women, even our wives, to visiting guests. This will be a great opportunity for Tiblina to serve a young, handsome man like you instead of a wretched poor devil later in life. As far as being defenseless, let me tell you something: Beware! Men are amazed at her capacity to survive, protect herself, and overcome the worst of hardships."

"All right, I will pay the extra ounce, but with one condition; I want to talk to her in private before we leave."

The purchase of Tiblina was also contingent upon both brothers providing an extra camel, archery, and provisions for her to travel along. They accepted the conditions except the one concerning her food supply.

"Let her feed on the horse's blood. It is cheaper."

Additional haggling ensued until Amur finally gave up, unconditionally accepting Sikin's demands.

Sikin had read that Mongols enjoyed bartering and arguing as much as profiting from the results. For these nomads, the information really rang true. Still he shook his head in disbelief that a woman's life was worth less than that of a horse, or for that matter a bag of food, in spite of the fact that the women were the best providers for the family group. For this kind of treatment, men were constantly cheated on, for which neither the women nor the men were ever ashamed. In Mongol settlements, nearly all of them were beautiful and vivacious, and they always looked for the opportunity to "serve" their guests.

As agreed Sikin joined Tiblina outside the family hut, and after practicing the same courtesies Ivan McKinley was accustomed to when meeting a lady, he talked to her in a low voice to prevent the brothers from eavesdropping on their conversation.

"Tiblina," he said to the girl, "Amur and his brother have offered me your company in exchange for an ounce of gold. My only mission at the moment is to arrive at the Oasis of Dunhuang and I feel confident you would not object to traveling along as my guide and assistant. I promise not to ask for anything else but guidance and support.

Amur told me of your extensive knowledge and experience in crossing the Taklamakan and Gobi Deserts, and therefore I'm asking for your help."

Tiblina extended her arms as a sign of welcome and acceptance, while Sikin in return laid his upon hers.

"Where are you from? Where was your caravan going? How did you get lost?" she asked curiously.

"I was raised in a distant land toward the sunset, where women are not allowed to be purchased or sold, much less offered to strangers in the same fashion than food and shelter. As to your other questions I shall answer them in due time. I promise!"

She nodded, willing to wait. "You must understand," she said. "To these men, the value of a woman depends on how much she pleases her man, her ability to supply food, and shelter, and the capacity to produce children. Otherwise she becomes useless and burdensome, with no way to survive other than offering her body to any man willing to pay or barter for its use, then passing her earnings to the master of the house where she lives.

After the Khan's soldiers murdered my parents, I went to live with Amur and his family, always trying to earn enough money to avoid depending on them.

I was fortunate enough to learn from silk merchants and caravan drivers many lessons in survival, and as I gained experience, merchants traveling towards Turpan and back hired me as their helper. I had to earn my keep somehow since both brothers had tried to use me for their pleasure on countless occasions under threat of abandoning me out unless I cooperated but I always refused. They claim that a beautiful female doesn't deserve to live around men like them unless she is willing to fulfill their wishes and do as they say which I refused to accept. By earning a little here and there I don't have to depend on their support."

Tiblina grinned happily. "Do you see now? They are disappointed and resent my disobedience, so they have seized a unique opportunity to make a profit and get rid of me at the same time. They have recognized your inexperience as a traveler and your need for help in crossing to Dunhuang, so I was included in the package."

She wagged a finger. "But they are not dishonorable men. To answer your question on whether or not Amur was telling the truth regarding this trip's treacherous conditions, yes, he was! It is quite a dangerous undertaking for anyone, but foolish for a person with little knowledge of the route."

"Why has the Mongol custom of 'pleasing guests' with their own wives and daughters persisted for so many years?"

"It has been a tradition carried down through generations." Tiblina answered simply. "Men believe that by the pleasure they provide guests with their wives and hospitality, the clan wins the favor of idols to multiply the yield of crops and their tillage.

When Mongku Kahn, the last lord of the Tartars, was informed about the custom of giving their wives to outsiders, he commanded under risk of heavy penalties that they desist from practicing such a bizarre form of hospitality. Upon receiving the news, the clans became very upset, obeying reluctantly for about four years. Then they held a council to deal with the matter, and decided to send an expensive gift to the Khan, along with an invitation to use their wives at his Majesty's discretion."

35

"What was the Khan's reaction?"

"He said, 'since you don't mind living in shame, do as you please!' Consequently he let them do as they wished."

Sikin felt a great deal of gratitude and admiration towards the young woman, not only because of the innumerable hardships she had had to endure to maintain her sense of dignity, but for her honesty with him as well. Sikin was convinced she didn't belong among barbarians; in fact, he thought it would be a good idea to teach her everything within his reach, and create the most worthy and educated woman on Earth. Education would surely enable her to become a better survivor among those people, he reasoned.

"There is something I'd like to know before we begin our trip," Tiblina said interrupting his thoughts. "Why are you so interested in Dunhuang? You're not going to send me back after we arrive, are you? I would rather die of thirst and starvation than come back to Amur's family. I am a hard worker, Sikin. I am an experienced guide, and my mother taught me how to decorate silk so I can create beautiful pieces and sell them for a living. There must be something I can offer besides my body, don't you think?" She gazed at him with desperate pleading eyes. "Please, Sikin, don't send me back to Amur."

"I will not send you back. I promise. Now I'd like to ask you another question. Why aren't you like the others? If your parents were like everyone else around here, why were you raised differently?"

"My parents belonged to a sect of Nestorian Christians," Tiblina replied, "and according to the teachings of the Friar, it was a man's duty to protect, feed, and honor his wife. Father set this example in the way he treated my mother, and for that reason, my beliefs differ from those of Mongols and Tartars. I was brought up learning from their good examples, and now it is impossible for me to accept anything less than what they taught me."

"Ah," Sikin said thoughtfully. "As I remember, the Nestorian Church was a community of eastern Christians that followed the teachings of Nestorius, Archbishop of Constantinople. Did you know he was condemned as a heretic by the council of Ephesus in 431 for advocating that Christ could not have been human and divine at the same time, and that such belief was the reason why Nestorian societies in order to escape persecution established themselves in Central Asia?"

"I don't understand what you are saying. Your words are too full of twists and turns. Besides, what is Central Asia?" Tiblina asked perplexedly.

"It is the name given to this area by those beyond the Tamir Mountains."

After listening to Tiblina's predicament, Sikin realized, that the adopted young woman had been nothing but a prisoner living under the rules of a most cruel and barbaric social system.

Instead of benevolence being the reason for her adoption, Sikin believed she was victimized and used as a slave by Amur and his brother. They simply couldn't justify keeping her any longer after she refused to accept their advances.

To start a mutually rewarding association, and as a gesture of good faith, Sikin offered to compensate Tiblina, which she refused claiming he was doing enough for her as it was.

No man had ever treated her with decency and respect, much less kindness, Sikin thought, since those attributes were non-existent among men and women of that culture. He also suspected that the story of Tiblina bringing bad luck to whoever married her, was merely another excuse for Amur to take control of the young woman's life. The Mongol not only kept her parents' property that rightfully belonged to her, but their beautiful daughter as well.

Sikin couldn't comprehend how the nomads could survive for centuries living in such a harsh environment, morally unrestrained, and without respect for each other's rights and property. Yet he also realized that in Ivan's world eight hundred years later, living conditions in many places was not that different - proving once again man's unwillingness to improve his ethics for his own sake.

"To put your mind at ease," Sikin said, "let me explain the reasons for my trip to Dunhuang. Then we should go see Amur to secure our share of the bargain and get on with our trip.

The oasis of Dunhuang was chosen as my destination by a wise man I dearly love. Its purpose was never revealed, yet I expect every aspect of my mission to be noble and productive, as well as inspiring and stimulating. I know this must sound bizarre, but until you discover who I am, where I came from, and the reasons for my mission, further explanations will be confusing at best. Therefore, in the same manner I trusted my mentor, I ask you to trust me."

Tiblina had no choice but to take his word. She nodded affirmatively, and both went inside the yurt to get their voyage under way.

By then, both brothers had all the conditions met: Two camels completely loaded with a small ax, two scimitars, a Saracen saber, archery equipment, blankets, dried horse meat, two skins filled with melted snow, two leather flasks filled with dry mare's milk, and a horse to ride and feed from his blood.

The dry mare's milk, Sikin learned from Tiblina, was a paste resulting from boiling the milk and skimming the cream off the top, then pouring the remaining liquid into another vessel, which was exposed to the sun until it dried to a yellow paste. Every morning they would place a half-pound of the stuff inside a small leather flask shaped like a gourd, add water, and as they rode, the milky paste would dissolve back into yellowish milk they would drink.

Having received much more for an ounce of gold than he ever anticipated, Sikin offered an extra ounce for all the silk pieces painted by Tiblina, but since the brothers' wives usually sold them to merchants returning to the Pamir range from the east, the men firmly disagreed.

After more intensive bargaining, the Mongols agreed to sell half of the stock for the same price, which Sikin reluctantly accepted, provided they would package the material well enough to protect it from exposure to the harsh environment.

That afternoon, the young couple left the nomad settlement en route to Dunhuang, one with dreams of discoveries and adventures, the other to conquer freedom at any cost - a feat totally unheard of in the Middle Ages, particularly in that barbaric part of the ancient world.

The tiny caravan had proceeded just over a mile when Sikin realized he didn't know how long the voyage was supposed to take.

Unaware of the concept of a calendar, much less the knowledge of numbers, distances, cardinal points, geography, the marking of time, and so on, the girl couldn't explain it either.

Once he deciphered her ways of expressing time, Sikin realized that they were months from reaching Dunhuang, and his estimate didn't even consider unexpected delays. Would their supplies last?

They rode silently along the edges of the "Land of Death," an expression commonly used to identify the Taklamakan. Tiblina exuded an air of confidence, her relaxed familiarity with her homeland combined with joyous exhaltation at her newfound independence. Sitting on the wooden seat atop the camel, bouncing back and forth to the rhythm of the animal's awkward stride, Sikin began to comprehend that Tiblina's presence was much more valuable than all the precious stones he carried inside his bag. He could see the young woman was one of those extraordinary persons fortunate enough to have a sense of destiny and purpose – not unlike himself. "No encounter is ever accidental," he recalled his grandfather saying.

As the caravan continued its gradual journey through the Land of Death, Sikin remembered another conversation he'd had with his grandfather.

The old man had stated that any social or political system regardless of its time and place in history, would never carry enough power of persuasion, brutal or otherwise, to suffocate the human spirit. Nothing could fully oppress humanity's endless quest to achieve equal and inalienable rights to choose its own destiny and express it. Even if the majority accepted in resignation a fate imposed by force, there would always be those dissenting at their own risk for their God-given rights to soar through the heights of the human experience.

The old man had a knack for using complicated and

sometimes poetic statements to express his simple thoughts, claiming that these issues had always being ignored, therefore resulting in humanity's ageless conflagration against its own design.

Influenced by Tiblina's predicament, Sikin had discovered another reason to justify his mission; help a woman whose free spirit refused to remain stifled in suffocating traditions.

And now that he found such a profound meaning to their encounter he felt compelled to do something lasting and noble for her. But what could that be?

Should he offer her the precious stones upon his departure to America? No, he thought. Riches would only temporarily satisfy her physical needs at a time when she was desperately trying to reach a more challenging and meaningful existence. But hampered by ignorance, Tiblina would always remain incapable of reaching a higher level of understanding and insight, qualities so vital in making the right choices in life.

Sikin reflected upon these issues over and over, and each time his resolve to offer education was reaffirmed. *Information,* he thought. *Eight hundred years of it!* He had an arsenal of knowledge to share even though Ivan had just finished high school, and his education was limited by the standards of his day and age. But in his role of Sikin, he was nothing short of a genius! Therefore, why not teach her as much as he could? Omitting, of course, information a person of an ancient mind set would find impossible to absorb.

First of all, Sikin thought, he would explain why knowledge is so pivotal in determining a person's fate. She must understand the importance of applying her strongest effort and dedication to that end.

He would begin by teaching her a western language. Not English; yes Italian, so she could communicate with the few Europeans traveling the road and express herself more eloquently than in Mongol or Chinese. Then arithmetic, so she learns to count, calculate, and use numbers as an aid to represent ideas.

Also measurements, to understand proportions, dimensions

and a basis for comparisons; Astronomy, to prevent her from making decisions based on astrological superstitions; Climate, so she could comprehend the development of weather phenomena and dispense the notion that the climatic process emanates from a capricious deity; Geography, to acquire a sense of placement in relation to the people of other lands; and the basic physiology of the human body and to apply simple cures for common ailments.

As a Nestorian friar had taught her religious values, he would make sure that "pagan ideas" were not intertwined with her Christian education. He would also teach her lady-like manners to create a positive impression when meeting foreigners, and to accentuate her God-given beauty. Finally, a little psychology to help her evaluate the reactions of others, to also understand her own emotions.

Sikin could have added more subjects to the list, but Tiblina interrupted his train of thought to ask the reason for his silence ever since they left the settlement.

"Do you regret my coming along?"

"Not at all! I just prefer to talk while sitting on solid ground, rather than from camel to camel. Don't worry!"

Satisfied with his answer, she didn't say another word.

Suspended in the western skies, tiny particles of dust lit by the rays of a gorgeous sunset, lavished upon the young couple a rich array of warm colors. And since the temperature in the Taklamakan had already begun its gradual descent for the night, they decided it was time to rest the camels, start a fire, and camp for the night.

Tiblina went after brushwood while Sikin gathered sticks and hemp rope to secure their portable felt tent.

That evening, their meal consisted of mare's milk, dry horsemeat, dates, and enough water to wet their lips. As Ivan, the young man might have found the fare repulsive, but along with foreign tongues, Sikin found he had adapted *somewhat* to Silk Road cuisine. The same did not hold true for Silk Road manners, however. He forced himself not to grimace as Tiblina attacked her horsemeat like a sailor, wiping grease on her sleeve and chattering cheerily with her mouth open.

Sitting by Tiblina's side following the meal, Sikin asked the young woman to listen very carefully to what he was about to say. He began by telling her how difficult it may be for her to understand.

"I've made a commitment to teach you certain arts no other human being knows, including the Great Khan. Coming from a far away land, I am versed not only in what he calls the "seven arts", but also in many other disciplines unknown on this side of the Earth. I intend to transform you into the wisest, most intelligent and attractive woman this land has ever known."

Tiblina's eyes widened as she listened attentively.

They spoke of the moon, the sun, and the stars and what their place was in the universe.

"I thought the tiny lights covering the sky were flaming gods from far away."

"If so, why do they remain in the same spot night after night, instead of burning and disappearing altogether?"

"I don't know." Tiblina replied. "That's what everyone says."

Sikin talked about the many marvels existing in his distant land such as aqueducts and flameless lights. Tiblina stared at him in wonder.

"I don't trust any other man except you," she said confidently.

"Why is that?" Sikin asked in surprise.

"After noticing an amusing accent in your speech, and realizing that your garments were unlike those worn by camel drivers, I decided to search your belongings. I found precious stones no camel driver could ever own. In fact, to keep Amur and his brother away from them, I didn't say a word to either one. Furthermore, Sikin, any person foolish enough to travel this land with so many riches and no protection has to be either crazy or from another world, and your sore butt tells me you haven't been on a camel in a long time."

At that Sikin had to grin at her observant nature. In truth, his behind had never been so sore.

"Besides, no man, whether Mongol or Tartar, ever treats a

woman the way you do." She concluded.

Sikin blushed from embarrassment as he listened to her talk. The woman was considerably smarter than she appeared.

"Are those good enough reasons to trust whatever I say?"

"You are an entirely different sort of man, and my only hope for freedom. So I risked coming along, rather than staying back in the settlement. Your voice and eyes and gestures do not show the lying ways of merchants. These are good reasons."

So much for psychology, Sikin thought.

Tiblina paused for a moment. Then she dug a tiny sack filled with a white powder from one of her pockets and said, "You know what's inside this little pouch?

Most warriors use this powder to kill themselves before they get captured. I stole it from Amur's brother and brought it along in case we want to kill ourselves during the trip."

Sikin's mouth dropped open. "Kill ourselves? Why would we ever do that?"

"If we get lost in the desert," Tiblina said gloomily. "I would rather kill myself than die of thirst. You see, once a person becomes disoriented, he will never find the path again. The wind erases every hoof or foot impression in the sand, and then you are entirely at the mercy of this abominable land."

Sikin promptly realized that he didn't know the woman at all. The vulnerable, innocent image Tiblina conveyed did not reflect the person she was. Along with her rudimentary and unpolished manners, she showed the unmistakable traits of a survivor, decisiveness, bravery, and true grit. Even though Tiblina considered her life worthy of sacrifice in exchange for an opportunity to free herself from abuse and oppression, she must have kept her capacity for endurance well under cover to avoid being considered a threat by her adoptive parents.

"Have I scared you?" The girl asked.

"No, you just caught me by surprise with that remark."

Tiblina wanted to hear more about the wonders of his world. Sikin on the other hand tried to explain that to grasp freedom one must forever abandon that land and travel to those far away countries in search of a more brilliant and better future. He

43

wanted her to understand that regardless of how hard he tried to teach her about those worlds, unless she committed herself with the same energy and optimism she applied to escape bondage, his plan will never work. Sikin knows how to train her, but again, the importance of time was most critical, since he didnt know how long they were going to be together.

She expressed to Tiblina the need for her to listen to him completely and carefully.

"You must give yourself a chance! Tiblina, it's now or never!" Sikin gazed at the girl earnestly.

Smiling, she looked deep into his eyes. "I know exactly what you mean, Sikin. After visiting places like Kashgar, Karakorum, Dunhuang, and others while guiding merchants from beyond the Tamir Mountains, my curiosity has been awakened just by listening to their fascinating stories. On the other hand, I have yet to hear about a land where women can exist without being considered a beast of burden."

She shook her head and poked at the fire, watching the sparks fly into the night.

"When I was little, the good Nestorian Friar opened my eyes by teaching me about the existence of more beautiful and better places to live, and I've always wanted to visit them some day.

Following our conversion to Christianity, my parents planned to visit a church in the Land of the Lakes called Saint Mark, but I was too young to travel that far, so they decided to wait until I was older. When they were killed I thought my chances of visiting those fabulous places had ended forever. Our lives were totally different from Amur's, who came pilfering like a vulture after he heard about their deaths. That event, Sikin, marked the beginning of my darkest moments."

Tiblina realized the importance of the education Sikin could provide for her and offered only her friendship in return.

"Are you my friend?" She asked timidly.

"Of course I am your friend! What else have I done but worry about your future?

Let's concentrate on preparing your path for freedom, so you'll never have to depend upon the favors of strangers and manipulators. If we don't accomplish this task before I return to my homeland, I'm sure the most important part of my mission will stay unfinished."

Tiblina couldn't grasp the purpose of his so-called mission, nor the reason for a departure. Therefore, she asked him the obvious question again.

"In due time I will let you know all about my past," he answered "and my future. Meanwhile, let's crawl inside the tent and try to get some sleep."

Inside the yurt, Sikin positioned himself at a prudent distance from her. Temptation was the last hurdle he wanted to contemplate at the moment, and a woman even as savage as Tiblina most definitely could ignite a young man's instincts too quickly to reconsider.

The following morning they welcomed the dawn of a new day, as the wondrous dunes of the Taklamakan, painted by the early morning sun, began to acquire a profusion of colors that unfairly disguised its evil reputation.

The day was cold, but there was no wind. Sikin peered blearily from the tent watching as Tiblina walked to the resting camels and pulled from a black bag a hanful of dry dung that she used to start a fire and heat water to brew tea.

As the fire began to crackle, Sikin emerged from the tent.

"Buon giorno Tiblina! Un bel di, eh?"

"What did you say?"

"I said, 'Good morning! What a beautiful day this is!"

"Buon giorno, amico Sikin!" She replied with a smile.

"And where did you learn that phrase?"

"That's how western travelers usually greet each other."

"What do you think about such a gorgeous display of colors?"

"I love it! But I also think you are too overconfident in this kind of environment. Don't you know that there are evil spirits out there waiting for someone to get lost?

If at any time a person becomes disoriented, a strange voice would speak to him from all directions. Then, the confused and desperate victim follows the whims of these ghosts, whose

45

intentions are none other than to disorient him even further until he is totally lost and at the mercy of the desert spirits. After a few days he dies of thirst, starvation, and sun blisters."

"Why did you have to tell me such a frightening story?" Sikin asked, secretly amused.

"Because two contradictions come to mind every time I stand in front of this desolation, one is how beautiful and inspiring it can be at times, and the other; is an intense fear of dying of thirst. How can a person experience two opposite sensations at the same time? And yet, I do."

Obviously this wasn't the first time she had felt intimidated by the desert's awesomeness, Sikin thought; and for good reasons. The Taklamakan's huge and active sand dunes had tormented travelers along the Silk Road for centuries. In the folklore of the Uyghur people, its name meant: *Once you get in, you'll never get out.*"

"I have witnessed death in the desert many times," Tiblina continued solemnly. "The image I always tried to convey whenever I served as a guide was one of confidence, while deep inside I trembled like a leaf. Perhaps some day I'll be able to earn a living doing something less dangerous and more rewarding."

"That is precisely my point!" Sikin answered reassuringly. "By the way, not that I want to change the spooky subject, but what's the surprise menu for this morning?"

"Another ration of dry milk and hot water," she replied. "But within a day or so, we should be passing by a group of gigantic sand dunes where rabbits, gerbils, field mice, and jerboas live. Then you should be able to hunt for fresh meat."

"Me?" Sikin gulped. Naturally she expected him to do the hunting. He was the man and she the woman. It took him several moments to catch her trembling dimples and the twinkling in her eyes. She was teasing him.

"Among those rodents," he said, "which ones are you planning to catch? Not the mice, I suppose?" His grandfather's magic apparently didn't extend to the mere notion of having to eat the little critters.

Tiblina giggled. "Oh no! I was referring mostly to rabbits, since it is almost impossible to catch mice with bow and arrow." She paused, and then spoke lightly.

"By the way, have you ever had mice?"

"Of course not! And I have no intentions of starting either." Sikin said, his stomach churning.

"Why not? They taste sort of sweet. We ate them occasionally at Amur's. His first wife used to fry them in horse lard. Their children loved it!"

Her dimples deepened. "Do you want to know what happened to a white tiger that was moving through the banks of the Tarim River?"

"Did you also fry the cat?" Sikin asked sarcastically.

"Too big to fry, but we did kill the beast and had it roasted for the day's last meal. By now I'm sure you know we eat anything with four legs around here, including tigers. And so will you, if you get hungry enough!

Now, I think we should pack and continue toward the huge dunes. I'm sure we will be able to catch some fresh meat along the way. There is also a water hole for the animals, as well as tamarisks, nitre bushes, and reeds for them to feed on prior to the climb."

"Can we fill the skins with more water?"

"We will become sick if we do. The water is bitter, so only camels and horses can drink from that well. But there is another one farther down the route we can drink from and fill our skins before continuing to Turpan."

The lonely travelers packed up their tent, wrapped a bundle of dry brushwood to take along, and climbing atop their camels, began their second day's journey, this time tying the horse to one camel's tail by a tether line.

He had studied camels, and remembered that the Bactrian beasts from the wild steppes of Central Asia differed from Arab dromedaries in that they have two humps instead of one. They also had shorter legs, and since they live through cold winters, their bodies would grow a thicker coat, which was then shed in masses during the spring.

These camels fed on the thorny, bitter plants of the area, they drank only occasionally with many days in between, carried loads of up to five hundred pounds, and could walk twenty five miles daily for three consecutive days without food or water.

Since they don't store water in their bodies, it was produced during dry periods by the oxidation of fat accumulated in their humps.

Walking on their soft and widely spread feet, which were naturally adapted to stroll on sand, these camels could easily ride one hundred fifteen miles during a fourteen-hour day. However, since Sikin and Tiblina were in no hurry, it made more sense to take short breaks during the afternoon heat than to continue without an occasional rest.

By mid-morning, as the small caravan continued its slow trek toward the Oasis of Turpan, they found the Silk Road completely covered with sand as a result of the recent storm. Under those conditions only experienced drivers could determine the safest course in the right direction; if they chose wrong, panic could threaten the caravan with total disintegration. In a typical scenario, no one will remember the right path to follow. Every direction would look alike as the traveler's sense of orientation ceases to exist. Discontent and fear take hold of the group's morale, and in no time, every rider is heading in a different course. In this way, thousands of human lives had been lost in misguided attempts to cross the Land of Death.

On this day, though, most of the ever-present floating dust had virtually disappeared. The sunrays were intense and the skies became unusually clear. It wasn't yet noon and it felt as if the sands were on fire. Noticing Sikin's face turning red, Tiblina who was wearing a silk scarf folded in a Saracen manner over her head and shoulders for protection, brought both camels to a stop and pulled another one from her saddle bag to cover Sikin's head.

Not finding words to express his appreciation, he kissed her hand. Tiblina furrowed her brow, perplexed after such action, then looked at him and smiled shyly.

After riding continuously throughout the afternoon, she

pointed toward the eastern horizon, where the enormous sand dunes were already discernible, saying that they should be reaching the foot of those hills before dark. Once there, they would spend the night by the waterhole to allow the beasts to drink through the night.

Sikin's head was swirling. He had been perspiring profusely during the entire day, had little to drink, and had reached the initial stages of dehydration. He could no longer recognize her voice or make sense of what she saw in the horizon, all he could see was a blurred outline of the sand hills.

Once again, Tiblina brought the beasts to a stop, climbed off the camel, and went to his aid.

"How sick do you feel?"

Trembling and incoherent, Sikin couldn't make sense of her words.

To provide badly needed protection from the hot sun, she laid him on his back atop a blanket spread alongside the camel. She poured water over his head then fluttered her scarf to induce cooling by evaporation. Finally she had him drink small sips of water until he was gradually able to swallow more.

In no time Sikin began to stabilize to the point he was ready to continue. Since the Mongol tongue lacked words to express abstractions, Tiblina resorted to kissing his hand instead, just as he had done to her. Then she helped him climb up to his uncomfortable seat atop the camel, and soon they were back on the road smiling at each other.

It took most of the day to arrive at the waterhole, and Sikin by then wasn't feeling well at all. Weak and confused, he tumbled off the camel and sat dizzily on the hot sand while Tiblina poured more water over his head and into his mouth.

The sun's intense rays became more lenient as the huge ball of fire began to set over the horizon, offering both much needed relief.

The next morning they intended to climb over loose sand for several hours so the young couple planned to depart shortly before sunrise to avoid the horrendous midday heat during their climb. According to Tiblina, after reaching the summit of the enormous dune, they would begin their descent into the Turpan depression, which Sikin claimed to be the deepest on earth - over five hundred feet under sea level, and widely known for its unbearable high temperatures on sunny days.

That evening Tiblina took care of most chores, allowing Sikin to recover gradually from heat stroke, and by the time she had finished lighting the fire, he was already expressing frustration at not being able to teach her anything that day.

That evening as if a powerful source of energy had overtaken him, Sikin began to talk about arithmetic - the meaning of numbers, their uses, names, and so on. Tiblina gave him her most undivided attention, and since he wanted to make up for lost time, they did not retire until late that night.

The following morning, after a good night's rest under cooler temperatures, Sikin awoke to find her milking the female camel.

"Who's drinking it?"

"You are! It is the best way to prevent heat illness from coming back. You should be glad we brought her along."

"How does it taste?"

"Thick!" She replied with a smile.

"I'll bet," he said, repressing a grimace.

He knew that camel's milk was also used in the brewing of *hoormog*, an alcoholic drink, and to make cheese. It was known for its wild and obnoxious taste, thick consistency and yellowish color. Any mammal that can live without water for ten days or more, survive over a month without food, and doesn't even sweat unless the temperature reaches one hundred twenty degrees or above, must produce the strongest, most concentrated kind of milk among all mammals.

He asked her how much water she thought the camels had drunk from the hole the night before, and her answer translated into the equivalent of twenty gallons at one sitting.

"Are you now interested in camels?" she asked mischievously.

"Not necessarily, but I'd listen to what you have to say."

"Come in close, and I'll show you how these creatures

survive the Land of Death."

She pointed at the camel's eyelashes.

"Look. The reason they are so large and thick is to keep the sand from damaging her eyes. When I touch her muzzle, watch how she instantly shuts the openings off. You see? That's how she protects herself against breathing desert sand. And during the shedding season, she'll produce enough wool to knit several blankets for a large family."

After strong hesitation, Sikin finally agreed to drink the yellowish beverage, in respect and sincere appreciation for Tiblina's advice.

Besides camel's milk, he also ate a thin slice of dried horsemeat and a chunk of the same kind of tough bread Amur had offered upon arrival at the yurt, except this chunk, was even harder. The Taklamakan's rate of humidity rarely climbed above five percent, so everything was dry; food, fabrics, even Sikin's own skin.

After loading their camels, they were ready to resume their approach towards the gigantic dune that loomed before them.

In his nausea the day before, Sikin had barely registered the imposing silhouette of the huge sand hill. But now that he had gained control of his senses, the young man couldn't figure out how in God's name they were going to climb through five hundred feet of loose sand.

Meanwhile, despite the annoyance of having to carry on a conversation from the swinging chairs of moving camels, Sikin used the short trip to review Tiblina's arithmetic lesson, which she had absorbed to the smallest detail the night before.

As anticipated, they reached the base of the dune early enough in the day to escape the worst of the heat. Any other creature attempting to climb the hill besides a Bactrian camel would have sunk hopelessly into the sand. These unique animals' feet had wide soles, and their toes were interconnected by cushions that distributed their thousand-pound plus weight evenly over the loose sand; hence, the double-humped camels were most capable of walking through sand dunes without sinking or losing their balance.

In contrast the horse presented a pathetic picture. Virtually being pulled by a rope, the distressed animal panted desperately for every meter climbed, foaming incessantly through his mouth and hide, and often, collapsing flat on his belly.

Sikin was fully aware that the purpose of bringing the beast along was to drink his blood, and to sacrifice him for meat if necessary. Such a thought has been bothering him ever since they left the settlement. If camel's milk tasted like an emetic, drinking blood from a live horse sounded even more disgusting.

As their climb continued at a snail's pace, Sikin found the camels' dexterity, sense of balance, and brutal strength exhibited by these animals absolutely amazing. In one instance, he was tempted to stop to give the exhausted horse a break. Tiblina flatly refused, claiming that if they stopped, the horse would collapse, and there wasn't enough strength in five camels to haul the animal uphill once his legs had given up. In fact, if it weren't for the camel's pulling power the horse would have sunk into the sand much earlier.

Again Sikin deferred to her expertise, and they continued the gargantuan effort to reach the top.

By midday, the caravan was only half way up. Fortunately, the sand was becoming more compact toward the summit, so they decided to stop for a moment to allow themselves and the beasts a deserved break.

Tiblina went to check the horse's legs while Sikin, using the camel's shadow for protection against the punishing sun, stood by the animal's side until it was time to resume the climb.

Examining the heat blisters that had formed on his neck and face, Tiblina fed him a sip of water in a vain effort to quench his unyielding thirst. Then she asked him to stop lecturing for a while in order to keep his lips and tongue from drying up and cracking. Sikin felt as if flaming torches had been applied to every part of his exposed skin, and his eyes felt bloodshot and irritated due to the excessive dryness and glare. Again, he blamed Old McKinley for not planning his trip more judiciously.

In his confusion, he inwardly berated the old man for not supplying sunglasses, suddenly realizing that sun spectacles didn't exist during the Middle Ages, and much less in the Steppes of Central Asia.

From their present location to the next stop; at least a week of traveling under similar conditions still awaited. *How do the locals keep their vision until old age?* He wondered. Tiblina didn't seem to be bothered by any of his afflictions. How could she look so healthy and strong after using so much energy and eating such an awful diet throughout her entire life? Yet, how ravishing and fit she looked!

Perhaps the McKinleys ate the wrong foods in spite of the wide variety of choices at the grocery store, but then, where would he find mare's milk, horsemeat, and pharaoh's mice? Could it be the water, or the lack of it? What about the dusty air they breathed, or their uncomplicated lifestyles?

"Let's try to reach the summit before it gets hotter!" Tiblina exclaimed, interrupting his musings. "You'll get used to these hardships sooner or later!"

Employing one of his greatest assets, self-discipline, Sikin climbed atop the beast in virtually no time, mentally ready for their next attempt to reach the summit.

The horse, somewhat recuperated, didn't have to depend on the camel any longer, but although the sand was more packed, his legs still sank half a foot for every step.

Tired and a great deal slower than before, the camels reached the top in roughly twice the amount of time it took them to arrive half way up.

Once at the summit, Sikin could find no words in any of his newly learned languages and tongues to describe the sensation of wonder and fear he felt as he and Tiblina gazed at the infinite amplitude of earth colors reaching as far as their eyes could see. Flat depressions and sand dunes, which Tiblina said could be circumvented from then on, occupied most of the visible landscape. Fortunately, no hike in sight seemed to be as steep and massive as the one they had just climbed.

Their next challenge was obviously the descent. This time, the horse would be on his own as, if necessary, it would be much easier to pull the animal out of trouble going downhill than uphill. As Tiblina explained, the chances of getting partially buried were just as great, but the solutions were more workable.

Now, way past noon, the blazing sun was just as hot if not hotter than the day before. Sikin's thirst made him feel anxious and frustrated. In his life as Ivan, eight hundred years later, he'd always taken water for granted, like so many others who are used to satisfy their needs without impediments, as if by the mere fact of their existence, nature owed them an effortless fulfillment of their wants. *Never again,* he thought with resolve, *I'll be taking anything for granted.*

In roughly half the time it took them to reach the top, their descent finally came to an end.

"How far is that waterhole with drinkable water?"

"A good two days barring unexpected trouble."

Sikin groaned. "I just checked our water supply, and it is good for only one more day. How could we have used so much? Where has it gone?"

"I used quite a bit trying to keep your body wet. Besides, water slowly disappears when is so hot and dry. Don't tell me you are worried. Are you?"

"I'm not worried! I just feel desperately thirsty. Perhaps I should have stayed longer at the settlement allowing my body to become better acclimated."

Tiblina shrugged. "Why don't you lie down and take a break? I'll head for those tamarisk bushes and catch some fat gerbils. They are usually active during daytime."

"Gerbils? What do we need gerbils for?"

"For tonight's dinner, silly! Slowly roasted, they are delicious!"

Tiblina grabbed her bow and arrows and ran towards the dry bushes.

Sikin didn't dare express an opinion this time. He would either get used to her eating habits, or die of starvation. He climbed off the camel and took a couple of sips, but his thirst was relentless.

By late afternoon, Tiblina had not yet returned from her hunting expedition. And Sikin, waiting patiently, agonized over

54

the worse possible scenarios.

After what felt like an eternity, he finally saw the girl's shadow moving away from the bushes. She was carrying half a dozen dead rodents, and even though Sikin felt like hugging and kissing her, he refrained from doing so to prevent misunderstandings.

The gerbils, beige in color, perfectly matched the desert sands. The forsaken rodents measured about eight inches in length, had very large eyes and ears, elongated hind limbs, and long hairy tails.

Tiblina remarked that they moved by jumping leaps, lived in boroughs with numerous exits and were only active during the day.

"Those creatures look disgusting." Sikin said doubtfully. They look more like mice, rabbits, and kangaroos all mixed together."

Tiblina shot him a hurt look, but held her tongue. Sikin did not offer to help, nor did he watch as she deftly skinned the little animals and skewered them to roast over the fire pit.

Between his endless thirst, the roasted rodents and his frustrated attraction, the young man was at the very edge of losing his sanity.

The gerbils proved tough and chewy, but edible.

That evening, following the unusual roasted meat dinner, Sikin re-kindled his lectures. And as he talked, his thirst began to abate, perhaps a sign of his body's initial adaptation to the lack of water. He'd read that this generally happens when a traveler suddenly switches from conditions of abundance to those of deprivation, not allowing the body enough time to become physically acclimated. Thus the nomads would cover themselves from head to toe to prevent moisture from evaporating and sunrays from penetrating.

The next couple of days passed uneventfully. Sikin experienced the same desolation, heat, glare, and dryness, and the persistent thirst he had thought to be abating recurred like an immutable agony, especially after midday.

Their water supply had dwindled dangerously, and still there was no sign of the small oasis.

As Tiblina continued to show confidence and hope in their endeavor, Sikin was recalling her story about how she used to reassure merchants and travelers of her experience by faking an expression of confidence, when in fact she was more scared than anyone else.

In light of that, he asked her to be sincere about her feelings.

"This time I feel no fear," she replied, "because we are together, and I know we make a good team. Don't worry, Sikin, I'm not putting up a front!"

That night a windstorm began to rage early enough to interrupt their lessons. The whistling winds produced strange noises and the roaring sand blasting against their tent, was loud and scary enough to cause them a terrifying and sleepless night. "What can we do for the camels, the horse and the load?" Sikin asked. "Shouldn't I go out to make sure they are clinging tight to the ground?"

"You must remember this is their natural habitat." Tiblina replied. "Those animals are accustomed to the harshest conditions. They will seek protection by closing their eyes, laying low to the ground, and placing their rears against the wind. Besides, what would you accomplish by going out? It is so dark, gusty, and miserable, you won't even be able to see your own hands, much less the animals. Instead, by walking away from the hut, your sense of direction will become distorted. Imagine spending this ghastly night, blind, disconcerted, and unable to re-trace your way back because of the blowing dust!"

"What if the storm lasts for several days? Are we going to stay inside this trap without any water, waiting patiently for a burial?"

"It's better than the alternative." Tiblina shrugged.

"What would happen if we moved under these conditions?"

"I am sorry, Sikin, but the truth is that we can't." Tiblina shook her head. "We wouldn't be able to force the animals to stand. They just won't move, even if we whip them. Their behavior is relative to the storm's intensity and to its sounds. So forget doing anything besides being patient and sitting tight. At least I'm sufficiently familiar with the area to resume our intended course, even if the sands change the appearance of every point of reference. But if we left with no sense of direction, we'd better be ready to die in three or four days."

"Why didn't Amur fill more skins with water? Maybe they wanted to kill us, then follow our footprints and steal everything but our rotten bodies."

"Thirst must have gotten the best of you! They loaded the minimum amount of water needed to reach the waterhole and I used quite a bit to cool you off.

You must keep in mind that water is our heaviest load. The more we carry the slower we move, and the less we can bring of everything else. It's just a matter of getting used to it. Soon you will be able to survive with much less."

Luckily the sturdy tentposts held, but neither one slept much during the blustering night. Furthermore, they couldn't even determine daybreak except by guessing. It was pitch black by night and the darkest gray by morning.

The winds began to show signs of abating toward late afternoon the following day, allowing both to leave their refuge momentarily in order to take care of their personal needs, fetch a skin, and bring some food inside.

Camels can sense a dying storm; in the same mysterious way they detect an approaching one. Widely known as the desert's lifeline, the supposedly dumb creatures are accurate weather forecasters. If a handler is perceptive enough to understand certain behavioral patterns, such as lying low for no reason, or standing up when a storm hasn't shown evidence of weakening, the chances of successful survival are increased. No wonder Tiblina kept a constant vigil on them.

Cooped up inside, with nothing else to do but wait and see, Sikin decided to keep up with his lectures, dedicating day and night to teaching, among other things, art, not only its historical significance as a form of human expression, but also as a means of communication. He explained the evolution of music by singing songs. Then by drawing on the sandy floor with his index finger, Sikin taught her Roman and Arab numerals, and their application to express quantity, sizes, distances, and so on. At times, Sikin had to hold back his speed and coverage in order to avoid confusion and frustration in the girl.

Little by little, after enormous efforts put forth by both, Tiblina began to realize the critical importance of human knowledge by comparing what she had learned in just a few days to what she didn't know before.

Sikin marveled that, although he and Tiblina were diametrically opposed in culture, and distant from each other relative to time and place, they shared so many similarities. Their human values were almost identical, and they shared a mutual curiosity for the unknown. Their appreciation for human dignity in the midst of a dark age where the lack of it was endured and accepted by the common people made the pair a genuine rarity for the times.

These qualities, coupled with a keen sense of destiny, helped form their essential driving force.

As Tiblina focused fixedly on the numeric characters she was copying and recopying in the sandy floor, Sikin watched her enraptured.

She was a nonconformist living in an age universally known as one of the most unproductive in human history...rebellious against oppression when such a disgrace was generally accepted as a necessary evil...compassionate in an era where such human quality was almost nonexistent throughout her world...naturally inquisitive during a period where brute physical force was far more important than the development of the mind.

Was Tiblina the only woman in her world with enough courage and conviction to focus and shape her own destiny, despite the widespread barbarian rule? He wondered.

The truth, he suspected was that there were many; but few shared her determination to accept full responsibility for challenging the firmly entrenched establishment.

History had proven time and again, that threats of change aimed at ingrained social norms, regardless of their moral and humanitarian benefits, always trigger negative reactions from the powerful ruling class. No wonder it had taken well over eight hundred years for women to begin their emancipation from prejudice and misunderstanding, Sikin thought. Yet, even in Ivan's day and age, little or nothing had changed in Tiblina's part of the world.

By early evening the winds softened, but since it was too risky to travel at night, they decided to stay till dawn and determine their new course of action at first light.

Before supper, they left their shelter to sweep the sand off their beasts, dig out their halfway-buried tent, and light another fire.

Afterwards, the skies became so amazingly transparent, that they lay on the sand gazing at the starry firmament.

Using the simplest terminology, Sikin tried to explain the nature of the sun, stars, planets, even the roundness of the Earth. The latter Tiblina categorically refused to believe unless it could be proven, thus marking the first time she had rejected any of his teachings.

At this Sikin began to comprehend the insurmountable nature of his project to turn his friend into the most educated person on Earth. It would be difficult, if not impossible, to present her with a credible and understandable picture of spatial distances, when she didn't even know how to visualize the length of one mile, nor the meaning of concepts such as; millions, thousands, years, magnetic, atmosphere and more.

He needed to limit most subjects to the intellectual capacity of a third grader, and realistically, even a third grader of Ivan's time, needed three years of full-time schooling to comprehend the basics. Even cramming into her mind eight hundred years' worth of culture in less than two were hypothetically possible, everyone else would be illiterate by comparison. In fact she could very well be accused of witchcraft for her ability to 'divinate' weather, cure diseases, explain physical phenomena, and so forth.

Alas, Sikin realized, Tiblina lived in an era where only a fortunate few had access to higher levels of education, while the rest of the population lived immersed in abject ignorance and superstition. As an educated woman she would always pose threats to society's powerful elite, whose lifestyles generally thrived upon the ignorance of the masses.

In my zeal to help, Sikin thought worriedly, *I could be creating a monster!* The last thing he wanted was to cause Tiblina harm. Aware of the potential danger for a contentious woman to express herself freely and withut constraints, and in recognition that an intelligent person like Tiblina would advocate such behavior, he considered it irresponsible to shape her into a "social heretic."

With this in mind, Sikin decided to tone down her education to suit the era, giving priority to her physical, emotional, and spiritual life while nourishing and preserving her sense of mission and curiosity.

A renewed focus on Arithmetic would enable her to compute much faster than the rest of the population, since they still relied on archaic means of counting and calculating. Showing Tiblina basic concepts of business, such as the true meaning of money, the value of savings, investing, spending, bartering, and so on, would turn her into the shrewdest among all dealers. As for Geography, he would cover only those nations and places she had visited, planned to visit, or knew of, since Sikin was convinced that her refusal to believe in the roundness of the planet left little room for major advancement in this area. He would still offer some tenets of social behavior to help her understand human relations, her position relative to others, and ultimately the reasons why most people conduct themselves differently as part of a group than as individuals.

Since the Nestorian Friar based her basic understanding of Christianity on previous teachings, Sikin wanted to examine her faith and convictions more closely, in order to verify that she was spiritually well equipped to discern and evaluate the different religions and beliefs.

For last but definitely not least, he wished to cast firmly in her mind the divine and timeless truth that human wisdom is invariably flawed unless rooted in total submissiveness and accountability to a higher power, and therefore to distrust those portraying themselves as divine messengers in their own right, since such charlatans are nothing but direct reflections of their own greed and vanity, two of the qualities best representing the root of all evils.

Henceforth Sikin amended his idea of "turning Tiblina into the most educated woman on Earth," to a new ideal; "The wisest user of common sense around."

"Why don't you keep talking about the stars?" Tiblina asked breaking his prolonged silence.

"It's late now. Let's continue tomorrow." Sikin said pointing at the tent, politely conveying his need for a good night's sleep.

The next morning, neither could discern the rising sun due to the cloak of dusty haze that usually covers the Taklamakan, a day or so following a severe storm. This phenomenon, Sikin recalled, resulted from microscopic sand particles floating in the lower atmosphere at altitudes of some ten thousand feet, occasionally impairing visibility to less than twenty-five yards. Unfortunately, this time it appeared to stretch as far as a quarter of a mile.

"Can you determine our position?"

"No, I can't," Tiblina replied.

"You told me horses detect water at a distance. Would it be possible to let the animals decide our course and just follow them?"

"Yes, if we were closer to the waterhole, but we are not."

They stared silently at each other, trying to suppress their innermost fears and choose the wisest course.

"We will drink some horse's blood. It should satisfy our thirst for another day or so," Tiblina said confidently.

"Aren't you concerned about the animal? Wouldn't he need water immediately afterwards?"

She shook her head as if frustrated by his lack of sense.

"Sikin, if the situation reaches a point where we must decide who lives and who dies, shouldn't we begin by sacrificing the horse?"

"Of course, it's just that the idea of drinking blood bothers me immensely."

Impressed by Tiblina's resourcefulness and lack of

squeamishness when it came to matters of survival, Sikin realized that the lives of Ivan and his American peers were nothing but a bowl of cherries in comparison to her world. He had to admit he was learning as much from her as she was from him.

Ivan's priorities were focused on graduating from school, finding a job, and earning enough money to marry, buy a house, and enjoy a few luxuries here and there. Financial success had been his life's most coveted destination.

Shouldn't those trivial pursuits be re-assessed upon my return? He wondered. *Shouldn't my values and priorities be re-evaluated at that time?*

Sikin suddenly felt shame at Ivan's immaturity and gross incompetence to deal with some of life's most simple challenges. *Ours is such a meaningless existence!* He thought trying to justify one reason for Ivan's Utopian lifestyle.

We have a precious opportunity to live in a free country and develop the endless possibilities of our human potential. And yet, we let it slip through our fingers by following ordinary and meaningless trends.

Tiblina approached holding two mugs filled with warm fresh blood.

"How's the horse?" Sikin asked gulping in horror.

"The horse is fine, Sikin. He is used to this. Why are you so serious? Are you worried about our fate, or about the blood?"

"When should I drink it?" He asked in complete resignation.

"At once! Tonight at the latest," otherwise, it will get lumpy and hard to swallow.

"Perhaps I should wait till morning. Look! My tongue is not swollen, and I am still coherent. Even if it takes another agonizing day to reach the well, I'll still be able to make it."

After drinking her cupful to the last drop, she looked at him in the eyes and said, "I'm not the one with the problem, Sikin. You are! I know I will survive, whereas I'm not so sure about you. Once your mouth becomes swollen, the color of your tongue changes to white; your body begins to jerk, and desert dreams take over, it is too late."

"How can I tell when the crisis is near?"

"You can't. It just creeps on you. Now drink!"

"How about camel's milk instead of blood? He asked, begging for an alternative.

"It would work, except she's dried up."

"If I reached a crisis, would you tie me to the camel's chair and take me along, or would you leave me to rot?"

"If you threaten my life by becoming a burden; yes! I'll leave you behind and let you rot." Tiblina says somberly.

"It's your call, Sikin. You, and only you, must decide whether to live or die a most horrible death." Her remarks were so blunt and morbid, that they left him no choice but to drink the swarthy stuff. As a sage once said, "Timing is the only element that separates the coward from the brave," and Tiblina had timed her words perfectly.

He held his breath and drank until the cup was empty. Then he took several deep breaths, quelling his nausea. He had to keep the liquid down, or the effort would be futile. He realized the problem was in his mind, not his belly.

That night before retiring, Sikin thanked God for the opportunity to live another day, and for allowing him the chance to survive the ordeal. Even then, the young man still had the rusty aftertaste of blood in his mouth and a lingering sense of repugnancy.

Both slept deeply until daybreak, when the haze, though still firmly entrenched, had lightened up enough to put them back on track. Again, the caravan took off. No unusual events occurred during the morning, and thankfully Sikin's symptoms didn't get any worse.

By afternoon, Tiblina noticed a slight increase in the horse's speed. "Sikin!" She yelled. "We must be close to water! Haven't you noticed a faster stride?"

Sikin didn't know whether to laugh, cry, or get off his camel and kiss her hand, since by then, the young man had almost reached the end of his rope. This time he was riding in front so Tiblina could keep an eye on him. The young man was swaying from side to side as if he had lost control of his balance. He also had more blisters on his face, ensuing from further loss of fluids.

In order to distract Sikin from the effects of dehydration, Tiblina chattered on about her initial determination to choose their present course instead of traveling through the Silk Road to begin with.

Sikin sat on the swaying camel, recalling what he'd read about the desert's water resources. Oases of the Taklamakan were fertile tracts of land that subsisted wherever a permanent reserve of fresh water was available. They varied in size, ranging from two to three acres around small springs such as the waterhole they were approaching, to vast areas of irrigated land. Underground water sources accounted for the existence of most oases, including their springs and wells. Artesian-type oases were supplied from sandstone aquifers whose intake might be more than five hundred miles away. Most of their inhabitants were sedentary people whose survival depended solely on the fruits and vegetables they grew, such as peaches, apricots, dates, figs, and cereals like millet, barley, and wheat.

After their long days of unbroken desert travel, the breathtaking greenery of poplars, turangas, oleasters and camelthorns arose in the distance like a vision of Paradise. And as the descending afternoon sun poured its rays upon the luscious landscape, a refreshing contrast between life and oblivion began to renew their thirsty hearts.

As the weary caravan approached the perimeter of the oasis from the southwest, Tiblina pointed out six saddled horses and two loaded camels assembled in one spot. The camels were sitting, and the horses grazing. "Who could they be?" She asked aloud.

"The saddles look like those used by Mongol warriors, but where are they?"

As she spoke, she unsheathed her scimitar with one hand and pulled the dagger from behind her goatskin belt with the other, then moved up in front in order to lead the way.

"The last thing we need is a confrontation with thieves," she muttered.

Sikin nodded, his senses on alert. He knew marauders

plundered caravans at will all along the Silk Road. Often merchants hired armed mercenaries for self-defense. He felt for his own knife, wondering how much help he would be in a battle. What if he were wounded?

The oasis measured about ten acres in size, and it offered copious shade. Sikin felt he had reached the land of Eden after visiting Hades.

Finding no signs of life, Tiblina stopped about thirty yards from the animals. Her first priority was to fetch the water. She grabbed an empty skin and marched through the thick vegetation, leaving Sikin resting alongside his camel. The sun hadn't set yet, and there was enough light to move around safely. Upon reaching the spring, Tiblina searched in every direction for signs of the animal's owners, then bent forward and closed her eyes. After touching the water with her lips, she drank to her heart's content as she waited for the skin to fill. She ran back to Sikin immediately, but at first allowed him to take only short sips at a time. Then he gradually began to drink more.

To relieve the pain and discomfort caused by his blisters, Tiblina ripped off a handful of leaves from a nearby bush, dipped them in water, and applied them over his face and neck, while the animals strode nervously towards the spring to satisfy their thirst as well.

Suddenly they heard the sound of voices speaking Mongol, and as the talkers drew nearer, both could easily understand the conversation among several men. Instantly Tiblina moved alongside Sikin and with saber in hand, she stood ready to face their next adversity.

Obviously patrolling the Silk Route, six Mongol warriors appeared at a short distance. Over their usual clothes they wore protective leather shields treated with a form of lacquer that made them impermeable to water and impervious to penetration by arrows, swords, and knives. They also wore helmets with metal tops, and sheepskin earmuffs on wintery days. On their feet they wore leather boots they never took off regardless of conditions. Overlapping iron plates similar to fish scales sewn into the boots protected their legs. Each of the warriors carried a battle-ax, a scimitar, a lance, and two versions of their most famous weapon: the Mongol re-curved bow, which was designed for long-range use from a ground position. Drawing one hundred seventy pounds of weight, it was much stronger than the best quality contemporary European bow, the English longbow. They also kept a lighter one to be used while on horseback.

Sikin had read that these fighters were so self-sufficient they even carried a flint stone to sharpen their weapons, along with needle and thread to repair almost any kind of equipment while in the battlefield.

Showing no signs of aggression, their leader, followed by his five subordinates approached Tiblina.

Blatantly disregarding her *ready to kill* position, he asked:

"Unto what earthly power do you pledge allegiance?

No doubt acknowledging her inability to survive a fight against six heavily armed men, Tiblina replied without hesitation,

"Unto the mighty Kublai Khan, the world's conqueror and most powerful of all monarchs."

After assessing her reaction with his subordinates, the chief asked for their names, where they came from, and for what reason.

"We are caravan drivers lost during the windstorm," she responded reassuringly. "My husband developed severe heat illness so we stopped here to rest and recuperate. Please forgive him; he can barely speak." She shot Sikin a look that said *'play along and stay quiet.*

"We are looking for silk. How much are you carrying?" the leader pronounced in a deep resounding voice.

"How much do you need?" Tiblina asked.

The chief warrior explained that they only needed enough to repair the silk underwear they wore to protect their bodies against arrow penetration.

Contrary to popular belief, Sikin recalled, silk was such a tough material, that even if an arrow penetrated the human skin, the fabric would often hold. The warrior could then draw the arrow from the wound by pulling on the silk. The fabric could also prevent poison on an arrow's tip from entering the bloodstream.

Since the leader could easily have killed them and taken all their belongings, but had acted judiciously instead, Tiblina answered, "We have some silk I have painted, but it's all we have to barter for food."

"We will give you food! You give us silk!" The intimidating chief replied.

Nodding acquiescently, Tiblina opened the package protecting the silk scarves and presented it to the group leader.

"You keep the most valuable ones," the Mongol commanded. "Give us the simplest pair."

Looking both surprised and relieved, Tiblina offered him double the amount in exchange for protection during the night, which the leader refused to accept, saying that he didn't need any more, and that they were planning to stay overnight anyway. They would leave the following morning at the crack of dawn.

During the negotiation, one of the warriors pulled out a small container filled with sheepskin fat and offered it to Sikin to cover his blisters. Sikin accepted it gracefully. In Ivan's time, the grease, called lanolin, was still extensively used as skin protectant and conditioner.

After sunset, one of the warriors approached the couple to offer them a hand pitching their tent, and during that evening Tiblina and Sikin who was by then feeling much better were invited to join their group to exchange stories by the fire.

Delighted to be alive and impressed by the men's demeanor, Sikin could not associate their conduct with their reputation as primitive savage barbarians.

He tried to recall what he'd studied about these ferocious tribesmen.

Up to about the year 1206 AD, the Mongol nation had been comprised of rival tribes throughout northern Asia.

Temuchin, who later on took the name of Genghis Khan, emerged as the leader of all peoples living in felt tents.

His supreme leadership and genius as the founder of the Mongol Empire, laid the groundwork for a profound change in world history.

The neighboring Chinese Empire and the Central Asian states, both militarily weak and decadent, as well as the decaying Arab-Turkish society of the Middle East, inevitably surrendered to Genghis' much superior army. Eventually the Mongol domination stretched from the China Sea to the Dnieper River in the Ukraine, and from the Persian Gulf almost to the Arctic Ocean, with the city of Karakorum as its capital.

The Silk Road re-emerged as the main link between east and west, primarily due to the protection afforded by the Mongol army against the menacing hordes of thieves marauding in the area.

Sikin marveled at the fighters's self-sufficiency. In addition to their protective armor, each one carried a full set of tools and spare parts, ropes of various sizes, cooking wares, dry sinews for sewing leather, and a waterproof skin bag in which to keep their clothes dry while crossing large bodies of water at which time they would tie all their equipment to the horses then swim alongside the animals in groups of eight at a time.

In the opinion of some medieval historians, the Mongol military superiority resulted from their sheer numbers. Sikin could see clearly this was probably an excuse to cover up European inferiority in the front lines. According to more accurate accounts, quality, not quantity was the key to their solid line of military successes.

The conquest of Khanbalik (Beijing) in the year 1215 offers a good example. Sikin thought.

When the magnificent imperial Chin capital fell into Mongol domination, the ramparts around the city boasted a length of thirty miles. The Chinese had six hundred thousand warriors fighting the war. The Mongols had only seventy thousand.

After the death of Genghis Khan, his empire was divided among the sons of his primary wife and their heirs. His third son, Ogodei, who later became Genghis's successor, ruled the Khanate of East Asia, including Outer Mongolia, Manchuria, Korea, Tibet, parts of China and today's Indochina. Ogodai's nephews, Mongku and Kublai, conquered nearly all of China.

The Khanate of Turkistan was ruled by Genghis's second son, Jagatai, and extended from what is known today as the autonomous region of China westward to the Aral Sea. After 1370 the western reaches became part of the empire controlled by the Mongol leader Tamerlane, and so the Khan's rule was then extended to the western world as well.

By 1231 Mongol armies had overrun Iran, Mesopotamia, Armenia and Georgia. The Iranian Khanate established by Hulagu -self promoted, as II Khan - and brother of Mongku and Kublai, comprised the areas Ivan knew as Iran, eastern Iraq, western Afghanistan, and Turkmenistan. In 1395 the Khanate broke down into small states, all ruled by Iranians.

The Mongol Empire under Batu Khan, another of Genghis' grandsons, surged westward. Batu established the famous "Golden Horde," and by 1241 his armies had reached the coast of the Adriatic Sea, close to modern Venice. Europe was felicitously spared by the death of Ogodei, when Batu withdrew his forces to participate in the selection of a successor. The Golden Horde ruled the area that is now southern Russia until the late fifteenth century. In 1480, by refusing to pay tribute to the Horde, Ivan III Vasilyevich, grand duke of Moscow, ended Mongol domination in the region.

At the time Ivan Mc Kinley became Sikin, Kublai Khan, then emperor of China, had just transferred its capital to today's Beijing. From there he ruled as emperor of the Yuan dynasty as well as Great Khan of the Mongols until the year 1368, when the notorious Ming Dynasty replaced the great Khans of China.

Fulfilling human history's seemingly endless vicious circle, Genghis's biological descendants became attached to material possessions, alcohol, and debauchery, losing as a result their sense of purpose and leadership. By neglecting their fundamental values, the Mongols brought about their own downfall.

At sunrise, awakening to the sounds of the receding warriors, Tiblina and Sikin found themselves alone again. Now supplied with extra food from trading with the Mongols, they decided to stay three extra days before continuing to Turpan.

Like an island surrounded by treacherous seas, the small oasis was the perfect place for rest and recuperation. Sikin took advantage of their free time to continue tutoring in whatever subject they found interesting.

Four days later, Sikin's blisters had dried up almost entirely, and the agonizing thirst was assuaged. He felt fully recuperated, in good spirits, and grateful to Tiblina, as they left the oasis on a clear morning, carrying enough water to last a little over a week. According to her predictions it shouldn't take much longer than that to reach the outskirts of Turpan.

During a sunny afternoon, while crossing the worst section of the Turpan depression, Sikin noticed on the distant horizon a couple of unidentifiable black spots.

Distorted by the waves of heat rising from the sand, the undulating spots seemed to emerge like dark shadows floating over a body of water, three quarters of a mile away.

"Have you ever experienced a mirage?" He asked Tiblina, stupefied. "Look at those two spots. What do you think they are? To me they look like a couple of bushes floating on a lake."

"Sikin, there are no bushes and no lakes in this part of the Taklamakan."

Moments later, the spots coalesced into an identifiable image, two camels, apparently traveling by themselves.

Where are their riders? Sikin wondered. As they drew closer, he had his answer. Atop the camels were affixed two decomposed bodies with their hands cut off and daggers deeply plunged into their chests. The corpses lay on their broken backs, facing the midday sun, tied to their saddles by ropes that bound their necks to both legs on the opposite side of the animal. Sikin and Tiblina dismounted their camels at a prudent distance from the ghastly scene. Afraid of finding more ugly surprises as well as a nauseating stench, they carefully covered their mouths and noses before advancing towards the victims.

The corpses, one relatively young and of dark skin, the other an older man of Asian descent, had been tortured and killed several days before. Tiblina felt so revolted that she couldn't watch. Sikin, though horrified, took the time to search their bags, finding them empty except for a carved wooden figure of a wolf, which he retrieved to show the girl.

On the sight of it, Tiblina turned as pale as the sand beneath her feet.

"Are you sick?" Sikin asked.

"I'm all right. I am just shocked."

"You see, the head of a wolf is one of many symbols representing Mongol supremacy. It has been their tradition to chop off the hands of thieves upon their capture. I'm almost certain those two thugs were caught in the act by a Mongol patrol, So, I can assure you that the perpetrators of this grisly punishment were the six warriors we encountered at the oasis." Tiblina said somberly.

"They didn't look like savages to me!" Sikin said dubiously.

"They don't have to look like it to act in kind." She replied. "The Mongols impose their law at any cost in order to set examples, thus keeping others from repeating the same offenses."

"Why don't we bury them and keep the camels?"

Tiblina pursed her lips. "Sikin, No one buries the dead around here, we reduce them to ashes. And if I'm right that the warriors did this to set an example, the last thing we want to do is challenge their intentions. Those camels will eventually end up in an oasis somewhere or perhaps crossing a band of thieves, which was exactly what they had in mind in the first place. We don't need the camels, so why not forget the whole episode and keep going? We should be joining the Silk Route in no time."

By late afternoon they were approaching the ruins of the ancient city of Jiaohe, west of Turpan, which had been decimated by the Mongols in their westward conquest fifty years before.

Tiblina suggested they spend the night among the relics, and in the meantime draw water from the city's abandoned artesian well to satisfy the thirsty animals. After retrieving over a dozen heavy pails of water, Sikin poured one over his head. The bath felt so refreshing that he decided to fill another and go after Tiblina.

71

SPLASH! "Sikin!" she squealed in mock anger entirely taken by surprise.

In the midst of their laughter, Sikin suddenly caught his breath. Somehow, the dripping dark hair accentuated her fine features, giving the attractive young woman the most feminine and captivating look he'd ever seen in her before.

As she laughingly wrung out her wet clothes, Sikin realized how well they were getting along, and how much affinity they had developed in less than a month. Once again, the young man allowed his imagination to run wild with fantasies as far-fetched as taking her back to America on his return trip.

What would the McKinley's neighbors' reaction be like after discovering a lovely young woman with the face of an angel, but the mentality and mannerisms of a barbarian, living in his house? What would Lisa, Ivan's girl friend say? Would Tiblina welcome the change? Would she ever adapt to a lifestyle eight hundred years yonder? Suppose she became an overnight hit after relating her incredible saga either in Mongolian or in ancient Italian at media press conferences? Would she add credibility to Ivan's teleportation stories?

Chances were she would be branded a fake - some kind of publicity stunt to market a new soap that cleans and shines dry hair after being exposed to sand and dust.

"Would you like to eat some goat cheese?"

Sikin returned to the reality of the thirteenth century. His thoughts turned from Tiblina to Turpan. He knew the oasis grew the sweetest grapes in the world, as well as the juiciest of watermelons, and that most local folk lived in homes with shaded arbors to survive the heat of the day in comfort. He couldn't wait to eat real food, especially after losing considerable weight due to dehydration and to the "negative appeal" of their meals. *The image of a watermelon sliced in half, dripping the reddest and sweetest juice* created in Sikin's mind another kind of mirage most difficult to erase.

"Sikin, I asked if you wanted goat cheese?"

"Of course I do!" He replied trying to conceal his innermost fantasies with a smile.

In anticipation of better days, of fresh cool waters running everywhere, and of his soul being renewed by the colors of nature, Sikin and Tiblina left for Turpan early the following morning, his desires to discover new experiences and experience new discoveries rekindled.

Always maintaining a keen sense of awareness, they approached the oasis without mishaps.

The large haven appeared as an explosion of color against the monotonous white and beige of the Taklamakan on its southern side, and the black and white world of the Gobi Desert beyond its eastern borders.

CHAPTER *Three*

THE OASIS OF TURPAN

A journey is never too long or too short,
like life, distance is a state of mind.
Anon.

Situated along the southern foot of the Tien Shen (Celestial) mountain range, the Oasis of Turpan, at three hundred feet below sea level, was in those days the lowest and driest town on the face of the known earth. As early as 52 BC it was established by the Han dynasty as an important Silk Road passageway and garrison town. By the time Sikin and Tiblina arrived, Turpan was already two thousand years old.

The oasis, which in antiquity measured about twenty acres in width, had multiplied its size many times by the use of the *Kariz*, or underground canals, an ancient system of irrigation invented in Persia and brought into the city by the travelers of the Silk Road. Nearing the ancient town, Sikin saw rows upon rows of large pockmarks along their route. Those were the holes through which men descended to clean their kariz, which brought irrigation water from the Tien Shen Mountains. Hundreds of kariz converged in Turpan, some of which had been dug as far back as hundreds of years B.C.

At the edge of town, Sikin noticed a short, skinny man running as fast as his legs allowed. The little fellow was wearing a thick leather belt, riveted with dozens of small bells that jingled to announce his approach to the next station. He was part of the efficient communication system in the Mongol world. There were three main levels of correspondence, which could be interpreted in Ivan's language as "second class," "first class," "On His Imperial Majesty's Service," or "Top Priority."

Runners to relay stations located three miles apart carried second-class messages. This system allowed messages to travel the distance of a normal ten-day's journey in only one. At every station a log was kept on the flow of mail, and royal inspectors patrolled every route.

First class service was conveyed on horseback, with relay-stages every thirty miles.

Non-stop dispatch riders who carried a special tablet bearing the sign of the gerfalcon to grant them safe conduct conveyed the most urgent and important messages of Kublai Khan's empire. As he drew near each post, the messenger would sound his horn. Then the ostler would bring out a freshly saddled horse, to which he transferred and galloped straight off. According to Marco Polo, these courier horsemen usually traveled three hundred miles in one day.

Turpan seemed so isolated; yet as caravan commerce thrived, the melon and grape oasis became one of the most important cultural crossroads in the world.

Sikin was enthralled by their surroundings. The combined sounds of different languages, of bells clanging from carts taking women and children to market, and the gurgling irrigation ditches refreshing the ambiance with cool mountain water and carrying the perfume of flowers downstream, painted a most harmonious picture. The tastes were as sweet as the sounds and sights. Almost everyone was either munching on Turpan's sweet melons, or eating its grapes.

Sikin found the surroundings active but relaxed, a feast for the senses. He relished the luscious look of fresh produce transported in woven baskets. He marveled at the different types of wheeled carts crammed with children, goats, the elderly, kettles, rolls of silk, mulberry leaves, furs, spices, large rodents and more. All these goods would be stuffed inside a boxy gurney not larger than twenty square feet, some pulled by the family strongest and others by a yak. And since most everyone knew each other, groups in animated conversations would halt in the middle of the road, totally oblivious to traffic and log jams.

In the marketplace, vendors brewed and sold fresh mint tea from felt kiosks. Cheese, milk, deer meat, wild boar, and a wide variety of birds were also sold or bartered.

Watching her children play, a mother of six sold cooked regional meals, such as handsomely curled fried wheat noodles called *sanga*, and *shoe sole bread* that her clientele had to dip in tea in order to eat. Sitting in front of her house on a blanket spread full of rice, an older woman plucked gravel from the grain. Nearby, under a grape arbor, she kept a bed where she took naps during the heat of the day.

Under a felt canopy, seated on a Hotan carpet, a scribe wrote on rice paper her client's wishes, while in the next stall, a group of children took calligraphy lessons from an older woman dressed in an exquisitely embroidered silk tunic.

In addition to bartering, paper money was widely used and readily accepted in business transactions. Foreigners unfamiliar could have interpreted the haggling among Silk Road merchants with their customs as adversarial, when in reality their aggressive gestures were nothing more than a good-natured part of the act.

Mongol warriors roamed everywhere. Turpan had escaped destruction by the invaders due to the citizens' cooperation and lack of resistance towards the conquerors. It was in everyone's best interests to maintain stability in such an important crossroad of the Route.

As they continued their gradual tour of the oasis city, Sikin became fascinated by a number of cloth merchants who were throwing their material into a fire to prove to interested buyers the wonderful properties of the cloth.

"My goodness!" he remarked. "These people know of the existence and usage of asbestos! How fascinating!"

"What did you say?" Tiblina regarded him blankly.

"Oh, nothing. I'm just talking to myself."

They strolled by dozens of guesthouses offering food and shelter to weary and dusty travelers.

Sikin identified followers of familiar and unfamiliar religious sects. Muslims prayed to Allah kneeling on their kilim prayer rugs. Asian Buddhists wearing orange tunics displayed their shiny sun-tanned scalps. Numbers of faithful streamed in and out of a large Nestorian Christian church. Sikin saw no evidence of poverty anywhere in the lively town.

Farther down the road, dozens of camels and horses occupied an area generally used by travelers to feed and refresh their animals, and on its opposite side, various forms of shelters, mainly felt huts, had been erected by transients for temporary stays.

After finding space inside the large community of travelers, Tiblina and Sikin pitched their tent, unloaded the beasts, and brought them feed. A shallow stream of fresh water crossed through the center of the lot where the animals were held.

Coming into the oasis Sikin and Tiblina had noticed hundreds of goats descending from the mountains and into town. Led by nomads and their trained wolves, the large herd was heading toward one of the irrigation canals, a routine carried out daily for generations. While the animals drank the nomads would sell fresh milk and cheese throughout the city, sometimes till late at night. Food was plentiful, so in spite of their slow and sedentary ways, none of the locals seemed famished or undernourished.

Since their camp occupied the liveliest and noisiest section of the city, tutoring was temporarily suspended. Transients gathered over a common fire to cook their meals and exchange gossip and conversation. Sikin wanted to listen for as much information as possible. Tiblina, on the other hand, was happy to relax.

Their answers to questions of identity and relationship

remained the same: they were husband and wife, modest merchant traders. This prevented the inquisitive from paying too much attention to Sikin, and hindered any man from making inappropriate advances to Tiblina.

Their deepest concern was the prospect of having to cross a stretch of the feared Gobi Desert to reach the road to the oasis of Hami. They needed approximately one month to reach Hami, which was located mid-way between Turpan and their final destination, the oasis of Dunhuang.

Next morning, Sikin accompanied Tiblina to market in search of silk decorating materials and a roll of the fabric to take along for painting, with the idea of offering her works of art in exchange for paper money while in Dunhuang.

While strolling through the countryside on their way to market they passed by dozens of mulberry trees, which produce the only leaves the weird looking white silkworm will eat. Silk, Sikin knew, is a fibrous substance produced by many insects, mainly in the form of cocoons; except the webs and nests formed by spiders are also of silk. However, the fibers used for manufacturing purposes are exclusively produced by the mulberry silk-moth of China, where the industry originated around the year 2640 B.C.

According to legend, Si-Ling, wife of the famous Emperor Huang-ti, encouraged the cultivation of the mulberry tree, the rearing of worms, and the reeling of silk. This empress devoted most of her life to the care of silkworms. Asian scholars also credit her with the invention of the loom. The Chinese guarded the secrets of her valuable art with vigilant jealousy, and many centuries passed before the culture spread beyond China.

Years later, the cultivation of the silkworm was started in India, where, *according to historians,* the eggs of the insect and the seed of the mulberry tree were smuggled concealed in the crown of a Chinese princess.

The first observation of the silkworm in western history occurred when Aristotle spoke of a great worm that had horns and looked very different from all others.

The silken textures, which at first found their way into

Rome, were outrageously expensive, and their use by men was deemed an effeminate luxury. From an anecdote of Aurelian, who detested the use of silk and forbade his wife from owning a single piece of the material - we learn that silk was worth its weight in gold.

Having mastered the art and skill of silkworm rearing, two Persian monks who had lived in China all their lives arrived in Constantinople invited by Justinian to teach their secrets to the emperor. Impressed by their knowledge of such a peculiar art the monarch asked them to return to China in an attempt to bring back to Europe the material necessary for the cultivation of silk, which they smuggled by concealing the eggs of the silkworm in a bamboo cane.

From the precious contents of that tube brought to Constantinople in the year 550 AD emerged all the varieties of silkworm known to the western world for the next one thousand three hundred years.

Sikin smiled to himself in the realization that those rare silkworm eggs could very well have come from a grove such as the one they were walking by.

"How do you decorate silk?" Sikin asked Tiblina.

"Years ago mother taught me two different methods. In one, I use oil dyes to hand paint and adorn the fabric, and in the other I use stencils."

She went on to describe her techniques, which had been applied by the Chinese for thousands of years.

"I assemble the screen stencil by stretching silk over a wooden frame. On this fabric is the design to be stenciled. I then paint the areas that are to remain white with stuff similar to gum, which makes the silk impervious to the color of the ink used. I place the stencil on top of the surface to be adorned, and scrape a puddle of ink from one end to the other with a flat leather tool. This forces the dye through the open areas of the stencil onto the material underneath. I then lift the stencil and continue to apply others in the same fashion until the piece is finished."

That evening, sitting around the fire with their neighbors, Sikin asked an older Turkman, who was traveling with his two sons and their elderly Abyssinian servant, enough information about the silk market to rekindle his curiosity about the quality and value of Tiblina's works.

"Concerning exquisite works of art, there are not enough this side of the Tamirs to satisfy the gluttony of wealthy Venetians," said the Turkman. "The finest Chinese pieces are only adorned with Oriental motifs, so traders rarely find silks that would satisfy the tastes of wealthy and knowledgeable Europeans. There are small silk filatures in Venice and Milano. The Sicilians have also planted mulberry trees to compete in price against Oriental merchants. But there is no comparison either in the quality of the fabrics or the artistic merits of their pieces. The Italians lack the secret techniques applied by Chinese artisans for thousands of years, and in my opinion they produce nothing but mediocre works.

I know a Florentine priest who wanted to order an altar cloth of the finest of silks, embroidered with religious motifs especially designed for his church. After years of searching everywhere in the country without any luck, he traveled all the way to Saxony and bought a gorgeous altar cloth made of the finest linen."

"If I show you a piece of work adorned by my wife would you give us your opinion as to its quality?" Sikin asked.

"It'll be my pleasure!" replied the Turkman. "I've been in this business all my life, first with my oldest uncle, and now with my sons. I know quality when I see it. And if it is a mediocre piece, I'll be the first one to tell you."

In a moment, Tiblina returned with a large, colorful scarf edged with fine silk filaments. The center bore a lotus flower with golden threads marking its contour, surrounded by a field of some of the flowers grown in China. The raised textures of the embroidery conveyed an almost multi-dimensional image throughout; little space remained for more ornamentation. It was without a doubt an extraordinary piece of art and craftsmanship!

Holding it in his hands, the Turkman ran his fingers over the scarf, paying special attention to the gold threads. After turning it around, bundling it, and stretching it, he placed it against the light of the fire. Finally he brushed the piece accross his face to feel its resiliency and softness.

"Young man," he pronounced, "rest assured your beautiful wife is worth her weight in gold. This is the kind of work I see in places such as Kublai Khan's palace in Shangtu or at His imperial court in Khan-balik. If we were going westward, I would buy it at any price. Then I would turn around and sell it in Europe for well over a hundred times what I'd paid."

Impressed with the merchant's comments Tiblina folded the scarf and ran back to the tent. She had never being praised for her work before, but remembered her mother saying that she was passing on the secrets of the past and that in due time her work would be appreciated for its beauty and value.

That evening, Sikin told her that he'd do everything possible to make sure she went to Venice following Dunhuang, and after noticing a great deal of surprise in her expression, he asked if she understood what it all meant to her.

"Suppose that after all our efforts I finally settle in Venice just as you said," she replied. "Let's assume I could begin supporting myself immediately. My life wouldn't be under bondage anymore. No one could use my body and get away with it. I would never be sold, enslaved, bartered, or abused again, and hopefully my painful memories will begin to fade.

Yet, if I settle down there, do you really believe a man like you would ever become interested in a woman like me? To them, I will always be a barbarian. Also, women of the west are entirely different in looks, education, culture, and traditions.

The fact that I'm foreign and so different from the others might make most people feel uncomfortable in my presence, and chances are that they'll ostracize me from society. Don't you see how small the odds of my being accepted really are? I might never be able to blend in and have friends, much less marry and raise a family!"

Sikin shook his head in disbelief. "I understand your concerns, and you may be right, but I can't imagine that the Venetians wouldn't love you. You're beautiful, talented, intelligent..."

Tiblina held up a hand to hush him.

"Since you also come from a different land, perhaps you can help me out with some answers. What would happen if you were not allowed to return to your country? Would you learn to love what you call desolation, savagery, ignorance, and backwardness? Would you look for a wife and friends among those whose traditions you find primitive and uncivilized? Would you learn to drink blood from a horse? If dying of thirst represents my most terrifying fear, living in isolation would be just as bad!"

Sikin nodded emphatically. Tiblina couldn't have expressed her anguish more convincingly. She would miss her land and her traditions, and even though she enjoyed Sikin's support, they both knew his stay was only transitory. Then what? Alone again?

He hadn't realized until that very moment how eloquent and perceptive she was, even though she had to combine her known languages to better express herself.

"Tiblina," Sikin said taking her hands in his. "If your main concern is whether you'd be able to find decent, loving, and supportive friends in a foreign land, the idea you would be rejected is pure hogwash! Being so exotically attractive, your features will turn western men inside out. Your so-called barbarian background is a secret you needn't reveal to everyone who crosses your path. Besides, those are not your roots. If people ask where you came from, just answer, 'My parents were from the steppes of Central Asia, and after they died, I decided to change my surroundings and come to Venice.' Tell them you are considered an expert in silk painting and came to take advantage of the great opportunities Europe has to offer. You don't have to lie to tell the truth, and there is nothing wrong with adding or taking away a little ornament here and there."

Tiblina raised an eyebrow, but Sikin noted a slight grin lightening her features.

"As for values and life styles," Yes!" He continued, "you will experience shock and confusion for some time, but then you'll make adjustments in order to blend without losing your identity. You'll speak Italian, have an excellent education, the demeanor of a lovely princess and your values will exceed by far those of most Western women. My goodness girl! How could you possibly be alone?

Finally there is the question of religion. If you were Buddhist, Moslem, or for that matter an atheist, I could understand you would have trouble being accepted in Venice, since the Catholic Church exercises absolute power in that city, as it does in most kingdoms of Europe. But your friar friend has already built a noble Christian foundation in your heart, so you would be fine. Let's continue with your education, and you will be assured of a place anywhere in the world. I promise!"

At this Tiblina smiled broadly. "All right," she answered. "I'm ready. But you still haven't answered my questions about how you would accept life under barbarian rules and traditions if you had to."

Sikin paused for a moment to gather his courage, and then replied, "first of all, if I had to stay in this land of yours forever, I wouldn't let you slip away no matter what. I'd get used to each and every torment, including hideous cheeses, leathery breads, camel's milk, and horse's blood. And to tell you the truth, I don't know how I am going to handle the inevitable return. The more I know you, the more I like you. And the longer we are together, the less I want to leave."

He quickly kissed her on the cheek, and then backed off, half surprised, half frightened at his own boldness. "I'm going for a walk," he said, and hurriedly disappeared into the night. He had felt attracted to the girl ever since he'd first laid eyes on her at Amur's hut. Yet, he had decided to prevent at all costs any passionate involvement in order to save her the suffering of an inevitable separation. How strong was his determination? Only time would tell.

Early the next morning, they were awakened by the sounds of merchants preparing to leave, the smell of mint tea being brewed, the whining of camels refusing their loads, wheels crushing the path underneath, and the loud voices of children at play. Both overslept for the first time since they'd left Amur's settlement.

The air was crisp and the sky was clear, a great day to visit the grottoes in the nearby Flaming Mountains. They decided to stay another day in paradise before facing the frightening black and white Gobi Desert.

Carrying a skin filled with fresh water and a basket full of dates and figs, Sikin and Tiblina mounted the horse, expecting to arrive at the canyon of the Flaming Mountains shortly before noon. There, they would stay overnight, returning to Turpan the following morning.

Sikin revealed his worries about the safety of the camels and their belongings.

Tiblina assured him that travelers and merchants protect each other's property around the camp. "No bandit in his right mind would dare enter and pilfer around. You've seen the kind of punishment they might expect if caught."

They traveled along the eastern bank of a river that led to a canyon beneath the yellow mountains where the Bezeklik Grottoes had been built. As they rode, Sikin and Tiblina asked each other a multitude of questions concerning the existence of those mysterious caves. Sikin had read about them in his research, and Tibina was able to fill in details and local lore.

The most significant commodity carried along the Silk Route was not silk, but religion. Buddhism came to China from India, where it originated in the year 400 BC, with its greatest impact occurring during the fifth and sixth centuries AD. Encouraged by an increasing number of merchants, missionaries, and pilgrims, the new religion spread slowly eastward through the oases surrounding the Taklamakan, where devotees built large numbers of monasteries and grottoes.

The hills surrounding the deserts were mostly of sandstone, with streams and rivers carving cliffs that could be relatively easily dug into to form sacred grottoes decorated with elaborate paintings. An abundance of funds was always available to finance the work, particularly from wealthy merchants asking their deity for protection or wishing to give thanks for a safe desert crossing. Gifts and donations were seen as an act of merit that would enable the donor to escape rebirth into this world.

Among the illustrations of Buddhas and Boddhisatvas, the walls held scenes of everyday life at the time, and in many of the murals and frescoes the donors themselves were clearly depicted. The best-known and finest examples were the Mogaku grottoes of Dunhuang. The building of the caves was not only confined to the borders of the Taklamakan, however. Sikin recalled there was a large cluster in Afghanistan, including the world's second largest statue of Buddha, towering two hundred fifty feet and dating back to 300 AD.

In Ivan's time, at the Bezeklik and Mogaku grottoes, archaeologists discovered a walled-up library of books written in Sanskrit, Chinese, and Tibetan, as well as thousands of manuscripts often written in less widely known languages. Among those, was one believed to be the world's oldest printed book.

Of the most important Chinese inventions, crushing the bark of the mulberry tree into fibers and pounding them into sheets accomplished the making of paper, dating from around 200 BC. Later on it was discovered that the quality of the product could be much improved with the addition of rags, hemp rope, and old fishnets to the pulp. Paper was soon widely used in China then spread throughout the rest of Asia.

Upon arriving at the foot of the gorge, Sikin and Tiblina tethered their horse to the trunk of a tree before climbing a huge limestone staircase built along the edge of the cliff. The stairs led directly to a path carved alongside the steep slope that linked most of the caves on that side of the mountain.

A total of eighty-three different caves and grottoes existed in the surrounding areas many dating back to 400 AD, built almost eight hundred years after Buddha's death.

According to legend, Buddha, "The Enlightened," lived in Northern India during the sixth century BC. Gautama was his family name, and his personal one was Siddhartha. He was born to a noble family of ancient lineage, the Sakyas. Therefore, the title by which Siddhartha came to be known was "The Sage of the Sakyas" or Sakyamuni.

What is known of the Buddha's life is based primarily on the evidence of canonical texts, which were written in the ancient Hindu language Pali. According to these records, his place of birth was Lumbini, near the small city of Kapilafastu on the border between Nepal and India. At the age of twenty, after witnessing sights of suffering, sickeness, and death, the young nobleman renounced his life in the palace and left in search of enlightment. Legend has it he achieved it at Bodhgaya in Northern India, and gave his first sermon at nearby Sarnath.

He spent the rest of his life traveling, teaching, and spreading his philosophies.

The new religion experienced tremendous growth in India, later spreading through the Northern edges of the Taklamakan and south from Bengal to Afghanistan. By the seventh century AD, the small kingdoms of the Tarim basin had been entirely won to Buddhism and to the Indian culture, and Sanskrit became their religious language. Even in Ivan's day, the Sarnath Lion capital is imprinted on India's currency, and the Buddhist Wheel of the Law on its national flag.

First the kingdoms of Kashgaria, Yarkand, and Khotan in the West, Tumusk, Aksu, and Kizil in the North, and Turpan and Dunhuang in the East, became centers of Buddhist art and philosophy – hence the murals, sculptures, and paintings found inside the thousands of grottoes in Central Asia. Buddhism also had a strong pacifying effect on other belligerent cultures in the steppes. Once a nomadic tribe adopted the Buddhist faith, they no longer exhibited their tough, barbaric, and war-like qualities.

The first grotto they entered emitted the distinctive odor of incense. They stood in awe before a fresco depicting princes from the Central Asian states in lamentation after Sakyamuni, the Buddha, entered Nirvana. They had gathered to express their grief by crying, beating their chests, piercing themselves with swords and knives, or cutting off their noses and ears. The mural depicted their devotions to the Buddha, and the garments and customs of the different nations along the Silk Road, as well as the history of cultural exchange among them, circa 400 AD.

Before their conversion to Christianity, Tiblina's parents had been fervent followers of the teachings of Buddha. Therefore she could explain in full detail the meaning of the frescoes, as well as those of other paintings, some of which had become so deteriorated due to environmental factors that it made their recognition almost impossible.

After leaving the first grotto, they entered another one where the entrance was larger and its interior much deeper. There, the cavernous sounds of praise and the humming of chants lent an air of hallowed mystery. Four monks with bare scalps; dressed in orange tunics and sitting in the lotus position, sang and prayed, seemingly oblivious to the presence of the couple.

Painted in a wide array of colors, a heavily adorned altar held a statue of Buddha with offerings of fresh fruit and meats placed at its feet. The acrid smoke of incense was so strong that Sikin began to cough, thus forcing them to leave the cavern.

Sikin and Tiblina had to walk alongside the cliff for almost half a day before arriving at what she claimed to be a very important cave.

Using her newly adopted vocabulary, she explained the significance of the frescoes inside.

"That painting bears a striking resemblance to the one inside our Nestorian Church," she said, pointing. "I can still remember the friar telling me stories about some of the persons depicted, and as I grew up the same legend became progressively more serious and complicated. It took me a long time to understand its profound meaning. The central figure in the fresco is Mani," she continued. "On the right side is Jesus, and on the left is Buddha. The others surrounding the three include Zoroaster and all the prophets from the time of Adam until that of Mani."

Tiblina continued to explain the rest of the story, while Sikin, captivated, listened attentively to her interpretations of the friar's teachings. She had an amazing memory, and expressed herself in articulate and descriptive manner.

The cave temples held a unique position in the development of Buddhist architecture, and intense devotion was deeply reflected in the wall paintings of the rock-cut caves. The artists, through arduous work, had created the most impressive wall frescoes dedicated to Buddha, his saints, and his legend, as well as astonishing displays of local societies, their royalties, knights, ladies, monks, artists, and so on. Besides their artistic value, Sikin realized such works of art provided a wealth of historical information. The frescoes displaying people with light skin, blue eyes and blond hair, for example, showed that this ancient culture was more Indo-European than Mongol.

Among the thousands of frescoes found by archaeologists in the centuries that followed, each one conveyed its own message. The painting with the images of Mani, Jesus, and Buddha that Tiblina described was the creation of the Uihgur Turks who had been driven from Mongolia into the Northern oases of the Taklamakan circa 840 AD. They practiced a religion known as Manichaeism, until their acceptance of Buddhism crystallized several years later. In the meantime, following prevailing traditions, they created works of art with their own Manichaeistic motifs.

Manichaeism was a "dualistic" religious movement that claimed the world, or reality, as we know it consists of two basic, diametrically opposite and irreducible principles that account for all that exist, similar to the biblical account of God and Satan.

Founded in Persia during the third century AD by Mani, who was also known as the "Apostle of Light" and "Supreme Illuminator", Manichaeism was long considered a Christian heresy. The movement was a religion in its own right because of the consistency of its doctrines and the structural inflexibility of its institutions, as well as its character and unity throughout its relatively short history.

Southern Babylonia - now Iraq - was Mani's land of birth. Later in life, with his "annunciation" at the age of twenty-four, he obeyed a heavenly order to manifest him publicly and proclaim his doctrines; and so began the new religion. From that point on, Mani preached throughout the Persian Empire against the King's wishes, for which he was condemned and imprisoned. Following twenty-six days of trial, which his followers called the "Passion of the Illuminator" or "Mani's Cucifixion," he delivered a final message to his disciples, dying around the year 280AD.

Mani viewed himself as the final successor in a long line of prophets, beginning with Adam and including Buddha, Zoroaster, and Jesus.

From its inception, the Manichaean Church was dedicated to strong missionary activity in an attempt to convert the world. The faith spread rapidly throughout the Roman Empire, from Egypt into Northern Africa, where the future Saint Augustine temporarily became a convert. Vigorously attacked by the Catholic Church and the Roman State, it disappeared from Europe almost entirely by the end of the fifth century.

The most peculiar doctrine of Manichaeism was to know oneself, which meant to visualize one's soul partaking in the very nature of God and coming from a transcendent world.

This knowledge enabled a person to accept that despite his or her abject present condition in the material world, he or she never ceases to remain united with the supernatural by eternal and intuitive bonds. Therefore, according to that doctrine, knowledge was the only way to salvation.

*   *   *

Sikin gazed at the extraordinary depiction of the world's prophets to that time. "Why did the friar tell you the story of that painting?" He asked Tiblina.

"I suppose since there were so many cults and religions flowing through the Silk Road, he wanted to make sure Christianity remained strongly rooted in my mind," she answered. "He thought by explaining the basic principles of Buddhist and Moslem doctrines, I would never fall as he said, into a 'trap of religious fanatics.'"

"The friar was certainly a good man, wasn't he?" Sikin responded with an approving smile.

"He saved my soul." Tiblina replied simply.

Shortly thereafter they moved to another grotto farther down the trail.

Finding an atmosphere of solitude and tranquility, they decided to stay for the night inside that cave, thus keeping those eerie sensations from disturbing their sleep.

After they lit their oil lamp, thousands of bats suddenly swooped from a distant corner, flapping against the yellowish boundaries of the grotto. Sikin momentarily entertained the gruesome delusion of being surrounded by vampires - an unpleasant sight to behold before bedtime.

"We should have brought weapons to defend ourselves!" Tiblina said warily.

"Defend ourselves from what?" Sikin asked. "They are just harmless bats!"

"Not bats, bandits!" Suppose thieves decide to hide for the night inside our cave? What do we do then?" She shuddered apprehensively.

"Stop worrying!" Sikin said soothingly. "You're just jumpy from the eerie surroundings. Let's quit talking and try to get some sleep. Shall we?" He blew out the lamp.

"Turn it on again!" She pleaded nervously. "I saw something down there."

"Why don't you close your eyes and stop tormenting yourself?

"Sikin, will you please turn on the lamp?"

The lamp back on, she pointed at a round object partially concealed behind a rock. After venturing a peek Sikin retrieved a bag filled with sand. She grabbed the mysterious package and began to pour its contents through her fingers until an object the size of a date stopped the flow.

Her eyes alight as if possessed Tiblina inserted two fingers into the sack and pulling out a heavy, almost transparent stone she asked; "What do you think this is?"

"Oh my God it is a diamond!" Sikin screamed jubilantly.

"A diamond?"

He explained that it was the hardest and most valuable substance on earth, and that emperors and kings from all over including India and China revered its actual and symbolic strength.

"Am I rich, Sikin?"Asked the innocent barbarian.

"Will you please quiet down?" Sikin cautioned.

Tiblina's heart was pounding so hard she could have easily passed out.

"To heck with my life in America," Sikin wondered aloud. "If it sparkles in the dark, imagine it under sunlight!" He exclaimed to Tiblina, who continued dwelling in a state of wonderment.

Sikin didn't need the precious stone, he had enough wealth as it was, and besides, his stay was only temporary. Yet he craved for it. Even the idea of staying in that forsaken land; seriously crossed his mind.

After spending the night inventing excuses to justify finding, taking, and owning the gem, both friends fell asleep holding each other's hands.

At the crack of dawn they rolled the covers, left the cave, and by the time they were mid-way down the cliff, both noticed a couple of Mongol riders entering the grotto. Once they had reached the bottom of the gorge, Tiblina and Sikin could hear the warriors screaming profanities at each other.

A cold sweat dripped down Sikin's brow, wondering if they fought about the stone.

"Let's leave before they find us!" Tiblina urged with a sense of rush.

"I think we are in trouble." Sikin replied somberly. "We shouldn't have stolen it."

"They'll never know we took it. Besides, we didn't steal it!" Tiblina replied defensively. "There's no way a couple of warriors could own such a valuable stone unless they had pilfered it from someone else. Besides, the friar once said that a thief who steals from a thief is not guilty of any crime, so I suggest we keep the rock."

While Tiblina and Sikin were munching on dates and figs down at the bottom of the gorge, a strange-looking creature that was eavesdropping on their conversation approached them from behind.

"Alms for the sick!" Implored the ugly hunchback.

Horrified at the frightful face of the leper, Tiblina tossed at him the leftovers, dragged Sikin to the horse and galloped away, arriving at the camp late afternoon. Most merchants were gone, and nothing was missing. What a sense of relief!

"Sikin, you two must leave immediately!" The loud voice of the Turkman was heard at a distance.

"What's going on?" Tiblina asked apprehensively.

"Two disgruntled warriors came to chop your hands off in retribution for stealing their property, an accusation no one here took seriously, so we told them you were gone. The Turkman answered.

"They were furious!" One of the sons said clenching his fists.

"I hate to be in your shoes," whispered the other.

Even the Abyssinian servant asked them to hide somewhere else for the night. It was time to worry.

Inmediately, Sikin and Tiblina began to pack their belongings as fast as they could when suddenly, they found wedged between the camel's wooden saddle and a thick blanket underneath, a note written in Italian, addressed to *the interesting young couple.* The document read:

Distinguished travelers:

Please excuse my indiscretion for omitting your names while addressing this note, but personal and moral obligations compel me to implore most humbly, and as a last resort, for the assistance and good offices of wayfarers.

I am willing to offer a generous reward for a service I desperately need. If interested, please meet me shortly after sunset at the inn located behind the kiosk of the scribe. It shall be my pleasure to welcome the two of you as my guests for late afternoon tea.

Please come.

Forever thankful,
Curzio da Ponte.

Sikin wondered whom this Signore Da Ponte might be when Tiblina insisted they meet with him and find out.

Early that evening, a lady of advanced age opened the front door of the inn, welcoming Tiblina and Sikin inside without even asking who they were or what they wanted.

In a courtyard heavily protected from the sun by a canopy of vines, a gentleman dressed in western attire far too elegant for the surroundings walked forward to greet the visitors, assisted by his ebony cane. After giving the lady a gentle indication to leave them alone, he offered them a seat.

The man exuded an aromatic fragrance hard to identify. His perfectly groomed grayish goatee and polished mannerisms conveyed the demeanor of an educated, wealthy Italian aristocrat.

First, he bowed and kissed Tiblina's hand. Confusing his politeness with intimacy, she did not appreciate the gallantry until Sikin indicated with a smile that it was acceptable. Discreetly ignoring her reaction, the mysterious gentleman warmly shook Sikin's hand, which was also an unusual form of greeting for that part of the world.

After an exchange of pleasantries, the man addressed them in his native Italian.

"Please allow me to reveal my story first. Then I shall present the reasons for requesting the honor of your presence.

I was born into a noble and immensely wealthy Venetian family. When I was about your age, I decided to consecrate my life to the pursuit of lucrative and adventurous challenges rather than giving into the hedonism, luxury, and trivialities, so commonly pursued by those who have everything. I learned young to always question people's sincerity and honesty of purpose, and to carefully select my friends because my family was constantly pestered by the meaningless adulation of sanctimonious parasites so prevalent in Venetian aristocracy during those days."

Da Ponte's eyes twinkled, and he stroked his goatee as he continued.

"In my early thirties I married the kindest woman in all

Venice. Of humble extraction, sincere and simple, Mirella became my best friend. She was the kind of human being whose personal fulfillment depended upon the happiness and contentment of her loved ones. She was a dream come true for any man wishing to share the rest of his life with a wonderful mate. Yet, I wasn't able to achieve personal fulfillment in marriage. In fact, I never fully realized the meaning of such expression. I had everything a young man could ever ask for, affluence, prestige, a great confidante, a noble and decent family that had miraculously survived power struggles, politics, conspiracies, greed, envy, and so on. Being aware of my good fortune, I should have fulfilled my obligations as husband and father, thus dedicating my entire life to such an honorable calling. However, my longing to escape confinement was overwhelming. Rather than achieving compromises here and there in order to save my treasures, the lure of becoming emancipated from what I considered a most boring and meaningless existence compelled me to relinquish my duties and old traditions. In this light I presented my irrevocable dilemma to those I loved, thus inflicting upon them unnecessary grief and heartaches.

Mirella reluctantly accepted my cruel and selfish conduct as an inevitable result of growing up under a dishonest and impersonal social system. As always, she fully understood my wants, and therefore suggested I do with my life as I wished, as long as the family was well provided for, and as long as I kept in contact with our daughters at least once a year.

Unlike most husbands in Venetian aristocracy, our male ancestors followed the time honored tradition of staying close to their wives and family, hence the same was expected of me."

The old man shook his head ruefully.

"I must have made her life miserable with all my nagging and complaining about my insatiable need for freedom and adventure. At last, drained and disillusioned, without even asking my destination, she finally opened the gilded cage, allowing me to escape into the real world to conquer the glories I wanted so much to achieve. Our two daughters were raised in the midst of the upheaval, and to make things worse, I virtually abandoned them during their childhood. Sylvana our oldest, married a Dalmatian nobleman. Mariu the youngest was, and still is, a mirror image of her father, but with much more common sense than he. She is feminine, refined, intelligent, and a born rebel against all forms of parasitical existence. In fact, her noble qualities are rarely seen among women anywhere.

I tried unsuccessfully to visit them during short periods of time every year, but my trade made it almost impossible. Now that my youngest daughter is about your wife's age," he smiled at Tiblina, "I want to return and beg their forgiveness for all the grief I have caused."

"A laudable goal," Sikin said. "But how can we help?"

"Allow me to finish my tale, and you shall see," replied the Venetian.

"Refusing to use the family's wealth for personal support, I decided to go out into the world and make a fortune on my own, which I have achieved in quantities exceeding my wildest expectations.

I began by joining a Turkish merchant who needed someone to assist him while traveling the Silk Route. I worked for the man during a trip that lasted two and a half years. I also made invaluable contacts East and West, learned the tricks of the trade, as well as the disciplines of physical endurance and survival, and gained sufficient knowledge and experience to venture forth on my own. This I did six months following my return to Venice.

On the next trip, I went alone. This proved one of the worst blunders of my life, since I almost died of thirst and starvation while crossing the Gobi in an attempt to find the Hexi corridor to reach Cathay.

Fortunately, two Italian merchants found me lying unconscious by the road. They fed and brought me back to life, and in appreciation I decided to join them, thus developing a close friendship and a lucrative association that has lasted almost a lifetime. Together we traveled to the farthest corners of the earth. At last I was leading the kind of life I always wanted, and

I exploited it to the fullest.

Several years ago, the two brothers and I arrived in Sudak, and from there we traveled to Surai, where we traded for a while. Shortly thereafter, a civil war broke out between Barka and his cousin Hulagu, making it impossible for us to return by the same route we came. We decided to make a wide detour toward the East in order to avoid the conflict, and thus we found ourselves stranded in Bukhara for over three years. In that city we were rescued by the arrival of a Mongol ambassador from Hulagu who informed us that the great Kublai Khan would be delighted to meet us, for he had never seen Latins before in his life.

We decided to take the Northern track of the Silk Road through Turpan, Hami, Dunhuang, and then across the Gobi through the Hexi corridor towards Khanbalik, where we were scheduled to meet with the Great Khan. The crossing alone would have taken several months to complete.

Weeks before arriving in Turpan I came down with a fever, and by the time we reached the town, I was too weak to continue. By mutual agreement, the two brothers proceeded to meet the Khan on their own, while I stayed behind recuperating. It took me weeks to get well, and I wouldn't be alive if it wasn't for the delightful lady you met at the door, who generously took care of my convalescence. Of my three manservants, two succumbed to illness, and the third disappeared with another caravan two months into my stay. Hence I find myself alone. After living in the Oasis for over a year, an official emissary of the great Khan personally conveyed a message on behalf of the two brothers, asking me to meet them in Dunhuang in approximately five months. They should be traveling via the Southern route back to Venice by now, and according to the emissary they were in dire need of my personal influence with the Roman clergy for an important but undisclosed reason. I consider it my moral duty to help them out, but as you can see, I am too feeble to venture towards Dunhuang entirely on my own."

By then, Sikin had no doubt in his mind that the brothers

Curzio was referring to, had to be Matteo and Niccolo; the father and uncle of Marco Polo.

"I also feel a deep sense of urgency to see my family after all these years." Curzio continued. "If I am unable to go now, I could very well never see them again. I wish to receive their blessings and forgiveness before is too late. Do you understand? I have asked other caravans for assistance and in spite of offering them generous compensation for their services they always see my presence as a potential encumbrance to their mission. Therefore, I'm still waiting for a merciful soul to take me along and allow me to join them on the journey.

So there you have the most important reasons to solicit your good offices. I would sincerely appreciate your mercifulness in taking me with you. If you will, my deepest gratitude will be yours forever. No price could ever be higher than that of never seeing my wife and daughters again.

As a reward I promise to make your dreams come true. In fact, I shall do anything possible to bring your wishes to reality. You have my word of honor!"

Their eyes met...

"Signore Da Ponte, with your permission, may we ask for a moment of solitude?" Sikin asked.

Bowing, the old man withdrew to await their decision in the house.

Sikin spoke softly; "I do not care for the idea of accepting money from a desperate man with a conscience in distress. If we decided to help him, it should be from compassion, not for personal gain. Tiblina nodded emphatically. "The friar has said many times, just as you have, that no encounter is ever accidental. He taught me to consider mutual needs every time I meet someone unexpectedly, and then to try to uncover the reasons for such an encounter by finding common grounds. Sooner or later the underlying cause for the coincidental meeting will become clear." She pointed to herself and Sikin. I know our meeting occurred for a reason, and so it was with the Mongol warriors, and the same with my parents and the Khan's funeral procession. As much as I hate to admit it, I believe the reasons for that tragedy will become self-evident sometime in my life. Of this, I am fully convinced."

Sikin knew that Tiblina felt the man should join them.

With apprehensive gestures and a broken voice, Signore Da Ponte approached the young couple like an innocent man awaiting judgment.

"Signore Da Ponte, would you honor us with your presence in our trip to Dunhuang? We are looking forward to sharing your extensive experience in these matters." Sikin said, bowing slightly in an attempt to keep the gentleman from feeling like a mendicant. Even if it was an act of mercy on their part, they wanted him to feel a welcomed guest.

The old man handed Sikin his cane and in a demonstration of gratitude, he embraced them with wide opened arms and teary eyes.

Tiblina's eyes grew moist as well. She hadn't experienced a hug like that since she lost her father, she later told Sikin.

Da Ponte begged them to stay at the inn for as long as they wished, an invitation they accepted on fears of being caught for stealing the diamond.

Two days later, the caravan of three resumed their trek toward Hami, the next large oasis after Turpan, one to two months away depending on conditions. The incident with the warriors was behind them, but still memorable.

The Gobi desert, Da Ponte reminded the travelers, consisted of the Kashun, Dzungarian, and Trans-Altai Gobi in the west, the Mongolian Gobi in the Center and East and the Ala Shan Desert in the South.

The Tien Shen mountain range to the west and the Pei Mountains to the south, rising to elevations as high as five thousand feet, Sikin knew, bound the Kashun Gobi.

The desert had a corrugated look with a complex maze of wide hollows separated by plateaus and rocky summits. The terrain was stony and waterless, though salt marshes existed in the secluded depressions. The grayish-brown soil was filled with coarse gravel in some areas and sandy salt marshes in others. Vegetation was as rare as in the Taklamakan, and the few varieties of salt-resistant saltworts and halophytes had a grayish-brown appearance as well.

Winters were severe, more so towards the North where temperatures dipped into the forties and fifties below zero; during summer the heat climbed to one hundred fifteen degrees.

Drainage in the Gobi was largely underground. Subterranean water was widespread and of such good quality it allowed cattle raising in some areas. The desert served as a habitat for wild asses, camels, wild horses, gazelles, and antelopes. Nomadic herders would migrate as far as one hundred fifty miles a year between the extreme points of pasturelands. Somewhat unlike the Taklamakan, the Gobi was just as treacherous.

As they were riding through the outskirts of Turpan, Mongol felt yurts, and Chinese clay houses built from crude brick, lined each side of the path leading to the Silk Route. The sight of families waving goodby through their windows gave Sikin the chilly impression he was embarking on a trip to eternity.

Da Ponte took along his two best camels. One, he loaded to capacity with a European tent, and provisions including dry meats, flasks of honey and olive oil, and leather bags containing dry fruits and giant figs gathered in Bukhara.

Following years of experience in such matters, the nobleman knew how to travel in style. The load also included appropriate attire for the road, a tricornered hat to keep sunshine off his head and face, soap made of volcanic dust, razors and scissors to groom his beard, a wide array of small bottles filled with aromatic oils for personal use, pillows stuffed with goose feathers, a mandolin, bottles of wine, hard liquor, and various distinctly unnecessary items. His loaded camel must have weighted in excess of seven hundred pounds. Concealed inside a smaller bag, Da Ponte carried enough precious stones to raise the eyebrows of the Great Khan himself. He had coated the gems with a brown substance to disguise their identity, so they looked just like gravel from the Gobi.

From the right side of his leather belt hung a polished scimitar and a dagger, and from the left, a fancy Saracen saber with its handle encrusted in diamonds. Wondering about how daring or foolish the man was to carry such precious cargo into areas rife with bandits and murderers, Sikin expressed his concern. "Son," the nobleman replied, "I'll be glad to show you the saber at our next pause. You will notice that the diamonds in the handle form the silhouette of a wolf, which is the symbol of Mongol supremacy. Hulagu Khan presented the piece to me while I was stranded in Bukhara in exchange for a beautifully decorated Murano crystal urn. His emissary advised me that the value of the saber is not in the handle, but in the message it conveys. I have used it as a diplomatic passage ever since. In fact, the mere showing of it has opened countless doors and provided golden opportunities."

Da Ponte laughed grandly. "On one occasion I was approached by six armed horsemen that insisted on searching our load with the sole intention of plundering everything of value. When their leader noticed the engraving on the handle, he fell on his knees begging for mercy. Shocked and horrified, the remaining bandits jumped on their horses and galloped away, leaving their boss smothering in a cloud of dust."

"Amazing!" Sikin Replied. "Perhaps I should teach Tiblina everything I know about precious stones, *especially diamonds.*"

Da Ponte inclined his chin toward Tiblina, who rode ahead of them humming a cheerful yet exotic tune. "I am really curious about your unique relationship, he said. Would you consider me intrusive if I ask what kind of association the two of you share? You don't behave like the usual married couples I meet."

"Not at all," Sikin answered. He went on to explain the details preceeding their encounter with Da Ponte, as well as Tiblina's history and backround, emphasizing that there was no intimacy in their relationship even though they shared the same tent. He also confessed his love for her and the reasons why he had decided to remain detached; omitting, of course, that the land to which he was returning would be eight hundred years into the future.

"My boy," Da Ponte said when Sikin finished, "you either must possess wisdom beyond my ability to appreciate to act so irrationally, or you are the king of fools. If you love the girl, go on and tell her! Don't waste such a unique opportunity! You'll never find another like her." The man stroked his goatee thoughtfully.

"Believe me, son, through the years I've had the chance to meet ladies at every social level and background, from the most beautiful and smart, to the ugliest and most brainless. And yet never have I met one I could honestly describe in the same manner you have depicted this girl."

He paused, and then spoke excitedly. "Would you allow me to help out with her education? My contribution could be substantial, coming from an old man who has learned lessons to last many lifetimes." His eyes twinkled. "I may be able to offer you a lesson or two as well.

Learning from the hidden past of an astute fellow could become an invaluable asset to a good listener. Unfortunately most people your age refuse to pay attention to the trials and vicissitudes of an old sage. You cannot imagine how much I wish I could share my experience with my daughters."

Sikin smiled enthusiastically, for the old man reminded him of his own grandfather.

"Thanks for offering your help, Signore Da Ponte. I think it is a great idea, especially if you speak to her in Italian."

"Bene," said the old man. "Good. And now you will please address me as Curzio. I am to be your friend, as well as a teacher, no?"

"Grazie, Curzio," Sikin answered, honored by the old man's gesture. Eager to hear some of his stories, Sikin asked the elegant traveler if he had ever seen the Great Khan in person.

"Ah!" said Curzio, lighting up. "I have indeed, but at first only at a distance. At the time I was disguised as an Oriental merchant during my first solo trip to Khanbalik. Knowing of His Majesty's curiosity for Latins, I'd never felt safe giving away my identity. He is an *incredibly powerful* monarch and a God to his people."

"Would you mind telling us about it?"

"It'll be my pleasure, but I'd rather wait till tonight when we are more relaxed. Why don't you join me this evening for supper?" Curzio asked grandly.

"We'd be delighted," Sikin responded, amused at the formal invitation. He fully expected the travelers would eat together every night, though they would each draw on their own food supply.

Tiblina, who had remained unusually silent throughout most of the day, asked if everything was all right.

"Everything is fine," Sikin replied. "I just wish you could understand the language better and share in our conversation. As of this moment, if you don't grasp everything we say, just ask! Don't worry. Curzio will understand."

But everything wasn't fine. Two riders desperately trying to approach them were catching up from behind.

"It must be a Mongol patrol," Curzio observed confidently.

"I'm sure they are looking for the stone," Sikin added in trepidation.

"What stone?" Curzio inquired suspiciously. "Is there something you haven't told me?"

"It's a long story, Signore Da Ponte." Sikin replied. "We think they are after a precious stone we took from a grotto."

"A thief who steals from a thief is not guilty of any crime" Tiblina said reassuringly.

"But nonetheless is a thief!" Curzio said contemptuously. "Perhaps the two of you were not as sincere as I thought."

"Please give us a chance, Signore Da Ponte. We will explain everything, I promise! That is, if we survive."

"She's the same woman described by the leper," roared the one-eyed warrior pointing at Tiblina.

"What about the old man?" asked his subordinate.

"Let him watch his grandchildren bleed to death while we chop their hands off!" Shouted the one-eyed warrior, wrestling Tiblina to the ground.

Outraged, Sikin jumped the hefty soldier from behind, and pointing a dagger at his throat, he whispered menacingly, "Let her go, or I'll bleed you to death!"

With a brutal blow to the stomach, his partner knocked Sikin breathless against a rock.

"Let me go, you filthy animal!" Tiblina screamed at the top of her lungs. "You stole it first. Now it belongs to us!"

With amazing dexterity, the young woman removed the one-eyed soldier's helmet, and sank her teeth into his left ear, making the victim swear enough profanities to rattle the ghosts of the Gobi.

Motionless and undisturbed, Curzio watched the skirmish from the seat of his camel with dignified curiosity.

To save the one-eyed soldier from Tiblina's fury, his partner raised a scimitar in a final attempt to decapitate her. All of a sudden a loud voice was heard, "*Surrender in the name of the Great Khan!*" The nobleman shouted displaying the diamond-encrusted saber.

Panting and horrified, the warriors bowed to the old man in repentance.

"From whom did you steal the stone?" Curzio asked adamantly.

"From a caravan thief," responded the one-eyed man trying in vain to control the bleeding.

"You shall return to your patrol immediately!" Ordered the nobleman. "And always remember that a thief who steals from a thief is not guilty of any crime." Curzio said, winking an eye to Tiblina. "Therefore since my children are innocent, I order you to leave them alone!"

As the warriors left and the dust cleared, Da Ponte asked to see the stone.

"Mmm…it is a diamond indeed," he said examining the gem against the light. "It is of a very poor quality though, and with so many flaws, I wouldn't trade it for my camel.

Why in God's name would you risk stealing something just because it shines? Shame on you!" Curzio said aloud. "And for goodness sake, if it doesn't belong to you…hands off next time!"

That night, the breathtaking transparency of the evening sky was astonishing, and the stars looked so dazzling that the nobleman decided to hold his dinner reception outside. By the time Sikin and Tiblina got to his tent, Da Ponte had already spread an ornate silk rug on the ground where they would share food, drink, and conversation. The fine Oriental carpet was so exquisitely finished, that both guests were hesitant to sit.

To gratify their sense of smell, Da Ponte had incense burners on the four corners of the piece. Sitting on his goose-down pillow, the host opened up the banquet by singing old religious melodies accompanied by his mandolin. After playing a dozen pieces, he set the instrument aside.

"This mandolin was built especially for me as a farewell gift by its maker," he said. "I received it on the day I left Venice for the first time. It has been my best friend and confidant for the past twenty years. I play it every time I need to see color in my surroundings. Its beautiful sounds add brilliance and vitality to an otherwise empty and silent existence. And, like a good friend, it never talks back about my blunders, nor recounts character flaws I should have corrected, nor does it allude to the kind of life I should have chosen instead. It shares my most treasured memories, and without reproach it answers my sorrows with its music.

But enough of this sentimental subject!" he exclaimed. "Let us drink! This bottle of Vin Santo was presented to me by my good friend, Pope Clement IV!"

Sikin and Tiblina gazed at each other in wonder as the old man filled three crystal goblets with the sweetly scented liquor. Tiblina recognized and knew the liquor could be dangerous.

"What is that stuff you are pouring?" She asked coarsely.

Gently ignoring her remark, Curzio went on "May this moment be a prologue to the birth of a loyal and sincere friendship among us three," he pronounced holding his goblet aloft. "May God grant us faith and courage to bring our mission to a successful and meaningful ending. May Tiblina continue to exhibit the same grace and enthusiasm in her quest for freedom and to my new friend Sikin, may God offer the wisdom he so eagerly pursues. Salute!"

Supper consisted of smoked wild boar meat, dried figs, and peaches from Bukhara, and mare's milk with honey for dessert. Sikin judged it a great dinner for being in the middle of nowhere.

He observed Tiblina, who had never experienced a meal presented so elegantly. Understanding this was her first encounter with class and finesse, Curzio was intentionally teaching the girl politeness and etiquette in a most subtle and effective manner. Tiblina, on her part, observed the nobleman closely, imitating his gestures. Her natural grace went a long way in preventing awkwardness even when she erred.

After supper, Tiblina went back to the tent to boil some tea.

"Son," Curzio remarked when she was out of sight. I certainly hope to discover someday who you really are. I sense a strong premonition that you come from a most alien and fascinating culture, so different and extraneous to ours that it makes of your presence an absolute wonder."

Sikin couldn't believe the incisiveness of the old sage's perception. He also realized that although the time was unsuitable to disclose his true identity, it was possible that he would have to reveal it sooner or later. In the meantime he simply grinned politely and tried to change the subject for a less complicated one.

Tiblina returned offering freshly brewed tea, her hair handsomely braided, and her face looking more radiant than ever. Instinctively, she had assimilated her first lesson in femininity and social refinement.

With the fire burning a few feet away, the two men sat on the carpet next to each other while Tiblina reclined on her back, stared at the magnificent skies.

"Sikin told me you have actually seen the Great Khan, and that you were going to share the story with us," she said to Curzio. "Why don't you begin by telling us how he looked?"

Curzio closed his eyes as if picturing the monarch.

"Of middle stature, proportionate body, fair complexion, reddish at times. His eyes black as charcoal, and his nose well shaped, but conspicuous," he said. "Now, perhaps you would enjoy listening to the story of my journey to the city of Shang-tu, and my visit to the Khan's summer palace? I am sure you will find it fascinating!"

"Yes, please, Curzio," Sikin and Tiblina echoed. "We are

all ears!"

"Very well, then." The nobleman arranged himself comfortably, as if for a long tale.

"The city was built by the reigning Kublai with the intent of erecting his summer palace in its midst. Constructed of marble and other magnificent stones, the palace is awesome in its elegant design, and marvelous for the skill displayed in its achievement."

Again he narrowed his eyes in recall. "The halls and chambers are gilt, and the teak floors are covered with hand-woven Persian rugs. The furnishings are of carved sandalwood, and the cushions intricately adorned with images of the battlefield and wild animals.

The Khan's favorite pastimes are falconing and conquering lands. But don't consider him a reigning brute. I regard him as a genius. The man is exceptionally savvy, decisive, intelligent, and knows the frailties of the human spirit well. He uses these qualities in the most tactful of manners to ensure absolute control over his pursuits. He understands and conducts government well. When provoked, however, the Great Khan can become the most ruthless of barbarians.

His Majesty built the palace with the front entrance overlooking the city and its rear facing a gigantic wall that encloses the palace sixteen miles around.

Surrounding this fabulous edifice, gorgeous meadows watered by small streams abound, nourishing hawks and other birds the Khan likes to hunt and eat. Deer, goats, and antelopes graze inside the enormous compound, waiting to be chased and caught by His Majesty.

He also keeps a handful of leopards that are carried by their keepers during his inspections or hunting expeditions. Often when a deer or stag appears, he orders them released, thus amusing himself as the cats seize and kill the prey. This he later feeds to his hawks.

The Khan keeps twelve thousand horses and mares, all of them white as snow," Curzio went on. "Of their milk no one is allowed to drink except for the direct blood descendants of

Genghis, the father of the Mongol Empire. So great is the respect shown for these creatures that even when they are at pasture in the royal meadows and forests, no one dares to stand in front of them or look them in the eyes.

Every year on the twenty eighth day of the moon cycle during the summer months, Kublai Khan departs to a nearby place to perform certain sacrifices. Profoundly versed in the arts of magic, the astrologers in his service ask the Khan to honor the idols and spirits they worship by scattering in the wind the milk taken from the white mares.

When the sky becomes stormy with rain and winds, the seers climb up on the roof of the palace where the great Khan is in residence, and through their mystical powers prevent the rain from falling on it.

Traditionally they never cleanse their bodies or change their raggedy outfits. Always filthy, and with begrimed faces, they live in absolute squalor and stench.

These men are addicted to the horrible practice of cannibalism. When a culprit is sentenced to death, they carry off the body, dress it on the fire, and devour it. However, they do not consume the bodies of persons who die of natural causes."

"Do you believe that account to be true?" Tiblina asked.

"Oh yes! I've seen it with my own eyes." Curzio made a sign of the cross in the air.

"Tell us some more about the Khan's way of life." Sikin said.

"Allow me to relate the story about the time I was invited to attend his public court and eat at the royal banquet.

The Khan's table, elevated above everyone else's, was set on the palace's northern side, for His Majesty always faces South. On his left sat the Empress, and on his right, his many sons and grandsons as well as a multitude of blood relatives, all sitting at lower levels so their heads are never above the monarch's feet. At an even lower level sat the wives of the nobility and military officers. I should also mention that not everyone attending the banquet had tables. Hundreds of envoys sat on carpets along the halls and outside, all waiting for a chance to bestow their gifts upon the Emperor.

In the center of the hall lay a magnificent fixture that looked at first sight like a square chest. It had exquisitely carved figures of animals and gilt on each wall, and inside it, a huge ceramic vase gilded in pure gold was filled continuously with buckets of liquor. Next to the chest, four smaller receptacles filled with mare and camel's milk were available for those not wishing to drink alcohol. More containers filled with enough liquor to satisfy the thirst of another ten to twelve persons were placed in front of every single guest. Needless to say, the quantity and richness of his Majesty's table was incomprehensible.

At all doorways in the grand hall, two enormous officers stood guard, one on each side of the threshold. They held large staves to prevent guests from touching the doorsill with their feet, a sign of bad luck. If any person were found guilty of such an offense, the giants would proceed to undress the wrongdoer and inflict a number of blows. The only way for the victim to stop the punishment and recover their garments was by paying an outrageous fine.

The numerous attendants serving His Majesty were compelled to cover their noses and mouths with handsome silk veils in order to keep their breath from contaminating his food.

After the gorging was over, comedians, dwarfs, and jugglers, performed for the Great Khan and his company. Then a large band played until the monarch stopped drinking, which also served as an indication to his guests that the party was over."

Curzio laughed. "At the end of the festivity, since everyone went his way in an inconceivable state of intoxication, the threshold ruling was temporarily waived to prevent the attending guests from going naked."

The nobleman yawned, politely covering his mouth.

"If you two don't mind listening to my anecdotes, I will be delighted to relate them at another time. But for the moment please accept my apologies, since this old man's only wish is to retire for the night."

Tiblina and Sikin were left in such a state of amazement that neither said a word for the rest of the evening.

The days passed insignificantly. Sikin and his friend chatted constantly, as if they couldn't find enough subjects to talk about. Tiblina participated in the conversation, but her limited education kept her mostly listening, learning, and asking questions.

Da Ponte grew more intrigued by the couple's attitude toward each other every day. More than once he remarked to Sikin that he couldn't understand the logic behind their detached relationship, and that nosiness was driving him crazy.

Aware of Curzio's inquisitiveness and knowing deep inside that the moment of truth had to be drawing near, Sikin contemplated the possibility of telling the truth in the likelihood of further ramifications.

He felt tormented by questions…

What if they refuse to believe the story? Will they make fun of me? Accuse me of madness – or sorcery? Perhaps is unwise to consider this move.

Realizing he might be opening a risky dialogue, perhaps irresponsibly, Sikin resisted revealing his true identity at that moment. After all, what would it gain?

But Curzio had begun speculating that Sikin was a reincarnation of a person from a higher realm. The sun never set without him making remarks, or asking bizarre questions about who Sikin was and where he came from. The issue was not "if" anymore, but "when and how."

If Curzio believed in the existence of aliens from another world and in reincarnation, Sikin reasoned, he was sure the old man wouldn't have a problem accepting his story. He had doubts Tiblina would though. If the girl wanted evidence of the roundness of the planet, God only knew what kind of proof she'd ask for this time.

The passing days were pleasant. A windstorm began to form one morning, and by midday the caravan found it virtually impossible to continue. The same series of events they had experienced in the Taklamakan awaited them in the Gobi, except this one presented even more serious challenges.

Following a sudden darkening of the sky, they decided to

stop and take cover inside their tents. Sikin helped Tiblina with theirs, and then intended to help Curzio. But once again he found the old man's display of stamina and determination in pitching his own tent amazing. In spite of his ailments, he moved at the speed of light. Nothing seemed too heavy or difficult to handle. Unlike other well-to-do travelers of the Silk Road, Curzio Da Ponte seldom hired servants for the journey. He claimed they were a nuisance, and worse than traveling with relatives

The grayish scene grew frightening as particles of blowing salt, dust, and gravel irritated everyone's eyes, and the animals tried in vain to find refuge from the barrage of flying debris. They made camp.

Once inside their tents all they could do was sit and listen to the sounds of rock fragments blasting the tent walls and to the incessant moaning of the relentless wind.

"Sikin, I feel sorry for Curzio," said Tiblina. "He's all alone inside a tent with no one else to share his thoughts. How could a mandolin become a friend? How can he share life with a piece of wood? It must be appalling! Don't you agree?"

"If you feel that way, let's have him for supper this evening." Sikin replied. "We owe him one, you know? The man is such a refined and thoughtful person. Haven't you noticed he uses twice the amount of words to express the same thoughts I would? It seems such a contradiction to find someone as polished and educated as him, dealing with the harshness of this brutal environment. Sometimes I wonder if he is deliberately punishing himself in order to placate a deeply seated sense of culpability."

Sikin paused at Tiblina's uncomprehending look.

"Unaware of their natural inclinations, some people go through life wasting precious time and energy searching for vague ideals and following deceptive dreams. Later in life, tired of chasing meaningless pursuits, they become bitter and dejected. They usually blame circumstances such as luck or perhaps others for their failures, seldom looking for answers deep within themselves. Our friend is certainly not a frustrated and bitter person, on the contrary he is a joy to be around. Yet some of what I've just said could very well apply. Don't you think?"

Tiblina dropped her eyes uncertainly and merely smiled.

That evening, under a barrage of flying gravel and debris, Curzio crawled toward their tent on time for "dinner", which consisted of their usual unappetizing menu. Sensing the moment to be perfect, Sikin decided to reveal his true identity right after supper.

"My friends," he began. "There is something very unusual about me that I'd like to share with you, in the hope that our friendship will either stay the same or grow even more after you listen to my incredible story. First of all let me say that there is little I can do to prove its veracity, so please don't ask for evidence. I only want you to understand and accept my account as the absolute and unquestionable truth."

Both listened quietly and patiently to Sikin's amazing story, and as he finished, Curzio couldn't conceal a grin any longer.

"What an opportunity for knowledge!" he exclaimed. "What a privilege to participate in such an extraordinary event!"

Tiblina however, appeared to feel betrayed and disappointed. She asked questions such as; do you have a wife in that other world? Can you stay in ours indefinitely? Were you much older when you left? Then she asked if he would take her along when he returned to his own time.

Sikin hesitated to offer an answer until Curzio, always perceptive, interrupted them to offer his opinion on various unrelated subjects.

Despite Sikin being the only person she had learned to trust, the young woman remained discreetly away from him during the next few days as if keeping the new puzzling and mysterious *friend* in quarantine until she fully grasped the significance of his revelation. Even the nobleman, who never missed an opportunity to offer free advice, didn't say a word regarding their *unusual* dilemma. He simply kept an eye on Tiblina's sad expression as if it broke his own heart.

Perhaps resulting from his unfulfilled mission as a father, Curzio clearly felt deeply concerned about Tiblina. Sikin

111

believed the old man had found that rare second chance that often crosses our paths undetected, and wanted to mend his past by caring for her.

Finally Curzio drew Tiblina aside, speaking slowly so she would understand. "Girl," He said, taking her hands. "I promised you an opportunity to attain happiness and a much better life in a different world. Sikin came, as he said, from another dimension with a pre-determined purpose neither of us could ever understand. You must have faith and trust that everything in life has a good side, no matter how ugly it might look at that moment. For unknown reasons he cannot take you along, so try to enjoy his company and learn from his vast knowledge while you can. Remember that enlightenment is the ultimate power. I know how difficult it is for you to understand my words, but please trust me! Continue to show your eagerness and optimism with the same devotion, and somewhere down the road you'll be reaping the fruits of your dedication and sacrifice."

It was getting late, and Curzio, very tired, was about to leave when they insisted he stayed for the night. Darkness and blowing gravel presented clear dangers to anyone venturing outside.

Accepting their invitation, the old man approached Tiblina, stamped a kiss in her cheek, and walked to the farthest corner of the yurt to lie down for the night.

Early the next morning, he withdrew quietly to bring back a handful of dried figs from his supply bag. By then, the wind had calmed down considerably, and a floating layer of brown dust conveyed a somber and colorless picture of the surroundings.

Sitting by the hot brazier, the old man prayed for a safe journey to Dunhuang, Sikin's mission to exceed everyone's expectations, for a safe return to Venice, for his family's forgiveness, and for, as he said, "my newly adopted daughter to fulfill her dreams."

After the meal, he looked at his young friend straight in the eyes.

"Sikin, I promise never to ask unsettling questions about the future," he said. "I know it could make you feel uncomfortable."

Then he took on another of his diatribes.

"From the time of creation, God has kept man from peeking into the future to prophesize his fate. If we knew the inevitable ahead of time, no one on the face of this earth would have enough courage to experience life. Our existence would center solely in deviating from the inextricable road to extinction. Our Creator instead, has bestowed upon us a quality called memory, which allows us to improve and rectify the course of our existence by learning from the lessons of the past. Yet, in their eternal quest for destruction, the forces of evil influence mankind to disregard most experiences worth remembering. We seldom search the past for reference and enlightenment, and by ignoring it we navigate through life like a mariner adrift wishing we had what we never will...the complete control of our destinies." Again Sikin smiled at how much Curzio sounded like his grandfather McKinley.

"I often compare life with the Silk Road," the old man went on. "Adventurous, unpredictable, dangerous, and at the same time fulfilling and worth experiencing, especially for those who listen with an open mind and are passionate enough to appreciate the colors and sounds most simply can't detect.

We would do well to imitate the blind man who relies on his walking stick and the rest of his senses to feel what lies ahead, which can only be achieved by remembering what he left behind. Perhaps if we didn't care so much to stimulate our senses with what we can touch and see, we would live in closer harmony with Creation and ourselves.

My dear friend," he finally concluded, "I have mentioned these philosophical truths to show you the reasons I would rather play by the rules of God and Nature than by my own. I couldn't care less about future methods of bringing water into homes, the foods they eat, their ways of moving from one place to another, and so on. Tell me only what's morally relevant about humans living eight hundred years hence. Are they any different? Are they better creatures? Has poverty and famine been eradicated from Earth? Have we stopped exploiting one another? Those, and only those, are the answers I want to hear about the future."

113

Understanding little of what Curzio had said, and anxious to continue their journey, Tiblina interrupted his preaching to insist they get ready to leave as soon as possible.

Realizing the importance of good or at least "less bad" weather, both men stood up to begin their packing routines and continue another day of trekking.

Except for their provisions running in short supply, the weeks that followed passed uneventfully. Although the quality of their meals began to deteriorate due to the lack of fresh food, Curzio continued to follow his daily ritual of laying down the silk rug, eating supper while the incense burned, and taking short sips of his luscious, consecrating wine. He continued to act and talk as an aristocrat, opportune with gentlemanly manners and propitious with suitable remarks.

The old man and the girl had clearly grown quite fond of each other. Tiblina began to feel a sense of belonging, Sikin thought, and Curzio one of meaningfulness. Everytime he referred to her as his "newly adopted child," she would grin with contentment.

Every single night, the men sat to discuss everything imaginable, emphasizing philosophical and conceptual comparisons between twentieth century humans and those from the Middle Ages. As agreed, Sikin ommited anything related to mankind's material achievements.

Gradually, Tiblina became more attracted to their talks, finally reaching a point where she was able to participate in simple conversations.

Sikin and Curzio agreed that inner growth had remained relatively stagnant in the last eight hundred years and that most notable achievements throughout this period were materialistic and mundane. Only weak attempts had been initiated to discover and nourish what lies within. Consequently, people continued to endure the same inconsequential and sorrowful existence they had from the beginning of time.

They also determined that the most effective way for humanity to break this vicious cycle would be to search more avidly for inner knowledge and fulfillment, and less eagerly for external excitement and stimulation.

Curzio maintained that one obvious reason for his generation to neglect its moral obligation in passing down wisdom and experience to the next, was the degrading conditions of ignorance prevailing among the masses.

Sikin interrupted by saying that unless the admonitions of the past were honestly divulged and respected by the present, not much could be expected of the future.

"In my world," the young man continued, "the printed word is often available to every citizen almost at no cost.

The teachings of the past could be found everywhere, and yet the great majority of people couldn't care less. Humankind has wasted thousands of years living like moral morons, instead of pursuing an alternate course in life. I regret to say that humanity's ethical mediocrity has not only prevailed through the ages, but that it has improved in sophistication as well. It seems as if an evil power has successfully managed to obliterate from our consciences the onus to learn from the wisdom of our ancestors."

Days slowly passed by as the small caravan continued its long journey along the base of the Tien Shen Mountains en route to the oasis of Hami.

As an important stage in the crossings from the Kansu province to Central Asia and the West, the Chinese had occupied the oasis since 73 AD, dominating the territory until 763 AD, when the Tibetans overran the Chinese toward the Northwest. In the ninth century it came under the rule of the Uighurs, and in the thirteenth century, Tiblina's day, it was already under Mongol control.

With hardly enough water left to reach the oasis, the group decided to stop at the small sheepherder's village of Uruklik, on the outskirts of Hami. Drawing near the settlement, they noticed a handful of yurts and shelters as well as hundreds of grazing sheep. The village well, situated near its center, was easy to find. The wind was relatively light, and plant growth was rather sparse, denoting the proximity of autumn.

As the visitors dismounted to fill their vessels, they were

cautiously approached by a small group of curious children.

A young girl of about twelve, wearing an ornate headband, a colorful woven sweater, broad black pants, thick leather shoes, and a handsomely embroidered V-necked leather vest buttoned at its center, introduced herself in fluent Italian as Parizat. She was the daughter of a herder who owned three hundred heads of goats and sheep. Not the least shy, the girl asked for their names, destination, origin, and business.

Parizat showed them where she and her prolific family lived by pointing at a house built of sand brick and clay, perched atop a rocky promontory overlooking the desert.

"How did you learn our language?" Curzio asked.

"According to my parents, Italian is the only tongue that brings prosperity to the family," she answered. "They claim that if we speak the language of rich merchants, our wares will be sold faster than our neighbors, and at a higher price. Therefore they made sure we learned it just as good as our native Kazan."

Leading Curzio by the hand, she took her new friends uphill to visit the family home and meet her relatives.

Followed by their camels and the horse, the group climbed arduously up a steep, rocky path leading to the house's front entrance. Thick sand-brick walls supported the structure's convex roof. Its front door, a solid hardwood plank, shielded the residents against the elements. The village population, another twenty families, had dwelled next to each other for generations, sharing resources as members of a single clan.

In front of the open porch, two of Parizat's three brothers and their friends played a game in which they wrapped sand in cloth to make a ball. One of them stood in the middle of a circle. The players around the circle had to try to hit the person in the center with the ball. If he got hit, he lost. If he caught the ball, the boy who threw it must drop out.

Using his father's bristle brush, Parizat's oldest brother was grooming the newly grown winter coats of three horses and two mares while they grazed quietly at a nearby pasture. Sitting on a large blanket, a sister carefully bunched summer barley for further storage, bread making, and to complement her father's beer brew recipe, which included the use of hops obtained from a local relative. Inside, a very old lady sitting atop a pile of sheepskins wove woolen sweaters, which, according to the girl, were to be sold at a bazaar in Hami at the beginning of winter. The lady was Parizat's grandmother, who spent countless hours creating the most imaginative and beautifully woven garments sold in all of Hami's bazaars.

An older sister breastfed her newborn baby while the husband, another herder, worked the fields from dawn to dusk.

In an adjacent room, Parizat's mother knelt in front of a brazier stirring an appetizing goat meat stew. A round opening in the ceiling, ten feet above the fire, helped dissipate the smoke and mouth-watering aroma of fresh home cooking.

An iron container set above a small gravel pit was filled with fresh well water to be used for cooking, drinking, and brewing tea. A clay crock wrapped in straw and filled with mare's milk was suspended from the ceiling by a winch-like contraption that raised and lowered the basket when needed.

A chamber used by Parizat's immediate family as a sleeping room was accessed through a large opening in the thick wall. Layers of woolen blankets piled over a large slab served as a common bed. An adjoining room was packed with food staples, pots full of lard, rock salt stored in clay containers, and a pasty malodorous cheese the grandmother ate to alleviate her pain from "old bone disease" during the cold of winter. Shelves were heavily stocked with salted meats, and way back in a corner, covered with cloth to keep the annoying desert flies away, a honeycomb rested against a large earthen jar full of beer. Adding to the fetid smell, rancid butter was stored inside small, shallow pots for further use as rubbing liniment for aches and pains. Though another opening through the roof helped disperse the sickening scent outside, the emerging stench was most intolerable.

One by one, Parizat introduced her family members, including a billy goat she kept as a pet. Her sister's ages seemed to fall somewhere between their late teens and early thirties. Being single the next youngest after Parizat lived with her parents, the others with their respective families in dwellings nearby.

An access through the rear wall led to a huge heap of black rocks Sikin recognized as coal. These were sorted by size and burned outdoors whenever strong and lasting heat was needed. The yard also held an earth oven used to bake *nan,* a hard-as-rock traditional bread.

The dwelling's rear window faced the Tien Shen Mountains toward the South, allowing the sun to project its warm rays inside to soothe the cold of winter. The home was close enough to the desert to feel its tepid, up-slope winds, and far enough from the base of the mountains to escape the commonplace avalanches during the snowy season.

A brown pony grazing nearby awaited his mistress Parizat to take him for a ride.

"His name is Libek," she announced with a sweet smile. "During summer I ride him up the mountains where it is so magnificent. We talk and talk all the time and never get tired of listening to each other." Parizat mounted and galloped away for two hundred yards, and after making a sharp turn, she returned to her waiting friends, exhibiting the confidence and grace of a seasoned horsewoman.

"Child, when did you learn to ride so well?" Curzio asked.

The girl answered by extending her arm two feet from the ground, indicating she must have been a toddler at the time.

"Forgive me for being absentminded, but could you repeat how many relatives live in your house?" Sikin inquired.

She answered by showing off eight fingers. "In one room my oldest brother, his wife and son sleep; the second room is where my grandmother, father, mother, sister, and I sleep; and in the third one we welcome our guests. That is where you shall stay tonight, after dinner, of course!"

The group accepted graciously.

"Which is your favorite season?" Tiblina asked.

"Spring," she replied, "because that is the time when nature turns green and the sheep and the goats have their babies. It is also the season when we visit relatives in Hami, and they come back to visit us."

Parizat narrowed her eyes in curiosity.

"How big is the city you come from?   Is it larger than Hami?"

"Oh no! I come from a village the size of yours." Tiblina answered. "However, I have visited much larger ones. When I was a little older than you Parizat, I began working for trains and caravans, first as a camel driver, then as a guide. Those trips took me to the most fascinating and sometimes dangerous places."

"Hami is the only world I know bigger than our village." Parizat said with a sigh. "Will you tell me about those faraway lands later? Perhaps I will visit them someday, but regardless of how beautiful they are, I will always return to where I'd enjoy life the most, and that is right here with my family."

"Of course I will," Tiblina replied looking into her dark eyes. "The world is full of exciting places to visit, and having a loving family awaiting your return makes you a very fortunate girl! I certainly hope all your wishes come true someday."

The young girl followed Tiblina all day long, relating in the minutest detail stories of her life in the village. She inquired about the customs of women in other lands, how they dressed, lived, and so on. Somewhat shyly, she also asked about boys her age living in those faraway places. She listened in awe as Tiblina described her journeys to Khanbalik, Karakorum, and other large communities, but the one that fascinated Parizat the most, was the Celestial City of Kinsay.

At suppertime, Parizat's family and their guests gathered around the brazier's fire to share conversation and the last meal of the day, which consisted of a most delectable stew-like dish, followed by tea and pieces of nan dipped in honey.

After everyone finished eating, and to ensure that no one else took the lead, Parizat asked Tiblina to retell her story about the Celestial city of Kinsay.

Tiblina, somewhat self-conscious, began by describing Kinsay as one of the largest cities she had ever seen, measuring about one hundred miles around, heavily populated, yet void of poverty. She said it was called the Celestial City because of its beauty and grandeur.

Surrounded by lakes and canals, its citizens float around all day visiting neighbors, marketing their wares or waiting to start a conversation with the right person gliding by.

"Ahh, La Serenissima!" Exclaimed Curzio. "Kinsay sounds just like my beloved Venice!"

"Go on, Tiblina," said Sikin, gesturing to Curzio to hush and give the girl a chance to shine.

The Venetian put a hand to his mouth and nodded encouragingly at Tiblina.

"The markets were filled with pheasants, quails, ducks, geese, fresh produce, and pears so sweet each weighed about ten pounds. Also there were delicious peaches and pomegranates.

The citizens of Kinsay are kind, peaceful, and quiet. Weapons and soldiers are unwelcome, and they dislike the presence of the Great Khan's officers.

There are public baths in every street. The families who frequent them are accustomed to bathe in very cold water since childhood. Servants of both sexes attend these baths. They claim this practice is good for their health, and for those strangers who cannot bear the shock of the cold; there are apartments in the compound with hot water available. All these people bathe themselves daily before each meal."

"Oh boy, that's punishment! No way, I'll ever do that!"

"Ignore him Tiblina," Curzio said. "So far I haven't seen him taking a warm one either."

She gazed at Sikin and smiled.

"There are also incredibly beautiful gardens, some of which are miniature replicas of famous sites and paintings carefully maintained to produce pleasure to the eyes and the spirit.

These Chinese gardens can never be completely observed from a single vantage point because they consist of isolated sections that must be discovered and enjoyed as the person walks through. The visitor must follow the paths, walk through tunnels, ponder the water, and finally reach a gazebo from where a fascinating view often appears. They have a saying: 'Unfold the landscape as you do a painting on a scroll.'"

"Tell us about girls my age!" Parizat said excitedly.

"Children are educated by their elders and by teachers appointed by the Great Khan. At any time of the day when they are not busy learning, they play all sorts of games, either in the squares, gardens, homes, or in the streets. Many girls follow the curious custom of walking with feet shaped like a pointed lotus bud, encased in exquisitely embroidered, excruciatingly tiny, lotus shoes, which never measure over three to four inches in length. This they achieve by breaking and binding their feet into the shape of that flower bud."

"Why do they hurt themselves like that?" Parizat inquired.

"No one knows for sure," Tiblina replied. "Some believe this custom was brought about by men to keep control of their women, others believe it was a form of flirting. There are as many legends, myths, and fantasy tales explaining the origins of foot binding as there are cultural excuses to accept such a painful eccentricity."

Tiblina paused to regard her listeners, whose incredulous faces were fixed upon her raptly, as if trying to extract further richness from the story. Suddenly and unexpectedly she found herself empty of words.

Even Curzio, who had been in Kinsay innumerable times, stared in silent amazement at his newly adopted girl. Pleasantaly surprised, Sikin, too, noticed in his friend the first sign of a radical transformation. Her phrasing of the story, the perfect articulation of words which weeks before had been totally absent, and her perfectly contrived dramatic gestures as the tale unfolded, had the audience on edge.

With the exception of Grandma, who by then was sound asleep, Tiblina's small audience begged her to continue. But the hour was past midnight, the fire almost gone, and everyone was tired; good enough reasons to close an enchanting evening. The three guests, accompanied by Parizat, went to their designated room in anticipation of a sheltered, safe, and comfortable night's rest, which they all considered a most welcome reward.

By early mornig, Parizat and her family had already provided the travelers with the necessary supplies to continue their expedition, thereby avoiding an intermediate stop at the strategically located oasis of Hami, where, according to the girl's father, most passing travelers were exploited by unscrupulous merchants who charged exorbitant prices for low quality food and supplies.

In a sincere gesture of appreciation, Curzio and Sikin paid generously with paper money for the family's hospitality and services.

Shortly before departing, the Italian nobleman called Parizat to his side. Holding her hands, he said to her in his usually ornate language, "Child, in remembrance of our brief, yet genuine friendship, allow me to present you with a small keepsake. In this realm of bleak desolation, your sincere trust and generosity brought much needed cheerfulness to our tired and hungry hearts."

Everyone watched Parizat open a small package containing a wooden box inlaid with dozens of precious woods of different grains and tones. Curzio described the object as a "musical box," one of the newest achievements in Italian craftsmanship, which had been presented to him by a merchant friend from the city of Sorrento.

A very happy Parizat asked Curzio what he meant by musical box.

Smiling, the old man rotated a lever protruding from the instrument, thus producing before a joyful group, the musical notes of an old Latin melody.

Sikin found Parizat's expression of joy and wonder nearly indescribable.

The adults tried to steal a glimpse of the fantastic machine, while the little ones squeezed through the crowd to see and touch her enchanting present.

Leaving unforgettable memories behind, the three visitors resumed their final journey to Dunhuang, which they expected to take another month filled with excitement, uncertainty and adventure.

CHAPTER *Four*

JOURNEY TO DUNHUANG

"No coal, no fire so hotly glows, as the secret love which no ones knows."
Quote from Sigmund Freud's "The Interpretation of Dreams."
Published April 1913

C urzio dedicated his tutoring to teach Tiblina the standards of etiquette, refinement, manners, politeness, verbal pleasantries, and social conduct in general, paying special attention to the gregarious Venetian environment.

Conversely, Sikin devoted his training to simple conversations, using most of his free time to help her adorn silk scarves, which by then amounted to dozens of new pieces to add to those taken from Amur's house.

The Italian and his newly adopted child got along as if they had known each other forever. Tiblina took upon herself the responsibility of watching after his health. Three times a day she brewed medicinal teas to help him recover from another bout with the fever, which fortunately didn't last long. She prepared special meals using some of the herbs and spices he carried in his overloaded camel, which supposed to alleviate symptoms and reduce the frequency of his relapses. Sikin recognized Curzio's ailment as malaria, possibly contracted during a trip to the Nile several years earlier.

Tiblina admired the old man, considering him a gentle, wise, and highly educated person, with much insight and common sense to share, but worried he was doomed to carry a feeling of culpability for the rest of his life.

Interested in his short-lived family life, Tiblina asked Curzio about every detail concerning his two daughters, especially the younger one, who became the apple of his eye even before birth. By doing so, Tiblina created a unique opportunity to learn the complexities of European lifestyles, traditions, and family settings. She paid special attention to the means women used to survive on their own in a society where most of them were supposed to function within a domestic environment.

After weeks of traveling, the heat became somewhat bearable, but the cold of night made early awakenings much harder to endure.

Curzio was wearing his tri-cornered hat more frequently to protect his head from the low temperatures, which he thought debilitated the rest of his body, and created a need for extra food and wine, of which he had little left.

Now in the winter of life, Curzio realized that indeed, all things could be possible, but always at a price, and whether or not it was worth paying his, he often said, only time would tell.

The nobleman never stopped dwelling in the past. Sikin worried about home and his own future in America, while Tiblina kept her mind busy designing scarves, and improving herself.

Sikin realized that Tiblina desired and needed him more each day, as he desired and needed her.

As they approached the Hexi Corridor linking the Silk Route to Khanbalik and other great cities, defensive garrisons located at a distance of *two arrow shots* and linked by a huge wall, loomed in the distance. Forces of the Great Khan to protect the trade route manned the watchtowers. According to historical speculation, Sikin recalled the garrisons were built first. The wall between them was erected next by filling wooden frames with soil from the Gobi. The soil tamped firmly, resulting in a tightly packed wall upon removal of the frame.

The structures that made up the Great Wall of China were built in separate stages by different dynasties. The Qin (221-206 BC) began the project with the purpose of keeping barbarians and Huns away. They had four options to survive those savage Nomadic tribes. They could carry out military campaigns to drive them out, create defensive garrisons, and conduct diplomatic attempts, including the development of economic ties. Each of the first three alternatives was enforced unsuccessfully at different times. The Chinese considered themselves at a higher human level than those "people with the heart of animals who lived at the edge of the earth," and as a result, no treaty of fair equality was ever reached. Thus they resorted to the fourth option...the building of walls.

They rebuilt some sections and extended others across the Gobi to protect the legendary Silk Road that played such a vital role in the flourishing markets along the route. Even the powerful Chin Dynasty, the one defeated by Genghis Khan, endured harassment by the Huns for centuries.

Sikin realized the Great Wall was far from complete. After Tiblina's time, the Ming dynasty that overthrew the Mongols or Yuan dynasty built the more lasting portions. In fact, most of what Ivan would see was the remnants of such walls. He found it interesting that on only two occasions were the barbarians able to conquer and destroy the ruling dynasties inside the walls, and in both instances those reigns had weakened from within as a result of apathy, indifference, and internal corruption.

There's another lesson from the past, eh Grandpa? He thought.

The wall crossed three different regions, the Western end crossed the Gobi Desert, the Central section spanned the Ordos Steppes where the Yellow River follows a meandering course filled with mud, and its Eastern side ran all the way to the Pacific Ocean.

Overall, the wall wouldn't have existed without millions of workers and slaves dying from the brutality of forced labor, disease, and suicide. The outsiders were savages, but those inside were just as cruel.

When it was finished, the wall stretched about three thousand miles, thus the Chinese expression, "the wall of twelve thousand li" – one *li* being about a quarter mile.

In Ivan's day engineers calculated that the material used to build the Great Wall, was sufficient to assemble one measuring eight feet tall and three feet thick all around the Equator.

As the small caravan continued to move along the wall's perimeter, Curzio as always, used the opportunity to offer a "dissertation" about the origins and reasons for the structure to exist.

"This wall represents a perfect example of history's ongoing tendency to repeat itself," said he. "It proves beyond the shadow of a doubt that in spite of how well protected citizens might think their country is, unless they are morally and patriotically inspired, no military might in the world will be able to prevent its destruction.

The reason this great nation collapsed at various times under the threat of savages, my dear friends, was due to its own moral infirmities, civic negligence, government corruption, and the people's loss of will power to defend something indefensible and unworthy of sacrifice. Always keep in mind the Old Persian proverb that says, 'History is only a mirror of the past, and a lesson for the present.'"

They camped next to the wall during the days that followed, always trying to keep the lowest possible profile to avoid thieves.

One morning, Sikin who was riding in front, spotted at a distance what seemed like a huge caravan traveling toward them. As they drew closer, they could see hundreds of soldiers marching in single file. They were Mongol warriors on foot and horseback followed by hundreds of loaded camels, asses, horses, and covered carriages.

He wondered aloud if they were part of a military maneuver. Frightened by the awesome sight, Tiblina suggested they hide to avoid a life-threatening encounter.

As the horde drew closer, Sikin noticed six horsemen pulling away from the group and galloping toward them at full speed. Tiblina made sure her Saracen saber was within reach and Sikin felt for his dagger. Curzio on the other hand, didn't bother to make the slightest defensive move.

Upon arrival, the group leader approached the old man first, asking for his identity, their destination, and their business. Cool, and collected, the Italian answered each and every question.

"To whom do you pledge allegiance?" Sikin asked the leader.

"We are the scouts and forward guards for the Royal Caravan and its Mistress, and we have orders to bring you in for questioning." The warrior quickly snapped back.

"Did you say Mistress?" Curzio demanded. "Do you escort a caravan with a woman in charge? Define yourself!"

Reluctantly, the soldier explained that a Persian princess who had come to meet the Great Khan's oldest son, Temur, was returning home. He also said that her father, the Sultan of Savez had offered the Princess to Temur as a candidate for future wife. "She is the youngest and most exquisite of his twenty five daughters," added the soldier.

"Savez?" Oh yes, I remember that Persian City," Curzio said to the young couple. "Savez is the town from where the three Magi set out to worship the infant Jesus. They also lie buried there in three beautiful sepulchers, inside square buildings with finely carved roofs.

It is said that their bodies are still intact," continued the old man. "They were known as Gaspar, Melchior, and Balthasar. But since most citizens in Savez are Moslems, no one knows for sure who the Magi really were. Their graves have become sources of innumerable stories and legends. The townspeople believe they were three kings from the Orient who lived hundreds of years ago. Others have mixed Christian hearsay with their myths, thereby creating their own legends."

"Stop talking and follow me at once!" the warrior said impatiently.

"First, tell me more about this Persian Princess." Curzio

asked pushing his luck. "If ten years ago Hulagu Khan subdued all of Persia, captured and beheaded Caliph Abbasid, and eliminated his court along with all the Saracen Royals, how can a Persian Princess be alive a decade later?"

"The Sultan of Savez is the Saracen who helped the forces of Hulagu Khan take Baghdad," the nervous warrior replied. "For that reason alone, he was the only one allowed to live after the conquest. Following Hulagu's death last year, his first son, Abaka il Khan, who took over the reign of his father, asked the sultan to send his most beautiful daughter to Khanbalik and meet Kublai's son Temur who was then looking for a suitable wife."

"As a provision for surrender," Curzio said clearing his throat. "You must first inform Her Royal Highness that I was a friend of Hulagu, and that I'm related to the Pope of Rome."

"I don't care to whom you are related!" The aggravated soldier yelled. "You must give yourselves up unconditionally, and do it *now!*"

"Curzio, you must be out of your mind!" Sikin said finally. "How dare you annoy the Khan's fighters? Do you know what you're doing?"

"I want to meet the Princess!" interrupted Tiblina. "I want to step inside her carriage and see how she looks. I also want to learn everything about her engagement."

"For goodness sake Tiblina, this is not a social call! Sikin said authoritatively.

"Just think of it as another adventure to tell your friends." She replied jokily. "Stop arguing, both of you!" Curzio demanded. "I must find out from the Princess whether she had seen or heard about my friends while at the Khan's court. I'm anxious to know what I had missed by not being in Khanbalik with them. I would also ask Tiblina to offer her a scarf and see the Princess's reaction to its beauty. Let's face it, these Saracens want to do business with every merchant on the road, and these arrests are nothing but scare tactics to weaken their will to make a profit."

"Finally," Curzio said gazing at the heavens. "I also want Sikin to appreciate the elegance and natural beauty of Persian women, as I'm sure that unless she looks as magnificent as an angel, the sultan wouldn't dare offer his youngest daughter to Kublai's first-born."

At that remark Tiblina shot him a jealous glare.

"You must also remember that the Saracens are shrewd," Curzio continued, "and that they move around with great skill and distrust. They wouldn't mind peddling their souls to gain influence, acquire more wealth, and of course, own the most sumptuous women on earth."

Taking charge of the situation seemed to give Curzio a fresh and revitalized look. His spirit of adventure, natural curiosity for the exotic, and a deep desire to rekindle his good old days, energized the old man.

The large caravan continued its gradual approach toward the group of travelers. In order to prevent an ambush from the rocky cliffs above, hundreds of horsemen and foot soldiers flanked the royal entourage on both sides. Leading the gigantic procession, two-dozen heavily loaded camels carried drinking water, food, clothing, furnishings, and provisions. Next in line, another group of camels rigged with wooden chairs and bright parasols carried in luxury and comfort the sultan's personal emissaries and their assistants. Draped in colorful blankets and fully loaded with encampment supplies, twelve Arabian dromedaries followed. Behind the festively attired animals and riding their Bactrian beasts, a dozen musicians, some with drums and tambourines, played tunes sung by black-veiled servants and chaperones.

Next, pulled by nine powerful oxen, a six-wheeled gurney heavily decorated with carved ivory ornaments transported the caravan's most precious cargo, the Saracen Princess and her staff. The royal coach looked like a massive jewelry box with windows on every side.

The African ebony carriage wheels had sackcloth covering their rims to ease the discomfort of a bumpy ride.

Personal attendants and eunuchs traveled inside the carriage to accompany the Princess while Saracen foot soldiers dressed in full regalia and wearing ornate turbans used large wooden poles to support a silk canopy large enough to protect the entire carriage from the sun's heat.

Four Moorish eunuchs of monumental size sat with crossed arms on two stalls on the carriage's top, protecting the royal passenger underneath. They wore broad white silk pants tied around their waist by sapphire-studded sashes and to each ankle by golden rings. Their magnificent chests were partially concealed by a tightly fitted black vest, and their heads elegantly arrayed with lavish white turbans.

Following the magnificent coach, slaves on foot carried spare parts and weapons such as bows, arrows, lances, knives, and swords to be used by the warriors on horseback. Behind them, large numbers of Chinese slaves pulled heavy carts loaded with camping equipment and Persian tents, which were deployed every time Her Excellency wished to stretch her legs, take a short stroll, have tea, or meditate in solitude before retiring.

As they drew close to the convoy, Sikin began to wonder whether the summons for questioning was related to the incident of the stolen diamond. If charged with thievery he thought they could lose their hands or even their heads to the ax-man. Sikin, just like Ivan, was over sensitive enough to become obsessed about situations over which he had no control, always expecting the worst, he was wrong most of the time. Curzio however, appeared to feel no fear, striding confidently as if the whole scheme was going his way.

As the large caravan came to a halt, Tiblina all excited couldn't wait for a *visit* with the Princess.

Upon reaching the gurney's luxurious entrance, two of the Sultan's dignitaries dismounted their parasol-sheltered camels and ordered one of the eunuchs to enter the coach to invite Her Royal Highness to meet the visitors. Sikin, Curzio, and Tiblina were ordered to prostrate themselves and keep their eyes fixed on the ground until the Princess expressed her wishes. Looking at her in the eyes without implicit consent, even though her face was partially covered by an almost transparent veil of silk, was a "justifiable reason" to apply, if she so desired, the summary penalty of death by decapitation.

At the moment Sikin thought it was time to return to

America, Tiblina although scared, seemed to welcome the whole affair, while Curzio, fresh as a head of lettuce awaited reverently the emergence of the Persian Princess.

Silence reigned while all men kept their eyes away from the entrance except for the eunuchs.

Time passed, and sweat began to trickle down Sikin's brow. He was committed to invoke his immediate return if a life-threatening situation unexpectedly emerged. All at once, the eunuch returned. Since the chief eunuch was mute, his tongue having been cut off prior to assuming his "privileged position," the anorchous man bowed to the visitors pointing toward the entrance. Three emissaries led the visitors into the Princess' *majlis*, or sitting room, inside the giant carriage.

Silk arabesques of great length and vivid colors hung from the ceiling, forming undulating patterns that provided a sense of lavish comfort. Delicate fabrics printed with Islamic calligraphy covered the walls.

Adorned with flowers and curvaceous designs, layers of Persian rugs covered the wooden floor. On each side of the chamber, dozens of large cushions served as seats for the servants and chaperones, and in the right corner, a *bukhoor*, or incense burner stood unused.

The room was crowded, yet the delicate smell of sandalwood permeated the stuffy air, conveying its predominantly feminine character. At left, a short plump eunuch stood with his arms crossed. Blind from birth, he had always worked inside the women's quarters. In the center and toward the rear, a red divan held the reclined figure of a slender woman in her early twenties. She wore a flowing chemise embroidered in gold, open at the bosom and fastened at the neck by a jeweled brooch. Her wide pants were of the whitest of silks, narrow and cuffed at the ankles. Her hair was adorned with innumerable thin beaded braids and covered by a skullcap inlaid in pearls and emeralds. She also wore two impressive diamond earrings.

The young woman undeniably had the coveted looks of a princess.

Her white complexion alluded to a person seldom exposed to

sunlight, and her broad black eyes created a contrasting and provocative look. Her lips carmine red added an outburst of soft sensuality to an already radiant personality.

The three visitors prostrated themselves as they were told. Sikin's apprehension was obvious, and Tiblina's hands were icy cold. Curzio, on the other hand, maintained his usual composure until Her Majesty opened the encounter by asking the visitors to raise their heads and stand up.

"Welcome in the name of Allah!" the Princess said amiably. "Would you be kind enough to state your business?"

"Peace be upon the great prophet Mohammed and unto Her Royal Highness!" Curzio began. "First and foremost, we humbly beseech the Princess' mercy and forgiveness for such an impolite interruption."

The Venetian nobleman bowed grandly, clearly at ease, a true aristocrat displaying the elegance and finesse worthy of the occasion.

"Your Highness, before I bring forth the reasons for our presence please allow me to introduce your obedient servant."

Applying the most extravagant and delicate manners, he gingerly unsheathed the notorious saber once again, holding it sideways by the blade to indicate he meant no threat. Bowing to the Princess again he gently raised its handle for her to behold.

After introducing himself by name, Curzio spelled out all his nobility titles, making sure the Princess understood their meaning, thus impressing the young woman with a deliberately exaggerated lineage.

"The Great Hulagu Khan," he continued, "whom I personally befriended while in Bukhara, asked my two Venetian friends and me, to go straight to Khanbalik on a mission to meet his brother, the Great Kublai, who desired to acquaint himself with an influential Latin person. Unfortunately, due to illness I couldn't continue, thus regretfully staying in Turpan.

My two colleagues arrived in Khanbalik over a year ago, and now they are on their journey back to the West. The Great Kublai was thoughtful enough to send his royal messenger to Turpan, seeking my presence on the oasis of Dunhuang in order to meet my dear friends as they travel back to Venice. Hence, Your Highness, I implore Her Majesty's attention to know if by chance she had become in contact or heard about two Italian merchants while at the Khan's court in Khanbalik. They went by the names of Niccolo and Matteo Polo.

Your assistance in this matter will be immensely appreciated, not only by my friends and the Great Khan, but by this humble servant as well." After a brief pause and in a well-acted gesture of humility, the nobleman swept off his odd-looking hat, lowered his head in a conspicuous bow, and remained staring at the floor patiently awaiting the Princess' response.

Changing to a sitting position from her reclining pose, the Princess clapped her delicate hands once, as an indication to the obese eunuch to bring tea and food for her guests. Then she looked at Curzio and said, "I know your friends. What's more, they saved me from slavery! I shall be indebted to them forever, as both were instrumental in convincing the Great Khan to sanction my return to Savez."

Sikin felt immense relief as he listened to the Princess, realizing once again, the futility of anticipating too much.

"Indeed, Your Highness!" answered Curzio in amazement. "How did this happen?"

"After becoming quite fond of me," she answered, "the Great Khan made certain I stayed in the palace until his son Temur decided my fate. He wanted to see Temur married to a young woman who could give him a son. According to the Prophet's mandate, however, a bride shall not meet her future husband in person until after the wedding. Therefore Temur knew about me only by reference and gossip from the Great Khan's wife and concubines.

"Meeting your friends was purely coincidental. During our first casual conversation, they made me aware of His Majesty's sudden change of heart following Temur's decision to postpone marriage indefinitely. They warned me about the Khan's desire to keep my body for his own pleasure instead. As you can imagine, had the Great Khan possessed me as his concubine, not a wife, I would have disgraced and humiliated my father and his house.

Aware of his lecherous scheme, your two merchant friends told the powerful monarch that although my father, the Sultan of Savez, was only a servant after being defeated by Hulagu, he still carried enormous influence in the highest spheres of government. Using this and other powerful arguments, they were able to convince Kublai that it was more prudent to maintain cordial relations with the sultan, than to alienate him by keeping his daughter hostage.

The great Khan accepted their advice, and glory be unto Allah, I am returning home!

The two merchants left Khanbalik two days after our caravan to meet an important friend in the oasis of Dunhuang. Now I can clearly see who their friend was."

"Your Highness," said Curzio earnestly. "May the Prophet Mohammed honor your sincerity of heart and faithful devotion to your father the great Sultan of Savez. From the depths of my soul, I thank Thee for such a valuable piece of information."

"Who is the lovely young lady?" The Princess asked, gesturing to Tiblina. "And who is he that looks so manly?"

Sikin blushed, wishing he didn't have to respond to such an unexpected tribute to his figure.

"She is my adopted daughter, and her name is Tiblina," answered Curzio. "Well versed in Latin languages and very much acquainted with the Silk Route, she is also a great artist. The man's name is Sikin, and he comes from a mysterious distant land none of us would ever be able to visit. He is a wise young chap well versed in the seven arts and beyond."

"What is her art?"

"Silk painting, Your Highness. Tiblina creates marvelous pieces worthy of Monarchs and Princes for their unique quality and beauty. If it pleases Your Majesty, she would like to bestow on her a most exquisite piece."

Almost instantly, Tiblina pulled from her bag a lapiz lazuli-colored scarf with its center shaded in turquoise, embroidered with orderly geometric floral patterns, and decorated with gold threads at the edges. She handed it to Curzio, who in turn offered it to the Princess.

The Princess's eyes opened wide as she examined every detail of the exquisite piece.

Addressing Tiblina, she said, "Never in my life have I seen a more beautiful scarf!

"You must be a very kind person gifting it to me." At once she pulled off her diamond earrings and presented them to Tiblina, who froze, so shocked she didn't know whether to accept them or not until Curzio nodded in approval.

Immediately the eunuch appeared with gold trays stacked with figs, dates, hazelnuts, oranges, various cheeses, an appetizing mix of almonds and honey, dry quail meat, and two varieties of tea, mint and flower of cardamon.

After the attendant laid the trays on the carpeted floor, the Princess took a couple of dates and invited all present to participate in the suddenly improvised banquet, which lasted till after sunset.

Delighted at the reception, the travelers couldn't find words to express their sincere relief and gratitude. They had not eaten that kind of food in months!

Their conversation was engaging, the subjects fascinating, and their rapport so genuine that the Princess ordered her emissaries to set them up for the night, along with personal attendants and plenty of food. The servants were also told to feed their camels and horse, as well as to gather all provisions necessary for the party to continue their journey, including a jar filled with rose water for Curzio's personal use.

Three white tents were assembled that evening especially for them. Inside, large Persian rugs along with colored cushions covered the floors. Trays filled with dry fruits, bread, and hot tea, were placed on tiny tables, while servants waited patiently outside to fulfill their wishes.

The three met inside Curzio's tent till past midnight, talking about every subject imaginable, until Tiblina, disappointed at not being able to ask the Princess herself, begged Curzio to describe what a Persian royal wedding looked like.

He began by saying that among the Saracens, their royalty in particular; the union is generally pre-arranged by the father of the bride regardless of her age.

"She is forbidden to speak to or see her future husband except through a window or an orifice in the wall, until after the wedding," he explained. "Both could have played together as children, yet after puberty they would not have been allowed to see each other again. In the meantime, the mother of the groom, his sisters, and close relatives describe everything she wants to know about her future husband.

When the time of the engagement arrives, the formal announcement is conveyed verbally through her personal messengers who wearing their best garments announce the event to future guests home by home, receiving food and gratuities in return as rewards for spreading the good news.

The groom and both parents offer gifts to the bride, all of which become her personal possessions. The bride's dowry usually depends on her family's financial position, and in the case of a princess, it could be clothes, jewelry, houses, slaves, land, or even a sizeable fortune…

When the wedding day finally arrives, the bride wears everything new from head to toe, colorful but not loud. Perfumes are blended especially for her, including a hair cream made with powdered sandalwood, musk, rose water, and certain spices. Also special blends of incense are mixed for the occasion. Bakery goods, meats, and all kinds of food and fruits are also offered.

During the last week of maidenhood, the bride spends her days and nights confined to a dark room wearing the simplest attire. This custom is supposed to increase her beauty for the wedding day. Before this incarceration she is visited by a large number of friends as well as those who had performed duties, or offered services throughout her life. Traditionally they come to collect a token or ask for her continued support.

Exempt from the dark room experience, the husband also rewards those who served him. He stays home during the last three days, sharing presents and compliments with loved ones and friends.

The marriage takes place after sunset at the bride's home or palace. However, she does not appear at all. Only her proxies do. After the ceremony she retires to her apartment, while the groom and his male companions hold a feast that can last as long as three days.

Official surrender of the wife is adjourned until the third day following the wedding. At that time she is beautified, perfumed, and then taken by female relatives to her new home. There, she meets her husband's friends and relatives.

If the newlywed wife belongs to a higher social class than her husband, she remains seated until he shows up. Then she waits for the husband to address her first, after which she may speak to him as long as her face remains concealed behind a veil. Before she takes it off, the husband, as proof of love, must bring a gift equal to his worth.

As of that moment, and as evidence of universal hospitality, the master of the house opens it for three weeks. All are welcome to eat and drink to their heart's content while taking pleasure from music, dancing, and poetry. As long as the house remains open to the public, eunuchs keep the tea hot and the bokhoors burning.

The newlyweds stay home during that time and see no one. Afterwards, the wife welcomes her friends and relatives who come to express their good wishes."

Curzio finished his account with a word of warning... "Never compliment beyond reason the master or mistress of a Saracen home for something they own, whether ornaments, carpets, jewelry or artwork, since they will feel obligated to give it to you!"

"What's wrong with that?" Sikin asked.

"When they return your social call, you will be obligated to pay them back with whatever they admire the most, and believe me, they will find something of equal or better value!"

At dawn, the three were ready to resume their journey. They found their beasts rested, fed, and loaded, as ordered by the Princess. Leaving the bowing attendants behind, they departed towards the last segment of their journey.

Tiblina, with the earrings concealed inside her boots,

couldn't stop fantasizing about an opportunity to wear them.

Continuing towards the oasis, they found this portion of the road much more traveled than anticipated. Occasional encounters with merchants coming from farther East, kept them busy talking and exchanging information. Weather news and gossip were swapped, warnings heeded, humors spread, and bad news sounded more dismal the farther they traveled. Oftentimes a midday encounter lasted through the night and into the following morning.

One common quality among these desert souls was their inexhaustible patience. No one ever hurried. Even camels moved slowly, becoming mean and irritable when pressed. Something about the barrenness of the surroundings seemed to instill in these wanderers a need to remain in perpetual slow motion and isolation until the end of time.

Monks from various Eastern sects also crossed their paths, as well as occasional bandits, whom they unfailingly frightened away by being aggressive instead of submissive.

Ever eager and dedicated, Tiblina continued faithfully to undergo her daily tutoring. She was now speaking flawless Italian and acting with refined manners. Guided by her newly adopted father, she used every opportunity to market her wares, which were sold to the highest bidder. She learned how to present, praise, and glorify her work in front of prospective customers, and the days didn't have enough hours left to produce more pieces. As a result, Tiblina was running out of inks and other materials she hoped to obtain while in Dunhuang.

Curzio became progressively tired. At times they had to stop abruptly to allow him some rest. He was bent on taking Tiblina to Italy, and she couldn't wait to see the land of lakes of which she had heard so much.

Unlike the patient caravaners, the passing of time tortured Curzio. Empty days and silent nights exasperated Da Ponte to no end. His "inspiring and meaningful" surroundings suddenly became real, barren, inhospitable, raw, and utterly despairing. Absolute freedom, as he once visualized was no panacea after all. At one time he thought freedom was the key to bliss, young

Curzio was too immature to sense the dangers of its abuse. He couldn't conceive as a youth that whatever a person worships in life sooner or later will become his or her master.

How would the young man characterize him eight hundred years hence? How would his culture judge him?

Curzio knew he had to pay back and was ready for it. He needed to be at peace with himself, even if it was at the expense of his entire fortune. Nonetheless, money was not the answer. His family didn't care about his riches, and obviously didn't worry much about the man, either. Why should they? He hadn't seen them in years. All he had left were memories of his autonomous and unrestrained past, along with the financial success achieved entirely on his own.

Not knowing what would become of the remainder of his life, much less his wealth, assuming responsibility for Tiblina provided him a sorely needed sense of purpose. Perceiving the inevitable, Curzio didn't want Sikin to leave either. More than ever he needed the young man's company and support.

Sikin felt mixed. He was enjoying his *transcendental experience*, but felt puzzled and overwhelmed about how and when to end his mission. Frequently he worried about whether the "return button" would work as promised, and often he would shiver when imagining the remote possibility of failure.

Weeks following their encounter with the princess, the three found themselves closer to Dunhuang.

Located in an oasis in the Kansu Desert, Dunhuang was at the far Western end of the Silk Road before entering China. Thus was the first trading post reached by foreign merchants who were traveling into Chinese territory, and during ancient times the junction where the two branches of the Silk Road converged.

The city-oasis was a great center of Buddhism from 370 AD to the beginning of the thirteenth century. It was the main entry for Buddhist monks and missionaries traveling from the kingdoms of Central Asia, becoming a focal point of pilgrimage later on.

To the West lay the feared Taklamakan Desert and the Tarim

basin, to the North the Gobi, and to the East Chang-an, or Xian, the oldest capital of China. Salt, gravel and huge sand hills surrounded the town, particularly around its Western perimeter.

All kinds of exotic imports reached China through Dunhuang, including enormous volumes of silk, vessels of gold and silver along with techniques for working those metals, fine glass, fragrances, spices, exotic animals such as lions and ostriches, fruits, artists, dancers, musicians, painters, and more.

Prior to their final approach into the region, Curzio took time to brief the couple about the town, its grottoes, caves, monastic communities, and the idiosyncrasies of its mixed population.

He went on to say that traveling alongside the Tang Ho River, at about a half-day horse ride from the oasis, there were scores of cave temples hewn out of a cliff by Buddhist monks eight hundred years before. Known to the locals as the Mogaoku Caves, they were filled with one of the most extensive and exquisite collections of Buddhist paintings and sculptures in existence.

"How many are there?" Sikin asked.

"Well over five hundred. They are known as 'The Caves of a Thousand Buddhas,' and it took monks over a thousand years to complete them. All the work was done on site. Nothing was brought from other lands or built somewhere else.

Tiblina learned from Curzio that the caves had been discovered by about six hundred years ago by Chinese traveler Xuan Zhuang who crossed the region with the intention of obtaining Buddhist scriptures from India. His travels recorded, and those who had the fortune of reading those manuscripts could easily visualize Chinese life in those days."

"Have you seen them?"

"Yes I have, Sikin. Ensuing from my way of life, I've had innumerable opportunities to experience what no one else on earth has, and now I'm beginning to wonder if they were worth the price I've paid."

Curzio swallowed a mouthful of mint tea from a skin, and then continued.

"As you age, Sikin, the universal quest to find purpose in life may torment and confuse you. Don't ever let that happen! Remember, it is entirely up to the individual to augment or degrade his human and spiritual dimensions. Our mission as human beings is not to find a reason for living, but to make the best out of our lives. Separate yourself from the deceptive perspectives of crowds. Interpret life from your own viewpoint, and don't allow plurality to coerce or influence your values and decisions. Always balance carefully their interpretation of success and failure, the standards of which are usually established and manipulated by self-serving interests and from this cause are equally fraudulent."

As Curzio found himself again buried knee-deep in one of his endless and convoluted sermons, Sikin surprised him with a question.

"Had you known beforehand your present fate, would you have changed your life's direction and stayed with your family instead? Or would you have continued being obstinate enough to persist in your objectives?"

"To be honest," he said stroking his beard, "I think I would have done it regardless. On the other hand, Sikin..."

"Enough now, Signore!" Tiblina interrupted. "Now you must change the subject, for you know this kind of discussion affects your health."

Curzio stood, removed his eccentric hat, and bowed smiling at her gratefully.

A few days later, in the midst of a winter storm, the three finally arrived at the oasis of Dunhuang. Sikin sighed. This was his final destination. Perhaps his mission would soon be over.

Under blowing and drifting snow, all wrapped up in furs and woolen blankets, they rode along the town's main access road, deciding after such a miserable afternoon to find lodging for the night instead of camping outdoors.

Familiar with the town, Curzio led the group to a hostel run by a Chinese man and his three daughters. The lodge consisted of a large sand-brick structure, void of openings except for a narrow entrance that also served as depository for dirty fingerprints. Almost blocking the passage, thick woolen drapes

141

hanging from the inside prevented the cold air from penetrating. Indoors the patrons used a massive stone slab with cushions on top, for sitting and gossip exchange.

The air reeked of fried food and smoke. The first came from a large kettle filled with very hot lard, and the other from burning wood and coal for warmth.

To the left a narrow hall accessed ten rooms, each of which had a straw mattress resting atop a wooden slab, covered with layers of blankets. The contraption was supposed to be used as bedding for a large family.

To the right a large rectangular table with rustic benches on each side served as the eating facility for all guests. Lodging prices were reasonable and included two meals.

Curzio, already familiar with the owner and his daughters from previous voyages, thought the connection could help him locate the two Italian brothers. Even though the town was large and heavily populated, word had a way of traveling at the speed of lightning.

Timing was his main concern. Were his friends already in the city? If they were, had they been there long? Or had they gotten tired of waiting and left? After traveling from Turpan in such delicate health, the possibility of not returning to Venice distressed him. He begged Sikin and Tiblina to escort him to Italy vowing to pay whatever price they asked. Sikin reassured him that with positive thoughts he would make it.

They spent the rest of that night in the room with the largest slab, where the aroma of cassia boiling inside a pot concealed the stale air with a sweet and gratifying scent.

Since there were no windows for light to enter, they slept till mid-morning the following day. Hungry but rested, they joined a few of the guests at the dining table for a meal of fried lamb chops, cheese, milk, and mint tea.

After the inn's owner indicated he had no news regarding the arrival of two Venetian merchants from Khanbalik, the three decided to walk the town, each in a different direction, asking questions, eavesdropping on street conversations, and searching for clues to the two merchants whereabouts.

Curzio planned to visit several establishments known to him from previous trips. Sikin followed the town's main drag to the north and Tiblina to the South.

As previously agreed, they gathered at the inn by late afternoon. Tiblina was suffering from frostbite in her left hand, which one of the Chinese girls brought back to life by rubbing it with snow until it began to hurt. Then she wrapped a small blanket around it to bring back color and circulation.

That evening, while they discussed the day's developments, a strange Chinese man who was visiting with other patrons overheard their conversation, and interrupted them.

"May I shed some light to your dilemma?"

"Of course, please do so!" Curzio answered.

"By the end of the last moon, as I was selling my goods in one of the open markets, a large group of Mongol soldiers, guides, wagons, and foreign merchants, marched noisily down the street. Rumor has it that those travelers came all the way from Khanbalik as special emissaries of the great Kublai Khan, and that they were traveling west."

The weird man paused as if trying to remember more details of the incident.

"You should look at the granary as the wealthy leave their beasts there."

"Great idea!" The three answered almost at once.

"May I ask the gentleman for a favor in return?" The slender man asked with a cynical grin on his face.

"Please go on," Curzio replied cautiously.

"I am an opium merchant, and ever since the Mongols invaded our land, the poppies market has suffered acute shortages. Some say is because of heavy usage by the conquerors; others believe the dwindling of crops was caused by bad weather. Opium use increases considerably during the winter, you see, and the colder it gets the more I sell. Unfortunately I am running out of stock, and the heaviest season is yet to come. Some merchants arriving from deep inside China bring along opium to sell or barter in exchange for favors, food, or services, and I was just thinking, 'if those travelers are indeed your friends, might they be interested in selling me some?' They looked to me like wealthy, influential merchants. All I ask from you is to present on my behalf this modest proposal."

"Naturally we'll pass your *modest proposal* along if we find our friends," Curzio said spadishly. "The rest is entirely up to them to decide, of course."

"Of course," agreed the wicked merchant.

Sikin wondered if there was a person left in town who would do a favor expecting nothing in return. In Dunhuang, profit was the ultimate motivator and universal standard of measure, the talk of the town, the grease that helped loosen values, and the catalyst that changed decent citizens into mercenaries.

That evening before retiring, Curzio told Sikin and Tiblina about the dreadful experiences suffered by opium addicts.

"I'm willing to bet my entire fortune that this blabbermouth doesn't touch the stuff. He just sells it and keeps the profits. He gathers gossip as well as disgraceful information, which he then uses for extortion to his own advantage. The man is nothing but a parsimonious criminal.

I strongly suggest the two of you visit the market described and look at the appalling sight of dehumanized men and women laying on the floor, smeared in their own feces, hungry, and freezing to death, not even knowing who they are anymore, all on account of this magic 'maker of dreams'

"Have you ever tried it?" Tiblina asked shyly.

"Only once," said Curzio clearing his throat.

"For unknown reasons some persons acquire an unmanageable addiction after trying it a few times, while others don't. I didn't want to run the risk, so I decided to quit after the first try.

At the beginning, it gave me a feeling of peace and well being I had never felt before. Nothing bothered me. I felt pleasantly drowsy and oblivious to the surroundings. I experienced dreams that seemed so authentic they felt real.

I remember flying like a bird in one of the dreams. It was absolutely wonderful to survey the colorful panorama below. I felt inmense peace. Then, all of a sudden I couldn't flap my wings anymore. I began to fall at an arrow's speed toward hundreds of sharp swords aimed at me by diabolical looking creatures. After crashing, I saw my entrails scattered all over, my eyes perforated by pointed blades, and my head dangling from the tallest sword. Detached from my remains I looked at the gruesome scene. In panic I screamed for help, but only an echo answered. Upon awakening, I felt intense anxiety and trepidation. My heart beat so fast; I thought my chest was breaking open. Terrified, and with my mouth dry as the desert sand, I began to tremble like a leaf, and after a while I began to vomit. The whole episode was so frightening that I swore never to touch the stuff again, and to this date I have fulfilled my promise."

The next day, on awakening to a crisp cold morning, the three decided to take their animals to the granary for forage, and rest.

The granary consisted of a large structure built of clay and sand bricks, sheltered by a thick thatched roof. The facility was sufficiently large to hold numerous bundles of dry oats and meadow grasses. Next door, another dwelling stored carts, provisions, wheels, repair tools, and spare parts.

Two young twins helped with the chores, while an older man, assisted by a cane, walked back and forth supervising, complaining, and giving orders. In his late eighties, the man had lost all of his teeth. He was almost blind from cataracts but his hearing was as sharp as the cold wind outside. His eyes were of a grayish color, and his upper back was markedly hunched. Dressed in a soiled woolen robe, the blind boss kept his feet warm by wrapping his sandals in heavy socks, giving his legs the appearance of thick stumps.

"Our beasts need food and rest," Curzio told him, "and we need information."

"I don't give free information to anyone, first tell me what you want then we settle. Then I'll give you an answer. You agree?"

Curzio stated his questions, and after agreeing on a price, the old caretaker nodded briskly.

"Now I remember them," he said. "Two merchants, accompanied by servants, guards, guides, carriages, camels, and horses, came in several days ago to rest their animals, repair damages to one carriage, and grease their wheels in order to continue their journey West. A great deal of work for my two assistants! And totally free of charge!" He snorted angrily.

"You don't seem like the type of businessman who does anything for free," Curzio remarked. "May I ask why we have to pay so generously for a piece of harmless information when you didn't charge them at all for so much work?"

"Didn't you know those merchants were carrying a *paiza* as personal emissaries of the Great Kublai Khan?" The caretaker grumbled.

"I do not know this word," Sikin said.

"A paiza is a golden tablet one foot long and four fingers wide that is presented to special individuals by the Khan himself to make sure they are provided with everything necessary to continue traveling, whether horses, food, lodging, guides or services, all free of charge!" The man snapped.

"What did the tablet say?" Asked Tiblina.

"It says, 'by the strength of the eternal Heaven, Holy be the name of the Khan. Let him that pays him no reverence, be killed.' It frightens me every time someone shows up with a royal tablet. They could ask for everything I own if they so desire, and with no recourse on my part. Thankfully, I had not seen more than a handful in recent times."

"Where were these influential travelers staying?" Tiblina asked.

The caretaker narrowed his eyes greedily. "That is a different question from another person. The answer has to be renegotiated."

Once again, Curzio took paper money from his bag and gave it contemptuously to the man, who tucked it quickly in his pocket. Then he said, almost in a whisper, "I am supposed to return everything in good repair to the red and yellow mansion located one li after turning toward sunset from the first street before passing the open market. The property is owned by a wealthy merchant who goes by the name of Han, and is shared among his friends and acquaintances."

"Good," Curzio replied. "When can we come back for our possessions?"

"Don't be in such a hurry!" Snapped the old man. "If you are continuing to the West, you must consider purchasing one of my carts along with two asses to make traveling more comfortable and efficient. This offer is just another way of assisting my customers, of course. If you need further assistance down the road, I will charge for it separately."

"It might not be a bad idea to have another cart," Sikin said. "I'll buy a sturdy one at the right price. But I don't have paper money. I can only pay you with precious stones."

"How can I trust your honesty when I know nothing about those rocks and much less about their value?" Asked the caretaker suspiciously.

"In the same way we paid you ahead of time for information which might not be correct."

Sikin pulled one of the less valuable pieces from a bag and showed it to the man, who brought it less than an inch from his eyes.

"A big cart for a small rock!" He cackled loudly.

"Not any different than paying with paper for valuable information." Sikin replied.

The stingy character called his assistants, and after arguing with them in Chinese, he decided to settle for two small "rocks" instead of one, to which Sikin agreed, since he knew their value was not any greater than that of a cart and two asses. Upon closing the deal they left the granary for the center of the city riding on the new cart.

Far from being a paradise, Dunhuang differed from most oasis towns. Daily life was much more agitated and demanding. Most persons were rude, and couldn't care less about each other. Cheating foreign merchants and among themselves encompassed all levels of society. Petty theft was also rampant, in spite of the Khan's measures to avoid pillage.

Wealthy husbands used countless opportunities to enjoy the

company of young women, who incessantly looked for rich men to please in exchange for presents, money, or whatever suited their fancies.

Curzio was convinced that one reason the Khan's forces seemed reluctant to control such excesses was because the citizens wealth eventually came his way through taxation. Why would he interfere with profits?

In a community of almost two million people where most dwellings were heated by burning wood and coal, the air was heavily polluted by a noxious brown cloud that covered the entire city throughout the winter. There was no clean air to breathe within miles beyond its limits. The deeper the Tang Ho river carved its way into town, the more it looked and smelled like raw sewage. Nevertheless, thousands of shanties filled both banks for miles, allowing neighbors to reach one another by small canoes.

Vegetables, fish, and other commodities were sold from all sorts of buoyant contraptions. In the early morning thousands of merchants floated without direction until their stock was depleted.

Most huts and shacks had small wooden docks that enabled their dwellers to fish, wash clothes, and scoop water for drinking and cooking as well as bathing during the summer.

During hot days ladies would wash their hair in the river while others sat on the docks letting the sun to dry it as they watched their children swim and play in the murky waters.

As the travelers moved along this section of the river, Sikin could see everything from Buddhist temples, statues of idols, and lusciously fertile gardens, to brothels and funeral parlors. The area truly provided a colorful display of life in motion.

"Do you want to know what I've been missing lately?" Sikin asked suddenly.

"I miss home, my friends, mother and father, Grandpa, the dog. I miss my real life!"

"I know you must return home some day," Tiblina said, sadly interrupting his nostalgia. "But will you be able to come back again?"

"If I were to choose my next destination; yes!" Sikin answered. "If Grandpa does, then I don't know. He is very faithful to his ancestors and will do nothing to upset them."

"I have saved a bottle of wine to toast my Italian friends. How about using a little to warm up our hearts?" Curzio said, sounding falsely jovial.

"Yes, of course! Let's toast for Sikin's prompt return." Tiblina said.

Making their way through the thick colorful crowds, they finally arrived at the market from which they would follow the directions to Master Han's red and yellow mansion. They had no trouble, for the building was unmistakeable.

The enormous mansion was built of yellow-colored brick and dark woods. Each of the many windows had beautifully carved hardwood gratings imbedded in their frames for protection against trespassers and thieves. Its unique roof was comprised of interlocking red tiles that would allow rainwater to flow to the gutters and into an underground cistern for storage and daily use.

During the dry season servants had to go to the river for water, which they carried into the house two wooden buckets at a time. They bore the containers hanging from a rope tied to each end of a wooden rod, the center of which rested against the servant's neck and shoulders. They would hold the heavy rig secure by laying their arms along the length of the stick. Sometimes more than one hundred containers were brought in during one day.

After passing several servants carrying water inside, the three hurried towards the entrance of the red and yellow mansion. As they walked along the path leading to the front porch, two Mongol guards approached warning them loudly not to come any closer without permission.

Taking off his hat in a gesture of friendship, Curzio indicated that they were good friends of Matteo and Niccolo Polo, and that they had come to visit them from afar.

Suddenly the front door swung open, and two men dressed in the elegant garb of Italian merchants came out to see what was going on.

"Niccolo! Matteo!" shouted Curzio joyfully.

"Curzio!" The men ran to receive him and the others with hugs and kisses, ushering them into the mansion with a thousand questions and exclamations.

Sikin could not believe he was meeting the father and uncle of Marco Polo. Wait till Ivan tells everyone at school, Sikin thought to himself. "Would they accept it as true?"

"I worried we'd never see each other again!" Niccolo said throwing his arm around Curzio.

"This is short of miraculous. Didn't I tell you that God was on our side?" Matteo exclaimed to his brother.

"Now my dear associates," Curzio said proudly, "I'd like you to meet those whom the hand of the Almighty God placed in my path at a time when I most sorely needed support. Niccolo and Matteo, please meet Sikin and Tiblina."

"Welcome, Sikin and Tiblina! Consider yourselves our guests of honor." Niccolo exclaimed eagerly.

"Thank you, Signore. We are pleased to share this occasion with Curzio's good buddies," Sikin responded gratefully.

"My young friend comes from a far away land none of us will ever be able to visit, since he flatly refuses to disclose its location," Curzio said, winking genially at Sikin. "However, his posture has not hindered our sincere relationship in any way, and I do expect from both of you the same attitude in return. I'm sure you will enjoy his company as much as I have."

"Gentlemen," Sikin said inclining his head. "Please consider me at your service, although I don't know for how long, since it is quite possible I might have to depart unexpectedly." Perplexed at such a statement, the two brothers looked at each other with raised eyebrows. Was Curzio in his right mind befriending such an eccentric young fellow? What kind of person comes from nowhere, and goes back to nowhere on a whim?

Curzio interrupted their unspoken curiosity by introducing Tiblina as his newly adopted child and loyal confidante. Once again, both brothers gazed at each other in amazement, clearly wondering if their old friend had lost his mind while convalescing in Turpan.

Almost immediately, Tiblina extended her right hand to Niccolo and Matteo, which they kissed eagerly expressing admiration for her exotic beauty. Shy and unpretentious, she conducted herself with the deportment of a well-bred lady of noble birth.

Both brothers examined the young couple unashamedly.

"Aren't they different?" Niccolo whispered to Matteo.

"Mmm, they certainly are." Matteo muttered, scratching his hat.

Meanwhile, walking through the mansion, Sikin noticed it was filled with priceless possessions; granite and marble sculptures, Oriental prints and paintings, Venetian crystal ornaments, Persian rugs, huge china cabinets exhibiting masterfully decorated ceramic pieces, silver candleholders, as well as intricately carved hardwood furniture so massive, Sikin wondered how they were able to move them around.

Tiblina's eyes and mouth opened wide in astonishment, and she clung to Sikin's arm as the two followed the three babbling Venetians. Each of the various rooms had been built and decorated differently from European to North African styles. A mansion more luxurious and ostentatious could not be found anywhere else in the province of Tangut.

Finally they entered a courtyard large enough to hold a Chinese garden during the summer months, but since winter was already in full swing, the two lady gardeners were polishing silver pieces instead.

There they joined the other honored guests in the mansion besides Niccolo and Matteo. The guides, soldiers, and servants who had accompanied them from Khanbalik were lodged in quarters especially designed for attendants and staff.

An entourage of servants dressed in bright white uniforms appeared. One brought chairs for them to sit, another, a silver tray filled with fresh fruits, and a third, a complete tea set he placed upon a table covered with a most exquisitely arrayed tablecloth. Sikin counted more than twenty servants standing ready to serve and please the guests.

Master Han, Niccolo informed them, was a gregarious Chinese merchant who boasted of buying and selling the most valuable pieces of art on the Silk Route, and as such, he had made an enormous fortune. Although he was out of town, he had made the mansion available for the exclusive use of his guests. Unmarried and without family, Master Han looked for the company of friends and acquaintances for fulfillment. He couldn't bear solitude, and if he found his house empty, he became anxious and depressed. Constantly needing conversation, he often gave large parties just to "keep in touch." A consummate philanthropist, Master Han shared his riches with the less auspicious in a variety of ways. Therefore, most citizens either knew him personally or had heard of him.

Tiblina continued to inspect the mansion in awe. She had never realized there could be so much luxury and beauty inside a home, or anywhere else for that matter, and she could barely express her wonderment at being a part of it. With eyes wide open, she marveled at every ornament, accessory, and furnishing displayed. Curzio, quite amused, couldn't take his eyes off her, and after the servants brought in chairs, he had to tell her to sit or she would have remained standing indefinitely.

Three ladies wearing long aprons, carrying pitchers full of hot water, a basin, and white towels, approached the visitors and removed their boots so they could wash and rub their feet before supper.

Shortly thereafter, the visitors found themselves without shoes their feet washed in warm scented water, and then rubbed in perfumed oils. They sat languidly across from their hosts making comments about the incredible surroundings.

Sikin couldn't believe he was sitting across from Marco Polo's relatives.

He detected in Niccolo's features a slight resemblance to a poster of Leonardo da Vinci that Ivan had fixed to his bedroom wall. Niccolo spoke Italian with an accent, and his mannerisms were more Chinese than European. He was also tall and slightly hunchback.

Would Marco Polo look like his father? Sikin wondered. I

certainly hope he's not short and chubby like his uncle!

Sikin noticed that the back of Matteo's head was awfully flat; so flat it looked like a dinner plate. Sikin also wondered whether Matteo's over-sized gut was the result of gluttony, because his body, shaped like a pear, had a pot belly so large that it hung over his sash.

How could this man survive the desert on meager rations is beyond me! Sikin thought with a tad of gentle wit.

Unlike his brother, Matteo spoke Italian with the right intonation, and his sense of humor kept everyone around always in good spirits.

The Venetian merchants were happy to see their old friend enjoying life at its best, at least for a while. As Southern Europeans generally did, they communicated by making eloquent hand gestures and elevating their voices to be sure their opinions registered. Their enthusiasm was so great, they frequently screamed at each other.

Concentrating on the surroundings as she was, Sikin doubted Tiblina was even aware of their conversation. He could not take his eyes off her either, delighted by her grace and inquisitiveness.

After exchanging gossip and news at a rapid clip, Matteo Polo told Curzio the main reason they wanted to meet.

"My dear friend," he began. "Shortly following our arrival in Khanbalik, we had the unique opportunity to meet the Great Kublai Khan. The monarch became so fond of Niccolo and me, that he began to consult us for advice on certain matters, especially those relating to Christianity, the Pope and the lifestyles of Westerners, Latins in particular.

Desperately seeking meaning and truth, the powerful man felt moved by our conversations regarding the Christian faith to present us with a most unusual request, which would be impossible to achieve without your personal help.

He has written a long letter in Turki, which he has addressed to no other than the Pope himself, requesting his Eminence to send one hundred learned men to teach his people Christianity, Western science, and the Seven Arts: rhetoric, logic, grammar, arithmetic, astronomy, music, and geometry. He also asked the Pontiff to procure him oil from the lamp of the Holy Sepulchre in Jerusalem. His Majesty is considering the possibility of reversing his previous religious practices of idol worshipping to the ways of Christianity, and for that reason, he has asked us to deliver the sealed document to the Pontiff in person.

In light of this, we were asked to travel with his golden tablet, which is more of a magic wand than a tablet of gold and has served its purpose to no end.

Hence, here is our question. Would you be willing to lead us through your infinite pool of influential contacts in order to reach Pope Clement in person?"

"Never in our relationship has any one of us refused to satisfy the needs of the others," Curzio replied. "Therefore, my dear friends, I am at your service as of this very moment."

Shortly after sunset, two attendants offered to serve freshly cooked food in the main dining area, and since the remaining guests were not eating at the mansion that evening, the menu was read aloud and selections were ordered. Almost immediately, the head sevant asked the travelers to follow him to their appointed rooms. The luxury of enjoying private accommodations was the last wish on Sikin's mind, and undoubtedly the most welcome of all day's events.

* * *

As Tiblina entered the dining area all decked out, her hair combed and dressed, her lips rouged, her fingernails cleaned; a pulsing conversation suddenly came to a complete stop. Sikin stood up like a soldier at attention. The brothers Polo stared at each other in wonderment, and then resumed ogling Tiblina. And Curzio, walked toward her, kissed her on the cheek, and said to the others, "Gentlemen, in good conscience, please answer this question. Why would any honorable man worth his lineage, leave this angelic creature to rot and waste in this infamous and desolate environment?"

Waiting for an answer that never came, he continued.

"I hereby refuse to let it happen! At my age, I certainly regret some of the crazy things I have done in my life, but this time, my friends, I shall do only what's right. Tiblina will accompany us to La Serenissima. She clearly doesn't belong around here. In Venice, I shall make certain she's given the right opportunities to capture her dreams."

The men seemingly couldn't move their eyes away from her. Self-conscious and overwhelmed, Tiblina sat down with the finesse of an accomplished lady, conducting herself as a seasoned aristocrat. Their succulent meal came to an end, and Curzio asked the young couple to please leave him alone with his two friends, to discuss an urgent matter.

* * *

Walking through the mansion, Sikin couldn't decide whether to treat Tiblina like his buddy, or hold and kiss her hand to cross the threshold. Her transformation left him speechless.

Tiblina had tears in her eyes as thoughts of Sikin's departure saddened her. She told him she was grateful for his rescue of her from Amur and how she would never forget his kindness.

Standing in front of him she gazed deeply into his eyes. "I had always idolized you as a friend, admired your sense of compassion as a human being, and deeply loved you for the man you are. Thank you for teaching me so much and for the memories you have left forever carved in my aching heart. I shall miss you, and all I ask in kind is for your solemn promise that if at all possible, you'll always think of me and you'll come back to see me again someday."

Softly caressing his face, Tiblina stood on her tiptoes, passed her fingertips across his lips, then kissed them fervently.

Embracing her passionately and delighting in the sweetness of her breath Sikin felt aroused by her firm bosom beating recklessly against his heart. The disconsolate woman, unable to control her tears any longer, ran back to her room.

Stunned, Sikin couldn't believe the magic of the moment. If as was said, memories come to life as they are recalled, he would always remember this one as the sweetest of them all.

Saddened and heavy of heart, he returned to the drawing room where conversation continued at an accelerated pace among the three friends.

At one point, Curzio interrupted to say, "My friends, it is very important that you listen to what I am about to request, and vow that you will use every resource within your reach to fulfill my last wish."

At this the Polos looked shocked. He held up a hand and continued.

"I know you all believe the reason I adopted Tiblina was to fill the vacuum created by the absence of my legitimate daughters. In a sense this is true, but that's not all. When a man perceives his mortality as I recently have, his mind begins to function differently. Money, power, and all the physical excitement in the world do not fulfill him anymore. If this person is wise, he will sense deep inside that there are much more important undertakings on the short road he has left ahead. Perhaps he realizes the possibility of encountering our Maker, to whom we owe such an infinite amount of excuses and explanations, or maybe he has finally grasped the futility of dedicating one's life to satisfying selfish desires.

In my case, this old man has determined to change course while there is time, and as a result I have decided to reward Tiblina's persistent courage, honesty of purpose, and goodness of heart.

Consequently, my friends, I have written my last will and testament in this scroll, which I entrust to you for safekeeping and presentation to the proper authorities in Venice in the event I die before reaching our beloved Republic.

The testament states among other things how I wish to distribute my fortune. It addresses first and foremost my legitimate daughters and longsuffering wife. Also included is an apology for all the misery I have caused them, as well as my last wish...*forgiveness*.

In this scroll I also ask my good friend Pope Clement to watch after Tiblina, making certain she receives the necessary support and education to be accepted in our society.

I intend to assign the precious stones and jewels I have carried along in my travels during the last twenty years entirely to her. Those gems became my symbol of personal security through rough times. I believe they rightfully belong to Tiblina, since they were taken away from her land. I carry them concealed inside the leather bag strapped to my camel's shoulder. They are heavily coated with clay for protection against thieves. Their value, which is high enough to make the Great Kublai envious, should provide plentiful wealth on which she may live the rest of her life in comfort and safety.

I also wish to pass on to my daughter Mariu half ownership of the silk operation in Sicily. And to reward my cousin's hard work and devotion to the business, I assign him the other half, which he so rightfully deserves. The remainder of my estate should be equally divided among my two daughters and dear wife.

A letter to His Holiness, requesting cooperation regarding the Great Khan's wishes as stated by the two of you will be included in the will, as well as my intention to pass ownership of the arable land I own in Southern Sicily, to our Catholic church.

I further ask you to please keep our conversation confidential unless I die on the journey. I want Tiblina to love and care for me as much as she has, without regard for future gains. In that way I know her love and compassion are genuinely heartfelt, and not a result of financial expectations.

Please introduce her to my youngest daughter. She will find a good friend in Mariu. In return I will ask Tiblina to tell my daughter about my life in this barren and inhospitable world, and how much and for what reasons I wanted to share my experiences with them."

Curzio paused as beads of sweat mixed with tears rolled down his pale chins. "Gentlemen, I'm afraid that's all for now."

The two brothers became as agitated as butterflies...

"Why are you so concerned about dying soon? What makes you think you will leave us on the way to Venice?" Matteo asked.

"I am a very sick man," Curzio answered gently. "Every day

that passes, I become weaker. It has been wondrous making it to Dunhuang. It will be a miracle if I make it to Venice!"

"Curzio, I agree with my brother." Niccolo chimed in. "Premonitions do not necessarily become reality. They are nothing but divinations inspired by our own fears. Nevertheless, my friend, count upon us. We will respect your wishes and carry on with the testament. You have our solemn word." He and Matteo nodded gravely.

Meanwhile, Sikin had been staring silently at the ceiling overwhelmed by a deep apprehension over the possibility of returning to his real world. He felt the time was closing in. Grandfather McKinley had specified Dunhuang as his final destination. Now, after listening to her confession of love, he knew it unfair to stay around Tiblina any longer.

His work here was done. By an act of providence, Tiblina will be accompanied by decent men of honor all the way to her "land of the lakes" where she would certainly find a worthy course in life. Even though Sikin would love to care for her, he realized he was no longer needed.

Curzio was finally on the way to fulfill his last wish, asking for his family's pardon. Bringing him from Turpan to meet his friends essentially completed that part of Sikin's teleportation mission.

The brothers Polo had achieved what they never thought possible; tempting the Great Kublai Khan to consider the ways of Christianity, opening as a result a dialogue between him and the Pope. In this case there was no further reason for his presence either.

What else is here for me? He pondered, wishing to find legitimate reasons to stay longer.

Gradually and painfully, he began to realize that the mission was over. Part of him wanted to return to a normal life as an American teenager, the other part longed to remain with Tiblina until the end of time.

Brokenhearted, Sikin wondered about the likelihood of another encounter with his friends from the Middle Ages. Imagining his task back home, he was deeply concerned about his credibility among peers. Would they accept his stories as legitimate accounts? Would his parents suspect he was suffering a mental illness? Would Grandpa feel proud of the results of his mission?

He could find no logical or easy answers, and the time of reckoning was around the corner. "If I made a decision to accept the gift of soul teleportation, then I must learn to accept the consequences," he said aloud.

Sikin returned to his chamber, went to bed, and took a moment to close his eyes and pray that everything would be right for everyone.

What if the 'return button' doesn't work? He wondered. *What if I don't say the right words to activate the teleportation of my soul? Perhaps I should rely on the same supernatural powers that brought me in, forget all worries, try to get some sleep and pray for a successful return.*

It was almost morning when totally exhausted, Sikin, finally closed his eyes, falling into a deep sleep.

CHAPTER *Five*

IVAN RETURNS TO AMERICA

*"We are more curious about the
meaning of dreams than about
things we see when we awake."*
Diogenes.

In New York, sitting on the comfortable rocking chair alongside Ivan's bed, Grandfather McKinley snored with his head down. It was four on Sunday morning. Ivan has been traveling for six hours, Yonkers time.

Rolling sideways, Ivan moved the pillow to accommodate his change of position. Grandpa, a light sleeper awoke immediately at the sound of the movement. Realizing Ivan was back from Dunhuang, he gently awoke the boy by touching his forehead.

Like a cat recovering from a lengthy nap, eyes still closed, confused and disoriented, Ivan stretched lazily. Then his eyes flew open. He sat at the edge of the bed scratching his head, gazing at his grandfather as if to ask, "Did all this really happen? Am I back?"

"How do you feel, son?"

"I can't really tell! I'm not sure what's reality and what isn't.

I don't even know whether I am at home, or at Master Han's mansion dreaming of it."

"Ivan, you are back where you belong," said his grandfather. "The dream is over! You are at home with your family! How long did your trip last?"

"Less than a year, I believe."

"Today is a holiday, so after breakfast let's go to the park where we can talk. I'm anxious to hear about it! But now you must go back to bed. It is only four a.m. You need the rest, and so do I. We'll talk later on." Grandpa McKinley patted Ivan on the shoulder, then shuffled out toward his room.

Incapable of staying still, Ivan scrutinized the room to make sure he was there. "Wow, what a resemblance to Niccolo!" He exclaimed gazing at the da Vinci poster. Then he threw off the covers, made up his bed, grabbed a change of clothes, and went for a shower to clear his mind. Then he tiptoed downstairs to the front porch, and sat on a wooden swing to watch the sun paint the early morning sky. In his heartfelt opinion there was no comparison to the explosion of colors from a Taklamakan sunrise, the stillness of the desert, and the fresh look of Tiblina wishing him "good morning" in broken Italian. His heart felt it would burst with longing and grief at the thought of her.

Later on he wandered inside, where mother was preparing a breakfast of eggs, sausages, and grits.

"No comparison to dried horsemeat and camel's milk," he said upon entering the kitchen.

"What was that, son?"

"Oh nothing, Mom, just mumbling."

Grandpa, who was helping set the table, peered closely at Ivan and smiled. "Good morning, young man! Did you have a good night's sleep? Any exciting dreams you want to share with us?" He winked facetiously.

"What are you guys doing this morning?" Father asked, entering the kitchen.

"Not much, Dad," Ivan answered. "Grandpa and I are going to take a stroll through the park this morning."

"Perhaps we can all go to the Polo Grounds and watch the

Highlanders beat the Orioles. Why don't you guys come along?" Asked Ivan's father.

"I certainly will!" Grandpa replied.

"What about you, Ivan?"

"Thanks, Dad, but I'd rather stay home and do some more thinking.

"Do some more thinking? About what?" His puzzled father asked.

"Son, you must keep his age in mind," Grandfather said coming to the rescue. "Ivan needs time to discover himself. Perhaps he is worried about finals. Maybe there is a girl in his life, or was...who knows? I'll go with you to the ball game. Let him stay and do whatever he wants."

As previously ordained by their Druid ancestor, he and Grandpa went for a stroll in the nearby park to share their thoughts about the trip.

The debriefing lasted until early afternoon, when the older Mckinley, realizing it was time to leave for the ball game, asked his grandson to write a diary while his memory was fresh with details, insisting it should be done as soon as possible.

"Should I tell Mom and Dad?"

"Oh, perhaps in a day or so, better sober up before opening your mouth, son. At this moment you are in no condition to express yourself credibly."

"Grandpa, you must understand before we go any further that my return to the past is an urgent necessity and one for which I would need your fullest support. Can I count on you? Please, Grandpa! Would you please say yes?"

Wearing a starched white shirt buttoned to the collar, gray knickerbockers, brown socks, and a gray beret, Ivan's appearance was as remote from Sikin's, as Grandpa was from approving another trip.

Ducks wading on the pond, birds nesting on the trees, lovers holding hands, and the abundance of color, contrasted sharply against Sikin's barren surroundings, and although Ivan has been back for a few hours, his heart was somewhere else.

Grandpa explained that his asking was unreasonable. These

teleportation experiences were simply not intended to become grounds for romantic encounters.

"You ought to realize that Tiblina has been dead for over eight hundred years, and chances are the privileges would be withdrawn if you use them to quench capricious desires. You must be very careful not to become emotionally involved. Always keep in mind that your job is to be a reporter, not one of the protagonists.

The responsibility vested in you, Ivan, is to spread the news by sharing your experiences with as many persons as you can. If you become obsessed with someone or something, your experiences could be considered biased, and therefore meaningless.

Suppose you encountered a situation where you had the power to rule a nation with all the riches, beautiful girls, and all the perks and privileges only absolute power provides, would you consider staying in the past forever?"

"Of course not! On the other hand, by not showing a more meaningful ending to our story, most listeners will not appreciate the vicissitudes encountered by this young woman when facing an entirely different culture, particularly during the Middle Ages. Was she ever rewarded for her moral values and virtues, or were those attributes widely ignored in those days?"

Ivan continued insistently. "Were Tiblina's struggles for fairness and justice, worth the potential harassment resulting from society's disregard for women's rights during that time? Would her successes and failures provide valuable insights to people of the twentieth century? Are men and women of modern times more compassionate and humane than their counterparts during the dark ages? Have we improved from our past in this respect? Are we better off, or are we worse than before?"

Grandpa opened his mouth to speak, but Ivan cut him off.

"Furthermore, if Curzio lives through the journey wouldn't you like to know the family's reaction to his act of contrition? Moreover Grandpa, do Tiblina's character and principles fall prey to the trappings of instant wealth?"

"All right, Ivan," Grandpa sighed. "I will call it a tie at this point, but only in principle. Suppose I agree to your conditions, how long do you propose to stay in order to bring this story to an acceptable conclusion? What if you decide to stay with her indefinitely, thus making Tiblina the central figure of your mission?"

"Who said she was the central figure of my mission? Yes, I was madly in love with the girl, as I still am with her ghost. But at least you should give me credit for being fair to our ancestors' wishes. I did what was expected, to the best of my ability."

"Please don't misunderstand me. You did admirably well. But at your age and under the circumstances, the call of the flesh can often destroy a young man's capacity to judge."

"Grandpa, I promise to finish the next mission as soon as our goals are achieved. Not an extra day, nor an extra minute.

Just think about how exciting it would be to follow their lives, not necessarily to their physical end, but to a more gratifying and meaningful completion than just a story full of uncertainties!

Since I refuse to consider our mission accomplished, I'm also willing to convince our ancestors of my motives for returning. Please let me bear this responsibility. I cannot be more truthful, and you must not doubt my intentions any further.

I'm still considered an adolescent according to age, but I have grown years overnight. My life will never be the same again, Grandpa. Your grandson has become an older person embodied in a teenager. I even worry about my ability to function like a kid anymore. I don't fit with grown up men, not with my peers."

Ivan gazed at his grandfather beseechingly.

"Just trust me! I shall not disappoint you. My next mission has the potential of becoming even more rewarding than the first."

After a short pause, the tired old sage replied,

"Please remember that you are my only hope for passing down our gift to future generations of McKinleys, and for that reason, I must think and act judiciously. Your request makes sense, but these issues are much more complex than anticipated. Being older and slower, I need more time to balance out my thoughts.

I shall give you an answer soon. As you know, I'm not supposed to go back to Stonehenge for guidance. Our Druid ancestor made it very clear: 'No further instructions shall be given, and no second chances will be allowed.' Therefore, Ivan, the full burden of responsibility rests entirely on our shoulders."

Grandpa peeked at his pocket watch. "Now let me go back to Finn before he becomes irritated. He always wants to be among the first to arrive at the ballpark.

Back at home, Ivan, who had enough artistic talent to draw by memory, began making sketches of the highlights of his trip. He started by drawing Amur's hut inside and out, their horse-driven carts, and the way people dressed. That evening he worked on Turpan and its streets until early morning. Then he slept for a couple of hours, and drew the grotto of the chanting monks, which took him almost half a day to complete. He wanted to draw Tiblina's face, but unable to sketch what attracted him the most, he decided that perhaps words would do more justice.

Sensitivity to acceptance by others was Ivan's most demanding personality flaw. In many ways this was not a positive quality, since he depended on others' perceptions of him to nourish his self-esteem and justify his niche in society. The fact he had to reveal his mission to a large group of friends worried him to no end. Moreover, since he intended to pen up to his parents that evening after supper, the prospects of rejection and mockery were already causing him acute anxiety.

In spite of feeling much nervousness and confusion, his mind had enough room left to dwell on one obsession, "The uncivilized girl Sikin had taught to be a learned lady, and who had left such an indelible mark on his young heart."

For dinner that evening, his mother had prepared Ivan's favorite recipe, shredded beef and dumplings.

Conversation at the table was lively, except for Ivan, who had remained silent throughout the entire meal, prompting his mom to ask if he was feeling well.

"I am fine," he replied. "If I have been unusually silent for the last couple of days, it is just because I have something important to share with you and Dad, and I don't have the slightest idea how to begin."

"Say it!" Grandpa intervened. "You must learn to confide in your parents. Besides, I am here to help you out."

"Help him out? Help him out with what?" Demanded his mother.

"Ah! That's it!" Said his father. "You must have told Grandpa already. I'll bet it must be something you feel bashful about, a new girl in your life, perhaps?"

"Yes and no, Dad. It involves a girl, but I don't know if you will laugh at me when I tell you how I met her."

"Oh! Don't be ridiculous," perhaps if I tell you how I met your mother..."

"Please, honey," his mom interrupted. "Let him talk. This is not the time to discuss ancient history."

"But Mom, said Ivan, this is all about ancient history!"

"You flunked the subject, didn't you?"

"No, Dad, I didn't." Ivan looked pleadingly at his grandfather who was sitting right across from him.

Nodding confidently, the old man gave the boy the encouragement and support he needed so desperately.

"Go ahead, son. We are all ears!" Said his dad patiently.

Ivan took a deep breath, glanced at his mentor, and looking at his parents in their eyes, he began to depict the saga, starting from the moment Grandpa revealed his incredible encounter with the swan until his awakening two days before.

After listening to Ivan for two hours, both parents looked stunned.

Finn asked Grandpa for an explanation for his son's "sudden attack of lunacy."

"This was a healthy young man until you began filling his head with those idiotic superstitions," he shouted. "Now listen to him! Our boy had become a nitwit overnight!

Why don't you go look for Cinderella in the grocery store

instead of the Taklamakan? For all I know she might be shopping for her missing shoe, and who knows? The two might fall in love with each other. Oh, God! I should have listened to my aunt. She was an honest believer... a true Catholic. Now my son's mind is under the influence of a lunatic!"

"You have no right to say such a thing!" Grandpa replied angrily. "I swear upon your mother's grave that my conversations with Ivan had always been honest and well intentioned. The boy shares the same beliefs I have cherished for over sixty years, and there is nothing wrong with that. The fact that everyone I know, including you, mocks my convictions doesn't give you the right to call me a lunatic. I am mentally competent and have more character than most people I know. I care for Ivan as much as you do. Furthermore, I care about future generations of McKinleys much more than you ever will.

As a child you were in no way influenced by my so-called 'idiotic beliefs.' Why don't you show the same attitude of acceptance toward him? The problem with most people these days are their refusal to consider real, anything they don't see, smell, touch, or feel. If I swear upon the Bible a thousand times that Ivan has told you the whole truth, you still won't believe him. The poor boy has been worried sick since yesterday anticipating this unfair confrontation."

Grandpa frowned, but did not cease his angry defense.

"You just said your Irish aunt was right when she wanted to separate us on account of my 'satanic superstitions'. Well son, tell us what I have done to hurt you ever since that aunt told you so? Have I ever led you down the wrong path in life? Have I ever said anything to humiliate or diminish you for not accepting my ideas and beliefs? Did I ever force you to accept my ideology? Since you know darn well all the answers are no, then why treat your son like a demented fool?

He took a deep breath, holding up his hand for silence.

"And let me ask you another question before I finish...

"Have you ever seen God? Do you know what Heaven or Hell looks like if they really exist? Have you ever touched his beard, or smelled his breath? Do you honestly accept every story in the Bible to be literally true? If your answers are no, then why do you believe so unequivocally in everything our man made church tells you?

You know why, son? Because it is our human tendency to believe in anything that provides the answers we want to hear. Even though there is ample room in our minds to store the unbelievable, the supernatural, and the existence of metaphysical dimensions, we just don't have the courage and open mindedness to endorse their authenticity, following instead, someone else's perceptions of what God's realm looks like.

My beliefs go beyond dogmatic faith." Grandpa continued. "They are based upon common and unique supernatural experiences few are wise enough to perceive and accept as genuine. Only individuals willing to extend their reach into the uncharted waters of creation and beyond will be able to comprehend what I'm talking about.

If you believe in the omniscience and omnipresence of God, you must also accept the existence of higher spiritual realms, legitimized by eternal and perfect energies that originate from a perfect and everlasting source. One capable of creating and manipulating inconceivable and miraculous events in our material world, rather than training your imagination to accept under fear of eternal damnation only what was blessed and approved by the religious establishment."

"I need proof!" Ivan's father demanded irately. "If you or Ivan can prove to Clare and me that his teleportation experience was in fact real, by God, I'll be the first one to offer support."

"Father, I didn't know anything about the Silk Road, nor about life in those days," Ivan said. "If I disclose certain events even most educated historians don't know about, would you then believe me?"

"That will only make me feel more inquisitive, Ivan, and then what? Where is that proof?"

"Now it is my turn," Ivan's mother said, "and I only ask for two concessions. First, if Ivan cannot prove the veracity of his supernatural experiences to our satisfaction, I insist he sees a psychiatrist immediately."

Ivan groaned. He'd been afraid of this.

"A young man of eighteen is old enough to discern between fantasy and fiction, and as his mother, I'm deeply concerned about his mental health. Who knows? The boy might be experiencing schizophrenic delusions." His mom went on, speaking as if he weren't sitting right there.

"Second, and most important, I would like to keep this whole affair a family secret.

All I want from a doctor is my son's mental evaluation, and if he has become unstable, then we shall take the necessary steps to correct the situation. If he is perfectly normal, I promise to leave the two of you alone with your trips, stories, and fantasies.

History recognizes that geniuses of the past have had occasional dreams as well as nightmares that felt as absolute reality, and in many instances, those mental images have served as sources of inspiration for the creation of the most wonderful masterpieces of art." Clare concluded.

"Are you thinking about Vincent Van Gogh, Mother?" Ivan asked.

"He was only one of them. In fact, he suffered from schizophrenia and depression. Therefore we must make sure you are not in that league, young man. Anyway, I certainly hope no one sees my requests as unreasonable."

"I agree Mom, I'm not afraid one bit."

"What about you, Grandpa? Do you think I'm too radical?"

"Not at all; if a psychiatrist shows to your satisfaction that Ivan is perfectly normal, you might be more receptive to his experiences."

"I think you are wasting our money dear!" Finn chimed in. "I'm sure Ivan's so-called abnormality is nothing of the sort, but a result of Dad's daily indoctrination and brainwashing. Just like those who believe in ghosts feel their presence, Ivan has become so impressed with my old man's superstitions that he cannot discern reality from fiction anymore. Had they become involved in activities like parchisi or football, instead of fooling around with the supernatural, all these delusions could have been avoided."

"Mom, I need to go to bed." Ivan said, having heard enough. "I have not slept well for the last two days. May I be excused?"

"Certainly! I'm sure we'll be next to follow."

As a result of the family's reaction, and to fulfill his mother's wishes, Ivan and his grandfather decided to suppress the stories from school friends, at least for the time being.

The next morning as usual, Finn left for work, Ivan for school, Grandpa to visit his Irish cronies and Clara, not as usual, hurried to the public library to find the names of accredited physicians specializing in the relatively new science of psychiatry.

Several days later, at dinner, Clare opened up another lively session...

"After an exhausting investigation, I discovered the name of a disciple of Sigmund Freud, whose research in the field of dream interpretation has made the Austrian doctor the most renowned psychiatrist in the world. The man is expensive, but according to my research, he is a distinguished pioneer in the field. I took the liberty of visiting his office in Manhattan and made an appointment for Ivan to see him next Friday."

"Then I should cancel the ball game that afternoon," Ivan said.

"I'm sorry son, but your mental health is much more important." She replied.

"I'll talk to the coach. I'm sure he'll understand," his father said supportively.

Thoroughly disenchanted, Grandpa remained silent throughout the evening. The following week, Ivan went to see Dr. Kalmann, a Viennese psychiatrist and former disciple of the "Father of Psychoanalysis."

In short order, the boy became virtually swamped with homework, finals, baseball playoffs, and social events, plus two weekly trips to the doctor's office, which took him hours to complete back and forth.

After reaching a diagnosis a month or so later, the good doctor decided to mail his findings in writing to Finn and Clara. The letter read like this:

After spending extensive time in session with your son, I became thoroughly convinced that the young man was not under the influence of narcotics at the time of his so-called "teleportation dream."

Such a possibility had to be ruled out prior to the application of psychoanalysis. Therefore, after discarding the use of narcotics as a main concern, one of the worse scenarios was in fact eliminated.

I also applied hypnosis as an aid to my investigations, based on the assumption that symptoms of hysterical patients are directly traceable to forgotten psychic traumas in early life, represented by undischarged emotional energy, which is usually sexual in nature, and often expressed subconsciously in dreams and nightmares.

My conclusion thus far: Ivan's condition is anomalous of hysterical patients. Nevertheless, I have made clear to the subject that dream interpretations resulting from pre-scientific views, as adopted by the peoples of antiquity such as his Druid ancestor, were in complete harmony with their view of the universe as a whole. They projected into the external world, as though they were realities, the things that in fact enjoyed authenticity only within their own minds. This determination brings to light the ancient judgement that someone who has just awakened from sleep assumes that his dreams, although they did not come from another world, did in fact carry him off into another realm.

Accepting the hypothesis that all the material that makes up the content of dreams is in some way derived from experience, we are presented with the indisputable issue that Ivan's subconscious mind must have been deeply influenced by someone exerting significant authority over him; hence the reasons for his vivid extracorporeal experiences.

It is also common knowledge in our profession that a dream usually represents the fulfillment of a wish, which proves itself in this case by Ivan's tendency to spend a great deal of time fantasizing about perfect love, heroism, chivalry, adventure, exotic beauty, discovery, as well as a multitude of desires common to the minds of healthy adolescents. Ivan's dreams however, were strangely realistic, filled with accurate historical data, extraordinarily detailed, and anthropologically challenging. Nonetheless I'm not implying that such unprecedented conditions are symptomatic of a disturbed mind, but rather a clear transparency of the patient's creative personality.

To conclude my diagnosis, Mr. and Mrs. McKinley, I will use a Freudian notion that recognizes the dreams of children and young adults to be pure wish fulfillment, thus inconsequential and scientifically irrelevant. On the other hand, the amount of historical information offered by the subject was absolutely astonishing and beyond belief. You must feel very proud having such an outstanding history student in the family. Please express my congratulations to your gifted son. In sum, I found the boy to be perfectly normal, even a genius.

Respectfully yours,
Heinrich Kalmann, M.D., Ph.D

* * *

The letter, which Clara read aloud to the family, prompted her husband to reassert his previous conviction that nothing was wrong with his boy's head, repeating once again one of his favorite lines, "See! I told you it was a waste of money!"

Being diagnosed as "normal" gave Ivan a needed sense of calm. Curiously enough his parents never mentioned his unusual experience again, since it was, after all, "just a dream."

Grandpa didn't say much. He felt disappointed and betrayed seeing such a marvelous experience being treated first as an emotional disorder and later as an inconsequential event.

"Science to most skeptics is a negation of the supernatural," Grandpa remarked, "rather than a medium to reach and understand its metaphysical origins and dimensions. Unfortunately, the kind of attitude exhibited by Dr. Kalmann only promotes the scientist's own impotence in accepting divine wisdom and enlightenment as an essential part of creation."

Following Grandpa's only remark of the evening, Ivan stood up, and with tears in his eyes, gave him a hug and a kiss.

"Finn," said Clara, "can't you see how beautiful it is to watch our son and your dad get along so well and love each other so much? Why don't we just leave them alone?"

"I still believe they should be playing checkers and talking baseball instead of messing around with their sanity, but if that's what you want, dear, then it is fine with me. Dad has always been different, and the truth is he has never hurt anyone, so from now on I won't fuss about it anymore. And by the way, Dad, I didn't mean to hurt your feelings. I just wanted Ivan to accept only what our church teaches, instead of struggling with contradictions that might eventually turn him into an agnostic. Yet, I also realize that the boy is already eighteen, and therefore should feel free to think and decide as he wishes, as long as he doesn't deviate from the teachings of our priesthood. Please forgive my rudeness. I truly didn't mean to hurt you."

"Don't worry, son." Grandpa replied with a smile "I still enjoy talking baseball with you. After all, what else is there to talk to you about?"

Since his parent's concerns were not on top anymore, Ivan felt free to propose another trip to the past. He wanted to know how she was fairing.

After innumerable discussions, both decided their next step should be to determine when the unavoidable voyage should take place. They had no doubt that another contact with the past was not only inevitable, but also reasonable under the circumstances. However, precise timing would be absolutely essential.

As a condition for another teleportation experience, Grandpa requested a detailed summary of Ivan's first voyage to preserve as evidence for future reference. Consequently, every time the boy had a free moment during the following weeks, he would lock himself inside his room to write pages upon pages of memories, including drawings, often working until the wee hours of morning trying to fulfill his grandfather's wish.

He frequently slept only three hours a night and still functioned normally during the day.

Six months flew by. Never again did Grandpa or Ivan bring up the subject of teleportation in front of Finn and Clare, and as far as they were concerned the incident belonged to the past.

As long as Finn had the time to talk baseball with family and friends, Clare the opportunity to visit the public library, Grandpa to chug glasses of lager bitter with his friends, and Ivan to continue preparing for the trip, the McKinleys' household was a joyful place to live.

Ivan was growing increasingly anxious about his voyage. Grandpa, who still expressed some apprehension about the coming adventure, should soon be deciding whether the next trip was warranted based on the quality of Ivan's written assignment.

One evening, while everyone else slept, the old man entered Ivan's room, tapped him on the shoulder, and whispered, "Ivan, wake up! I just finished reading your report, and must say I'm quite pleased, which means you should start preparing for the coming voyage very soon."

Ivan stirred sleepily, unable to believe his ears.

"Are you fully awake now?"

"Yes, sir, I am!"

"Then listen to my plan," the old man continued. "Sikin will emerge like a handsome merchant in his mid to late thirties, somewhere in the vicinity of the Palazzo da Ponte in Venice. You'll be fluent in four languages, articulate, sophisticated and very familiar with their customs and traditions. You'll be carrying precious stones and gold inside your leather satchel to be used entirely at your discretion.

Always use your head, my boy. Most definitely resist temptation, which this time may be difficult to elude.

I have chosen Curzio's neighborhood as your initial point of arrival, since his home was the most likely place for him and Tiblina to visit upon returning to Venice. That is, of course, if he made it back alive.

Casa da Ponte was situated along the western side of the Grand Canal, north of a wooden bridge that is known today as

174

the Rialto. Next to the Rialto was the Fondaco dei Tedeschi, a storage facility and inn owned by German merchants, which was also used to accommodate transients.

Approximately three hundred yards East, you should find a well-appointed pink palazzo with a wrought iron gate bearing the name *Ca'da-Ponte* on a polished bronze plaque."

"Grandpa," Ivan interrupted, "how do you know Curzio's address? Is there something else you didn't tell me?"

"I'm sorry for not saying this before, but preceeding your first departure I had dreams showing vague impressions of the location selected for your arrival. For unknown reasons, the same experience occurred to me a couple of nights ago. I didn't find this to be coincidental, so I'm using it as a guide. The same conditions as before shall apply, so the rest is entirely up to you, including time of departure and return."

Overtaken by surprise and widely awake by then, Ivan nodded in approval.

After kissing his grandson good night, Grandpa silently left the room.

Bursting with excitement, Ivan couldn't wait till the next morning to tell the old man he was ready.

"Could I leave tonight or tomorrow?"

"You can leave whenever you want," Grandpa said. "But if I were you, I'd take enough time to learn about life in Venice during the late thirteenth century."

As Grandpa spoke, Ivan recalled that stormy afternoon in the Taklamakan when the nomad spared Sikin's life.

"I think you are right," he said reassuringly. "I know this time will be different."

One evening a few months later, wearing his robe and carrying a small pillow to support his lower back, Grandfather entered Ivan's room, asking facetiously if he was awake.

"Are you kidding? How could I fall asleep when I'm waiting for you to come in anytime?"

"Now son, let's not get too excited. I know you must be anxious to be on your way, but before I forget, remember to say hello to Tiblina for me. Tell her how much I admire her courage and determination. Also, Ivan, please remember to be very careful when offering information about the future. Never open your mouth without thinking first. Your date of arrival will be approximately eighteen to twenty years following your departure from the oasis of Dunhuang.

Do you have any questions?" Grandpa asked.

"Yes, I do. What would happen to Ivan if Sikin gets killed?"

"After departing Sikin's body, Ivan's soul will return to you immediately; which, after all is where it belongs."

"Grandpa, I don't know how to act like a thirty year old man." Ivan said worriedly.

"I'd seen men in their seventies behave like twelve year olds. You'll be fine."

"Then I guess I'm ready!"

Part Two

CHAPTER *Six*

THE TELEPORTATION OF IVAN TO VENICE

"There was life and motion everywhere, and yet everywhere there was a hush, a stealthy sort of stillness, that was suggestive of secret enterprises of bravoes and of lovers; and, clad half in moonbeams and half in mysterius shadows, the grim old mansions of the Republic seemed to have an expression about them of having an eye out for just such enterprises as these at that same moment. Music came floating over the waters – Venice was complete..."

Mark Twain, 1869

F ollowing the set ritual as before, Ivan fell into a deep slumber as his grandpa placed a pillow against the lower back of the rocking chair, sat comfortably, and said his prayers.

Late into the night, and shrouded by the heavy fog so commonplace in Venice during January, Sikin stood motionless in the middle of a narrow street that passed in front of the German warehouse, just as Grandpa had described.

Only the trickling sounds of water washing against building foundations alongside the Grand Canal gave him a notion of where he was in relation to the water. While waiting for a feeling of direction he heard the sudden sound of wheels rolling against the pavement.

Momentarily, four men holding lanterns and driving their wheelbarrows emerged from the fog, barreling straight toward him! They came to a sudden halt inches from his toes.

Thank God it was not a horse driven carriage or load cart! Sikin thought.

One of the men asked him in Italian if he needed directions.

"I am a traveling merchant visiting Venice for the first time," he replied. "Can you tell me where the Fondaco dei Tedeschi is located?"

The shortest fellow in the group, who appeared to be the foreman, introduced himself as Paolo.

"Follow us!" He replied. "That's exactly where we work, and since there is so much quartz to be loaded, our master has us labor almost round the clock."

"Actually, I only asked for the warehouse as a point of reference. My final destination is the Ca'da Ponte. Do you also know where that is?"

"Just a short walk away, but you'll never find it in this dense fog," said Paolo. "Perhaps it would be wiser to stay and rest at the Fondaco until it burns out."

"You may be right, it would also be impolite to knock at someone's door this late at night, or should I say, this early in the morning."

Seemingly guided by a sixth sense, as they could barely see an arms-length ahead, they walked confidently towards the Fondaco.

As they entered the warehouse, the burliest of the men strode towards a wood stove to brew up some tea. "Would you like some?" He asked the newcomer, and introduced himself as Renato.

"Thank you, Renato. I'm feeling damp to my bones."

"Water is everywhere around La Serenissima," the stout workman said. "It even permeates the air you breathe."

"This is the best mint tea coming from the Saracen countries.

Try it and let me know what you think. My name is Caramello."
Said the wiry bald fellow.

They all sat facing each other across a long rectangular table
talking and sipping the aromatic drink.

"What business brings you to La Serenissima?" Paolo
inquired.

"It must be the carnival," interrupted Caramello, the tallest of
the group.

"What carnival are you talking about?"

"The one that visitors from all over come to participate in,"
Caramello answered. "Have you never heard of it? The tradition
began almost a thousand years ago, when our republic celebrated
its victory against Ulrico, Patriarch of Aquilea. It started with
dances and reunions, and later magicians, charlatans, and
acrobats joined in. It's grown bigger and better as time has gone
by."

"You are a very fortunate tourist," Renato said.

"Beginning the first day after Yuletide and ending around
Lent, you will have a chance to falsify your identity and do the
things you'd never consider doing unless hiding behind a mask."
Paolo chimed in eagerly. "Women go around wearing eccentric
costumes looking for romance, and to make things even better,
everybody is an equal. Ordinary people might very well be
wearing costumes made of expensive fabrics, so there is no
visible difference between a nobleman and us, or between a
promiscuous woman and a lady of rank. The government
prohibits wearing expensive jewelry in order to keep anonymity
as part of the fun."

"Ah, come on!" Said Renato, rubbing his muscular arms.
"The government promotes it so we can express our frustrations
in an innocuous manner. That way they keep us busy arguing
about what to wear, rather than paying attention to their
scandals." He shook a finger at Sikin. "Don't be shocked if you
see lots of people wearing *bautas* year round," he continued. "In
fact, during government holidays and special occasions, such as
the inauguration of a Doge, it is compulsory to wear them."

"What is a bauta mask?" Sikin asked.

"It consists of a black veil worn under a three-cornered hat to conceal the hair, ears, and neck. Occasionally a white mask is also worn to hide the upper part of the face, allowing the person to eat, drink, and talk without being recognized. The costume also includes a long cape. Both men and women, rich and poor, wear this garment. I'd say it is the most popular of all."

"You'll want one for sure," laughed Caramello. "By being able to engage in illicit activities, most foreigners feel as if they've died and gone to heaven. Some run through the Piazza San Marco singing lewd songs and wearing nothing but paper costumes. Others fill eggs with rose water and throw them in the path of beautiful women, or use real rotten eggs against unpopular citizens. Also, respected members of the aristocracy visit gambling establishments and brothels wearing bauta masks to avoid recognition."

"It sounds as if everyone has a license to violate moral codes!" Sikin said.

"Young man, you must remember this is the Serene Republic of Venice," said the short man soberly, "where everything is permissible as long as there is money to be made! The carnival is a profit maker for the local merchants. Everyone eats and drinks excessively. Nothing is done in moderation! Inns fill up to capacity with foreigners, and to keep their outlets well stocked, most shopkeepers work around the clock. Eateries are packed with patrons all day and through the night. On our positive side, we enjoy magicians, acrobats, fist fighters, dancers, marionettes, painters, musicians, and so on. To me, that's the best part of the carnival."

"As far as I'm concerned, the only bad part is the filth," said the quietest workman, whose name was Carlo.

"Imagine all these people overeating and drinking, then taking care of their needs. How do you think they dispose of it? The canal and the lagoon are their only choices. Besides their waste and vomit, they throw in food and garbage, which rots and bring rats. And to make matters worse, thousands of pigeons fly over the piazza eating leftovers and leaving droppings everywhere, especially atop the dome and around the cathedral.

The city looks and smells awful afterwards! We might as well close our eyes and wait till Carnival is over."

The bald worker, Caramello, asked Sikin where he came from.

"If I tell you I came from nowhere what would you think of me?"

"I would say you are taking our carnival too seriously already."

"Let's say that instead of wearing a mask to disguise my identity, I am here to disguise my nationality and let you beat your brains out to find the answer,"

All laughed at Sikin's remark. After several fruitless guesses, the men gave up trying to guess where he was from.

They talked, cracked jokes, and drank tea until the early hours of the morning.

Sikin felt at ease. The men treated the young merchant as if they had known him forever. But as the fog dissipated, he began to feel anxious about his coming visit.

"I think my time is up," he said. "I should gather my belongings and leave for the da Ponte residence."

"Keep us in mind in case excessive luxury, comfort, and pampering makes you feel out of place," said Paolo. "Remember that you are always welcome to use our modest accommodations."

"Thank you, gentlemen. Chances are I will be back for more of the same."

The workers got up and followed a path toward the back of the building, where they were supposed to load quartz all day long till after sunset. Now in full daylight, the fog having dissipated, Sikin began to walk towards the Ca'da Ponte as Venice awakened to another day. The sounds of horse-driven carriages and the shouts of children playing, the sights of elegantly dressed merchants greeting each other as they went about their daily routines and the chattering of women on their way to market, all seemed to gather energy from the rising sun and the early morning dew.

Sikin was glad he'd done some research this time.

The thirteenth century was the pinnacle of medieval civilization in Venice, he recalled, crowned by its gothic architecture and sculpture. Social groups such as guilds, associations, government councils, and monastic chapters proliferated, accomplishing remarkable autonomy. The strengthening of Italian city-states, the rise of secular education, the breakup of feudal structures, and the emergence of national monarchies all over Europe, climaxed in the birth of a self-conscious new age.

An energetic spirit that looked back to classical standards for its inspiration was paving the way to an era later known as the Renaissance. Such was the prevailing mood in one of the wealthiest and most prosperous countries in the known world, the Serene Republic of Venice.

Sikin finally found himself standing at the front gate to the da Ponte's palazzo. It was a pink three-story building, approximately seventy feet wide by ninety feet deep, which seemed to float on the water during high tide. It had glass windows on every floor, and a flower garden between the main entrance and the wrought iron front gate. Arrayed along the rear of the cheerful structure, multi-colored pilings used to tie boats and gondolas had been driven into the bottom of the canal.

Sikin's heart pounded as he knocked at the polished front door.

A lady in her late fifties wearing a scarf to cover her hair, and a black dress partially concealed by a large white apron answered the call.

"Buon giorno, Signora! My name is Sikin, and I am looking for a lady named Tiblina. Do you by any chance know where I can find her?"

"Certainly. Tiblina da Ponte lives here, but she is in Rome at the moment. Please come in and have a seat while I call my lady."

Sikin's heart thrilled at the thought he had found her so easily and plummeted simultaneously on learning she was so far away. He stepped into a large drawing room, brightly lit by the morning rays passing through the glass windows. The parquet floor was a work of art in itself formed with different types of woods, cut and inlaid in decorative designs and polished to a mirror-like finish.

Rich tapestries hung from the walls not only for decoration but to add extra layers of warmth during the humid winters. A massive door at the rear of the salon with large glass windows on each side, led to a balcony facing the water, allowing a spectacular view of the Grand Canal. In those days, Sikin knew, glass windows were available only to churches and to the wealthy.

A candle chandelier, made of blown Murano glass fused with eighteen-karat gold and tinted in pink, hung from the center of the ceiling over a round table surrounded by wooden chairs that were apparently carved in Asia and upholstered in Venice. The massive table rested on a large Persian rug of beautiful and intricate design. Against the left wall, a large vase filled with freshly cut indoor-grown flowers stood atop a wooden chest with drawers underneath. Suspended on the opposite wall, a huge Byzantine painting of a Venetian festival provided an allegoric ambiance to an already lively room. A framed mirror added a welcome glitter to the salon.

While Sikin awaited patiently the lady of the house, another servant, this one dressed in white with a black apron, approached and asked what she could do to make him feel more at home. She had brought tea and bread that Sikin instantly accepted.

He was growing more nervous each passing moment. The thought of soon seeing Tiblina had his hands shaky, and his head overcrowded with memories. The sound of steps coming down the stairs from the second floor made him swallow dry.

An attractive young woman in her mid or late thirties; richly coifed with a Venetian bonnet and wearing a lavishly decorated gown, extended her hand to the guest, which he graciously kissed.

"I am Mariu, Curzio's youngest daughter." She said vivaciously.

"My name is Sikin."

"Yes I know. The maid told me."

"I must confess this is a most pleasant surprise. It took me a long time to believe my father's story about you."

Gregarious, charming, and sincere, Mariu was clearly a person who would make anyone in her presence feel comfortable in an instant. She regarded Sikin directly and unhesitantly.

"I never thought you'd make it back," she continued. "The whole tale is so bizarre! Yet Tiblina has always had faith that some day you would appear unexpectedly and out of nowhere, and here you are! Let me take a look at you! She said you had the expression of an Adonis."

Mariu squinted appraisingly at Sikin, who blushed.

"Mmmm, I can see you have aged a little, though I must say you look quite different than I imagined."

"And why is that?" Sikin asked shyly.

"I thought you'd look more Asian; smaller in stature, and of a much darker skin and round face. But you are much taller, your mannerisms are polished, refined, yet masculine, and the subtle graying on your sideburns reveals an unwavering and fascinating character. And if I may say so without offending Tiblina; you are indeed a very charming and attractive man, Sikin. My dear sister is very lucky!"

"Thank you, Mariu," he responded bashfully, entirely taken by surprise.

"You will stay with us, of course," she chattered on. "Tiblina, my maids, and I are the only ones living in this huge palazzo. We'd love to have you!"

Silence reigned for a moment while Sikin tried to gather his thoughts.

"All right, Mariu, I accept, and thank you."

"Bene." She nodded happily. "Now fascinate me with the reason for your return."

"Why don't you first tell me about Curzio and Tiblina? Is she happy?" Sikin asked to deflect her question.

Mariu spoke evasively. "She has the kind of attitude that makes everyone around feel cheerful no matter what."

"What do you mean by 'no matter what?'"

The lovely Venetian shrugged. "Some tragic events have

taken place during the last several years. It is a long story; but there will be no better time to discuss it than now, while she is away." She sighed and began.

"During a rainy afternoon in October, some two years after they'd left Dunhuang with the Polos, two persons, soaking wet, wearing ragged garments and with faces so soiled they were virtually unrecognizable, showed up unexpectedly at our front door. The oldest was my father; the other one Tiblina.

How he made it back home through such deplorable conditions was unquestionably due to her dedication and loving care. It certainly was a miraculous event. I recognized him only by his voice and mannerisms. He looked totally emaciated.

Suddenly and unexpectedly, father fell on his knees begging and crying for forgiveness. The girl simply stared at the floor in embarrassment, not knowing what to say or do. It was a painful moment for me and especially for my mother, who at the time was bedridden with paralysis. My sister, her husband, and three children, who at the time were living in Dalmatia, never bothered to visit Papa or even offer us a hand. She claimed he deserved the punishment and should pay for his mistakes. Therefore, as of that moment, Tiblina and I took charge of the situation entirely on our own. It broke my heart to see such a strong man, who years before had carried such an air of invincibility, now begging for mercy. I couldn't help but hug the old relic and kiss his dirty cheeks, reassuring him of my love and saying that nothing in life could have taken away my affection and therefore never would.

Shivering from the cold, he thanked me. Then I called a couple of maids to help me take care of both.

At the moment I didn't have the faintest idea who the girl was. It didn't seem important at the time.

That same evening, I told my mother what had happened. She broke down and began to shiver, which I thought would make her illness worse, since she also had a weak heart. Mamma was the kind of person who believed that the Devil was a saint who never had an opportunity to prove it, and that evil was a direct result of our negative perceptions. She was naïve when they married, naïve when she opened the gate, and naïve throughout her entire life. A forgiving woman, she did not hesitate to welcome father into her room. Bedridden as she was, Mama held Papa's hands and asked him for a kiss, creating a bath of tears as a result.

My older sister's attitude was a completely different story. Pretentious, selfish, and condescending, she couldn't stand Papa for being, in her words 'a man who always tried to find himself in the wrong mirror.' She considered him undisciplined, lacking a sense of responsibility either as a husband or as a father, and a selfish, and incorrigible adventurer who placed his personal wishes ahead of everyone else's needs and feelings."

Mariu gazed at the ornate ceiling for a moment, then smiled sadly at Sikin. "I admit she wasn't all that wrong, but I also knew she was looking for a reason to stay angry with her offending father, and avoid eventually forgiving him. Even at his funeral, she did not attend."

At Sikin's stricken look, she added, "I'm sorry. Of course I assumed you must have realized my father had passed on." She paused then resumed her story.

"Unconcerned about her presence in the beginning, we took Tiblina for some kind of helper hired to assist Papa during the journey. We welcomed her as a temporary guest until the next morning, when we found out who she was and what had happened.

Father introduced her as his adopted daughter, which made me angry at first, especially after he mentioned that he had already assigned part of his estate to her. But after listening to their experiences, I realized that Tiblina was to him like an angel from heaven. Otherwise Papa would have died long before arriving in Venice. Tiblina and I became loyal and truthful friends, and in virtually no time we were much closer than my sister and I ever had been. Our unique relationship gave Mamma and Papa great satisfaction. They took delight in seeing our support for one another especially after the death of my husband.

Tiblina refused to let our maids take care of my father.

I remember her listening to his neck, lungs, and chest, and

according to the sounds she heard, Tiblina either gave him wine to drink, a hot bath, or a potion made with garlic. When his feet became swollen, she tightened them with wide bands of material, which, according to her, 'pushed fluids up his body.' She forbade doctors from seeing him, since all they prescribed was drinking enormous amounts of hot water to dissolve the bad humors, plus putting leeches all over his back and neck to get rid of bad blood.

She became so notoriously proficient at her vocation that soon neighbors came asking for her help and advice.

Tiblina claimed she had learned most of her remedies and techniques from you, as well as from personal experience in her former surroundings. She also helped to take care of my mother, though not as zealously as she did with Papa. In fact, Mama died three months before he did.

When she wasn't attending father, Tiblina visited the church sacristy to help with common chores, under one condition, that she was allowed to read their books. She also visited the Doge's palace to learn about the Republic's political process. I had never seen anyone with more hunger for knowledge.

I remember Tiblina saying she always felt an urgent need to help people in distress, especially orphans and abandoned women, and that as soon as the opportunity presented itself, she would attend the Salerno School of Medicine to learn the medical arts. She didn't care much for riches. To her, money was more of a servant than a master. When she left for Salerno, she took only the necessary funds to support herself while at school, later using a portion of what she left behind to open an orphanage.

Preceding her departure, being deeply involved in political affairs, we attended social engagements almost daily, which we still do to this date. In fact we have been invited to a masked ball a week from tomorrow, honoring a council member who has recently won election.

As you can imagine; wherever she appears her ravishing beauty and charming personality cause men to immediately shift their conversation to talk about her. Rich and poor, noble and plebeian, political figures, wealthy merchants, poets, artists, dozens of men have had tried in vain to lure her into their web."

Sikin couldn't help feeling his heart flutter with hope.

"So Tiblina hadn't married?"

Mariu continued blithely. "Can you imagine how attractive and tempting this woman became to the wealthy and powerful? Just imagine all those men, having all the resources to possess anything in the world, competing against each other like children. Tiblina referred to them as 'effeminate and spoiled.' Yet, she never showed the kind of vanity most women experience after constant flattery and adulation."

"You said she left for Salerno after Curzio's death. Will you please tell me more?"

"She went to the university bursting with ideals. There, she met the son of a prominent Genoan politician, a young man, named Tirso who was studying to become a sculptor. Before long, they got secretly married while attending school. A year and a half later, she gave birth to a boy she named after you."

Sikin's heart broke and soared. "So she did marry! And she had a son!"

Mariu smiled sympathetically at Sikin's expression of joy and regret.

"Venice and Genoa were at war," she went on, "so it was almost impossible for either one of us to cross borders. We didn't see each other for a while. The three moved to Genoa with Tirso's parents.

One day, Tiblina sent a message through one of our friends, a Dominican priest who traveled the territory as an inquisitor in search of heretics. He said Tiblina had fallen into disgrace and that her life was facing imminent danger.

Her husband Tirso, an idealist, had joined a group of disgruntled citizens opposing certain codes of law pertaining to the election of captains, the equivalent of a Doge in Genoa. According to them, the law gave absolute power to members of the privileged oligarchy, thus keeping the majority of the population away from government participation. Apparently, he became involved in acts of violence against powerful figures. He was accused of treachery and of endangering the sovereignty of the state. He was tried, found guilty, and executed."

Mariu's eyes filled with tears. "Not satisfied with their revenge, they accused Tiblina of witchcraft since according to rumors she had brought back to life persons who were supposed to die, and cured ailments that were incurable.

She was also charged as an accomplice to Tirso and his band of rioters, and for using incantations to turn a young decent man from a prominent Genoese family into a mutinous character who wanted to engrave his name in history at any cost. According to hearsay, Tirso's own father, campaigned to persuade the council to believe that Tiblina's wicked influence on Tirso caused the young man's downfall, placing in jeopardy not only the sovereignty of the country, but the immaculate reputation of his illustrious family as well.

Only then did we learn that, due to her foreign appearance, she was never liked nor welcomed by Tirso's father, hence the reason for their secret marriage in Salerno. In Genoa she suffered unjust embarrassments and vexations. Tirso's father claimed little Sikin wasn't his son's child, which was a perverted lie designed to punish Tirso for his disobedience in marrying Tiblina. The young sculptor hated his father for being a brute to his mother, who played the silent role of a statue, submissively tolerating her husband's transgressions as she felt was her duty to the sacred vows of marriage. Tirso also disdained his father's unscrupulous ways of surviving political intrigue, and hated his tyrannical and condescending treatment of him, as well as others of lesser status. In spite of his indignation, he obeyed his father's wishes and commands, except when joining the rebellion that cost him his life.

Young Sikin was never accepted or treated with love either. On the contrary, they kept him and his mother at home purportedly to avoid a 'scandal,' although sooner or later an explosion was bound to happen. Knowing our friend, she wasn't going to put up with that situation indefinitely. I am convinced that only her child's safety kept her from setting the house on fire or worse.

The father's contempt for mother and son became more vicious and bizarre after Tirso's execution, to the point where she seriously considered running away with the boy after killing her father-in-law. However, before she had the opportunity to end his life, Tiblina was apprehended, tried, and found guilty of treason, heresy, and witchcraft, which all combined carried a sentence of death at the stake."

At this Sikin gasped. Mariu held up a hand. "Significantly enough, the church was never allowed an opportunity to try her for heresy and witchcraft. Thank God those allegations were proven contrived by a group of power brokers and adulators on behalf of Tirso's father and had absolutely nothing to do with religion. As a result, inquisitors were expelled from her trial, which was something unheard of in judgments of that nature. Nevertheless, she was convicted of treason.

While she was in prison awaiting execution, little Sikin was abducted from his grandparent's home. No one has ever found a trace of him. Most people believe that he was killed.

Otherwise, he would be around thirteen by now. Only our family's influence with the Roman and Venetian clergy helped us save Tiblina's life.

After years of exhaustive searches, no documents were found anywhere in the church concerning the child's abduction, proving once again that their accusations were never based on evidence found by inquisitors, but by a government tribunal, with the intention of setting an example to an already disgruntled populace, or to placate the anger and grief of a greedy powerful family.

One cold night, in physical and emotional pain, famished and distraught, Tiblina returned to our home. It took our servants and me almost four weeks to bring her back to life. Dominican nuns came in every morning to pray for her and the little boy. Members of our community showed up from every corner of the city to offer their support. Some brought images of their patron saints. Many of her so-called 'effeminate admirers' came in and out of the house almost constantly.

For the first time, I felt Tiblina was appreciated for her

wisdom, generosity, and courage, and not for her looks or wealth. Unfortunately, no matter how hard we all tried, she never returned to the person she had been. She had enough courage and an earnest desire to bounce back, but the wound was too deep to heal.

A few months later she finally began to work on the project of the orphanage. All of our friends, neighbors, and acquaintances offered their help for no ulterior motive besides personal satisfaction in becoming part of such a noble endeavor. Priests from local churches prayed publicly for her success, and many wealthy merchants donated money and services.

I had never seen anything like it. It seemed as if she had to go through hell before fulfilling what she considered her life's mission. The cooperation and goodwill of our notoriously narcissistic society was unbelievable.

She hired persons with her same inclination and dedication; some worked for free, others for pay. Tiblina was finally on her way to fulfill her dream: building and managing a home for abandoned women and children. All of us helped in the undertaking while she traveled all over the country searching for clues. She is convinced little Sikin is alive, though others are at best skeptical.

Her lovely hair is already showing signs of graying, perhaps as a result of so much grief and suffering." Mariu felt silent.

"Why is the church involved in solving the puzzle?" Asked Sikin. "Is that why she went to Rome?"

"If for any reason the boy was abandoned after the abduction, we assumed they would be the only ones who could have saved the child from starving in a ditch, being sold into slavery, or 'adopted' for further exploitation by persons without scruples. A widely accepted notion suggests that documents were purposely destroyed to cover up an illegal adoption. Others don't believe the church was involved, since nothing relevant has shown up in their records.

Another theory proposes that the boy was killed by hired hands, though no evidence or trail has ever been found. If the boy happens to be in an orphanage, he will be dismissed at age fifteen. This scenario is driving Tiblina insane, since it would be almost impossible for her to find him afterwards. The purpose of her trip is to continue searching through endless piles of documents, begging every priest and cardinal for their help in finding the boy.

Through the years no sensible lead was ever dismissed or questioned. Friends who previously offered support are the same ones assisting in the search today. We all have used our personal influences, contacts, money, and everything imaginable to find at least one relevant piece of evidence. Most have reached the point where they think our effort is fruitless. Yet, they refuse to let her down, so we all continue our blind crusade, hoping that some day our faith and dedication will pay off."

"What can I do to help? Can you think of anything?"

"Not at the moment," she said. "Although coming from the future, you might be able to toss in some new ideas."

"When is she supposed to return?"

"It also depends on weather and road conditions. I would say perhaps in a week or so. Oh, Sikin!" Mariu's eyes filled with tears again. "I can't wait to see her face when she sees you!"

Embarrassed, Sikin lowered his eyes then tactfully changed the subject. "Mariu, may I ask a question about your father? Did his friend the Pope ever send the one hundred learned men to the court of Kublai Khan?"

"No, he did not," she said sadly. "Pope Clement died before their arrival in Venice. The newly elected pontiff only sent a couple of Dominican monks who quit before venturing too far into the region. But I was told both of the brothers Polo along with Niccolo's son Marco left for Jerusalem to gather a bottle of oil from the Holy Sepulchre to take to the Khan."

"Now tell me about your life, Mariu," said Sikin. "Your father talked constantly about how proud he was of his younger daughter."

Mariu smiled, flushing a pretty pink. "I loved him dearly in spite of his transgressions. But if you want to know more about my life Sikin, there's really not much to be said. I'm at peace with myself. I enjoy numerous friendships. Not having to care for my parents, allows me the freedom to come and go as I please. Yet, I am deeply concerned about loneliness. There is no one else left but a few cousins and aunts, and of course, Tiblina. I always wanted to have children and raise a family, but my husband died of an accident shortly after our marriage."

"I am very sorry Mariu, It must have hurt you a lot."

*　*　*

Mariu and Sikin spent most of the day talking and getting to know each other. Later that afternoon they went for a stroll around the Piazza San Marco, where he had the opportunity to meet some of her acquaintances. In spite of her elevated social status, Mariu was a simple person, and at every encounter Sikin was introduced as her distant relative from the Germanic countries. Kind, accessible, and with a wonderful sense of humor, Mariu conveyed from every angle an air of feminine softness. Men felt at ease in her company, and most female friends considered her a role model. She gave the impression of being exactly who she portrayed. Her social circle included men and women from all walks of life, and she ignored the petulant snobbery of some aristocrats whom labeled her gentle disposition abhorrent.

The next two days served their growing friendship and in no conversation were the subject of Tiblina and her tragedy left out.

One evening, after experiencing a terrible nightmare, Sikin awoke agitated, with his heart beating out of control.

Later on at breakfast, he shared his unusual experience with Mariu.

"Last night," he said somberly, "I had an unusually horrifying dream, so vivid, that I woke up in the middle of the night drenched in sweat. Since then, I have tried to erase the incident from my mind, but the nightmare keeps coming back."

"Do you mind telling me? I might be able to help,"

"In the dream I was a very young child sitting by the shore of a lake located in a park across our street. Ducks, geese, and swans were swimming in the water. After noticing a swan rapidly approaching, I stood up, and frightened, I ran to the bench where my mother sat waiting for me. But to my dismay she wasn't there anymore, even though she had promised to stay and watch me until I got bored. Terribly scared, as the swan kept getting closer and closer, I screamed for help, but no one answered!

Lost and horrified, I ran towards the bushes as fast as I could. All of a sudden I felt a cold hand grabbing my throat and another covering my mouth. Horrified, I recognized the man with icy hands to be my grandfather, warning me to shut up, to do exactly as he said, or he'd chop my head off.

Removing his hand from my mouth, he pulled a knife from his waistband and dangled it in front of my eyes. Although his image was blurred, I could see his right ear was missing.

Mariu," Sikin said after pausing for a moment. "Grandpa has both ears, and he is one of the kindest persons I know. Why would he appear so ruthless in this nightmare?"

"Because it was only a dream! If I were you, I'd try to forget about it."

"You might be right, but I believe we should also try to see the difference between simple dreams and supernatural revelations. Although I cannot swear this one came from the Otherworld, its vividness and realism were beyond belief, and the fact there was a swan, makes me wonder about Grandpa's experiences at Stonehenge. I have had nightmares like everyone else, but believe me, this was entirely different."

"What happened afterwards?"

"Bewildered, I sat on the window ledge facing the lagoon racking my brains for clues. Then, a sense of urgency and anxiety began to set in."

"Another revelation, perhaps?" She asked skeptically.

"It could very well be. I just need time to figure it out."

Gaily trying to relax him, Mariu asked if he wanted to view his father's collection of exotic precious gems. He followed her to her mother's bedroom, where she opened a small wooden coffer containing a magnificent array of jewels and precious stones.

"Father collected these from his travels to the Orient," she said.

Even though Sikin was not a gem connoisseur, he faked paying attention by asking all sorts of questions.

Quite perceptive, Mariu asked if there was something wrong.

"Absolutely not!" He fibbed. "But perhaps if you will excuse me for a moment, I'd like to go to my room for pen, ink, and paper."

When he returned, she smiled as if she knew his sudden change of heart had something to do with the nightmare.

"You must be feeling better, aren't you?"

"Yes, I am, but I need your help!"

"You can count on me, Sikin. Just tell me what you need."

"Would you give me the name of Tirso's father and his address in Genoa?"

"I can give you his name, but I don't know where he lives."

"I just came up with a plan so wild you might think I've lost my mind. First of all, you must promise to keep my visit to Venice secret. This will be absolutely necessary!

"What are you talking about?"

"I am seriously considering a scheme to uncover the truth, but it will be essential to keep the idea under cover, not only from Tiblina, but from everyone else as well, at least for now. You see, I thought of an alternative for gathering information as to where the boy might be. Although my methods might not be considered legal or ethical in certain cultures, they are highly effective. Since in this case I'm a firm believer in the end results justifying the means, I'm ready to take chances and do whatever it takes to solve the mystery."

Sikin grinned eagerly. "To begin with, I'll be moving elsewhere in order to avoid an encounter with Tiblina. Please forgive me for acting so abruptly, but I'm sure you'll understand my motives. Late tonight I'll be meeting with some friends who might offer me a hand and if so, I may have to leave Venice temporarily. But no matter what, I promise to keep you informed."

"All right, Sikin, since you sound so encouraging, I'll try to get you as many facts as I can."

Sikin couldn't wait to lay down his strategy, and Mariu, inspired by his excitement felt an infusion of hope into what appeared more and more like a dying cause.

During a gorgeous afternoon, the pair went for a gondola ride to the small village of Burano, where they could keep a much lower profile than in the city.

That same evening before retiring, Mariu handed Sikin a piece of paper containing valuable information about Tirso's parents, their address, and a series of useful hints. Afraid of experiencing another nightmare, Sikin couldn't sleep that night.

Shortly before sunrise he began to walk towards the German warehouse. There was no fog that morning, so he found it easily.

Partially dilapidated because of humidity and neglect, the old brick building, closed at the moment, seemed to have been carving here and there its own deterioration.

Striding nervously back and forth, Sikin awaited anxiously for signs of life.

Soon he heard the sound of approaching wheelbarrows. As he'd hoped, it was the same group of workers he'd met a couple of days before.

Paolo, the short foreman exclaimed, "Welcome back Sikin! You must have gotten tired of living in luxury!"

"Would you join us again for some tea? Come on! Let's go inside."

"So you finally decided to stay with us?" said Caramello, rubbing his baldhead.

"Not really," Sikin said seriously. "I thought since you boys are so familiar with what goes on in town, this could very well be the right place to start looking for a very special kind of person."

"There isn't much poor people like us can do for variety, other than keeping track of the town's scuttlebutt and sharing it with friends," said Paolo with a cheerful smile. "Shredding the rich to pieces is fun! To mutilate certain characters without going to prison is even more fun! Therefore, Sikin, rest assured that you have come to the right place to obtain the hottest information of what goes on in our town, in addition to the best counseling money can buy."

In an instant, they were all sitting at the same table as before.

"I'll try to be precise, however, at least for now, or until we reach an understanding, you men must promise not to dig any further for reasons as to why I'm seeking your help, nor ask certain questions, even if you feel compelled to do so. If all of you agree with my initial conditions, I am willing to pay generously to whoever tells me where to find the man I'm looking for."

"Uh-oh. Sikin is involved in illegal activities and wants to liquidate a 'snoop' before the word gets to the authorities." Caramello said jokingly.

"Shut up!" Paolo said authoritatively. "The rich merchant is serious and has enough money to prove it. So let's listen to his proposal before you start cracking jokes."

"All right, my friend. We are all ears!" Said the quiet one, Carlo. "How much are you willing to pay for what?"

"Five ounces of gold to find the man. Five more ounces if he agrees with my terms," said Sikin flatly.

"Don't make us wait any longer, stranger! Throw us the bait!" Bossy Paolo insisted.

"I want to hire a person whose loyalty crosses the limits of self-preservation," Sikin began. "Someone ambitious for money, but not greedy enough to covet my treasure.

So strong he could fight and knock out three men, all at the same time. And exceptionally smart; wise enough to make no mistakes. Capable of running like a gazelle, crawling like a snake, and killing anything or anybody whenever he is told, without looking back, or asking why.

This man must be an angel of heaven, yet, proficient in the use of swords, sabers, and knives...compassionate and obedient, but ruthless when circumstances call for it...tenacious to enter an enemy camp at the risk of his own life, but faithful enough to always remember he cannot serve two masters at the same time.

Finally, he must be as well-acquainted with cities like Venice, Rome, and Genoa as if he was born and raised in them...

welcomed and trusted by every scoundrel, thug, and hoodlum in the underworld, yet he shall look pious enough to become an inspiration to the clergy...and so sophisticated in the criminal arts, he could carry out the most gruesome crime and make it look legal and evenhanded."

Well, gentlemen, at the moment I cannot think of any more qualifications. I hope this gives you an idea. Go find me the right person, and we'll do business." He scattered a handful of tinkling gold coins across the table.

After regarding each other gravely, they burst into laughter.

"It's carnival time fellows, and our new master wants us to become magicians!" Said Renato between guffaws. "You want us to do like Prometheus, don't you, Sikin? You'd like us to find a handful of clay and create the slave of your dreams, then tie strings to his head, arms, and legs so you can handle him like a marionette!"

Again, they roared, holding their sides.

"You know, Sikin? You are quite an amusing person," said Carlo. "I'd give anything to know what's brewing inside your head, but I guess you don't want us to ask, right?"

"That's correct."

Wringing his hands while staring at the floor, Paolo had acquired a sober and worried expression. Then, looking at his cohorts he asked, "What if I know the right person? Do I have to share my gold with you nitwits?"

"Of course you should," answered Renato. "Have you forgotten our pledge of allegiance? Suppose you need our help sooner or later. What then?"

"That's not fair!" The bald man pounded on the table. "I propose we ask the Master."

"All right," Sikin replied. "I'll tell you what I'll do. If I enlist your services day and night, I'll be willing to pay an ounce to each of you for every ten days of work, regardless of who finds the man, as long as you follow directions and obey my commands."

"How could anybody work day and night without rest?" Asked Carlo.

"You misunderstood me," Sikin replied. "I need you to be at my disposal all the time, not necessarily doing continuous physical work as you do when loading quartz."

"I'm all for it then," Renato answered rubbing his muscles. "Just tell us, who shall we kill?"

"No one at the moment, and hopefully never," Sikin replied. "So are you all in?"

Sikin acknowledged Paolo, as their capable leader and that he would be his contact.

No one voiced an objection, so at Sikin's request, they began to reveal their backgrounds.

Learning the "art of swindling" from a large group of wanderers, Renato, the group's burly storyteller, was a gypsy by birth.

Wiry, bald Caramello hadn't learned his trade from time-honored traditions. As an illegitimate child, he became an orphan beggar at a tender age, surviving all kinds of vicissitudes, including famine and disease, entirely on his own. As an adolescent, he got entangled with local hoodlums, emerging as an expert forger who knew when and how to open locks without using keys. Quite resourceful, Caramello was recognized as an accomplished contortionist who practiced his vocation in street presentations as well as in darker and more profitable ways, such as squeezing his slender body through wall cracks, roof fissures, and so on. In addition to his job at the German warehouse, Caramello prowled the streets and alleys of Venice during the early evening hours, always finding "small keepsakes" here and there.

Carlo, the quiet one, was the only group member asserting to be honest. Claiming to be the fastest runner in the world, he bragged about competing and winning every single race in town, especially the carnival's wheelbarrow speed contest.

Paolo, the short bossy fellow and group leader, was the fastest talker. He could sway an enemy to his camp by mere ear exhaustion. Self-educated and street smart, he had friends and connections everywhere. Always short of cash, Paolo fell into the habit of using favors as a form of currency. Knowing the intimate lifestyles of prominent citizens, he utilized contacts to move his interests forward. Paolo's favorite and most productive pastime was listening to rumors, which he passed along to the right ears at a suitable time, awaiting patiently for repercussions. Then he appeared as an uninterested innocent party willing to offer solutions to conflicts that wouldn't exist if it weren't for his interference in the first place.

Sikin was well aware that his newly hired crew would not hesitate to use their individual vocations against him under the right set of conditions. Likewise, he also knew the benefits of surrounding himself with the best talents for a given job. Plus he was perceptive enough to realize that an opportunity like this would not present itself again.

Before departing, Sikin wanted to make sure they all knew exactly what to expect. "I don't intend to reveal the purpose of my mission at the moment," he said. "However, you should anticipate it being a dangerous one. At first, we will be operating from inside an enemy city. Therefore, most of our actions will be illegal and consequently life-threatening.

Since we have just met, you don't know me well enough to realize I am first and foremost a rational, prudent man. I shall be the only one developing tactics and giving orders. Being conscious of your individual "talents", I'd like to encourage suggestions, but under no circumstance will I accept dissention. I will not tolerate disobedience, and I intend to accomplish my objectives at any cost.

Our assignment promises to be most noble and meaningful. There will be no quests for glory or treasures, since our ultimate objective will be strictly humanitarian. You will feel proud the rest of your lives for participating in such an elevating endeavor, if we succeed. Therefore, gentlemen, this operation might help save your souls from a certain road to hell."

Silence reigned for a moment until Caramello raised his hand. "When will you tell us about the mission? And another question; what makes you think we are going to hell?"

"To answer your first question, as soon as is prudent. My answer to the second one, ask your own conscience.

Your pay will start immediately after you find and hire the right man," said Sikin. "With my approval of course.

Let's meet again tomorrow night. Same time, same place. Shall we?"

All agreeing Sikin went back to Mariu's where preparations to welcome Tiblina were well underway.

After telling her about the meeting, Sikin explained his reasons for moving elsewhere.

"Sikin," she said, holding his hands, "even though you might be entirely guided by instincts, I have complete faith in your judgement."

Promising to keep her informed, he received his satchel from one of the maids, and with a reassuring smile, he kissed Mariu on the cheek and left, spending the remainder of the day searching for lodging.

Ultimately, the grapevine took him to a guesthouse owned by an older couple and located not too far from the German warehouse, where he intended to spend the necessary time to put his plan in action.

The following night, Sikin and his crew met again. After Renato brewed the tea, they gathered at the table.

"Boss, we have great news for you!" Paolo exclaimed.

"There is a fellow in town who might very well be your man. Even though I don't know him personally, I'm quite familiar with his story. If you don't mind, I'll provide you with a brief background, and in the event you decide to meet him in person, we'll ask our informants to find out his whereabouts."

Sikin Nodded happily.

"His name is Naguib," Paolo began. "A moor so tall you couldn't touch his nose standing on stilts. Charcoal black and strong as an ox, the man is obedient and loyal to the core. So powerful and handsome was he as a boy, his father sold him to the Caliph of Egypt, who was looking for an attractive slave to serve his youngest daughter; following castration, of course."

Sikin winced, as did the others.

"After hearing about the dreadful plans, the boy ran away from home to Constantinople, where he joined a group of smugglers and pirates as a deck hand. Naguib became so irreplaceable in the new job he was later promoted to the position of slave driver.

Following another good impression, his masters promoted him again, this time, to perform difficult and dangerous missions.

In light of his new assignment, young Naguib was taught piracy-related skills, such as the effective use of long - and short - range archery, the expert handling of knives, daggers, sabers, and stilettos, as well as sailing the different kinds of vessels common to the Mediterranean. He learned to swim underwater for such a long time without surfacing for air that adversaries gave him up for dead on countless occasions. Legend has it he swam from northern Africa to Constantinople without aid.

According to witnesses, his band was chased and caught once. Some members were condemned to the dungeons, while others died under the ax. Naguib, on the other hand, broke out of his cell, escaping farther West into Dalmatia, where he served another master who was involved in illegal and dangerous businesses such as extortion, theft, and blackmail. His job at that time was to safeguard the boss's family and his property. Living inside their mansion, Naguib slept during the day and stood guard at night.

One evening a group of thugs who were attempting to break into the house breached an entryway located opposite the post where Naguib stood watch. At the sound of approaching footsteps, the giant unsheathed his dagger with one hand, and grabbed his sword with the other, then stepped into the entryway. Suddenly five masked men, armed to the teeth with swords and daggers jumped the Moor.

The clamor awoke the master of the house and his daughters, who came down to behold the most incredible display of strength; Naguib disarming and killing the five men, almost effortlessly, one by one. He gained so much notoriety after the incident that his master loaned him to a Venetian friend, who was also involved in illegal but very lucrative trading between two nations at war, Genoa and Venice. His business was to buy weapons from the first one, then sell them back to the Venetians. Naguib's mission was to protect the lives of emissaries carrying out those dangerous duties within enemy territory.

One day he was caught and tortured by a gang of criminals who wanted him to talk. They threatened to cut off his tongue, but the loyal giant kept silent. He lost his tongue to the Nordic gang leader, who was notorious for taking pleasure in torturing and killing Venetians.

Despite such a deplorable event, he escaped and returned to La Serenissima, where he began to look for occupations similar to those he held before."

"How can a person who is unable to communicate be of any help in dealing with life-threatening situations?" Sikin interrupted Paolo.

"You'll see," the short man replied. "In spite of his diction not being very clear, you'll begin to understand after listening for a while. I should add that Naguib also knows how to write and use numbers very well, which complements his disability.

And boss, I really don't know what you ultimately have in mind, but according to your description, I'm almost certain this is the man you are looking for."

"All right Paolo. Go find him!"

Nodding affirmatively, they stood up and went to the docks for another tedious day of work. Three days later, Carlo knocked at Sikin's door in the middle of the night.

"Boss!" He yelled. "I have a message for you. Paolo has located the man, and he wants to see you now."

On arriving at the warehouse, Sikin noticed that everyone, including the Moor, was chatting, drinking tea, and waiting for him to appear.

He beckoned Paolo away from the bunch to determine how and where the man was found.

"Caramello located him with the help of a lady-friend who knew Naguib's last master," Paolo replied. "Disabled from the neck down, this now deceased master was totally dependent on him to satisfy most needs. Naguib was his personal aide, and he carried the crippled man in his arms anywhere he wanted.

Despite his imposing figure, the giant was most gentle and compassionate toward his last master, always pleasing his capricious demands. Though widely known as a very difficult person the master felt so appreciative toward his dedicated servant that on his deathbed the sick man asked a notary to grant full freedom to Naguib upon his demise, as well as a small legacy. Such a kind gesture changed the Moor's status from that of indentured servant to a free man.

Shortly after his release, Naguib began to work as an apprentice carpenter for the Royal shipyards, which was where Caramello found him boiling and bending large planks of hardwood to be used in the construction of galleys. When asked if he would consider a dangerous but better-paying occupation, Naguib's answer was unequivocal, 'Boredom is killing my desire to live.' Caramello told the Moor he didn't know exactly what kind of work you had in mind for him, but of one thing he was certain, 'Our boss scatters gold like bird seeds,' he said, using exactly those words."

"You boys have definitely earned a day's work." Sikin said to Paolo. "Here are the promised ounces. Please share them with the others, and tell Naguib I'd like to have a private talk with him. And Paolo, if he agrees with my terms, you may consider yourselves hired. Then, and only then, will I disclose the purpose of my mission."

Paolo nodded, grinning. "Boss, before I forget, we owe Caramello's lady-friend a reward for the information. He'll need an extra ounce in expenses."

Sikin rolled his eyes, but gave Caramello the coin as Paolo signaled his subordinates to follow him to the docks.

Sikin introduced himself to Naguib, who stood respectfully. He had to crane his neck to address the giant, and gestured for him to sit.

"You must be wondering why I wanted to meet with you. The truth is that I am committed to fulfill a solemn promise. No one else knows about my plan, but you'll need to be aware of my expectations so you can decide whether to accept the challenge. A child was abducted in Genoa approximately ten years ago from the mansion of a highly respected government figure and influential member of the aristocracy. His mother, who I've known for years, swears he is alive. I have my reasons to agree. Yet, based on available evidence, only a handful of people familiar with the case believe he is. No one, including those in high government positions has been able to provide the slightest clue of what really happened at the time of his abduction.

My scheme begins with us infiltrating Genoa and initiating a blind search for the most vague forms of evidence; clues, tracks, hearsay, or anything that might help us decipher the unsolved mystery. If I hire you, Naguib, it would be because of your proven record of honesty and loyalty to your masters. I would demand your full devotion to my mission, even if it puts your life at risk."

Naguib frowned thoughtfully, but remained silent.

"The other team members may be extremely helpful," Sikin went on.

"Except for Carlo, whose only interest in life is running, their aptitudes are far from law abiding. I've wondered if their jobs at the docks are nothing but a front. Therefore, Naguib, in order to keep them straight, I would need you to maintain an eye on their movements surreptitiously. All I owe these men is pay for a day's work. I will not tolerate greed, trickery, or backstabbing, either among them or against me. The same goes for petty politics and jealousies. I detest using you as an informer when we should be working as a team, but these men have what it takes to turn against me, and consequently the mission. Hence, we should keep them in check until I feel safe and comfortable in their company. I will anticipate your fullest cooperation at the first sign of foul play."

Naguib bowed his head solemnly.

"You will become my right hand and confidant in this pursuit," continued Sikin, "so first and foremost I ask you to be sincere. If you don't agree with a decision, tell me why, and we'll discuss it in private. Also, some of our conversations shall be kept confidential. Report only to me. The less you talk to others, the better our chances of success. Our mission is to find and bring back the boy to Venice, alive. I must confess, however that as crazy as it sounds, all I have to go on is a strong premonition, his grandparents' names, and the approximate location of their mansion. Do you have any questions or doubts about my judgement so far?"

"No, Sahib."

"Then let's talk about your reward. I can see some graying and wrinkling on you already. I also realize that you make an honest living working from sunrise to sunset. I wonder if you've had second thoughts about the meaning of freedom, when for all practical purposes you continue to be enslaved. Perhaps you've also pondered about what would happen to you when you grow old. Of course you'd be a free man! But what's the point in being liberated, if by that time, you are frail and poor, with dwindling health and no family ties. Furthermore, you'll be totally isolated from your countrymen, since most Italian masters will forbid you from coming into contact with their slaves. To make the outlook even worse, society will continue to look upon you as an inferior creature, because of your race and background."

Pausing for a moment, Sikin pulled a leather sack from a pocket, untied the knot, and spread a glittery array of precious gems across the table.

"Naguib," he said, "these might very well mean your deliverance from such a lonely and awful fate. If after working for me as I expect you will, we still don't have the good fortune of finding the boy, you will receive two ounces of gold per day of work, beginning tomorrow morning and thereafter, until I decide to call the mission off.

If fortune is on our side and we find the child, I promise to make you the absolute owner of all these jewels – in which case you will become the richest Moor this side of the Atlas Mountains, and the same condescending aristocrats who consider you sub-human will become your servants for a change.

As unfortunate as it might sound, but as real as the sun above our heads, wealth is the only aphrodisiac in the world, known to transform any individual, good or bad, into a venerable and distinguished personality. The wealthier you are, the higher your chances of being praised and glorified. By becoming the most powerful and dignified Moor in all of Venice and her neighboring states, you will become one of those exceptional human beings who won't have to pretend, deceive, or change colors in order to survive."

Naguib fingered an emerald, so large and radiant its magnificent light seemed to shine from within. "Sahib, I promise find child," he replied humbly in dismembered Italian.

Sikin felt a deep gratitude well up in his throat, but he could think of no way to show it. His shoulders came to the level of the giant's waist, so he couldn't express it with a hug. Handshakes were not customary, and a kiss on his belly was out of the question.

"I thank you, Sir," he quietly told the Moor.

Conversely, as a gesture of appreciation for such an offer and respect, Naguib fell on his knees, hugging Sikin to the verge of asphyxiation.

"Where can I find you within the next couple of days?" Sikin asked catching his breath.

"Shipyards, *Bucintoro*," he replied.

"All right," Sikin said with a smile. "Here is your pay for the day!" He handed him two ounces of gold.

Staring at the shiny metal in the palm of his hand, Naguib left in disbelief.

Wishing Ivan had a friend like him in whom to confide, Sikin returned to the guesthouse for a few hours of well-deserved rest, following a sleepless and stressful night.

Two days later, he visited the shipyards. The acrid smell of hot tar and pitch permeated the air. From higher ground, the huge work area looked like a forced labor camp where dozens of armed galleys were being built to fight the Genoans at sea. As the dry, deafening noises of striking hammers seemed to follow a rhythm of their own, hundreds of workers, sweating and wearing only loin-cloths, labored in the midst of a punishing hot humid day, obeying the boisterous orders of foremen and overseers. Sawing large pieces of wood, workers kept pace with their chanting, while near the water, craftsmen and artists added the final touches to shiny, polished galleys.

Walking through an area where workers were shaping and burnishing hundreds of massive oars, Sikin saw mental images of famished convicts, eight or more to an oar, rowing to their agonizing deaths by the inexorable, tormenting whip, cracked against their backs by butchers who derived pleasure from the mere sight of blood. And for those prisoners who collapsed under the excruciating heat, barbaric cruelty, and the awful stench of body fluids and feces, sometimes detectable as far as three miles away, another cruel fate awaited; they were thrown overboard, like rats waiting to be drowned.

Approaching the center of the hustle and bustle, Sikin passed under huge tents where women, using bone needles and waxed hemp rope, prepared enormous sails for immediate installation. Their hands were as rough as the rigging itself. He crossed through the middle of a large cooking area, where dozens of steaming kettles filled with some kind of aromatic broth hung above their individual fires, and the smell of smoke from roasting deer and fowl tortured the appetites of hungry laborers. Farther away, in a covered area, refined and neatly dressed men discussed plans and deadlines. They were government headmen hired to supervise the whole operation.

Sikin approached the open tent where master carpenters and shipwrights were discussing their plans for the coming week. So involved were they in the conversation that his presence was unnoticed for several moments, until the head of the group offered his sincere apologies for such mindless behavior.

"I am looking for a man who goes by the name of Naguib," Sikin said politely. "He is black, of massive body and difficult speech."

"Ahh, the lucky fellow who used to be a slave," said the master shipright. He pointed at a steamy hill rising above the surface of the water.

"That's where the planking is being formed, and the man you are looking for is in charge of boiling and bending strips of wood to build the hull of the Bucintoro. But even though his job demands considerable physical strength and endurance, the finished pieces require a painstaking process of shaping and shearing the planks to form a perfect fit. That's why Naguib is working for the Bucintoro project. He is one of our most reliable and meticulous carpenters."

"What is the Bucintoro project?" Sikin asked curiously.

"Our Doge's council has ordered the construction of the largest, sea worthiest, and most beautifully ornamented galley ever built," the man answered proudly. "She is to be christened at the annual regatta."

Sikin had read about the famous festival that originated in Venice to celebrate its "marriage to the sea."

"How long will it take to complete?" he asked.

"Perhaps another couple of years. She'll be a floating masterpiece," answered the shipwright.

"Signore; let me ask you a question. If for personal reasons Naguib were to leave his job temporarily, would he be able to return at a later date?"

"He could certainly try, but no guarantees!" Answered the man.

Moving through the disconcerting clutter of parts, tools, smoke, workers, slaves, noise and smells, Sikin finally found Naguib standing atop a scaffold. He was fastening and bending a hot plank of wood against a rib of what would hopefully become the hull of the most exquisite royal galley ever built, the Bucintoro.

After securing a hot steamy plank against the center of a beam rib, Naguib, his body drenched in sweat and steam, spotted Sikin waiting underneath the framework.

"Have you had time to think about our conversation?"

"Yes, Sahib. Naguib wants hear Sikin," replied the Moor.

If it's all right with you, let's meet tomorrow at sunrise in front of the Basilica. Just make sure you don't get in trouble with the boss.

"Not care boss," Naguib answered. "Care little boy!"

* * *

Aware of its historical significance Sikin arrived at the Basilica shortly before sunrise to watch the splendid array of blue and gold mosaics shine the light of the early morning sun.

The exquisite Gothic architecture, cupolas, steeples, columns, and capitals, all built of multi colored Carrara marble, made the magnificent cathedral look like a giant piece of jewelry formed with precious stones of all colors.

Enjoying a panoramic view of the breathtaking surroundings, and knowing that it was too early for Naguib to arrive, Sikin strolled toward the end of the piazza, sat at an empty table facing the Basilica, ordered *pannetone* dunked in milk, and in astonishment; watched La Serenissima come to life.

The scent of the Adriatic, the smell of freshly baked bread, of sausages, cheeses and fruits, the crispness of the air, and the massive amounts of flowers pearled by the the early morning dew, enthralled Sikin to appreciate more than ever, the miracle of being there.

Right at sunbreak, Sikin's heart pounded wistfully at the striking sounds of bells announcing early morning mass. Then, before the crowds began to fill the piazza, he returned to the basilica to meet Naguib.

Following a warm greeting, Sikin explained his plan.

"Our first priority will be to find the mansion of Gabriel Lombardo. Then we must design a scheme to find important pieces of information about the man, his habits and his secrets. I need to know the safest way to enter Genoa without being caught and have several plans of escape, in the event our strategy doesn't work.

Please be honest, Naguib, as capable as you are of handling difficult and dangerous situations, do you feel at ease with my judgement?"

"I look at eyes and know man is good, man is smart," Naguib said. "I like man."

Sikin blinked in surprise. "How can you say I'm competent just by looking at my eyes?"

"I not talk good," Naguib answered. "Read eyes well."

Sikin modestly accepted the Moor's assessment.

"How well do you know the town of Genoa and its surrounding areas?"

"Naguib go to Genoa much, knows well."

"What's your opinion on the safest way to cross the border into that country? Should we go as a group or individually?"

The giant knelt, found a small rock, and drew on the surface of the street a picture of what Sikin thought to be a banana. After realizing bananas were unknown in Europe at the time, he asked the Moor what it meant.

"This Italy," Naguib said. "Here Venice, here Genoa. Walk to Pisa here. Then boat to Genoa."

"Why not travel straight to Genoa by land?" Sikin asked, pointing out the route on the crude map.

"Better be merchant on Genoa boat. No ask questions."

"Oh! I see. The Genoese would suspect a Venetian ship of carrying enemy soldiers. Since they don't bother their own merchants arriving by sea, we should travel to Pisa by land first, and then sail to our destination on a Genoese boat. Is that right?"

"Yes, Sahib."

"How well do you know the coastline?"

"Good." The Moor grinned. "Good sailor. Worked on pirate ship little boy. Many years. Fight storms alone. Never lost ship."

"So you think our next move should be to organize our group and move on?"

"Yes, Sahib."

As they strolled by the Grand Lagoon, taking two steps for every one of his companion's, Sikin asked Naguib to point at the kind of boat they would need to carry out the mission.

"No boat here," the Moor replied with a smile.

"Must go Elba, Sardinia, Genoa."

The men chatted for a while, and even though the Moor spoke in short, thick sentences, Sikin began to understand him quite well. After agreeing to meet with the others at the warehouse the following night they went their separate ways.

Under the usual racket ensuing from all kinds of jokes they

meet again as planned.

Sikin asked for silence. Then, pointing at Carlo, he said, "I want you to take this bag to the Da Ponte residence, and ask to see Mariu. Remember, Carlo, Only Mariu, and no one else! When she asks who you are, just answer, 'I bring a personal message from a friend of your father.'"

"What else should I tell her?" Asked the quiet runner.

"Nothing! Just hand her this bag. It contains a few precious stones that she will convert into gold. Instructions are written inside. Simply leave the bag and get out."

"What if she is not home?"

"Ask when would be the most appropriate time for you to return, and then do so."

Carlo winked mischievously. "May I ask the boss if this errand has something to do with our mission, or is he using me as a middleman to flirt with the woman?"

Following an explosion of laughter, Sikin wondered if these creatures ever took life seriously. Were their attitudes indicative of careless and irresponsible individuals? Having to accept their dubious lifestyles was one thing. Leading buffoons was another.

"Gentlemen, since I have no way to carry the needed ducats to pay for your services, my lady-friend will safeguard them until our mission is over. I know they will be much more secure in her possession."

"But we must get paid in order to eat!" Paolo objected.

"I will take care of the meals and all the expenses, and perhaps an occasional advance. But you will have to wait for the rest of the money until the mission is over."

"What if I get killed? Who receives my share then?" Renato asked suspiciously.

"Whomever you want. Just remember to notify me before we leave Venice."

"How do we know you are trustworthy?" Asked Renato, narrowing his eyes.

"You never will, unless I get a chance to prove it,"

"What if you die before telling the lady how much money you owe us?" Demanded Caramello.

"Naguib will take care of every detail during my absence."

"Why should we trust him?" Asked Renato.

"Look fellows," Carlo interposed. "We are antagonizing each other for no reason. Just because you are dishonest doesn't mean everyone else is. The boss is willing to risk his own life for 'an elevating and noble ideal.' My friends, let me ask you, when was the last time any of us risked a thread of hair for the sake of a decent cause? Never! I admit there are many risks involved, but don't you take a chance every time you cheat or deceive someone? The boss is willing to pay us generously. Keeping the money away from our pockets means we won't burn holes in them. Therefore, my modest proposal is to give Sikin a chance!"

"Boss, you can also count on me!" Paolo said, followed by everyone else.

With the trust issue behind them, Sikin moved on to reveal the purpose of his mission as well as his expectations.

He answered the men's questions as candidly as he could, thus creating the camaraderie needed for each member of the group to feel a part of the same team.

"Boss," said Caramello, "I have a friend in Isola d'Elba whose occupation is pitching oakum and scraping barnacles off of pirate ships. I'm sure he could give us an idea of where to find a vessel that would sail as efficiently as Genoan trade ship."

"What do you say to that?" Sikin asked the giant.

"I go Elba."

"All right, boys, Naguib and Caramello will go to Isola d'Elba with enough money to negotiate a good bargain if one appears. Please don't buy anything just because it floats. If you can find a way of using a ship only temporarily, then go ahead and close the deal. Otherwise we will all be saddled with a useless boat for who knows how long.

The giant and the forger nodded their agreement.

"Paolo, Renato, Carlo and I, will travel to Pisa by land. Then we wait for you somewhere along the coast."

"Boss," aren't you acting hastily?" Paolo asked. "What if they can't find a boat? Are we coming back to Venice to start all over again?"

"If they don't find a ship in Elba, we'll find one elsewhere in the Ligurian Sea. But regardless of what happens, we should always remain close to the Genoan border." Sikin paused. "How long should it take to reach Pisa by land?"

"About one week," Paolo replied.

"Good. We'll be saving valuable time moving by land. How do you propose we travel to Pisa?"

"The road is dangerous and rarely traveled," Renato replied. "There are gangs of gypsies and thieves everywhere, waiting for the next casualty to pass by. And if by coincidence they discover how wealthy you are, our chances of traveling without mishap are almost nil."

"Do you have any suggestions?" Sikin asked.

"Going to Rome first, then to Pisa, makes the route safer but much longer," answered the burly gypsy. "The next alternative would be to join escorted trains and caravans going west. With luck we might find one, and even if they don't go straight to Pisa, we could very well transfer from one train to another until we are close enough to the city."

"Are passengers allowed?"

"Most refuse to carry strangers for fear of taking someone who works for the law."

"Renato, be serious. Aren't you exaggerating a little?"

"Not at all, boss, I'm just telling you what to expect if we travel alone. I get paid too well to let you take risks. But I'll tell you what. Just give me a day or so, and I'll come up with something."

"All right. We'll meet again here in a few days."

"Boss," Paolo interrupted. "Regardless of how we enter Genoa, everyone should carry some proof of identity. We'll be in great trouble if they discover who we really are."

"What do you suggest?" Sikin asked the extortionist.

"Genoa is on good terms with Constantinople, so we can all pose as Levantine merchants. I would have no problem supplying documents to that effect."

"Perfect," said Sikin. "Does everyone agree?" He waited for a chorus of yeses, and then returned to Paolo.

215

"I also need from you a personal favor."

"Go ahead, boss. Those are also my specialty, romantic ones in particular!"

Sikin didn't need to listen to such an innuendo to recognize the short man's insight and skill at infiltrating private lives. In his own view, Paolo was the smartest and most determined stoolie around.

"I'm quite concerned about a young lady, who lives at the Da Ponte's Palazzo," Sikin said. "Her name is Tiblina, and she is my dearest friend. I am worried about her state of mind following an exhausting trip to Rome. She's being out of the city for quite some time, and I'm afraid she is not in good health. I want to know how she's doing. But most important, Paolo, you need to determine if she knows I'm in town."

"Have no fear, boss," answered Paolo pounding a fist on the center of his chest. "Feebleness of heart and spiritual malaise represent my two most precious sources of income, and the only way to keep starvation away from the table."

"Now you listen to me, Paolo! I want to make this very clear. Under no circumstance must you dare tell anyone in that house about my request. Do you understand?"

"Why don't you trust me?" Paolo asked. "Secrets and gossip are among the most valuable of all my assets. Besides, Sikin, I'm working for you now. Keeping my mouth shut increases my reputation and good offices in the eyes of one of my best clients." He grinned amiably.

A couple of days later, Paolo arrived unexpectedly at Sikin's boarding house. "I have just discovered some fresh and important information," he said pompously. "Or shall I use the words 'sweet and passionate' instead?"

"Be careful with your selection of words, Paolo," Sikin warned. "You might regret them later."

"No offense, boss! Fortunately for you, the lady doesn't know you are in town, so hopefully this should put your mind at ease. Her sister, Mariu, has already exchanged your 'rocks' for gold, and is keeping the ounces in a place so secret, not even her most trusted maid knows where they are."

Paolo sighed ardently. "Observing your lady from a distance helped me understand the reason for your obsession. How lovely and attractive signora Tiblina is! According to a maid, she relieves her torments by recalling the days when, in the company of Mariu's father and a young man she deeply loved, Tiblina crossed the Taklamakan Desert along the Silk Route."

Paolo winked. "The maid, who used to be an old flame of mine, believes Signora Tiblina suffers from hallucinations. Her unbelievable stories are much like those of Scheherezade from the book Arabian Nights which Tiblina used to tell to her little boy every night before bedtime.

I was told that she dedicates a great deal of energy to some kind of asylum for children she founded. But considering you didn't have much interest in this part of her life, I didn't ask more questions. Everyone feels she is in good health, and in spite of adversity, your lady has a very positive attitude toward life.

My lady friend said the two women she serves have enough stamina to drive her up a wall. Their home is filled with activity all the time. As a matter of fact, when I met my old flame in the kitchen, a cardinal, an acolyte, and a well-dressed couple were visiting, also a younger man who according to my source has been attracted to her for years."

"How old is this fellow?" Sikin flushed despite himself.

"I'd say probably five to ten years younger; of good breeding, handsome, and very wealthy."

"Who is he?"

"I don't know, boss. You told me just to ask about her health, and whether she was aware of your presence in La Serenissima."

"You're right. I suppose that concludes your 'fact-finding' mission."

"Yes, unless you want me to go back for more, and if so, you must give my lady-friend some kind of reward."

"All right, Paolo. That's enough for the day."

The short man hesitated. "Boss, before I go, and since we are touching on the subject, I'd like to bring up a topic that's been bothering me for some time. You might think I'm out of line by asking, but I also hope you understand my reasons for doubting."

"Speak, Paolo."

"I began questioning your intentions the first day we met," said the short man. "The more I know you, Sikin, the less I believe you came from nowhere and for no reason."

When Sikin didn't answer, Paolo continued. "Think about it boss. A person traveling with a small duffel bag loaded with gold, precious stones, and only a change of clothes, arrives in Venice impeccably dressed and way past midnight, searching through the fog for the Palazzo Da Ponte. The stranger has no idea what our carnival is about, which means he came from the moon. He disappears, and in less than four days the same enigmatic gentleman contrives a mission of benevolence that will cost him a fortune, for no apparent reason other than to impress his lady. He hires persons of dubious reputations because he values their skills. To everyone's amazement, almost overnight he develops a strategy to carry out his scheme. The mysterious traveler tells the newly hired band of thieves that his word is law, expecting them to risk their lives for a few gold coins, and all this in the name of perfect love?"

Paolo tapped his foot impatiently. "Would you believe such a sham if you were in my shoes? I might be a blackmailer, but I'm not stupid.

What if this operation of yours is a gigantic money-making maneuver disguised as a mission of love and compassion? How do we know the boy ever existed? How do we know those eerie stories about abduction, witchcraft, contrived marriages, and executions are real and not a false front to disguise some sort of grand scheme?"

He crossed his arms over his chest. "If you want my allegiance, why don't you prove there are no hidden ploys or gimmicks involved?"

Disturbed, but not surprised, Sikin found himself in a quandary. He could understand Paolo's point of view, yet how could he convince a hoodlum of someone else's genuine desire to do what was right? Attempting to persuade Paolo of the legitimacy of his intentions would be like trying to convince a thug that he is a wrongdoer. Understanding that exceptional people risk their lives and fortunes for the sake of others without ulterior gain was beyond Paolo's intellect and moral values. Unexpectedly, Sikin had stumbled onto the mission's first wrinkle; dissention and mistrust within the group, which as its leader, he couldn't afford to let spread.

"If I tell you the man who crossed the Taklamakan along with Tiblina and Mariu's father was I, would you then believe me?" He began. "If I tell you my love for her is so precious, I decided to return many years later, to make sure Tiblina is enjoying the kind of life she so deserved, would you believe me? For your peace of mind, Paolo, I am the man of her dreams. That's all I can say at the moment. I came with a single purpose; to make sure she is treated with dignity, fairness, and decency."

Sikin looked Paolo in the eyes. "This is the truth. There are no hidden schemes or subterfuges. If you believe me great, if you don't, I am sorry, but I will not lie to bring you on board. This venture is mostly about trust, love, and justice. As far as my identity and origins are concerned, I regret to disappoint you, but they will not be revealed until our mission is over, and I reserve the right to keep them secret even then.

If you doubt me, I would ask you to quit right now. Don't stay with a group you are eventually going to divide. No one has a right to do that. Don't try to start your own crusade without reason or cause. It will hurt everyone, including yourself. Have I made myself clear?"

The short man shrugged, clearly mystified as to why Sikin had lost his temper.

"Look, boss," he said calmly. "We could sit and argue for days, and neither of us will be satisfied. I will continue to harbor disbelief, and you, a feeling of betrayal. Therefore, I'd like to present a proposal, if you promise to let me quit without reason, questions, or punishment, I'll stay as loyal and faithful to the cause as you say you are. Then time, and only time, will put everything in the right perspective. What do you say to that?"

Sikin knew that neither of them wanted a serious confrontation. Paolo needed the money badly, and Sikin required him for cohesiveness. They agreed to make a concerted effort to collaborate.

A few days later, Paolo showed up with the false identity papers, asking for more money to satisfy the various links in the chain.

Late one afternoon, a message arrived from Renato, sent via a gypsy girl, asking Sikin, Paolo, and Carlo to meet him early the following morning at the produce market. The next day, after mingling with the dense crowds at the marketplace, they found Renato helping a gypsy family get their colorful carriages ready for a trip to Pisa. Two large groups who would be traveling with goods to sell along the way were preparing to leave.

The air was filled with noise and energy. Babies cried and children squabbled while their mothers yelled their heads off, trying in vain to control their unrestrained behavior.

The women wore colorful skirts and scarves, and most men white sweaty camisoles and thick dark pants.

They seemed to be roaming from an area east of Rimini to Venice, then South towards the Western coast, all the way to the island of Sardinia, where they would be spending the remainder of winter.

A wanderer himself, Renato convinced the gypsies to welcome his friends as passengers for a generous fee, which they initially refused to accept, suspecting Sikin and his friends were undercover law procurators of some sort.

Following Renato's introduction, Sikin decided to pay their fee in advance in order to gain some confidence. Food was included in the price.

In virtually no time, the caravan was under-way. Three large wagons were used as living quarters for families and pets, including trained rats for the children to play with, singing birds of all colors, and small domestic animals for food. Loud, colorful designs were painted and displayed all over the vehicles, including the cartwheels. Tied to the horses' bridles, dozens of flowers added an animated expression of life and color. Hanging from the side rails of their carriages, all sorts of pots and pans clanged and banged against each other announcing the presence of the caravan as it went by.

A smaller, fourth wagon carried a large inventory of woolen blankets, which were moved to its roof so the four passengers could travel indoors. Inside there was a hearth to heat water and warm up their meals, as well as enough woolen blankets to accommodate the guests during the ten-day journey.

Moving slowly, the caravan stopped at every opportunity to beg, sell, or steal, while a dozen dogs trotted beside the procession at all times.

Accompanied by their primitive instruments, group members sang lively folk songs to lessen the trip's monotony. Undoubtedly stolen from a wealthy home, an artistically decorated lute brought forth the most delicate of melodies.

When they reached Sardinia, the tribe would spend the rest of the winter and early spring living in caves. During this period they would steal, make, or buy goods to be sold or bartered on their way back to Rimini the following summer.

Their wandering route was the same year after year, generation after generation, and they had memorized every inch of road.

The first stop took place on the outskirts of Venice in an area where all sorts of people congregated to trade, barter, shop, or just talk. Shaded by their wagons, the women sold and bartered their hand-made goods, and farther away under the trees, fortunetellers practiced palmistry, card reading, and scattering of shells for curious pedestrians interested in clairvoyance and divination. Anyone buying items or seeking services from those Romany merchants and fortunetellers ran a certain risk of wasting their time, money, and possibly everything they owned including their clothing. Children were encouraged to stampede, pilfer, and wheedle at every stop.

The Romany spoke among themselves a dialectic corruption of various romantic languages. Contact between the gypsies and their passengers were virtually non-existent, except for Renato, who got along with his hosts extremely well.

During evenings, younger women breastfed their babies, while the older ones cooked on an open fire, foods Sikin and the others found almost impossible to digest because of the generous amounts of hot paprika and lard they contained.

After ten solid days of upset stomachs and aggravations brought about in part by unruly children pitching rocks against their carriage, pestering for money, and pulling nasty tricks, the passengers were more than ready to jump off and walk the remaining distance. On their late afternoon arrival in Pisa, they quickly departed from the group, except for Renato, who stayed behind wiping away tears over his farewell.

The four strolled around the city looking for a place to spend the night, but finding nothing available, they decided to walk toward the coast and sleep alongside the road. Waking up the next morning by the crystal clear waters of a river so quiet, they had mistaken it for a lake the night before, the group decided to jump in for a cold refreshing soak before continuing their journey.

By mid-afternoon they reached a village where dozens of vessels, anchored in a choppy lagoon accessing the Ligurian Sea, waited impatiently for their masters to jump on board and go fishing.

"Boss, how do you intend to find Naguib and Caramello?" Asked Paolo.

"Have you ever met his look-alike?" Sikin replied with a grin.

"Naguib is too conspicuous to go unnoticed. Let's offer a small reward to the person who finds him first. I am sure the whole village will become involved in the search."

Dozens of shacks built on stilts formed the greatest part of the small fishing community. Beneath them, the owner's small vessels were moored to pilings to prevent the incoming tide from taking them away.

Since there was no lodging in or around the settlement, they opted to stay inside an abandoned structure that had been long used for the salting and smoking of fish.

In spite of being vacant for a long time, and perhaps as a

permanent reminder of its lucrative past, the old building still reeked of rotten fish, which became distinctively acute after a rainstorm. It was difficult to get used to its concealed stench, but at least they had found a peaceful place to lie down for the night.

The following morning Sikin went out to offer the villagers two ounces of gold as a reward to the first person to reveal Naguib's whereabouts. First, he stopped by a netweaving facility owned and operated by a neighborhood cooperative, where industrious workers wove, repaired, and dressed fishing nets for the town's mariners, as well as those in surrounding areas. Three older men, one of whom was almost blind, treated the twine with creosote, while another group spooled the foul-smelling lines to make sure they were free of twists and knots. Another handful of workers laid out the finished nets to dry under the sun, where they would remain for several days until no longer soft.

When Sikin showed up, everyone was so attentive to his or her craft that no one cared to raise a brow or say a word, until he mentioned the reason for his call.

Soon thereafter, the news had spread like wildfire throughout the entire village, and in no time groups of children were already standing guard along the spit of land protecting the lagoon, waiting for the imminent arrival of the giant.

Women did their mending and knitting sitting outside their shacks to avoid missing the man who would hopefully make them rich.

When fishermen went out to sea on pitch dark and moonless nights, they yelled Naguib's name every time their boat encountered an unidentified vessel. It seemed as if every villager had suddenly found a pastime as well as a new and exciting way to make money. During the days that followed, the matter of Naguib became such an obsession to the small community that everyone was placing bets on something or other; the time and place of "apparition", the size of his fists, his shoes and so on. Children were improvising traps to literally catch the giant.

Meanwhile, Sikin and his companions waited for news about the two sailors, eager to leave the smelly building and begin their assignments.

Finally, one dark and foggy night, after listening to some sort of commotion coming from the shore, they left their shelter to find out the reason for such a fuss. When the boisterous villagers became aware of their presence, they raised their oil lamps, showing the face of a tall man who indistinctly looked like Naguib himself.

"Is this the man you are looking for?" Inquired the blind man who worked at the net factory.

"It's so dark I can't see very well," Sikin replied.

Suddenly, someone else's deep voice resounded in the darkness.

"This Naguib. Crazy fishermen here, Sahib?"

"He is the man!" Answered Sikin. And as the entire village watched the unusual event, he gave the gold to the blind man.

"How could a blind person find a black man in this darkness?" Paolo asked.

"Because those who see and hear don't pay much attention to what darkness conceals." Sikin responded. "Conversely, the blind man concentrates on what lies beyond the visible, and nothing else."

The villagers couldn't go back to sleep even after the excitement of discovery was over. Noise and conversation lasted until dawn.

As the "band of six" greeted each other, Sikin asked Naguib and Caramello to follow him to their shelter.

Upon entering the old fish house, the giant asked Sikin to let Caramello do the explaining.

"As long as you are present," Sikin replied. "Go ahead, Caramello."

"After arriving in Sardinia, Naguib and I heard the story of a rich merchant who had just lost one of his best captains to a homicide," Caramello began. "The faithful seaman was murdered in cold blood the night of his arrival."

"According to reliable sources, the captain's wife, a notorious sorceress, kept a former sailor as her lover. One evening, after returning unexpectedly from a lengthy voyage, the captain found them committing adultery. A fight ensued, and both men fought until the unscrupulous sailor plunged his dagger into the cheated husband's heart, killing him instantly.

The witch, stunned and horrified at the sight of blood, blamed her husband's employer for causing his untimely death, claiming that by taking him away for months at a time, she was compelled to seek the company of other men. Following the murder, the unfaithful wife went after the wealthy employer, accusing him of exploitation and abuse. After hurling at him all sorts of ridiculous accusations, she went on to cast spells on the frightened man, who had absolutely nothing to do with the killing to begin with.

Immensely superstitious, the rich merchant has not ventured outside his house ever since, for fear of meeting his former captain's fate."

Caramello grinned. "When I heard the story, I went to visit the rich employer disguised as a fortuneteller and diviner, and Naguib as my personal oracle and confidant.

'Signore,'" I began by saying. "'Coming from a family of seers, I have been advised by the spirit of my deceased uncle, a former prophet and soothsayer, to locate you at any cost.

Being a most reputable psychic and clairvoyant during his life on earth, my uncle predicted, among other things, the war between Genoa and Venice. I might also add that he was secretly employed by the Great Council and the Doge himself to forecast political events. He also performed acts of exorcism in cases similar to yours.

A highly perceptive man, my uncle also acted as a medium between the quick and the dead. During his apparition the night before last, he begged me to pay you a visit in order to prevent another wrongful death, this one resulting from curses and spells recently cast upon your body and soul.'

The old man's eyes nearly dropped from his head at that," Caramello added. "He turned as white as sailcloth and quaked in his velvet slippers."

"'Although I'm not here as a mediator between you and the witch, I have come to avert further tragedy and bloodshed,' I kept haranguing. 'Indeed, I am a stranger in your eyes, nonetheless I have been chosen by the universal forces of light to detect signals and vibrations from the otherworld no one else could decipher. Every time I sense messages disclosing harmful effects on people's lives, I intercede on their behalf. And that, Signore, is the mission of my life'"

"What happened then?" Sikin asked, amused at the direction he could see the story heading.

"After listening to my discourse, the superstitious merchant asked me for help in exorcising the curse. I went for the jugular. Facing the ceiling with my eyes closed and arms extended, I invoked the dissolution of the curse, reciting abracadabras and prayers. Then I sealed the lifting of the curse by asking the wealthy trader for his deceased captain's ship. 'Its use should be only temporary' I said to him. 'And those sailing it shall be the most compassionate Samaritans this side of the Holy Land.'"

Sikin laughed merrily.

"Falling on his knees and shaking from head to toe, the merchant begged me to find him the right seaman to perform the task as soon as possible. 'I shall find them!' I said reassuringly. 'And as an act of good faith, I shall accompany them until the mission of benevolence is finished. Then and only then shall your ship be returned, and the spell forever exorcised into a void.'

I swept my cape back on, and grabbing Naguib by the hand, I yelled to the top of my lungs, 'Oh, Prince of Darkness! Master of deceit! I rebuke you in the name of righteousness, and I beseech you to leave this man alone!'

As we were leaving, the merchant ran after Naguib and I shouting; 'Please be merciful, wise man! For God's sake, don't abandon me! You can have as many ships as you want for as long as you wish.' I spunned around, saying, 'Signore, being assigned the sacred duty of saving your life; I promise to find the right persons before sunset tomorrow. And for your peace of mind, we only need one ship.'"

Caramello paused for a moment trying to remember additional details of the encounter while Sikin, anxious to hear its conclusion, urged him to continue.

"Sorry, boss, but I don't have much else to say."

"Not much else to say?" I want to know what happened to the ship!"

"Ahh! The boat! Yes I'm sorry, I suppose you are talking about the Genoan trade ship, correct?"

"What trade ship?"

"The one we anchored at the mouth of the lagoon. Caramello answered.

"You mean the two of you got the boat right away and at no cost?"

"Many boats if boss wants." Naguib interjected.

The three roared with laughter.

"You are a fine company of rogues indeed!" Sikin pronounced.

Shortly after sunrise, Sikin and his men left their odorous refuge en route to the launch that would take them to the ship.

Genoan and Venetian trade ships were predominantly designed and built by Arabs during the Middle Ages. Unfortunately, Sikin knew, many were used for the slave trade along the East African coast. Their single triangular lateen-type sail looked very much like those used on the feluccas sailing the Nile.

The ship's largest disadvantage was the great length of its lateen yard overhanging the bow, which needed to be hauled in close to the base of the mast and swung across to port or starboard with every new tack. This proved a slow and cumbersome process.

Sikin studied their borrowed boat. The vessel measured about sixty-five feet in length and had a twenty-foot beam.

The bow housed a tophamper, a structure used for human protection under heavy weather, and the stern had a quarterdeck used by the captain and his mates while underway. Shaped like huge oars, two long wooden rods functioned as rudders from each side of the quarterdeck. They were cylindrical at the top, gradually flattening toward the bottom for better steering. The sail displayed a red cross, its middle painted with the words

"God is Love" written in Latin.

In lieu of a deeper keel, the vessel carried tons of rocks on its lower deck as ballast to balance the ship under heavy seas.

Since the tradeship's insignia symbolized the Serene Republic of Venice, they had to replace it with one from a friendly country. Also to avoid suspicion, they changed the name from *Madre di Dio* to *Il Genovese*.

Sikin entrusted the ship's command to Naguib, who would be delegating duties in due time.

While maneuvering the ship in good weather presented a challenge to the six sailors, it would have been an impossible task under less desirable conditions.

Already stocked with salt-pickled fish, dried fruit, bacon, flour, honey, lots of wine, and a few itinerant rodents, the trade ship was ready to sail.

CHAPTER *Seven*

THE TRAPPINGS OF GREED

At the Blackwall docks we bid adieu
to lovely Kate and lively Sue
our anchors weigh'd and our sails unfurled
and we're bound to plough the wat'ry world
Sing hay, we're outward bound
Hurrah, we're outward bound.
Anon.

T he crewmen dedicated the next few days to learning and memorizing their individual assignments. Sikin stood by the giant's side at all times, mastering the vessel's maneuvering, and offering a hand wherever needed. On one occasion, as the ship sailed towards its temporary anchorage, a sudden, squall exploded in all its fury, increasing seas to ten feet and winds to forty knots.

In spite of being just a skeleton crew, the six seamen did admirably well as the ship yawed, pitched, and took in water while bucking the large swells. Fortunately, the brunt of the storm lasted only briefly. Otherwise, the outcome would have been entirely different.

After a week of intense training, Sikin felt his men were ready to take over, so he called a meeting in the captain's quarters. The six crewmen crammed inside the cabin to discuss various options and ideas.

They sat facing each other across a long rectangular table, so packed with nautical items they had little room to put anything else on top. Lined up along its sides, seven chairs built of Asian teakwood and upholstered in a red velvety material, added badly needed color to the austere surroundings.

Used to measure the boat's speed in conjunction with a sand clock, a long, thin rope with knots tied every twelve feet remained half reeled on an old wooden spool. Old charts, showing almost imperceptible detail due to continuous handling, as well as a thick navigation log and a whistle, were piled up between two waxy candleholders.

In a vain attempt to cozy up the ambiance, a colorful tapestry showing in amazing detail the most important ports of the Mediterranean Sea, along with a smaller, more primitive illustration of the known world, covered the entire wall toward the rear. Suspended from the ceiling and hanging above an old briarwood desk, a brass oillamp shed just enough light to outline the most significant features of the seated men.

The stale, humid air, along with the unmistakable penetrating odor of mildew, reminded everyone of what death by asphyxiation would smell like.

Opening the transom windows to allow the ocean breeze to enter, refresh, and mask the musty air, Sikin couldn't help but reminisce about a book Ivan McKinley once read. The story told of an abandoned ship sailing through a violent storm, with the ghost of its murdered captain at the helm. Perhaps, either out of respect for the ship's murdered captain, or due to carefully concealed superstitions, the young man didn't sit in or touch the captain's chair. Leaning instead against the table's edge along with Naguib, he addressed the crew.

"Gentlemen, we shall set sail for Genoa on Wednesday when the moon is almost full. According to Naguib, the ship should be at anchor by Sunday or Monday, unless we encounter stormy seas or gusty winds coming from the land of Africa. Upon arrival, we'll board the launch and row straight to shore. Make sure you fellows take enough food and water to last a minimum of three days. Carry along your weapon of choice, also plenty of rope. Avoid crowds, and if by necessity you must respond to strangers, our story should go like this; 'We are all members of a Levantine family traditionally dedicated to the silk trade, and we came to Genoa in pursuit of new markets.' If we all answer the same way, no one will ever know the truth. If someone in authority asks for additional information, direct him to me.

As you know, we'll be searching for clues regarding Gabriel Lombardo, his habits, address, lifestyle, reputation, and his past in particular. Pay close attention to every remark and conversation you hear. The more we learn about this man, the better our chances of success. Once we have gathered enough information, I'll figure out the plan of action."

"Boss, if we belong to the same family what do I say about our relationship to Naguib?" inquired Carlo.

"If you are asked such a question, say he was our deceased father's personal attendant."

Early Wednesday morning, at the sound of the Moor's whistle, the four hoodlums awoke like a disciplined crew of sailors ready for duty, and by sunrise, they were underway.

They sailed Northeasterly for the greatest part of the crossing. Winds and seas were favorable all the way to Genoa, where they arrived two days later without mishap.

On anchoring at the mouth of the bay, they boarded the skiff en route to the deserted coast. They pulled the boat up on the pebbled beach as far from the tide as possible, always following Naguib's instructions.

Sikin assigned Caramello to visit a tavern, find a couple of lewd women, buy them drinks, and encourage them to talk about politics, politicians, and government figures, leading the conversation toward Gabriel Lombardo and his reputation.

Paolo, the group's rabble-rouser, and Renato, his "cousin", were to offer their services as tailors and garment makers to well-bred and elegantly attired aristocrats, with who they would gossip.

Sikin would portray a merchant with excellent connections in Saracen countries, as well as an expert in silk, who was willing to spend his enormous fortune on trivialities, investments, or both. Naguib would play a personal emissary from Sikin's supposedly personal friend, the sultan of Savez, and chief eunuch of the sultan's harem. Carlo will pose as a young protégé and intimate playmate of the sultan.

Sikin provided each group with enough money to play their roles for a couple of days. Then they would return to the ship to exchange information.

* * *

Caramello loved his assignment. Getting paid to have fun with lewd women was the apotheosis of his fantasies. He walked along the waterfront until he found a tavern; a malodorous establishment packed with intoxicated customers. Only two women were present, one serving wine and spirits, the other washing wooden mugs and cleaning the floor.

After sitting and ordering drinks, Caramello asked the charwoman why there were no other females around.

"Haven't you heard the news?" She asked. "The council has cracked down on prostitutes. They are forcing them to pay some kind of tax, or else stay home. The ladies claim their bodies are their own personal property and that no one else has a right to make a profit from it. But the procurators harass them to no end, making their lives so miserable they now work strictly from their homes." She paused and winked. "If you are willing to pay generously for a piece of sensitive information, I can tell you exactly where to go to have a good time. Do we have a deal?"

"Please don't misunderstand me." Caramello said. "I came to visit this place with only one purpose in mind; to enjoy good conversation with intelligent and talkative women."

"You must be crazy!" Answered the servant. "After spending months overseas, you come to Genoa looking for women to talk to? Heck, I'll be willing to chat all day for half price. Just remember…Conversation and nothing else! Why don't you come back tonight after closing? Then we can talk till our mouths bleed, and I won't even charge you! I'm dying to hear what kind of conversation you are after!" She laughed heartily.

"Madam, I shall return after midnight!" Caramello replied with a grand bow.

* * *

Renato and Paolo, acting as expert garment makers and fashion designers from the Middle East, were offering their services as "traveling tailors" to the oldest and most respected Jewish clothiers in the city. In those days Genoa was considered as *avant gard* in fashion design as Paris and Florence.

Renato was wearing a flamboyant garment with scalloped sleeves, buttoned from the collar to the hem, yards upon yards of fabric, along with an elaborate liripipe hat that extended its long point all the way to the back. Noticeably small for his large feet, the high-heeled shoes painfully elevated the swindler an extra four inches from the ground.

Paolo sported a jacket-and-hose ensemble so striking and colorful, that the short man could have been easily mistaken for a court jester. Unexpectedly they have found all the accouterments inside a moldy trunk at the captain's quarters.

Renato's proposal to the incredulous Jewish owner went like this, "Let us use your name and reputation as our introduction to prospective clients, and we'll bring you lots of business. We will go from mansion to mansion offering your distinguished services in the privacy of the customer's homes. We will take the client's measurements, bring them back to you, then deliver the final garment and collect the money."

"Are you some kind of authority in the fashion world?" The old tailor inquired scrutinizing their outfits.

"My brother and I are the most celebrated clothiers in Constantinople. I work as a liaison between him and our select clientele, or should I say as a moderator. You see, my brother Benniamino is a very shy person who cannot take complaints or rejection lightly. Yet he is also considered the most talented couturier in the country."

Paolo nodded modestly at Renato's description but stayed silent.

"In order to keep profits flowing," Renato continued. "I took over the position of spokesman for the shop. I handle ladies' complaints with silk gloves and charming flattery. Furthermore, gentlemen are appeased by my positive observations about their garment's unique style and character." Renato said touching his liripipe hat. "We dress Saracens as well as merchants from the West. To be honest, Signore, there's not enough light in a thousand days to fulfill our present obligations. We came to Genoa only temporarily and by necessity to accompany a very sick grandmother who needs urgent care. Benniamino and I will be spending some time with her, and if in the meantime we can earn some extra income, we'll be most grateful." Renato sighed deeply.

Astonished, the old garment maker asked them to come back in three days to meet his even older partner. "We are both Sephardic Jews, and that is precisely our problem. If someone else does the calling and we do the sewing and assembling, we could all make lots of money."

* * *

Sikin, Naguib, and Carlo, entered the old city of Genoa via the Porta Soprana, a door of monumental proportions built in 1155. After passing the cloister of S. Andrea, they took the inner path leading to Piazza Sarzano, where the spire of the church of St. Agostino appeared, covered with thousands of tiny multicolored majolica tiles. Naguib led them to the guild of the merchants, an exclusive society where the wealthiest tradesmen met to drink, contact women, talk, and cut deals. Wealthy Genoese and influential politicians were also welcomed at the guild. Here men of the world with enough means could purchase food and drink at exorbitant prices, and women of ill repute were allowed to negotiate their terms, insulated from taxes and repercussions.

As they crossed the establishment's threshold, two perfectly uniformed men asked the three travelers for the purpose of their visit.

Sikin offered his usual story, but since they were not suitably arrayed, their entrance was denied.

An elegantly dressed merchant who had accidentally overheard their conversation interrupted the steward, asking him for permission to talk to the strange visitors. The man introduced himself as Dino de la Francesca.

"I've heard you mentioning the Silk Road around Turpan," said the stylish man. "That's my favorite spot along the entire route. I always look forward to drinking the sweetest wine from those grapes."

De la Francesca turned to the stewards. "Please allow these men to be my guests."

"White men only, the slave stays outside!" One of them replied.

"Sorry, but I must decline," Sikin said. "This man is my friend. Naguib knows more secrets about the riches of the East than anyone I know. He came along to protect this young man, who happens to be the Sultan's protege and intimate friend. Do you understand?"

"I certainly do!" Dino said, waving off the steward. "Please don't take this man's insolence seriously. But perhaps we can all meet at the garden behind the guild. I don't think it would be prudent to shake up this place by bringing the three of you inside anyway. This way we can talk, drink, and eat to our heart's content."

In the garden, inebriated by the soothing sounds of water trickling from the fountain and the sweet scent of hundreds of flowers, the three ate and drank all kinds of exotic delicacies and delicious wines. Sikin and the merchant took control of the conversation by recollecting their bittersweet moments while traveling the Taklamakan, the grapes of Turpan, its underground canals and delightful cool waters, the luscious dates and figs from the various oases, its glorious sunrises and sunsets, the crowded city of Dunhuang, and of course, those damned unforgiving windstorms.

During their lively talk, the merchant said he was one of four brothers traveling the unknown world in search of riches and adventure.

As their nostalgia seemed to have flagged, Sikin asked if Dino was acquainted with the name, Gabriel Lombardo.

"Everyone in Genoa is familiar with that name." Dino replied. "Gabriel Lombardo has a pact with the Devil.The hypocrite would sell his own mother in exchange for more power and money. He has an absolute dominion of the government's grapevine, as well as great skill manipulating information for his own benefit and for the benefit of those submissive to him. A dangerous foe, and an unfaithful friend, Lombardo is feared for his influence and lack of scruples. In fact, I don't think he is liked by anyone, the brute has all the markings of an abominable person."

"Why do you ask?" Is he by chance a friend of the Sultan?" Dino stopped himself suddenly.

"No, he's not," Sikin said reassuringly. "Lombardo owes my best friend an explanation about an unpaid debt contracted over fifteen years ago, and part of my mission is to find out where he lives, meet the fellow, and negotiate on her behalf."

"My goodness, Sikin, It would be easier to reach the Pope!" Said Dino. "Personal guards are by his side day in and day out. God only knows what those butchers would do to protect him. Much of what I'm telling you could very well be hearsay, since I never had personal contact with the scoundrel. I've also heard he has gotten much worse following his wife's suicide several years ago."

"Suicide?" Sikin asked in alarm.

"A tragedy," said Dino.

"Some blamed appalling family situations, such as the abduction of his son Tirso's little boy, as one of the reasons for her self destruction. She never forgave her husband's implicit endorsement of their son's execution either, nor his repulsive servitude to the government that took his life."

Dino noted his companions' blank looks.

"The bizarre state of affairs began," he continued, "when Lombardo publicly accused Tirso's wife of instigating rebelliousness in his son's mind. He also charged the woman with adultery and witchcraft, claiming that her son wasn't Tirso's. What he never acknowledged was that Tirso's anger toward his father led the young man to participate in public acts of violence and insurrection long before he married the alleged witch. Following his son's execution, Lombardo contrived a scheme to destroy Tirso's widow by formally charging her with harlotry, sorcery, and witchcraft. As a result, she was tried, imprisoned, and condemned to die at the stake. Despondent and overwhelmingly grieved, the poor widow received at the same time the tragic news of her son's abduction.

Compounding the enigma even further, she disappeared suddenly from her cell a day before the execution, and to this day no one has ever heard of the woman again. Lombardo claimed the mysterious event demonstrated once again her satanic faculties. Nevertheless, it is common knowledge he lives in a state of constant anxiety, expecting her ghost to appear anytime.

After the drama, the man became obsessed with the elimination of every alleged prostitute and sorcerer from the city, affirming his 'devotion to the cause of human decency' in the community.

According to another dependable source, he used to be an assiduous visitor to a certain brothel, until his wife caught him in the act and threatened to expose his 'impeccable character' to the powerful clergy and the public ear. The scandal brought about a vicious campaign against prostitution solely instigated by him, with the transparent purpose of rescuing his already tarnished public image!" Dino laughed, and then shook his head. "Just recently, he proposed a law banning the ladies from public view unless they pay a ridiculously high contribution to the government. The man is a snake!"

"What happened to the little boy?" Sikin asked as Naguib's frown turned to a glower. Sikin raised his eyebrows questioningly, but the giant just shook his head.

"No one knows for sure," said the merchant blithely. "In my opinion, he had him killed, hence eliminating the last trace of his repulsive scheme."

After a moment of silence, Sikin praised his new acquaintance for such valuable information, and then pointedly changed the subject back to the Silk Route and their adventures on the road.

Dino proved to be educated and articulate; a person who knew what he wanted out of life and had the determination and courage to achieve it. In his early forties, he exuded the energy of a younger man. Gregarious, and with a great sense of humor, Dino had the knack of making those around him feel like old friends. From a large family, he had relatives all over Italy, although he was the only one living in Genoa.

"Shall we meet again to discuss some possible business ventures?" Sikin asked.

"Oh, I imagine we could," Dino replied.

"Are you interested in trading?"

"Only in manufacturing," responded Dino. "I'd like to quit running the route once and for all. Traveling East has become more dangerous than ever. Furthermore, sea merchants claim they can carry more weight a lot more easily, faster, and for less than we can do over land. I'd be most interested in processing fabrics in a city other than Venice, a neutral country perhaps. That is essentially my next objective." The merchant spoke enthusiastically. "Silk fascinates me. It always has. Besides, I'd like to establish roots, start a family, and live a more predictable life with my loved ones. I am tired of sharing it with camels and strangers, and I don't want to become another old merchant rotting in the desert."

"We have a lot in common," Sikin said. "Let's make sure we meet again in the near future!"

"I am here Mondays and Wednesdays for supper, and all day on Fridays," Dino replied.

Following the usual formalities, the three visitors left the guild.

"Boss, you really winged that meeting as good or better than any conniver would. I almost believed in everything you said." Carlo remarked.

Naguib, who had remained silent throughout, asked Sikin if he had noticed a tall man with reddish hair arguing with a group inside the guild.

"No, Naguib. What about him?"

Naguib narrowed his eyes. "Man red hair cut Naguib's tongue. Hit man, rich now."

Sikin's mouth dropped open. "Are you sure he is the same person who tortured you?"

"Never forgot face. Never forgot hair. Never forgot man!"

"Why didn't you tell me before?"

"Not good place to talk," Naguib answered. "Man not see me."

"Before considering any action against this person, I suggest we investigate his past to make sure. We don't want to threaten an innocent life. Don't you think?"

"Boss right," said the giant. "Then boss sure. Naguib already sure."

* * *

It was way past midnight at the old tavern by the waterfront. Caramello felt he had waited long enough for the charwoman, and was about to go elsewhere for information, when a female voice reached him from the rear of the empty saloon:

"Signore please stay! I'm sorry it has taken me this long to finish my chores. Aren't you anxious to hear me talk?"

"I'm out of time," Caramello replied. I've been waiting all night to ask questions about a widely known government official. I was willing to compensate you generously for reliable information, but perhaps I should go elsewhere."

"May I ask whom you are referring to?"

"I'm talking about Gabriel Lombardo," Caramello said, dropping his voice.

"After serving hundreds of patrons every day, you must have overheard slanderous remarks about this person. So set a price,

Signora, and tell me everything you have heard about this man."
Caramello said shaking some loose coins in his hand.

The woman eyed the coins. "Not until I know your reasons
for this inquiry," she said hesitantly.

"Just take it as mere curiosity." Caramello replied.

"Mere curiosity? How dumb you think I am?" She snorted.
"Many would give anything to see Lombardo rotting in a
ditch. His life has been threatened so many times, that they say
he always sleeps in a room brightly lit, with two armed men
standing guard inside his bedchamber. The man has countless
enemies, but he also has powerful friends and squealers all over
town, so if you appreciate life, I strongly urge you to return to
your ship, and forget all about Signore Lombardo. Take my
advice, and leave!"

"All right, Signora," Caramello said rising. "If that's what
you want, I'll go somewhere else with my questions. But take a
good look at what you are missing." He scattered several shiny
pieces of gold across the table.

As Caramello began to sweep the ounces of gold back into
the little sack, the woman, who had become increasingly nervous
watching them disappear, grabbed Caramello by his camisole. "I
won't let anyone else touch that gold. I'll tell you all I know.
Give it to me now!" She said urgently.

Gently and very slowly, Caramello withdrew a few pieces
from the bag, and began dropping them one by one in the palm
of her hand.

"I don't recall ever being so close to gold in my entire life,"
she exclaimed, stroking the metal. She held up one to the light.
"Look at that! Their yellow glitter is simply breathtaking. Now I
can understand why pharaohs and rulers took such great
quantities to their graves. So go on and ask me anything you
want." She clutched the coins tightly; her eyes alight as if
possessed.

"Why don't you begin by telling me everything you know?"
Caramello said.

In a hushed voice but with great enthusiasm, the lady began
to relate her story.

"Almost overnight, Lombardo became obsessed with a voluptuous Iberian beauty who was then working at this very tavern. Stella and I were good friends, so most of what I know comes from her. Everything else is gossip and hearsay."

"Do they still see each other?"

"She visits the mansion every time Lombardo sends for her, which makes Stella the only person with whom he shares anything in life. Needless to say, my friend is well aware of his qualities, or perhaps I should say cruelties."

"Was he always unfaithful to his wife?"

"He chased women all his life, and had a special knack for prostitutes," the woman replied. "Following his wife's suicide, he stopped visiting brothels and began summoning them to his home instead. One day the lady he called was sick, so my friend volunteered as a substitute. The man became so captivated that from then on he never called anyone but Stella. She hated him with a passion, but with a disabled mother to support she had little choice except to continue. She claims he is an unscrupulous monster, and like her, most servants despise his despotic manners as well.

His so-called friends and supporters will continue to exist for as long as they keep benefiting from his influential connections, as I am also certain they will turn against him at the first sign of weakness. The man has more enemies than a witch."

"Has your friend ever mentioned the disappearance of a child several years ago?" Caramello asked.

"It was atrocious. No one ever found the poor creature, much less his mother. Contrary to the beliefs of many, my friend is almost certain the boy was abducted, but not killed. According to Stella, the one person who truly knew what happened that day was Lombardo's coachman, and unfortunately he died recently. Loyal to his master, he never talked to anyone about the incident."

"Did Stella and the coachman ever talk to each other?"

"Of course they did. He drove her back and forth all the time."

Caramello returned to the ship to meet with his boss and the rest of the crew, and share their exciting progress.

Back at the captain's quarters, after a long and protracted debate, Sikin decided to move forward with a plan.

"Renato and Paolo will revisit the Jewish tailor, meet his associate, and try to obtain written credentials to offer their services door to door. If successful, a visit to the Lombardo mansion should become their next priority. If allowed to enter, they should memorize the surroundings inside and out, as well as study the most effective way to break into the mansion at a given time. They should also examine Lombardo's private guard, their weapons, and all things related to personal protection. In essence, their mission will be to develop a mental picture of everything they see.

Caramello will ask the charwoman for Stella's home address, in order to offer the woman a small fortune in return for her full commitment and cooperation with our plot.

Finally, since Mariu Da Ponte, who also owns a silk filature in Sicily, has been considering a partnership for quite some time, Sikin's group will be offering Dino de la Francesca their personal services as mediators between the two. We will also extract as much information about Naguib's torturer as possible,"

Sikin massaged his brow and called it a night. He was now trying to accomplish two missions at once: justice for Naguib, and finding the boy.

* * *

Two days later Paolo and Renato, "the clothiers from Constantinople", met the tailor's ancient partner, and both wondered how the pair of feeble men with trembling hands and extremely poor vision could be so widely acclaimed for their work among the well-dressed aristocracy.

After a long discussion in which every detail was fastidiously scrutinized, the garment makers decided to let the two fashion authorities from the East solicit business on their behalf. Renato proposed they visit Gabriel Lombardo as a first attempt to prove their "new method of selling."

Lombardo, not known particularly as a neat dresser, had made concerted efforts in the past to employ the services of the old tailors. The clothiers had chosen to stay away from controversial figures, however, especially those with armed escorts whose ominous presence intimidated other clients. In view of this, Paolo proposed to visit the man in his own environment, thus avoiding an embarrassing situation at the shop.

"Why are you so interested in this man's wardrobe?" Asked Simon, the elder of the partners.

"A mutual friend, whom we've known for years, told us about his shabby dressing habits. Knowing we are in town, she asked us to contact the man and convince him to improve his public image by correcting his appearance," Paolo replied.

"As long as he pays ahead of time and doesn't show up around here with his entourage, it will be fine with us," Jacob, the littlest partner, replied.

The following morning, both "couturiers", carrying as proof of competence a hand-written scroll, visited the impenetrable residence. Their next obstacle would be convincing Lombardo's guards and his retinue of servants to persuade the wretch to welcome the tailors and listen to what they had to say.

Perched atop a hill almost bordering the city limits, the mansion looked more like a fortress than an inviting home. It was built of stone and hardwoods, with a red tile roof. The surrounding gardens were in such deplorable condition that they made the compound look vacant and neglected. A tall stone barrier encircled the mansion, which was accessible only through a narrow gate. Between the gate and the house was a stagnant pond with a couple of ducks and a swan. On the opposite shore, unusually large bougainvillea bushes offered partial shade to a couple of dilapidated wood benches. The bushes were so neglected that they had only isolated clusters of leaves and no flowers. As they approached the gate, Renato and Paulo noticed a pair of mastiffs fiercely baring their shiny fangs. They trotted toward the visitors, growling.

Following the dogs walked a man so tall and massive they wondered who would be the biggest brute, him or Naguib. The giant carried a chain with a spiked iron ball at the end and clasped to his belt, black leather sheaths holding a saber and two daggers.

The intimidating creature asked what they wanted in a sonorous voice. Upon showing him the written scroll, Paolo and Renato solicited an audience with Signore Lombardo, whereupon he took the document back inside to ask the boss for permission to open the gate.

After a long wait the creature returned, accompanied by an impeccably dressed attendant who introduced himself as Lombardo's personal penman and assistant. Satisfied after a long interrogation as to the pair's identity, background, and competence, he cleared them to enter the mansion.

"I am quite concerned with Il Signore's public image," said the neatly dressed man. "A public servant so widely admired and respected should always represent his office with the utmost dignity and style. I have tried on countless occasions to convince both of your partners to offer their services to Signore Lombardo, but they always use their busy schedule as an excuse to keep our guards from scaring customers with their presence. That, in my humble opinion is nothing but arrogance and hogwash. Those avaricious pygmies think of nothing else but money, which means little in comparison to the personal need of our public servants to portray an elegant, graceful image at all times. I don't know if Signore Lombardo will be interested in your convenient services, but I will present your proposal anyway."

"Do you mind if we follow?" Asked Renato. "I'm sure Signore Lombardo will be pleased to know that we are the official tailors to sultans and maharanis, as well as other prominent citizens in Constantinople.

Please present to your master this unique opportunity to become the most unusually and tastefully attired leader in Genoa, and quite possibly in all of Italy. Wouldn't the privilege of dressing in harmony with prevailing fashions, make your master a trendsetter rather than a follower in matters of good breeding? If it pleases you, do convey our sincerest desire to place our talents and good offices at his disposal. Unlike our partners, our mission also embodies serving our country by elevating the images of our most prominent leaders!"

"Then will you gentlemen please follow me?" The attendant gestured grandly. "I'm sure signore Lombardo will be delighted to meet you. I must say yours is such an attractive and highly evolved approach to fashion, it could very well become the trend of the future. Who knows?"

Passing through the mansion, attempting to memorize the layout, they found servants polishing floors, cleaning ceramic ornaments, and covering furniture with large white sheets.

"Please excuse the mess," said the penman. "Our master is preparing a visit to the healing springs of the North. As you have probably heard, he suffers from periods of melancholy, which are attributed to the many depressing sights of poverty and misery so evident in the city. You see, Signore Lombardo is a man with a highly sensitive sense of compassion, who carries deep within his heart the suffering of others."

"Sort of a Jesus Christ, isn't he?" Paolo mumbled with a cynical smile.

"When is he leaving?" Renato interrupted with a grin almost impossible to conceal.

"We expect to depart within seven days, depending on the rains and road conditions. Now, will you please take a seat while I tell my master you are here?"

The penman disappeared into a large chamber, from which the tailors could hear a man's deep voice arguing with the assistant. The master was clearly upset that his attendant had allowed strangers to enter the mansion without his implicit consent.

Moments later, the door slammed open aburptly, giving way to the imposing figure of a tall, obese man, sloppily dressed with a missing right ear; lost during a battle against the Pisans, they'd been told. Gabriel Lombardo's manner unmasked him as a boisterous, vulgar human being. Ironically, his assistant introduced him to Paolo and Renato as *His Excellency.*"

Lombardo's questions about the tailors's credentials sounded more like accusations of incompetence than queries regarding their knowledge and experience. While he continuously boasted about himself, his penman remained staring at the floor in a vain attempt to mask his sorry assignment as assistant to someone who, in spite of being so widely disliked, encouraged constant adulation from each and every servant as a prerequisite for employment.

"Noble deeds are a statesman's greatest legacy," he intoned. "Personal appearance, though being one of his prerogatives, stands second to everything else in his political life."

The obese man ordered Paolo and Renato to submit proof of their work such as samples or sketches, as a condition for further talks. He closed the interview by snapping his fingers, and ordering the penman to lead the peddlers out. The assistant, faking a smile of admiration for his boss's distasteful behavior, asked Renato and Paolo to follow him to the front gate, where fortunately, the mastiffs were already tied to a tree.

Feeling a deep sense of relief, the two impostors left the mansion.

"Can you imagine what would have happened had they asked for a demonstration or specific questions about our craft?" Paolo asked, roaring with laughter.

"That's why Sikin chose us for the assignment! We can cheat any nincompoop in the world after this one." Renato replied, hugging his belly to keep the laughter from hurting.

"Of something we can be certain," said Paolo after calming down. "This buffoon has absolutely no idea of what's coming to him!"

Like children surviving a prank, they roared with laughter again and again.

* * *

In the tavern by the coast, Caramello met with the lady servant once again. This time he went after Stella's address, which she didn't hesitate to provide. At once he went searching for her house in almost total darkness.

The lady answering the door was a tall, attractive woman in her late forties with lots of gray hair for her age. Caramello introduced himself and offered a brief explanation of why he had come to see her.

Stella's home consisted of a rented room in a neglected terracotta house. It was furnished with a wood stove and two small bunks filled with straw. Lying in the one was her aged mother.

Following Caramello's request for a chance to discuss a very important matter, Stella invited the visitor inside, offered him tea, and asked him to sit on her bunk, since her mother was using the other one to mitigate the symptoms of gout by keeping her legs elevated.

After comments regarding Stella's friendship with the tavern lady, Caramello began his search for information.

"Have you ever had a child?" Asked the counterfeiter.

"I can't understand why you are asking me such a personal question, but I really don't have a reason to refuse an answer either," she said. "Since I'm sure you are aware of my profession, I will try to answer every question fairly. Beyond that, I have nothing else to hide.

Due to a fever that almost carried me to the grave, my one and only pregnancy ended in miscarriage. I have been barren ever since."

"Let's suppose for a moment that you did not lose the baby," Caramello said. "Three years later someone broke into your home and kidnapped the child. You spent 12 years of your life searching for him in vain. Moreover, since there was no evidence of murder, you lived in constant and agonizing pain the rest of your life. The tragedy never ended. Your wound never healed. What would you have done?

If I knew the perpetrator, I would have emasculated the bastard. And if I happened to be that woman, I'd be devastated."

"Then you understand what it has been like for Lombardo's daughter-in-law Tiblina," Caramello said.

Stella nodded, her eyes downcast.

"Sounds as Lombardo is implicated. What if he doesn't talk?" asked Stella doubtfully.

"Don't worry, we'll make him squeal one way or the other." Caramello said scattering a few diamonds across her ragged bed.

Mindful of the display, he continued:

"I came to make you an offer. If you accept it, these gems will be yours forever. Their value will allow you and your mother to live the rest of your lives without financial worries of any kind, and most important, you should not have to work in your 'profession' ever again."

Stella's eyes widened.

"Furthermore, as a complement to my proposal, we propose to move the two of you to another country on our ship, which is now anchored at the mouth of the bay. If you wish, you and your mother will sail with us to a foreign city where no one is aware of your past. You'll have an opportunity to begin a new life without shame or guilt. You will be able to move into a decent dwelling with the comforts any hard-working person deserves, and better yet, you will never have to face that monster again."

"What do you want me to do?" asked Stella.

"You must try to see Lombardo within the next two or three days," Caramello replied. "If he asks why, tell him you feel somewhat depressed and need his company, or for that matter say anything that will get the two of you inside the bedchamber. You must also tell Carlo Lombardo's answer. Carlo is the youngest of our associates, and he will be sharing this room until you blow the whistle.

"Being a fast runner, Carlo will relay your message to us in no time. Then, while part of our group goes to the mansion, Carlo will return to take your mother and personal belongings aboard the ship, where she will remain until everyone is back and we set sail down the coast."

"What if Lombardo finds out there is another man living in my room?" Stella asked, alarmed. "He has spies everywhere, you know."

"Just say a distant cousin came to visit your mother. Also tell him he is a homosexual."

Stella frowned thoughtfully. "Please continue."

"When the time arrives, Caramello said, four of our men will be waiting for you outside Lombardo's mansion. Enter as you always have, and tell him you are dying to go to his bedchamber. Lead him there playfully. We will give you ten minutes and then break in! My boss will take care of Lombardo, our giant friend will turn his humongous guardian to rubbish, and the other will be keeping Lombardo's guards from entering the chamber. You'll have plenty of time to escape before the fight gets nasty. In fact, we will let you know ahead of time when and where to go."

After pausing for a moment, Caramello asked confidently what she thought of the proposal.

"Only a fool would reject it, and believe me, I am everything but that. Count me in!" Stella replied excitedly.

"Your boss is not far off in his appraisal of that miserable creature. You fellows have no idea of what I have to go through in order to survive the brute. The man is capable of anything!

I wish I knew more about the little boy but frankly, even his trusted coachman refused to talk about the incident."

* * *

Sikin and Naguib headed for the guild to visit Dino de la Francesca.

After passing the steward's interrogation, they located Dino, who was pleasantly surprised to see them.

Following a lengthy conversation about topics enjoyed by both men, Sikin mentioned the possibility of a partnership in a silk filature near Sicily. He identified his faithful confidante Signorina Da Ponte as half owner of that business and relayed a short history of the operation. Dino became so interested in the idea that he even asked Sikin for Mariu's address in Venice.

"I'll be sending her a message," Sikin said. "Perhaps this will be an excellent investment opportunity for both of you!"

Sikin then asked his new acquaintance to wait a couple of

months before contacting the lady, saying she would be out of the city during that period of time. Otherwise, Sikin thought, he will be letting everyone in Mariu's household, including Tiblina, become aware of what was happening in Genoa, and he thought it would be prudent to keep Tiblina away from the action until positive news of her son's fate could be verified.

Pretending to be indifferent, Sikin inquired "just out of curiosity" about the red-haired man they had seen at the guild a few days before, mentioning his features resembled those of a distant relative living in Constantinople.

"The man's name is Leif," Dino replied. "His parents emigrated from a Nordic country, but the fellow you saw is Genoan by birth."

"What kind of a person is he?" Asked Sikin, as Naguib became increasingly nervous.

"He is a strange character who hangs around the guild every afternoon past sunset. Sometimes he disappears just as mysteriously as he shows up. However, he is almost always here after dark. According to credible sources, merchants involved in the white slave trade and in the contraband of weapons from Venice to Genoa hired him years ago to eliminate and punish adversaries. Supposedly he has saved enough money to trade on his own."

Dino shrugged. "Leif rarely talks to anyone, yet he carefully watches the movements of everybody around here. No one is afraid of him, but the man makes us feel uncomfortable in his presence. He obviously has a dark history, but here at the Guild we refrain from asking personal questions unless they are business related."

Then Dino shook a warning finger at Sikin. "I advise you to refrain from doing business with that one, my friend. Hundreds of Venetians, who crossed to Genoan territory in search of trade, were tortured and murdered by the man. He was also known to be responsible for abducting adolescents from Venetian orphanages and selling them for sexual exploitation and slavery somewhere else. That was his latest boss's most lucrative business."

"How could he get away with such crimes?" Sikin asked.

"His hatred against Venetians; a trait powerful enough to guarantee the safety of any criminal in this country. The politicians protect him. Sickening, isn't it?" Dino replied.

"Now he has enough tainted money to clean up his reputation and invest just like any reputable merchant would, and as long as his center of operations remains in Genoa, no one will confront or accuse him of wrongdoing. Yet, the man has more enemies than red in his head."

Dino frowned. "Being friendly toward monsters like Leif for the sake of trade has always being a part of my business, and believe me I've hated it! This is one of the reasons I jumped at your proposal the way I did."

"Suppose he ends up in Venice someday?" What do you think his fate would be?" Sikin asked idly.

"I'm sure he'd be severely punished once they identified him," Dino answered. "I certainly hope he is not the relative you thought he was."

"Certainly not!" Sikin responded.

* * *

Although Sikin had not seen a single sign of dubious behavior from anyone in the group, he stayed on the lookout for any form of dissention or misconduct. He found himself pleasantly surprised and encouraged by the men's attitudes towards him and his mission. Perhaps they were not as bad as he thought!

His meeting with Renato and Paolo became a revelation in its own right. He remained stupefied listening to their description of Lombardo, his qualities, and the pond in the front of the house, the swans, the bougainvillea bushes, and the amazing final element, his missing right ear.

Utterly amazed, he recalled the nightmare in which Grandfather McKinley had grabbed little Ivan by his throat, ordering him to be quiet. Then a pond, a swan, and ultimately, Grandpa's missing right ear. Flabbergasted, Sikin realized his dream had been in fact a revelation from the Otherworld, a divine manifestation from a mysterious realm that convinced him even more about the noble purpose of his mission.

That same evening, inside the captain's quarters, Sikin held his final meeting with the group. The time for action had arrived!

"Here's my proposed strategy," he said.

"Our fake tailors will draw a detailed sketch of the mansion and its surroundings right away. As soon as Carlo arrives with Stella's 'go ahead' message, Paolo and Caramello will accompany Naguib and I to the mansion, break in, and get hold of Lombardo.

Carlo will return to Stella's home to bring her mother and their belongings back to the ship. Being the strongest, Renato will watch for Leif on the outskirts of the guild. When the red-haired merchant appears he will bring him back to the ship using his own tactics. He will then become a prisoner until our arrival in Venice, at which time he will be released to the proper authorities for punishment.

Once we are all on board, Naguib will take command of the vessel, sail south to the tip of the peninsula, and then North to Venice, making sure the ship's name and flag are changed back to their original standing.

Immediately following our arrival in Venice, a message shall be sent to the Elban merchant who loaned us the ship, asking him to send a few trusted sailors to take his vessel back.

Paolo suggested they create an emergency plan in the event something went wrong. Sikin suggested they use Carlo to relay information between the two teams, thus providing an excellent method to work in harmony with each other.

"As a last resource," Sikin added, "and in the event one or both missions fail, we should all return to the ship immediately to devise another plan for a later date. Under no circumstance we should divide ourselves. That will be disastrous to both undertakings. Regardless of the outcome of our assignments, we should strive to regroup and stay together.

It amazes me that this long-awaited opportunity to do justice depends entirely on the good will of a stranger, Stella. Yet we must also realize that fate works in paradoxical ways, and ultimately our faith in the wisdom and power of the Almighty, and the conviction that sooner or later good shall prevail over evil, will become the unchanging elements that keep us aiming at a just and final victory. Let's have faith in ourselves and in the goodness of our mission. Allow your conscience to overflow with that feeling of peace and harmony that can only be achieved by consecrating our energies to noble ideals. This, my friends, is the essence of what fulfillment is all about."

After a couple of days with no news from Stella, Sikin and his crew began to grow anxious. Two sedentary days with nothing to do but wait and worry about why Lombardo was ignoring Stella before leaving town was enough to drive them crazy.

"Perhaps they had a fight!" Renato said worriedly.

"If they did, don't you think Carlo would have let us know by now?" Caramello replied. "Besides, do you really believe Stella would let an argument interfere with our plan? I'm sure she'd do anything to see the mission succeed."

Tired of listening to worrisome talk, Paolo walked toward the stanchions, and leaning his elbows against the handrail, the short man stood contemplating the sunset reflection in the calm waters. Moments later, he spotted the blurred image of a skiff approaching *Il Genovese*.

"He's coming," Paolo yelled. "Carlo is on his way to the ship!"

"Gentlemen," Carlo began, gasping for air. "I'm sorry about the delay. Stella wanted to wait for two of Lombardo's bodyguards to leave for the springs north of town. She thought the confrontation would be easier for us with less resistance. The only remaining guard now is Rocco, the big man with metal teeth. I have now delivered Stella's message to Lombardo, who wants to see her this evening before midnight."

"Did you say metal teeth?" Asked Sikin.

"Yes, boss. According to her, he lost his own in a big fight, so Lombardo implanted some sort of metal blades that look like teeth, which he uses to bite into his opponent's throat, bleeding them to death."

Naguib, who had remained silent all day, replied angrily, "Naguib more powerful. Naguib shatters teeth."

"Return to Stella's house immediately," Sikin told Carlo, "and bring her mother and belongings to the ship. Ask any cart driver in town for help carrying the old woman and the load across the city. Also, on your way over, stop by the tavern and inform the charwoman that her friend Stella will be stopping by the establishment sometime between midnight and daybreak. Ask the lady to make arrangements to bring her aboard our ship as soon as she gets there. Tell her that this is a matter of life and death to her friend. But don't say anything else! Remember, you are only a messenger."

Sikin and his team of three left for Lombardo's house early that evening. Hiding behind the bushes across from the front gate, they'll explore different ways to break into the mansion.

"Paolo," said Sikin, "when I give you the signal, go sit atop the stone fence and try to irritate the dogs and make them bark. This will hopefully bring someone out to check what's going on. At that time, back off to create the impression that the dogs were barking at a cat or at something inoffensive. After the person returns to the mansion, continue pulling the same trick over and over until no one comes out anymore. Then, throw some pieces of dried meat as close to the stone barrier as possible. On your signal Caramello and I will jump over the fence, muzzle and tie up the mastiffs while they eat their evening snack. And for goodness sake, don't hesitate to jump over and help us if necessary."

He turned to Caramello. "Try to remember from the drawings where the chimney leading to the hearthstone in the reception room is."

"See that square shadow over the left side of the roof? That's the one!" The bald contortionist answered.

"Right after Stella makes her way inside the house, you will climb to the roof and go down the chimney to the hearthstone. Then, go to the front door and open it. If for any reason this is not possible, come back right away, and we'll plan another strategy to enter the house unnoticed. Make sure the chimney openings are wide enough to go through and climb back out without getting stuck in the process and that there's no fire going on. Understood?"

"Yes, boss," Caramello replied. "I'll tie a rope to the flue and start my descent. If I detect a serious obstacle, I'll climb back to the roof and come back to you guys."

Following Paolo's prank, a person came out of the house to check on the restless mastiffs. The man was no other than Lombardo's penman, which walked toward the area the barking was coming from. Standing on a rock, he looked carefully across the fence, finding nothing alarming or unusual. Paolo repeated the trick three more times; no one came out for the last two.

The plan to restrain the animals worked out without a glitch, and the four men returned to the mosquito-infested bushes to wait for Stella.

Finally they heard the unmistakable sounds of a person walking toward the gate, and then ringing the bell for someone to come out.

Almost immediately, a uniformed servant approached the entrance, and without asking questions or even greeting the visitor, he allowed the caller to enter. As both were walking toward the mansion's front door, the dim light of the servant's oil lamp gave away the vague silhouette of a woman walking by his side.

"Caramello, go ahead and do your part!" Sikin whispered. "We'll be waiting for your signal."

The contortionist approached the fence, jumped to the other side, and climbed up the roof as nimbly as a cat. Then...silence. Absolute silence. Not even the screeching crickets were singing that night.

Suddenly Sikin and Naguib heard the sound of a soft whistle coming from the open front door. They recognized Caramello's signal but the bald man was so covered with soot, he was virtually invisible in the dark.

Slowly and quietly they entered the mansion. Sikin raised his eyes to a large loft about fifty feet away from the entrance, where the poor lighting revealed the shadow of a huge man standing with his arms crossed.

"It's Rocco, guarding Lombardo's chamber," Sikin whispered to Naguib. "All right, my friend, now it's your turn."

It being almost impossible for the giant to climb the short set of stairs leading to the loft unnoticed, he resorted to another trick.

Standing beneath the loft, Naguib threw a glass vase against the wall, prompting Rocco to lean over the banister to look for the source of the clatter. He held the rusty saber in his right hand, ready to chop someone to pieces.

Just as the giant with crushing bronze teeth was bending over, Naguib leaped almost to the top of the banister above, and grabbing Rocco by his head and ears, pulled him down to the ground floor along with ten feet of shattered balustrade. The thunderous crash sounded as if the mansion was crumbling to pieces.

Naguib stuffed his opponent's mouth with a large chunk of oakum he'd brought along from his previous job at the shipyards, and lifting the brute by the waist, he hurled him head on against the hardwood floor. Seizing the man by his head again, he pounded it several times.

Rocco groaned, stunned, but then let forth a bone-chilling growl.

In an instant Naguib whipped a dagger from his sash, and pressing its sharp point against Rocco's throat, he cut enough flesh to make him bleed. Leaning close to his opponent's ear the giant whispered, "Rocco moves, Naguib bites ear. Rocco fights, Naguib cuts throat. Rocco wants life, Rocco be like baby."

Rocco moaned and squeaked with fear, suddenly as passive as a mouse. Caramello and Paolo tied up the huge, whimpering man against the pillars supporting the loft, making sure the cowardly brute was completely immobilized.

The tumult had prompted Lombardo to open his chamber door and venture into the hall. Sikin, who was waiting outside the threshold leading to the bedchamber, jumped the heavy-set man, and locking the right elbow behind his back, he pointed a knife against his throat. "Open your mouth and you are a dead man," he hissed. "Now tell me! Where is Stella?"

Lombardo signaled with a head motion, and Sikin, followed by the others, pushed the man back inside the bedroom.

"Stella!" Sikin shouts. "Go!"

Naguib towered over the quaking Lombardo, who shivered in his nightshirt.

After Stella left the room, Sikin ordered Naguib to stand outside the door and make sure no one else entered. Also following instructions, Caramello and Paolo, bound Lombardo to a chair, filled his mouth with oakum, and tied a hangman's noose around his neck.

Drawing out his dagger, Sikin approached the restrained man, and piercing the top of his earlobe with its sharp edge, said in a firm, menacing voice, "You are going to cooperate with us. You will answer every question and behave like a civilized boy, or I'll cut off your other ear. If anything goes wrong, we'll hang you from that beam in the ceiling, and *poof!* Before you know it, His Excellency will be meeting the little boy he murdered years ago. By the time your corpse begins to turn purple, this mansion will be engulfed along with your body, in the wildest fire seen in Genoa since the last battle against the Pisans. Got it?"

Lombardo wiggled his head, petrified.

"Paolo, show him the pitch!" Sikin turned to his prisoner. "Do you find its odor familiar? We use it in Venice to set witches and sorcerers on fire, just like you intended to do to the child's mother. Now that you know how awful your fate might be, tell us in a gentle voice whether you are willing to cooperate." He yanked the stuffing out of Lombardo's mouth.

"I will," the man answered reluctantly.

"Then begin by telling us what happened to your grandson."

"The boy wasn't my legitimate grandson," Lombardo answered in a determined voice. "He was conceived inside that witch by the Devil himself, and I was afraid the little demon would eventually destroy me in the same way his mother did my son Tirso. So I had him killed," he concluded without visible remorse.

"Who did the killing besides you?"

"I paid the coachman to take the boy to the countryside and burn him at the stake, just like we do to sorcerers and witches around here. Being the most loyal of all the servants, I knew he'd do anything for me, and much more for a hundred ounces of gold."

"Naguib!" Sikin shouted.

The giant appeared at once.

"Rip that portrait of our friend off the wall and bring me the canvas. Then cut off his other ear and pour the blood into that cup."

Obediently, the giant followed his master's orders as proficiently as any good executioner would, leaving Lombardo screaming in pain.

Sikin dipped his index finger in the blood, and then wrote on the back of the canvas, *I murdered my own blood. I killed my grandson.*

"Caramello, take off his clothes and wrap him up in the canvas. Just make sure the bloody sign shows well."

Caramello grinned and began his task.

"Naguib, go to the barn and get a cart or something we can use to take this man to the council and hang him from the tallest tree in front. That will tell his cronies who their influential friend really was."

He turned to the prisoner, who had turned white with terror.

"Do you imagine how many of your adulating buddies will enjoy seeing you tried and executed for murder? Just think about the excitement all over town! Everyone screaming at the top of his or her lungs; 'Kill the scoundrel!' The city's prostitutes will be throwing rocks at you. And before you know it, His Illustrious Eminence, after being humiliated by his peers, will pass on to the next life wearing nothing but a stigma. Right on time to meet the Devil! Or, like you said before, the true father of the child."

Lombardo tried to speak, desperately shaking his head, but

could only make a feeble gurgling noise.

"Paolo, spread the pitch over the bed and drapes. As soon as Caramello and I cross the threshold with this man, set the whole place on fire."

"No Signore, no!" Someone began to pound at the bedroom door.

Caramello opened it to find an elderly lady servant crying, begging them on her knees not to set the house on fire.

"Signore, please don't destroy what has been my home for over fifty years," she wailed. "I know the truth, the only truth." The distressed old lady said.

"Tell us Signora," Sikin said kindly. "Be quick though. We don't have all night"

"Signore Lombardo handed the child to the coachman," she babbled. "But after finding out what they were up to, I decided to follow the coach and do everything I could to prevent this horrible murder from happening.

While driving the coach through the countryside, following his master's instructions, the old coachman secretly stopped at a hut where a relative of his lived. I found out she was his older sister. The woman held the child in her arms, and the three went inside. Moments later I heard the loud squealing of a pig being killed. I drew close to a window and watched the old man enter the hut through the rear door, carrying a piece of hide from the animal. By then, the lady had the little boy's head completely shaved. She had cut off his curly hair and was handing it to the coachman in a small bundle. He took it to the stove along with the pig's skin, slowly charring both to the point of making it unrecognizable.

He stuffed the sick blend inside a bag, went back to the coach, and returned to the mansion.

The coachman never knew I followed him, and I never said a word about what I had seen to anyone. Otherwise, the master would have pursued and killed the boy himself. Signore, this is why I have kept silent up to this moment. I have been praying for the little boy ever since.

I admit the coachman was his master's trusted confidant. But he was a noble and decent man. The master thought he could buy his soul, but he miscalculated the man's character. The coachman not only saved the boy, but made a fool out of Lombardo as well. I'm telling you the truth, Signore! Please don't set the house on fire. You must believe my word!"

"That bastard! That hypocritical wretch!" Lombardo shouted in agony. "He cheated me, and I believed it! He took my gold. My hundred ounces! I should have finished the job myself instead of trusting the coward."

"Good Lady," Sikin said, interrupting the frenzied man. "Please tell me something else. Did the little boy have any markings or unusual spots on his body that could help us recognize him after almost fifteen years?"

"He had curly hair, a dimple in his chin, and his mother's irresistible aqua-colored eyes," she answered.

"Signora, please try to remember. Was there anything else?"

The old lady squinted. "His father Tirso, a sculptor and carver by trade, gave the boy for his third birthday a miniature figurine of the infant Jesus to carry as a good luck charm. The piece was left behind when they took him, and I kept it as a memento ever since. Maybe he would remember it."

"Signora, what if I tell you his mother is alive, and that I am doing this search on her behalf? Will you let me borrow the little statue? It might become indispensable once the boy is found. I'll make sure you get it back. I also need to know where the coachman's sister lives. And of course, Signora, I will not burn down the house. You have my word!"

On leaving town, the lady servant said, "follow the road to the North, where you'll find a river. After crossing the bridge you will come across a narrow path that leads to the right. Walk this trail until you find a clearing with a holding and three huts. Hers is the one on the right."

After telling the good lady how much he appreciated her support, Sikin asked Caramello and Paolo to carry Lombardo to the cart Naguib had taken from the barn.

The lady disappeared momentarily, returning with the tiny sculpture. Holding it in the palm of her hands, she kissed it, and then handed it to Sikin, who patted her shoulder as a sign of gratitude and admiration for her courage. He slipped her several gold coins. Then he left the house to join Naguib and the others.

"Take this humiliating wrapping off my body! You are accusing me of a crime I didn't commit. I didn't murder the boy. I am innocent!" Lombardo yelled at the top of his lungs.

"That is precisely the point," Sikin replied. "Why don't you try to persuade those who know you as a scoundrel? Convince them you did not kill the child. Tell them he is alive. Tell them where the boy is; or better yet, invite the young man to your arraignment! Otherwise you might have to ask the coachman to return from the grave to attend your trial as a key witness. That, and only that, will get you off the hook. They won't believe your lady servant, of course. As a witness, her story would sound so ridiculously contrived they might suspect you are also paying her off."

"I'll make sure you miserable creatures pay for this outrage!" Lombardo screamed. "I'll have you executed for intimidating and abusing a member of the council. I'll make sure you pay for this audacity with your own lives!"

Naguib, who couldn't stand listening to his cursing and yelling anymore, stuffed his mouth with a handful of oakum leftovers.

It was early dawn when they finally reached the magnificent tree in front of the Council building. Carrying Lombardo on their backs, Paolo and Caramello climbed up and tied his hands and feet to the tallest branch, making sure the sign was readable from below.

Their assignment finished, the four rode in the cart all the way back to the coast.

* * *

Back at the ship, Renato prepared to visit the guild. In order to credibly present himself, he searched inside the captain's trunk for formal outfits to wear, and after finding a wide array of garments worn by mariners during official ceremonies; Renato tried one that fit him like a glove. The gypsy portrayed a uniformed officer with all kinds of decorations.

Renato thought it would be a good idea to take along some sort of wheeled vehicle, a large woolen blanket, and rope, to haul Leif back to the ship.

Off he went to the guild, armed with a wheelbarrow, fake identity, and wearing a garment that looked somewhat outdated and out of place.

After requesting permission to enter the trade association, the steward asked for identification of some sort, saying stiffly that the guild did not admit anyone except for active tradesmen, not mariners.

"May I suggest you find signore Leif, whom I came to invite on behalf of my master, Sikin of Savez, the Magnificent?" Renato said to the steward after detailing the purpose of his visit.

The steward, not knowing who in the world the magnificent man was, became so impressed with Renato's introduction, mannerisms, and exotic accent, that he went to fetch the red-haired man, who came almost immediately to meet Sikin's emissary.

"Signore Leif," said the steward. "This officer is here to invite you in behalf of his *magnificent master* to a banquet honoring some of the most influential persons in the city, including Gabriel Lombardo."

"And may I ask why your master is so interested in inviting me to his banquet?" Asked the red-haired merchant.

"My master is actively looking for partners of different vocations to participate in what could very well become highly lucrative plots," answered Renato. "Being well aware of your multiple experiences and attributes, as well as your willingness to take calculated risks His Excellency decided to include you on his list of prominent guests."

Following a barrage of questions regarding moneymaking opportunities in Eastern countries, Leif's incurable greed led him to accept Renato's ridiculous invitation.

After walking and talking amiably for a couple of blocks, Renato jumped the man, gagged him and immobilized him with the blanket. He dumped his tightly wrapped body in the wheelbarrow, and then covered it with grass to simulate animal feed.

After wheeling his cargo merrily to the vessel, Renato unwrapped the bundle and showed his human trophy to Naguib and the others.

While the giant couldn't take his eyes off his former torturer, Leif remained cold and indifferent.

The ship began to acquire a festive atmosphere. Stella and her mother had prepared food for the crew, which had grown from five to eight, including the coming prisoner.

Finally the noisy group ended their revelry for a few hours' sleep.

The next morning, after an early breakfast prepared by the ladies and devoured by everyone except the prisoner, Sikin addressed the group from the top of the stairs leading to the poop deck.

"My friends," he said.

"This incredible accomplishment wouldn't have been possible without your faithful participation as individuals and as a team. I'd like to express my heartfelt gratitude for your allegiance to the mission. Your gallant performance has left me virtually speechless. Your faith in each other has exceeded my wildest expectations, and your confidence in my judgement has made all of you worthy of my trust and respect.

Now more than ever, I am fully convinced that Tiblina's son, young Sikin, is alive somewhere. I cannot rest until my mission is successfully concluded. I am sure this decision will come as a shock, but tomorrow, you will be sailing the ship back to La Serenissima under Naguib's command, while I stay behind to complete the rest of the quest on my own."

He pulled a letter from his shirt.

"Paolo, I'd like you to deliver this envelope to Mariu. Inside, is a letter asking her to pay the promised amounts, plus an additional bonus to each and every one of you for such an unparalleled achievement.

Please familiarize her with the highlights surrounding our

successfully completed plan and ask for her cooperation in helping Stella and her mother settle in the city, as well as making sure they obtain proof of identity from the Venetian government. Remember to meet Mariu only in private. The decision of whether to make our story known to the child's mother shall be entirely her own.

I hope this mission has not only served the purpose for which it was intended, but has also brought a sense of justice and commitment into your lives, as well as the opportunity to ascertain your hidden capacity to do good. Paradoxically, even the most wicked of qualities, when applied to a good cause, can suddenly acquire a redeeming character.

Naguib, I trust you will return the ship to the superstitious merchant from Isola d'Elba who loaned it. Please send him a message of appreciation, explaining briefly the purpose for which it was used. Also ask him to send enough men to sail the vessel back to his country. Remember to include a note signed by Caramello declaring the curse has been vanquished. He grinned.

I sincerely hope your newly earned fortunes will exert the natural sedating effect needed to restrain your pursuit of wealth at any cost, hopefully turning the reckless and insensitive ways of your past into more responsible and ethical ones in the future. Whenever I return to Venice, my friends, I shall expect to find all of you involved in elevating and worthwhile endeavors. I ask you to pray every single day for the success of the mission, and to express your gratitude for being chosen to participate. May our Lord always keep you in the palm of His Hand"

Following his admonition, Sikin stepped down to the lower deck and asked for a launch and a volunteer to take him ashore.

The launch was soon lowered with Sikin and Carlo inside, with all on deck watching sadly as their former boss disappeared into the fog.

After running ashore, Carlo picked up his boss's duffel bag, handed it to him, and with a warm embrace, both said good-bye.

At well past noon, Sikin was walking the town in search of an inn where he could spend the night, when he noticed a large stable offering horses for sale.

"What kind of horse are you looking for and what's the maximum price you are willing to pay?" Asked the proprietor, a stocky man with a bushy beard.

"I'd like to buy a healthy, relatively young horse that could be taken to the ends of the earth if necessary. Don't worry about the price. Just try to find me a hearty, dependable animal."

"Wait here," said the man. I'll show you several."

As soon as the man entered the stable, a boy of about fourteen, who had been listening nearby, tapped Sikin on his shoulder.

"Signore, don't waste your time waiting for him," he said eagerly. "My father raises the best horses in Genoa. He sells most of them to the military big wigs. This man is nothing but a cheat. He feeds some of his animals a daily potion that gives them great energy, but as soon as they stop taking the stuff, the poor creatures become stupid and lethargic. Then, if a deceived buyer returns complaining, his answer is always, 'that kind of horse was the best you could get for the money. Besides, you were not supposed to over-exert him the way you did. If you want a good animal that can endure treatment like that, you'll have to pay a much higher price.' Usually the client will pitch in more money to buy the one he should have gotten in the first place."

Weighing the potential for dishonesty between the hairy man and the boy, Sikin decided to leave the stables and follow the young man to his father's horse farm.

After a long walk during which the young man talked of nothing but horses, they arrived at the stables, where a slender man was brushing the most beautiful Arabian that side of the Mediterranean. He had the color and sparkle of a full moon, widely set, large eyes, a long graceful neck, and a short back. The horse carried his tail with distinction and elegance, and his bright, lustrous mane along with his shiny coat, added to his refined appearance. His legs were as strong as steeples, and although his height wasn't great, his posture denoted one of the most handsome breeds in existence at the time.

The boy explained to his father that Il Signore wanted to buy the best horse in the world, so he had brought him to see Cicerone.

"Son, you know he is not for sale," the farmer said.

"But Papa, he is willing to pay any price for the right horse, and you said we need a new roof for our house!"

The man smiled apologetically at Sikin.

"You know how proud of Cicerone we all are, son. Besides, not everything in life is for sale. If your friend wants to buy a horse, he is looking at the wrong animal."

The boy asked permission to show the horse's strong and wide crowned teeth, which were as white as the animal itself. "You must also look at his coat, Signore!" He exclaimed stroking the animal lovingly. "Those are the best signs to determine their health and how old they are."

Like a child contemplating that toy he always wished to have and couldn't, Sikin walked around the animal several times, touching his shiny coat, padding him on the rump, and examining every feature. The more he scrutinized the beast, the closer he came to begging. He took a short stroll around the stable to cool off his head, but instead, he searched for a need and pretexts to buy it, realizing that another such opportunity will never present itself again.

The longer Sikin reflected on the possibilities, the more he wanted the horse, and the harder he tried to justify owning one, and the higher the price he was willing to offer. Finally, after stifling his own will to resist temptation, Sikin went after the boy and the farmer, who were working on another horse behind the stable.

"Signore!" He showed the farmer an emerald so bright it seemed to bear a light of its own.

"What is that?" The man asked.

"A precious stone," Sikin replied. "Have you ever seen one as beautiful?" He dropped the gem in the palm of the stunned farmer's hand.

"I have never seen anything so full of beauty and color. What would it take for a person like me to own one?" The boy's father asked.

"Only you can answer that question. I'm sure your wife has never seen anything like it either, so if you promise to bring it back, take it and show it to her."

Without removing his eyes from it, the man ran inside the house.

After a while, the farmer and his wife returned to the spot where Sikin and the boy were carrying on another lively conversation about horses.

"Signore, may I ask how much a stone like this is worth? I'd love for her to have one some day, but we don't have much to spend on luxuries."

The farmer's wife rested her arm around the farmer's shoulders, leaned her head against his neck, and with eyes transfixed on the stone, whispered in a warm, subtle voice,

"Darling, owning something that beautiful will make me the happiest woman on earth."

Staring at each other in resignation, the middle-aged couple tried to find a solution to their longing for the precious stone. With his will thus obliterated, the farmer decided to offer Cicerone in exchange for the emerald, which made Sikin's eyes sparkle like those of a young boy getting away with his most capricious desire.

"Forgive me for making an offer which might sound ridiculously low, and perhaps offensive, but please understand we know absolutely nothing about precious stones or their value," said the farmer.

"I don't know the value of this horse either," Sikin replied, "nor about the breed."

With their common sense obliterated, the men closed the deal. At the end however, the boy shook his head, muttering that his idea had just backfired. First, they lost their horse, second he would continue to sleep under a leaky roof; third, his father got nothing from the arrangement; and lastly, the only one gaining something was his mother, and it was nothing but a green rock. But the adults ignored him, happy with their deal.

Before attempting to ride the horse, Sikin asked the farmer

about his training, how he came to own the animal, and so on.

"As far as training is concerned," the farmer replied. "I have always used my own methods. By talking to him often, especially when brushing his mane, the horse learned little by little to recognize and trust me as his new master. Refusing to use force and much less a whip, I always tried persuasion, patience, and perseverance instead. I never failed to caress his neck whenever he did something right.

After some time, Cicerone followed me everywhere. I continued his training on a regular basis to the point where the horse looked forward to his workout every single day. Then, I began to teach him riding manners and obedience.

Please try to be consistent and gentle," the farmer continued. "Don't push him beyond his limits, and for God's sake, don't abuse the animal! If you treat him with affection he will pay you back tenfold. Keep in mind that love conquers everything. Cicerone is a very smart Arabian and eventually, the horse will see you as his loving master."

Later that day, with his new friend under the saddle, Sikin trotted toward the meadow where the coachman's sister lived, and after spending the night somewhere along the way, he woke up the following morning in a region so desolate that thorny scrubs were the only visible form of life. By morning Sikin caressed the horse's neck in appreciation for staying with him all night and in virtually no time both were on their way to the settlement.

He tied the animal securely to a log, and then walked toward a tiny shelter where dozens of cats and dogs were roaming around freely. He knocked at the front door a couple of times, and a feeble voice from within asked him to enter.

Darkness and filth were the most predominant features inside the room, darkness due to soiled walls and ceilings, filth from pigs living indoors.

Partially disabled from disease, the lady of the house excused herself for not standing up. The frail, toothless woman was dressed in rags, and her hair was so dirty, it resembled a wig made of bleached jute strands. As the pigs rooted in a corner, she stroked a white Himalayan cat sitting on her lap.

"Young man," she said. "Please blow the dust from that chair and sit down. You are my first guest in a long, long time. Would you be kind enough to tell me the reason for such an honor?"

Sikin, who very delicately declined to dust the chair and sit, explained his mission.

The woman paid close attention to what he had to say, then asked suspiciously if he was by chance one of Lombardo's henchmen coming after her fortune.

"Signora, let me put your mind at ease," Sikin answered, wondering what possible fortune could be hidden in such squalor.

"That criminal is locked up inside a damp, dark, dungeon where he will undoubtedly be spending a great deal of time. You have no reason to fear."

The old woman wouldn't stop scrutinizing Sikin from head to toes, and after deciding that he bore no ill intentions, she related her side of the story.

"The little boy, who we named Sakheem in order to conceal his real name, was staying under my protection until one rainy morning, two itinerant monks from the Penitent order knocked at my door to buy some food. I asked them in, not just for humane reasons, but also because they offered to pay for it. Shortly thereafter, as I was bringing the broth to boil, they noticed the little boy playing with my cat. You should know signore that during those days my house was sparkling clean inside and out." The woman shook her head sadly.

"They soon wondered why an older woman living alone and isolated, would keep a child under her care. I wasn't sure what to answer, but since they conveyed an authentic and virtuous image, and the boy's life was in imminent danger, I decided to tell them the whole truth about Sakheem, emphasizing the possibility he could be kidnapped or murdered if he stayed around much longer. After a long discussion they called the child over and asked him to accompany them to their hermitage, where he could spend a great deal of time playing with their animals, and also learn much about the world around him. They also promised a small pony if he went along. The boy, who hadn't laughed once since the day he arrived, smiled broadly at the monks, and then gazed at me for approval. I gave Sakheem a hug, and a kiss, and told him he was free to leave."

"What was the boy like?" Asked Sikin.

"The child wasn't afraid of anything or anyone. If he saw a pond and wanted to jump in, he'd go ahead and do it! Never feared snakes, bugs, darkness, or whatever. Hence the reason he was ready to join the first people to offer a little adventure." The woman smiled sweetly at her memories. "On the other hand, he was a most loving and polite little boy, perhaps too smart for his age. He missed his mother constantly, especially every night at bedtime and every morning upon awakening. Not a single day passed by without his asking when he would see her again, and the reasons she had forgotten him. I comforted the child with all kinds of explanations, though I never lied. Somehow he was certain she would find him someday."

"What happened then?" Sikin asked.

"After spending the night indoors, Sakheem and the monks left early the following morning, the hermits on foot and the boy riding an ass already overburdened with wares. That, Signore, was the last time I saw him."

"Do you remember which Penitent order they belonged to?"

"I was so nervous that I forgot to ask." The lady answered apologetically.

In appreciation for her help, Sikin offered the lady a gem she refused to accept, because, as she said, it was her moral duty to cooperate. Then she reached for a wooden coffer the size of a breadbox and opened it to reveal perhaps the most exquisite collection of jewels West of Persia.

"You see son," she cackled, "I might look indigent, but I am very wealthy. I'm showing you these gems because I detect an air of dignity and honesty in your character. If you ever find Sakheem, please tell him I have enough wealth to take care of my needs for the next hundred years, so he should not worry."

"What do you do with all those jewels?" Sikin asked

wonderingly.

"Enjoy their company," she replied. "Whenever I open the coffer, I take out the pieces one by one and lay them on the floor in front of me. Then, I begin to imagine the many comforts and luxuries I could otherwise be enjoying by converting them into paper money. At that moment and without fail, an overwhelming sense of insecurity compels me to save them for a more meaningful purpose; that of protecting my person against the scourge of abject poverty."

At Sikin's bewildered look, she continued. "You see, son, this treasure offers me immunity against life's unpredictable changes. It allows this old woman to savor that unique sense of confidence and distinction nothing else in the world is capable of providing. Likewise it allows me to fulfill my own destiny without depending on personal favors. If I choose to live in squalor and indigence, it is my own decision, and not due to circumstances beyond my control.

Finally their inner beauty makes me feel attractive and desirable once again. Those gems will never abandon me because of ugliness or stench, consider my person inferior, or take care of my needs unwillingly. They resurrect my spirit like no magic potion or miracle ever would."

She paused. "Now do you see, son? Being older and wiser has compelled me to become pragmatic about life, and more skeptical about the human condition. I have come to value our race, as well as those jewels, in a completely different light than before. For example, I learned to appreciate the company of animals *and* children more than ever, since they bestow on me a sincere, unconditional love, without surreptitious motives for personal gain. If these creatures come to me, it's just because they want to, not because they need to. These jewels make me feel safe and powerful enough to accomplish anything I want. Therefore, I decided to save them in order to preserve for as long as I live that reassuring feeling of everlasting invulnerability."

"Aren't you afraid some criminal might come in and wipe you out? What then?" Asked Sikin.

The old woman shrugged. "After so many years of existence,

I have become a firm believer in human fate in the same way those Muhammedan philosophers do; 'If it comes to pass, is because it was written.' Besides, I project an image of poverty to keep outside greed away. If no one comes to visit it is because there is nothing to take away. Children come all the time from everywhere. They joke about my way of life and my surroundings, while in return I offer them honey and bread, perhaps an occasional small gift or morsel. They continue to come again and again even if they leave with empty hands. Those youngsters come to hear the stories and fables I invent in order to keep my mind busy, and theirs dwelling in a world of fantasy."

"What will happen after they reach adulthood and become more susceptible to evil and wrongdoing? Would you then reject them?" Sikin asked the lady.

"I don't analyze life's contradictions anymore," she replied. "I just take things as they are presented and go from there. Perhaps you'll do the same when you reach my age."

Dumbfounded, Sikin thanked the woman for her invaluable help, and walking backwards without losing sight of her and the coffer, he opened the door, waved good-bye, and left staggering, either from the smell or because of such an uncanny experience.

Completely at a loss, with nowhere else to go for more facts, he decided to find the closest monastery and start all over again.

Following the advice of a priest from a nearby parish, Sikin traveled to the town of La Spezia, another coastal settlement South of Genoa, to visit the Monastero di Santa Croce del Corvo.

After asking innumerable times for directions to the monastery, Sikin and Cicerone finally arrived at the rocky outcrop where the white building in the shape of a cross was located. The view of the sea from four thousand feet above was breathtaking. Sikin dismounted and walked toward a rocky precipice where a kneeling monk prayed overlooking the ocean.

Mindful of his concentration, Sikin passed quietly, heading for the modest whitewashed church next to the monastery. He entered the tiny chapel through a narrow passageway, and then sat briefly in front of the crucifix symbolizing the Barefoot Carmelite Monk's dedication to their faith.

The peaceful atmosphere, interrupted only by the ocean breeze flowing through small wall openings offered a sense of serene freshness to the austere ambiance. Finding no one inside, Sikin left the chapel through the rear door, then crossed through a cemetery located behind the tiny church.

In the distance, Sikin saw another monk climbing the narrow winding trail that led to the graveyard. The barefoot friar, assisted by his long staff, was wearing a white robe restrained by a girdle. A pointed brown hood covered his entire head except for two small eye slots in the front. Sikin wondered how the men survived the heat of the day wearing scratchy woolen robes, head covers, and no sandals.

Anxious to find guidance, he waited for the friar's arrival and blurted out his inquiries apprehensively. Offering the traditional blessing, the monk introduced himself as the abbot of the monastery.

"Young man, haste is bad for you," the friar said. "We don't have biting dogs or poisonous snakes around here. Why don't you stay for our mid-day meal and share your concerns with the brotherhood instead of rushing onward? Remember that patience is not a vice but a virtue."

Sikin realized that his abruptness was uncalled for. He humbly changed his tone saying that it would be an honor to stay, since he hadn't had a decent meal in a long time. Then he asked the friar if he'd let him feed his horse.

"Absolutely!" The hooded man replied. "Behind the refectory there are plenty of oats and millet for our goats and sheep. Your horse is certainly welcome to share. Just make sure he is securely tied. We don't want him to fall off the cliff. I invite you to stay for the night, and if you accept, please feel free to use as much water as you need from the spring behind the olive grove."

Inside the monastery, the abbot led him straight to the refectory where food was ready to be served. Long, simply set tables stretched from one end of the room to the other. Wearing the same condemning outfit, another thirty-five monks waited for the Abbot to enter and say grace before their meal.

Following his prayer, the men ate in silence, except for one friar who read from the Holy Scriptures. When the brothers had finished eating the meager rations, another prayer session ensued. The message, which was read in Latin, seemed to pass through Sikin's ears like the ocean breeze, an uninterrupted palpable presence. When the session finally came to an end, they all stood including the new guest, who, affected by the sermon and the altitude, had almost fallen asleep.

Later in the afternoon, Sikin and the abbot met inside the cloister; a dark room barely illuminated by streams of light passing through the magnificent stained glass windows.

Beautifully carved fan vaulted ceilings, supported by round arches held by Corinthian columns gave the room an air of solemnity.

A massive wooden table stood in its midst, behind it, a bench resembling the throne of a feudal lord served as seat for the abbot. Purposedly built so that a visitor wouldn't stay longer than necessary, an austere hardwood chair across the table was the only extra seat available.

Sitting on the uncomfortable chair, Sikin offered the holy man a complete account of his mission. At the story's end, the abbot laid an arm on his shoulder. "Son, I don't intend to intimidate you with my personal opinion," he said. "But I fear you have an almost insurmountable task to accomplish. First of all, there is no such thing as an order of Penitents, as I am sure the lady at the hut didn't know. Penitents belong to a brotherhood of priests who believe in doing penance for the rest of their lives. Such fraternity occurs within the Orders of Franciscans, Benedictines, or any other. Therefore, here lays your first hurdle; finding out to which order the two Penitent monks belonged.

You also said they took the child to their hermitage, which leads to the possibility that the monks were hermits, either living on their own or as members of a small, isolated group. Hermit monks and nuns usually dwell in modest communities where they follow their own set of rules, often colliding against those of the mother church. They survive off the land, eating grasshoppers, drinking goat's milk, growing vegetables, raising their own cattle, and so on.

They rarely leave their lonely surroundings, and they always pay for food and shelter wherever they go, since most of them share a dislike for charity."

Sikin nodded, crestfallen. "The old lady said they paid for her hospitality. What else can you tell me?"

"Worshipped by many because of their divine healing powers, hermit monks usually end up surrounded by the sick, the dying, and the financially distressed," said the abbot. "Also by women, orphans, astray dogs, the curious, and hostile unbelievers, who dedicate their existence to proving that miracles are nothing but auspicious coincidences. I am not implying that Sakheem's care ended up in the wrong hands, but that he might had been adopted by persons incompetent to teach a child about the things of the world, such as numbers, reading, writing and history. I can't imagine how hermits could teach a youngster the ways of God and man when their main objective in life is to stay away from human knowledge and personal interaction. Perhaps after realizing their unusual predicament, the brothers would have given up the boy's care to a qualified institution, such as an orphanage or monastery. Who can tell?"

The abbot shook his head doubtfully.

"In a world filled with as many orphans as there are children, how will you possibly find a young boy whose name may have been changed several times? How will you identify an adolescent you never met as a child? The boy himself may remember little or nothing of his past. I detest sounding skeptical, but it wouldn't be fair to instill optimism over a seemingly hopeless situation."

"Then I shall have to rely on the grace of God," Sikin answered simply.

"So you shall," said the abbot.

"And now, changing to a more positive subject, perhaps you should consider meeting Friar Giovanni. He is young and one of the wisest brothers in our fraternity and the only one who could help you overcome such a painful burden. I strongly suggest you share his cell for the night. Stay with us for as long as you wish. I assure you that the friar will help you get closer to your Maker. I also recommend you abandon all human wants during your stay. Allow yourself to revitalize your tired body and disconcerted soul. Give it some time, and you will be able to hear the inner voices that only those persons in harmony with their spiritual selves are sufficiently gifted to appreciate. Our disciplines and way of life will clear your mind. If you give your entire self to the will of our Supreme Being, you shall begin to understand and appreciate the meaning of those voices."

The abbot's voice intensified as he spoke.

"Allow yourself the wonderful opportunity to discover your spiritual potential by detaching mind and soul from worldly wants and desires. Learn to live in absolute communion with your Maker without interruptions from the outside world. For your sake, Sikin, let Friar Giovanni become your religious mentor and brother in Christ while you are here. You'll never regret it!"

He paused kindly, regarding Sikin's surprised expression.

"Frankly, my son, there is no alternative to your dilemma. If you leave tomorrow, ask yourself where would you go next, and for what reason? Then, you'll see what I mean."

Before the abbot's admonition, Sikin wouldn't have considered accepting restraints of any kind, yet he had nothing to lose by staying an extra day or so, especially considering that meditation and prayer might help transform him into a physically and spiritually renewed man.

"Remember that anything in life is possible through faith." The abbot continued gently. "Faith is as much of a miracle as healing. Why don't you just try it? If, after a few days you still feel good about it, then by all means continue for as long as you want. Otherwise, we'll be glad to bless your departure."

Sikin considered the significance of timing on his mission one of his most important priorities. Yet, not having the slightest idea of what to do and where to go next, except to continue running around in circles, he decided to compromise for a couple of days, as long as he paid for room and board, which the abbot flatly refused to accept.

"All we ask, even if you have no intention of becoming a priest, is that you wear a disciple's habit while at the monastery," the friar said.

Following a short prayer dedicated to Sikin's enlightenment, the abbot laid a hand upon his head and left the cloister. That same evening after supper, the holy man introduced him to brother Giovanni. Since they all looked alike, Sikin's only way to differentiate one monk from another was by finely tuning his sense of hearing.

Brother Giovanni led Sikin to a cell austerily furnished with two wooden bunks minus pillows and cushions, where they became engaged in a lively and friendly conversation.

"Before letting our talk slide into another subject," Giovanni said authoritatively," I'd like to emphasize that while you are here, your primary responsibility will be to follow and obey the code of ethics provided in the timetable."

"What is the timetable?" Sikin asked.

"Written during the sixth century A.D. by St. Benedict, the timetable is a scroll with written rules and guidelines especially designed to make monastic and religious communities of all denominations more systematic and analogous to each other. Drafted after many years of confusion and disobedience among the different orders, the timetable was enacted canon law by the Pope in order to eliminate persistent violations and inconsistencies created by the various monastic groups, who followed their own vows, created their own codes of ethics, and modified age-old traditions at will.

And now, young man, let's leave this controversial issue aside and use this opportunity to present you with a series of duties and assignments.

One of your responsibilities will be to learn my techniques for decorating books, such as ornamenting the first letter of each chapter and so on. In this way you can help me with a project I had been working on for years. Then, from time to time you will become my assistant in the preparation of potions for the sick and the dying.

Since I teach catechism to the children of surrounding areas every afternoon, you will at that time go to the kitchen and offer your help wherever is needed.

You shall try to remain silent at all times except when praying, chanting, learning, or teaching. As you have already noticed, we try to keep conversation to a minimum around here.

Use this energy to learn our prayers and chants in Latin, instead of allowing your mind to wander unproductively.

Beginning tomorrow morning you shall begin wearing this hair shirt at all times." The friar pulled a thick woolen camisole from a trunk and handed it to Sikin. "This rough garment made of harsh woolen hairs is supposed to be worn between your naked body and the habit. The reason we all wear it is to make of its constant itching and discomfort a continuous remainder of our Savior's suffering on the Cross.

Forget manhood as long as you are a disciple. The only image you should bring to mind and heart is that of the Virgin Mary. No other female, including your own mother, shall take up that sacred time. This is a very important exercise for a young fellow like you.

You shall also stop considering food as a source of carnal pleasure. Its consumption has only one purpose, that of nourishing our bodies. There is plenty of water and wine to quench the thirst of everyone around, and to help segregate bad humors. Consequently, you may drink to your heart's content. The Devil, who is perpetually hovering around, is always waiting to enter an idle mind. Therefore, pray incessantly. Don't allow yourself to become vulnerable. You shall also fast as often as the timetable requires. Resisting the temptation to eat enables us to deal more effectively with evil provocations later on. Besides, your chances of feeling the presence of the Holy Ghost are much greater with a clean stomach than otherwise.

Before I continue, you shall promise to disclose any previous accusations of heresy, if any. And if by chance you were ever found guilty of such mortal sin, you must confess now, or forever be banned from entering this holy place!"

"No, Father, I have never been accused of crimes against the church," Sikin answered respectfully.

"Then, my son, why don't you stay for at least a week and allow yourself to experience, along with your brothers in Christ, what we believe to be a preamble to Paradise?"

"Do you honestly believe such a practice will help me find the boy?" Sikin asked skeptically.

"No one can guarantee that," the friar answered frankly. "Nevertheless, always bear in mind that in order to find others, you must first find yourself."

Sikin didn't fully understand the monk's last words, finding them too arcane for him to appreciate, but he nodded respectfully.

"If you decide to stay," friar Giovanni continued, "come to mass tomorrow morning wearing the disciple's habit instead of your usual attire. There, after a short and simple ceremony, the abbott will ask you to stand up and offer your pledge to fulfill the three sacred vows."

"Which are?" Sikin asked somewhat apprehensively.

"The first is that of poverty," the friar answered. "This means you shall not depend on material possessions to achieve spiritual wealth. In an effort to help you fulfill this vow, I will assume temporary guardianship of all your personal belongings, including the horse, until your time of departure. This trial will demonstrate to you that reducing or eliminating our dependency on material worth can only attain a peaceful and meaningful life.

The second vow is that of chastity, which means in part that you shall prevent erotic ideas and lewd fantasies from entering your mind. If an attractive or seductive woman crosses your path while you are a disciple, turn your eyes away immediately and start praying! Those kinds of thoughts are considered fornication even if they only exist inside your head.

The third and last vow is that of obedience. You shall obey God's commandments, as well as those of our order, thus sharing our conviction that there is only one purpose to life: That of finding and submitting yourself to the will of our Creator.

I'll be defining these principles in much more detail as you progress," friar Giovanni continued. "They are considerably more complex and cannot be fully understood with a simple explanation. However, always bear in mind that every time one is ignored or violated, you will have to suffer some sort of punishment in order to receive absolution."

"Father, can you tell me when I would be getting back my personal possessions? Please forgive my asking, but I have a fortune in gems and gold I intend to use for my mission, and I want to make sure you are aware of it."

"Son, I solemnly promise to return them intact upon request," the monk replied, staring at the ceiling and joining the palms of his hands in an expression of piety.

The next morning during mass, Sikin made his pledge to the brotherhood, promising to stay for a couple of weeks at the most.

He began his covenant by suffering perennial discomfort and exasperating itching all over his body while enduring hunger pains day in and day out. The absence of personal contact with normal sinners enhanced his feeling of total isolation. He worked like a slave from dawn to dusk, virtually eliminating his repressed romantic feelings for Tiblina. Since he dedicated three mornings a week to helping a sculptor build a new baptismal fountain at the marble quarries nearby, he wondered if the reason for his skin becoming so white was due to his contact with the stone or the continuous wearing of the hooded habit. Running long errands on a donkey and on foot down to the nearby town of La Spezia brought large blisters to his feet. At times, when he wasn't climbing up to the quarries or descending to La Spezia, Sikin helped a couple of friars fetch heavy buckets of water to irrigate their garden. He also helped clean up the kitchen and dust the pews of the church.

Waking up before sun break along with the others, he made a habit of walking up to the rock overlooking the sea and saying a few prayers in Latin before attending mass.

Finding the repetitious invocations in Latin meaningless and boring after a while, he dedicated that time to observing his surroundings with the utmost curiosity, particularly the comings and goings of a nearby anthill at the edge of the precipice.

While listening to Giovanni's teachings and exhortations during the evenings, he also learned the latest medieval techniques in the art of calligraphy and letter ornamentation. The wise friar was a perfectionist at everything he did or said. Nothing destabilized him more than the omission or transposition of minutiae. The use of specially prepared paints and brushes, some having only two strands of hair, exasperated Sikin to no end.

Sikin found the Friar's obsession with detail mind-boggling. Every time the new disciple learned a new prayer in Latin, Friar Giovanni had him repeat it countless times until the pronunciation became impeccable. He also learnt a special invocation for "the peace of the world," which made him wonder about the possibility of God suffering from some kind of hearing disorder.

Clearly dogmatic, the monk proved inflexible when it came to questioning traditions and customs. Chronically solemn, Giovanni claimed that diversions represented the most distracting and useless form of human expression. The Friar even calculated the amount of time dedicated to trivia to make sure he didn't exceed his set limits. It was no wonder the man rarely laughed, Sikin thought.

On his light side, the monk was the kindest and most sincere of persons. Never losing sight of the needs of others, Friar Giovanni dedicated a great deal of his time to teaching children and adults everything from Christianity to astronomy. No book or manuscript ever crossed his path without being carefully examined, hence his extensive knowledge of just about everything.

Voice coaching was one of his most beloved activities. The Friar applied his highly discerning ear to creating along with members of the chanting choir, the most exquisite sounds the human voice could produce. The monks' chanting unveiled music so beautiful that only God could deny its heavenly origins. Never left out of group activities, Sikin was pushed to his limits until the friar made certain he sounded right.

Deeply loving but not sweet-tempered, Friar Giovanni became such a fascinating character to Sikin that he always looked forward to their nightly sessions, during which he listened to the monk's dissertations and admonitions about everything known and unknown. His acute perceptiveness led Sikin to believe that Friar Giovanni had the capacity to read his mind. All in all, the friar was the main reason he decided to extend his stay for three months.

Sikin carried out his vows with so much care and dedication, most monks wondered if the lad was seriously considering joining the brotherhood. The only worldly thought he couldn't get off his mind was the formidable task of rescuing the boy. Otherwise, he stayed centered in absolute discipline, commitment, and a keen desire to learn by simple observation.

At length he began to recognize deep within himself strengths and weaknesses he had never before encountered. Enjoying a newly revitalized sense of awareness, Sikin began to treasure certain previously unnoticed qualities. For the first time, he appreciated the many tones of light rebounding from running waters, the infinite range of colors and shades deeply imbedded in nature's splendors, eternally available for the subjective mind to unveil. He began to sense the incontestable influence of human faith in shaping individual thought when practiced truthfully and from the heart. He developed a firm conviction that some form of timeless spiritual energy dwells throughout the physical universe, as well as a new belief that mysterious forms of transcendental power never before perceived was constantly reaching for his soul.

All those elements and others enticed Sikin to become less and less vulnerable to the logical and rational, and to rely more on intuitions and insight. The more extensive his degree of transformation became, the greater his tendency to harmonize with abstractions.

Giving up his unsuccessful search for credible explanations for life's inscrutable mysteries, Sikin decided to follow the Friar's admonitions to "rely on faith and you'll find the answer," or "discard your doubts, and savor the experiences brought about by new discoveries."

Inspired by a bolt of energy so authentic and uncorrupted, Sikin began to experience a new sense of oneness with the universe. As a result, he dedicated as much time as he could to reaching a higher level of communion with such an awesome entity, coming to rediscover, in due course, his own individuality. He also realized that the wisdom he so eagerly pursues; could only be attained by conceding to the ommipotence of God.

The idea of perpetual silence within the monastic community also made good sense to Sikin, who took advantage of the surrounding quietness to explore his inner world without interruption.

By beginning to recognize meaning and intent in everything, he was also able to differentiate mere coincidence from divine intervention.

Even after losing considerable weight, he felt physically stronger and spiritually renewed, with an inexhaustible amount of energy and enthusiasm.

He learned much about man's unsuccessful attempts to discover and believe in dignified reasons for his earthly existence, as well as comforting ones for his inevitable fall, thus applying again friar Giovanni's exhortation to "Search for, and submit yourself to, the will of God by faith alone."

Despite countless theories and philosophical definitions elicited by man to rationalize his earthly presence, none made more sense to him than a solid belief in the existence of a Grand Design, which according to Giovanni, "is the only course leading to the one and only truth."

The Friar maintained that seers, astrologers, learned men, enlightened intellectuals, false Messiahs, phony prophets, wishful thinkers, philosophers, doomsayers, religious peddlers, and an infinite number of opportunists, had offered throughout the ages innumerable answers to human dilemmas, the most notorious of which were those justifying human existence, and the likelihood of life after death. By adapting their self-serving interpretations of divine truths to the different levels of intellect, political conditions, social order and so on, those opportunists gained enough notoriety and acceptance in a society to entrench themselves in the most venerable and lucrative of niches. He also held the conviction that human capacity to seek and recognize divine truth, or its antithesis, dwells nowhere else but in the human soul.

He gave much credit to those who fueled by faith alone, dedicated their entire lives to the pursuit of truth through an ascetic and isolated life, as in the case of the monastic community. Likewise, he demonstrated that poverty and deprivations confer a sense of worth on values otherwise taken for granted, and taught that there was absolutely no difference between the pauper and the privileged in the eyes of the Great Entity, since everyone in existence will inevitably evolve into a different kind of reality, regardless of their present human roles.

Every evening before retiring, the wise monk asked if there was something Sikin wanted to discuss, and there wasn't a single night when Sikin didn't produce a list of questions, some of which were not answered to his satisfaction. As the Friar said, "We are not supposed to understand everything, though we are obligated to accept what's given, and accept it gracefully."

Of all the fascinating people Sikin met during his travels, the young Friar became by far, his most admired and well liked of all. Honest, loving, superficially shy, insightful, clear-minded, and strong as Samson, Friar Giovanni was one of the most faithfully committed men ever to cross Sikin's path.

Following his third month at the monastery, Sikin realized it was time to re-kindle his mission, and with that in mind he asked Giovanni if he had any new ideas or suggestions concerning his quest to find the boy.

"As a matter of fact, son," the Friar replied. "There is a religious community atop a hill overlooking the town of Cassino, founded by the followers of St. Benedict," Giovanni continued. "In it there is a group of priests solely dedicated to maintaining records of most activities taking place within Benedictine convents and monasteries. They record the names of citizens receiving charity, a full description of every pilgrim passing by, hospital services provided, baptisms, betrothals, last rites, and so on. And by God, Sikin! It suddenly occurred to me that someone in that group might be keeping records of activities such as the comings and goings of children! Suppose the two hermits saw the senselessness of raising and educating a child on their own. What would you have done if you were in their shoes?" Giovanni asked.

"First, I would have searched for a suitable religious fraternity or orphanage where I felt comfortable leaving the boy," Sikin replied. "Then I'd visit him often to make certain he was in good hands, and to tell you the truth, I would have chosen a Benedictine order to begin with."

"Then I strongly urge you to visit the monastery at Monte Cassino, which is by far one of the most respectable in the land. Ask our abbot to write you a letter of introduction before departing, in order to establish your credibility immediately upon arrival."

"Father, why didn't you tell me about the record keepers when we first met three months ago? I'm sure you must have known it all along."

"I suppose I did," Giovanni answered, somewhat embarrassed. "And please forgive me for doing so, but would you have stayed this long otherwise?"

Sikin flushed, knowing the answer.

"We've seen dramatic changes taking place during this time, and I feel very proud about the way you've handled them," the monk continued. "Keep in mind that from now on your mission will take a completely different course. First of all, the use of force and violence belong to the past. You will be applying good judgement and compassion instead of power, patience instead of conflict, faith along with logic, and prayer in lieu of anxiety. I'm fully convinced that you have the necessary qualities to finish your upcoming duties with the same integrity and dignity as in the past. By having faith in divine intervention and confidence in yourself, I'm sure you will find the final outcome highly rewarding.

Therefore, Sikin, keep struggling until you reach the final

objective, and may God help you and the boy find each other soon. Don't forget that the best part is yet to come. And of this, my friend, I am absolutely certain!

Tonight we shall offer a prayer of gratitude for your three-month visit to the monastery, for your crew, the coachman and his sister, the two hermits, and all the others. We shall also pray for the boy and his mother, and be thankful because all along on your mission, key events have fallen in place and will continue to do so time after time."

"Father," Sikin ventured. "Why should we give thanks for events that are yet to come? Aren't we stretching our faith too far?"

"Whenever the faithful prays." The Friar replied, "Thankfulness is expressed even before petitions are granted, and regardless of whether or not they will ever be. Such is the spirit of a true believer. Prayer represents the ultimate and most perfect form of interaction between God and Man; thus the reason we claim that faith is in fact a miracle."

Three days later, armed with the Abbot's letter of introduction, riding an overly rested Ciceronne, and carrying all his personal belongings, a completely transformed Sikin left the monastery and headed South toward the Benedictine community.

CHAPTER *Eight*

LOVE TRANSCENDS TIME

Love; The noblest delight of the human soul.
Excerpt, anon.

Sikin had heard of the town of Cassino, formerly Casinum, located at the foot of the mountain bearing its name inside the Italian province of Latium in central Italy, roughly a four-day horse ride south from Rome. In the year 529 AD, St. Benedict of Nursia had established the nucleus of his famous monastery at the summit of Monte Cassino.

Sikin rode his reliable horse toward the old Benedictine monastery, arriving on the eve of Epiphany. Either because of his letter of introduction or due to the spirit of the holy day, the friars with open arms welcomed him, and all resources available to them were placed at his disposal.

One evening, after spending long hours searching through their vast collection of handwritten scrolls, the Friar in charge of verification knocked at the door of the dimly lit depository where Sikin had been working day and night and asked if he could interrupt his search for a moment. Taking a seat next to Sikin on a hard wooden bench, the Friar made an observation that changed in an instant, the outlook of the mission from one of commitment and endurance, to one of realistic hope and good cheer.

He had discovered a record dating back five years, stating a convent run by Dominican sisters had to relocate two hundred boys due to a cholera epidemic that took the lives of thousands from a nearby city. Since forty of the older boys ran errands and did menial work for merchants and well-to-do families in town, it was decided to isolate the rest of the children from them in order to avoid contagion. But they were faced with the dilemma of resettling two hundred boys to other religious institutions, some located as far as southern Spain.

Despite their efforts, twenty-five of the forty older boys presumably contaminated, lost their lives to the disease.

According to the Friar, every boy included on the relocation list was identified not only by name, but also by his appearance, individual markings, special features, and personality traits. Included on the list was one boy of about thirteen whose description differed from the others in that he was tall for his age, of "apparent caucasian descent," with tanned skin, black curly hair, and blue eyes. The record states that he was given the adopted surname of Aurelio in order to eradicate every connection to the past, including his original birth name.

"Does this description match in any way the person you are looking for?" The Friar asked.

"His features resemble those of his mother," Sikin answered, "and the age is definitely close. His name had been changed to Sakheem in order to conceal his real identity and save his life, so is quite possible they changed it again for the same reason."

"I strongly suggest you visit the Benedictine convent of S. Agnesia alla Sperandia in Siena," said the monk. "You may uncover more details about the boy, such as the conditions preceding his adoption, and most important, find out where he was sent from there. Unfortunately our records don't provide much detail in this respect. Nevertheless, if the physical traits match, I wouldn't be surprised if you have found his footprints."

Sighing with relief, Sikin thanked the Friar for his help. The next morning, together again, Sikin and Cicerone traveled northward to Siena, passing by the city of Rome, where they spent two days of rest before resuming their trip to the convent. While crossing the gorgeous Tuscan countryside, they arrived at the top of one of three hills where the old city of Siena had been built hundreds of years before.

Of Etruscan origins, the old town used to be a Roman colony named Sena Julia. At the peak of its splendor during the Middle Ages, Siena was unrivaled in terms of riches, power, and beauty. Even in Ivan's day no other city in Europe embodied the Middle Ages better than Siena.

While in town, Sikin stopped for food and water at the Piazza del Campo, one of the most beautiful medieval squares in all of Italy. Then he visited the Duomo, a perfect example of Italian gothic architecture. Inside the cathedral, while staring at Nicolo Pisano's marvelous pulpit, so crowded with details of medieval stories, Sikin's mind shifted to his American hometown, wondering whether his recent transformation would continue to dwell in eighteen-year-old Ivan McKinley, or disappear upon return, as Grandpa said it could. If it stayed, how would his new perspectives measure up to those of his friends, teachers, and parents back in the USA? His conversation would be so incompatible with everyone else's that he would either have to accept being called a buffoon and a far-out eccentric, or keep his experiences to himself, which was not an option.

Was he obligated to report on his spiritual experiences, he wondered, or just the historical ones? Hearing his description of the overwhelming beauty of his present surroundings as well as of other medieval landmarks, would others accept that he had been there in flesh and bones? Why would anyone believe his stories when his parents so negatively received his first experience *Thank goodness Ivan lives in a civilized society*, he thought. *Otherwise they'd be burning me at the stake.*

Ivan had undertaken the role of Sikin in part to quench his desire for adventure and excitement, never considering the possible ramifications to his personal life. Would he have been better off staying in a socially acceptable state of apathy and ignorance instead of reaching for enlightenment at an age when most peers couldn't care less about serious matters? Conversely, it wouldn't be fair to his Druid ancestors to drag all that knowledge to the grave on account of his community's shortsightedness and misplaced priorities.

Sikin left the duomo and crossed the piazza to visit the Palazzo Pubblico or city hall where he climbed its steep bell tower all the way to the top. Once at the apex, he paused to catch his breath and enjoy the fabulous view of the city.

At a much slower pace he descended to the first floor to contemplate Simone Martini's fresco *Maesta* as well as Ambrogio Lorenzetti's *Allegory of Good and Bad Government;* a fresco depicting the dangers of tyranny.

At this, Sikin began his quiet monologue:

"Why is it that citizens from affluent societies tend to develop a sense of indifference toward those same values and traditions that once were considered pivotal in the formation and final consolidation of their social group? Why do they refuse to be fair and evenhanded toward people of lesser means who directly or indirectly contributed to their privileged status, when by doing so they are endangering their own existence? Paradoxically, this seems to me a perfect formula for any kind of organized government to bring destruction upon itself, since historically, social groups thriving on the exploitation of others haven't survived for long without suffering severe repercussions.

Why didn't my parents listen with an open mind to the merits of my experiences rather than labeling them as phony? The degree of complacency shown by my own parents tends to breed the very historical arrogance that hampers people from reflecting on their past, thereby forfeiting all their rights to have a voice in their future. They tend to consider themselves wiser just because they are older, which has absolutely nothing to do with knowing better.

Our history class is so passive and boring because it only teaches the dates, locations, and so-called "facts" of historical events. Those same incidents will never become relevant unless our teachers dare to challenge our minds with questions such as, 'would it be possible that a similar event could repeat itself in our era and therefore impact our lives?' 'Have I, as a student, learned from history anything that could be applied for the common good of our present community?' Or, assuming that a certain historical event was possible today, 'what would the public reaction be like?' 'What can we as citizens do to prevent at all costs a repetition of such and such disaster?'

Maybe I should become a history teacher!" Sikin/Ivan thought excitedly as he began to comprehend the message of Lorenzetti's fresco.

"Wouldn't it be interesting to compare current events to similar ones in history and offer alternatives on how to alter the course of the future? I could ask the students to portray the different characters in a given historical event allowing them to explain why they did certain things. Then I could ask the class to come up with examples of alternatives that would have changed the course of history for the better.

Sometimes I wonder why our Druid ancestor has bestowed on me such a responsibility. It could very well be that because of my role as Sikin, I have become too concerned about our culture's survival, and therefore my mind tries in vain to find simple, workable solutions to very complex issues. But regardless of what anyone thinks about my stories, I have learned the undeniable truth that apathy and complacency are a nation's worst enemies and therefore I should try my best to spread my traveling experiences as much as I can."

Interrupting his mumbling dissertation, a custodian from the real world, tapped Sikin on his head. "Son, you are gesturing as if trying to convey something very difficult to express. Also your face shows signs of desperate indignation and anger. Are you by any chance speaking in tongues? Can I be of help?"

Reddening with embarrassment, Sikin apologized for disturbing the peace of the establishment, blaming his "eccentric behavior" on a deep state of exhaustion that made him lose sight of where he was at the moment. Thanking the custodian for his concern, he left the Palazzo in pursuit of a decent place to spend the night before visiting the convent of St. Agnesia alla

Sperandia the following morning.

There wasn't a single bed available in town that evening due to the enormous number of pilgrims visiting the city in anticipation of a religious holiday, and as a result, Sikin had to spend the night camping on the outskirts of Siena. Tired, unwashed, and still embarrassed by the events at the Palazzo Pubblico, he regretted he would have to visit the convent looking like a beggar.

"Who's going to believe a stranger looking like this?" He mumbled the next morning as he knocked at the front door of the apparently deserted compound.

After trying repeatedly without response, he went behind the stone building and rang a bell that was hanging by a frayed old rope from the frame of the window upstairs.

"Sorry, but we can't feed anyone at this moment. Why don't you come back later?" The voice of a young woman yelled from within.

"Madam, I am not in need of food," Sikin called back. "I just want some information from the Mother Superior."

"She went to confession with the other sisters and won't be back till after noon." The voice answered.

"I am very sorry to inconvenience you, but could I have a drink of water?"

Following a moment of silence, a Benedictine novice opened the rear door.

"Don't you know the bell is supposed to be used only by those in dire need?" The young woman snapped. "Besides, how could you possibly be hungry and poor owning such a beautiful Arabian? You certainly don't look famished to me." She paused, admiring the horse.

"What's the name?" She asked.

"Mine, or the horse?" Sikin replied with a grin.

"Oh how I love horses!" She exclaimed. "But if the bishop ever finds me riding, he will become terribly enraged. You see, Signore, I spent the best part of my youth riding horses and rounding up cattle and sheep. Since joining the convent I have never had a chance to ride one again.

Sikin shook his head sympathetically.

"My name is Sikin, Sister, and the horse's is Cicerone."

"What else is Il Signore Sikin's business here besides water?"

"I want as much information as possible regarding the relocation of a child during the cholera epidemic, so I need to talk to someone familiar with every boy living in the convent at the time."

"Then you must be his father!" She said, scooping water from a wooden barrel into his cup. "Our well has the best water in the world. Perhaps that's why our children were not affected so much by the epidemic."

As she watched him drink, the young woman posed another question rather discreetly.

"Since there's no one around," she whispered, "Would you let me ride your horse just for a little while? Only for a moment, I promise!"

Sikin smiled his assent.

The novice squealed with delight. "Oh, thank you, Signore! My name is Emilia, Sister Emilia, that is. If you promise to keep my transgression a secret, I'll change my habit for pants right away. There are plenty of them in the cellar."

Transformed in an instant back to a farm girl, the young novice began riding the horse with remarkable dexterity up and down the nearby hills, behind the convent, and around the pond. Mindful of the young woman's enthusiasm, Sikin told her to continue riding for as long as she wished, provided he could use their bathing facility in the meantime.

"Just remember," he warned. "If the bishop catches you in the act, I won't be the one going to hell, do you understand?"

For the first time, Sikin had the opportunity to see his graceful horse in full array as Emilia's white scarf, blown by the wind, uncovered the delicate features of a young woman in her mid-twenties shimmering with joy.

The spirited novice said she had stayed behind to fetch water from the well, tend the garden, do the cooking, feed the animals, and spend any extra time fishing at the pond or dunking her feet

293

in its cool waters. Sikin accepted Emilia's invitation to stay for supper and spend the night at the convent. "You'll lick your fingers after tasting my cooking!" She promised. Joining the congregation after supper, Sikin explained his mission.

After listening attentively to his compelling story, every nun familiar with the children during the outburst of cholera, described the boy just as each one saw him. One said Aurelio missed his mother constantly, despite having been separated from her for such a long time. She added that initial efforts to find her were made in vain. "First," she said, the church records were useless since the boy's name was changed. He remembered his mother, and talked about a father who died in an accident, but nothing else. Worst of all, the two heretics who brought him, refused to say much in order to protect his life.

An older sister claimed that since orphans were the ill-fated results of abandonment, prostitution, neglect, abuse, war, death, and misfortune, they tended to develop emotionally detached personalities for the rest of their lives. "However," she said, "in Aurelio's case, for unknown reasons his devotion to her was much more pronounced than usual."

Passionately disagreeing with her remarks, a grouchy Mother Superior stated, "God always bestows upon His children the capacity to love and be loved way before they are born. Therefore, regardless of the many evil influences experienced during early childhood, those youngsters will always be perfectly equipped to recognize and appreciate His universal love later in life. Not all orphans are equally receptive to the influences of evil."

After repeatedly stressing their controversial views, a loud argument ensued among the other sisters, prompting Mother Superior to raise her voice demanding silence and civility from the group.

After a short pause, the authoritative nun, exhaling a sigh of relief, sat down while the steamy argument began to cool off. She invited Sikin to join her the following morning for a complete review of the convent's logbook. She also cautioned him against being over enthusiastic about finding the child, since most adopting institutions were not compelled to keep the children at the same location indefinitely.

Shortly before adjourning, another sister added that on the eve of epiphany, Aurelio always complained of missing a small figurine of the infant Jesus, lost as he said, "When the old man took me away from my mother."

Unable to conceal his euphoria, and openly disregarding the Mother Superior's words of caution, Sikin raised his arms, and with clenched fists, yelled at the top of his lungs, "It's him! I'm finally on his track!" He withdrew the statuette from his pouch and triumphantly showed it to the visibly moved sisters.

Trying to cover up their bashful smiles, the argumentative nuns, by then totally fascinated by Sikin's charming personality, asked the young man to relate more stories of his travels and adventures. Dazzled by his incredible anecdotes, the sisters violated their own rules of retiring at sunset, staying up late to listen enthralled.

As agreed, early the next morning Sikin visited the Mother Superior to help search for more substantial information regarding Aurelio's whereabouts.

"After last night's commotion," the dignified nun added apologetically, "I forgot to tell you that the boy had a name similar to yours, and that one of the bearded monks who brought him here, asked if we could give the child an adopted one instead."

"How long did the boy stay with the monks?" Sikin asked.

"Before I answer that question, let me offer you a brief recounting of those circumstances," she replied categorically.

"Living in a shack atop a hill overlooking a city never mentioned by name they also raised a few sheep and goats for their wool and milk, as well as a couple of ponies, one of which was offered to the little boy as a pet, under the condition he help out with daily chores.

According to the hermits, the little boy talked like a chatterbox. Unusually inquisitive, he learned to read and write, use numbers and conduct himself properly. You should also be aware that by the time Aurelio joined our family, he was already ahead of everyone else in matters of good breeding and overall education.

The hermits became so attached to the youngster that they refused to release him to just anyone, until one day they decided it was unfair to keep such a talented child living in isolation from the rest of the world. Therefore, they began to look for a nice orphanage where the boy could spend the remainder of his childhood years.

To make my story short, we welcomed Aurelio with open arms under the condition that the two renegades would have to come visit him once in a while during the first year, in order to make the transition smoother for the child. They had to walk for days to reach our convent, and they made their journey faithfully until we had to relocate him in order to save his life from the plague.

Now, to answer your question, I don't think Aurelio spent more than a year or so with them." The Mother Superior continued. "We were also concerned about the ongoing war against Sicily, particularly since armed mercenaries fighting on the side of Charles d'Anjou were constantly on the lookout for young recruits to help defend their cause. So we decided to relocate most boys at the monastery of San Anton and Santa Clara in Catalonia, an excellent facility for raising young adults that was founded in 1237 by a group of penitent friars. As I'm sure you know they are usually released at around age fifteen."

"What do these boys do afterwards?" Sikin asked.

"If the monastery has good connections with prominent citizens, they often find them work prior to their release. Sometimes they become apprentices of a craft, or if they have an outstanding personality and intellect, perhaps a rich noble family will offer to subsidize their education at schools of higher learning."

Sikin smiled hopefully.

"Please understand that this is not a common scenario," the Mother Superior cautioned. "Most children are not that lucky.

In my estimation, a common dilemma with young adults is their vulnerability to believing in any cause that sounds appealing. Therefore, mercenaries without scruples, well aware of their weakness, tend to seek their attention. I have never been able to understand how they can sacrifice young lives to satisfy their selfish desires for domination. It is such crimes to see some of our young men waste their lives that way, that we relocated them as far away from our perpetual battlegrounds as we could. I didn't want to see them fighting for the Anjous or for the King of Sicily. Neither cause was worth dying for.

I might add that most come back to visit their orphanages long after they leave, perhaps in pursuit of a warm sense of belonging, a familiar place where they can feel safe, or for faces they can trust." The Mother Superior shook her head sadly.

"Sometimes we hear tragic news about one of them following the wrong path in life. Others become productive citizens, though, and most make the best out of their circumstances. They all come back to visit us sooner or later."

"Are you implying that Aurelio will eventually come back?" Sikin asked hopefully.

"He might, especially after spending half his childhood here. Furthermore, the boy became so attached to those two radicals, that chances are he will return to visit them as well." She rolled her eyes heavenward.

"And now I'd like to inform you that last night, after checking our log for additional clues, we found nothing more of interest. I strongly suggest you make the Monasterio Santa Clara your next and hopefully final stop."

The Mother Superior pulled from a dusty shelf behind her desk an even dustier chart showing the known trails crossing the Pyrenees all the way into the Catalonian region, which Sikin copied on a large piece of paper as best he could.

Prior to his departure, Sister Emilia gave Sikin several sets of used garments to wear. She said they had belonged to one of the wealthiest men in the region. Upon his death one of the daughters had donated all his possessions to different religious institutions.

"Ours," she added, "ended up with the leftovers."

Back on the trail, Sikin and Cicerone first traveled North and then West bordering France's Mediterranean coast. They crossed the lowlands of the Camargue, the delta region of the River Rhone, where Sikin camped out for a few days while Cicerone interacted with the wild horses indigenous to those plains. They also enjoyed the company of migratory and sedentary birds such as egrets, herons, mallards, and wagtails, as well as thousands of other species of various sizes, calls, and colors, also indigenous to the region.

The Camargue, Ivan had read, a most unusual environment, hosts an immense diversity of wildlife. The low-lying salt plains, cracked and dried during summer, were covered with glasswort and salt crystals that horses love to graze on. By incinerating it, the locals created soda ash for soap and glass making.

Submerged during winter, vast areas of the Camargue wetlands not only became natural habitats for a wide variety of migratory marsh birds, but also offered large sections of fertile ground used throughout the centuries by local farmers for cultivation.

After several days of uninterrupted communion with nature, Sikin and his horse continued towards the town of Saintes Maries de la Mer, located at the Western tip of the delta on a thin strip of sandy ground often battered by the unpredictable Mediterranean. There, he visited a fortified church built one thousand years before, where he prayed for a positive encounter with Aurelio. He also visited the relics of Mary Salome, the mother of the apostles James and John, as well as Mary Jacobe, the Virgin Mary's sister, who came to gain converts following the death of Jesus. Sikin also went to see the statue of their Egyptian servant Sara, patron saint of the gypsies, which was traditionally covered with enormous piles of clothing.

Following two weeks of travel, he was already crossing the wild rocky coastal area known in Ivan's day as Costa Brava, trekking through its inlets, pine forests, and beautiful beaches. There, he spent a complete day running Cicerone up and down the packed sand, galloping in and out of the water until both were tired and soaking wet.

After a couple of days, they finally arrived in Catalonia, a rich, lovely land that had become an independent state many years prior to his visit, thanks to the good offices of the counts of Barcelona.

Since most locals spoke other languages besides Catalan, Sikin found it easy to move around the town and find the monastery, which was located a short distance from the Gate of San Daniel.

With cold, shaky hands, his stomach tied in knots, the loyal friend approached a large field bustling with wild daisies, where boys of all ages played games he'd never seen before.

Finding him visibly upset, a monk crossing his path at the time asked if he needed assistance.

"Certainly, Father," Sikin responded, trying in vain to conceal his anxiety. "I am looking for a boy named Aurelio."

"Aurelito! Aurelito!" The monk yelled, waving his hands at a group of boys who were playing some sort of soccer game farther down the field.

Following a brief pause that felt more like an eternity, a tall, handsome young man, with lightly tanned skin, pitch black curly hair, light-colored eyes, and with exotic features resembling Tiblina's, approached them at a fast pace.

"Aurelito," asked the monk. "Do you know this gentleman?"

"I'm sorry, Father, but I don't."

"My name is Sikin," said the traveler. "I have come to see you on behalf of your mother."

The young man's eyes flared angrily. "But my mother is dead! She was killed before I got kidnapped!"

"No, Aurelio!" Sikin said urgently. "Your mother is alive, and she has been desperately looking for you ever since you were taken from her."

Turning pale, the young man asked the baffled priest if the encounter was supposed to be some kind of joke.

Sikin pulled the carved figurine from his pocket, handed it to the boy, and asked, "Do you remember this?"

Aurelio slumped to the ground, and after carefully examining the piece he began to sob.

The monk, clearly unaware of the events preceding the

encounter, laid his hand upon the young man's shoulder.

"What's the matter, son?" he asked. "Do you think this man is telling the truth?"

"Where did you find it?" Aurelio demanded; his eyes transfixed on the object.

Sikin explained briefly the series of events leading to their encounter.

Still sobbing, Aurelio appeared trapped between a profound need to cry, and a youthful desire to jump with joy. He leaped to his feet and embraced the mysterious foreigner.

Totally caught by surprise, Sikin didn't know what to say, how to react, or for that matter what to do. He simply held the boy's head against his chest as the monk, in total confusion and disbelief, watched the touching scene.

"I'm too old to understand this whole drama without an explanation," said the monk, "so will you please follow me to a place we can discuss this matter more privately?"

Sensing that something unusual had just taken place, the oldest among a nearby group of orphans approached the boy.

"Is he your father, Aurelio?" He asked. Please tell us, is this man your real father?"

"No, he is just a friend I didn't know existed," Aurelio answered, wiping off his tears.

Upset by the group's sudden outburst of questions, the monk told them in an unmistakably firm tone to disperse and return to class, or risk spending the rest of the week polishing brass and mopping the floors inside the church. Then he grabbed Sikin and Aurelio by their arms and led them frantically into the building.

Inside the monastery, Sikin talked about the challenges and hurdles he had had to confront in order to find Aurelio. The priest remained silent, listening in awe to the stories preceding the encounter. The boy, on the other hand, never stopped asking questions.

Outdoors, they could hear some of the older boys pushing and shoving each other in an attempt to gain a foothold on the window ledge to eavesdrop on their conversation. The friar, already tired of their disobedience, stood up, and in an outburst of anger, yelled a warning to return to class immediately, or risk being whipped.

After the ominous threat, they boys scattered, allowing the men to finish their discussion.

Invited by the abbot to stay for as long as he wished, Sikin spent several days getting to know Aurelio in anticipation of an imminent departure to Venice, becoming in the meantime everyone's favorite topic of conversation and most solicited company.

Their talks covered a wide variety of subjects, including Sikin's adventures while traveling through the Silk Road across the Taklamakan with Tiblina; beginning the moment they met at Amur's hut, to the day he disappeared from Dunhuang.

Sikin's double identity and background, which he wanted to conceal from Aurelio at least for a while, did not surface at all during their conversations. The young man wanted to learn more and more about his mother, how she looked, her ancestry, values, upbringing, as well as the story of her friendship with Curzio Da Ponte. He also asked questions concerning his father Tirso, of whom Sikin did not know much. Moreover, the sad story of his greedy and cruel grandfather was also revealed.

What fascinated him most about his mother was her ability to survive the severity of the desert environment, as well as her courageous commitment to pursue her dreams in a world where most women were considered citizens of a lesser strain.

Sikin also told him about their frustrated romance, but he was careful not to elaborate or dwell on the subject. Aurelio, detecting some anxiety in his expression, did not pursue further details about their relationship either.

Evidently, the boy was much more mature for his age than his contemporaries, who considered him far too judicious.

One evening before bedtime, Aurelio asked his new friend to present on his behalf a written request for release so he could visit his mother. By doing so, Sikin would assume full responsibility for the boy's welfare. The Abbot would have to approve the document, which at the time formed part of a new emancipation practice created by the Benedictines in order to keep better track of the children and their whereabouts.

Without hesitation, both agreed to talk to the Abbot the following morning.

After a long pause, Sikin asked Aurelio if he wanted to ride Cicerone all the way to Venice.

"You mean me? Ride your beautiful horse?"

"Yes! He'll be a good friend during the entire trip, and besides being beautiful, the horse is smart, strong, and very mindful of his rider."

"I wouldn't feel right abusing your generosity," Aurelio replied. "Being his rightful master, you should be the only one to ride Cicerone."

"Aurelio, you don't understand!" Said Sikin. "I'm not only asking you to ride my horse. I'm begging you to accept him as a gift! You see, I must return to my native land after I bring you to your mother in Venice, and chances are we will never see each other again. Therefore, my young friend, Cicerone will become the only link left between you and me. Please accept him as a token of our new friendship. I want you to remember this moment for as long as you live."

"Sikin, it wouldn't make a darn bit of difference whether you give me the horse or not. I will always remember you!" Aurelio cried. Then he paused. "But must you leave? If you loved my mother as much as you said, why not stay with us and continue being my best friend for life?"

Holding his hands, Sikin replied, "Someday you will find out who I really am and the reasons I must leave. After that, I'm sure you'll understand."

Unwilling to accept another loss in his loss-filled life, Aurelio went to bed, covered his teary eyes with a pillow, and faked falling asleep.

Sikin felt devastated, but could only comfort himself at the thought of reuniting the boy with Tiblina.

Early the next morning, he went after the Abbot to request the boy's release, and also to find out where he could purchase a healthy horse.

The Priest said he was well aware of how much Sikin and

the boy meant to each other. He would not present any objection to Aurelio's release, but he wanted to see the boy that afternoon to finish the paperwork.

After asking a myriad of questions concerning Sikin's plans for Aurelio's future, the abbot recommended the stables down the hill as a high quality establishment at which to purchase a horse. He also suggested taking the boy along to make sure there were no language problems.

Sikin walked down to the stables, thinking about the impossibility of offering Aurelio the fatherly presence suggested by the priest. He also realized that providing the boy with the kind of environment envisioned by the friar would not present a problem, given the atmosphere at the Palazzo Da Ponte. Most definitely, Mariu would play the role of a loving aunt, and the maids whom had worked at the household for years, would make their contributions as well. The dynamism and joie d'vivre prevailing at the Da Ponte household would bring out the best in any adolescent.

The capricious Mediterranean produced two consecutive days of pouring rain; therefore delaying their departure until after the soil had dried up. Finally the sun came out, and a week later Sikin and Aurelio departed for Venice.

Everything was new to the young man, who couldn't wait to arrive at the next settlement or town to listen to the compliments about his stupendous horse. He also loved to engage in conversation when they crossed paths with young ladies of his own age, since Aurelio was very gregarious.

Well aware of his good looks, he grasped every opportunity to show with amazing elegance and finesse, his polite manners and good breeding toward the ladies.

Sikin, at the time roughly twenty years older than Aurelio felt that his new friend was not a child anymore as the priests thought him. His openness with people from all walks of life was nothing short of amazing for a young man who had lived most of his childhood centered in religion, restraint, and virtual isolation.

His openness toward Sikin brought up, among other subjects,

discussions about the entanglements of sex in the lives of adolescents, boys in particular, and even though the young man paid special attention to Sikin's comments, he implied many times that he'd known the answers beforehand. Sikin found he was utterly amused that he was offering advice to someone only three years younger than Ivan McKinley.

When Aurelio's future became their topic of conversation, Sikin used the opportunity to comment about the different alternatives available to him, saying that among the most popular trades and professions to chose from were those like education, metalworking, medicine, government law, and perhaps the one that suited his personality the most, decent and honorable public career, which in those days was as much of a rarity as in Ivan's day. Sikin insisted that Aurelio's family was influential and wealthy enough to catapult him into the public scene, and that the Republic needed young, decent men of honor to represent its interests.

Aurelio replied that he had always wanted to become a priest, or perhaps a merchant like Da Ponte, though not necessarily traveling to Asia. The young man also expressed his desire to develop into a prosperous man with resources to assist others, just like Signore Curzio had for his mother.

Sikin felt concerned that the boy had taken upon himself an unreasonable amount of responsibility, most likely inspired by feelings of gratitude, and not necessarily motivated by his own natural inclinations. Moved by the young man's determination, Sikin tried to insinuate other options in his mind. Showing an attitude of indifference, he noted that God generally assigns one or more callings to every human being, so every person should strive to discover his or her own inclinations before attempting to imitate others. He recommended that Aurelio ask his own conscience which alternative would suit his personality, personal values, and lifestyle the most.

Then, if you still feel called to become a priest, by all means, do so, he continued. "However, keep in mind the myriad of disciplines and restrictions that can be difficult to understand, much less willingly accepted by a person as gregarious and unreserved as you are."

Sikin also said that wealth in and of itself wasn't a panacea to the brutality and unpredictability of life, and that happiness and personal fulfillment were sometimes more evident among those with less financial resources than amidst the rich.

He cautioned Aurelio not to tie his vocations, natural abilities, and spiritual gifts exclusively to the pursuit of wealth, since at the end we must all pay a price for what we have done, or not done, with our lives. Sikin urged the lad to recognize that time, unlike wealth, is not only a gift from creation, but life's most precious asset as well. Its use should be judiciously studied and directed, for time is simply irreplaceable and impossible to stow away for future use as riches are.

On his part, Aurelio continued to use their journey to contend that his friend should consider Venice as his permanent home. At length Sikin decided to reveal his true identity, and when he did, the young man became so disconcerted that he asked for some irrefutable proof in order to believe his story.

"What kind of evidence do you want?" Sikin asked.

"Take my mother and I with you," Aurelio replied.

"I don't have that kind of power and you know it. Besides, if Mariu, her father, and Tiblina believed me, why can't you do the same?"

"Because it sounds too absurd to be possible."

"Aurelio, please listen to me. Sometimes you must accept the impossible as an intrinsic part of life, because when you do, the vastness of your own universe will expand by leaps and bounds. Just look at the recent developments touching your life. Did you ever envision them? Weren't they inconceivable just ten days ago? Wouldn't you say that the impossible has just taken place?"

The young man replied that those events were nothing but pure coincidence.

Finally, after a long philosophical struggle with the issue, Aurelio decided to accept Sikin's story temporarily, or until a sign of deception showed up.

Sikin welcomed the challenge, saying that whether he

accepted it as truthful or not was irrelevant, since their friendship was limited by time, and there wasn't enough of it left to be wasting it with arguments.

Baffled and confused, Aurelio stared at his friend and said that regardless of who he was, or where he came from, he would always feel love and gratitude in his heart for what he had done.

On a cold and rainy February afternoon, following several weeks of difficult travel through muddy terrain, and almost a year after he had left the city in pursuit of Gabriel Lombardo, Sikin finally arrived on the outskirts of Venice with Aurelio.

From there, they rode their horses to the inn where he used to stay, where the person renting them the room also agreed to provide food and shelter for the horses. Acting intuitively, Sikin decided not to show up at the Da Ponte mansion until he had a chance to test the waters.

The innkeeper said that if it weren't for the lady who formerly occupied that room being suddenly recalled to Florence, both would be spending the night somewhere else, perhaps sleeping in the streets or in a piazza. He reminded his guests that the first week of Carnival was about to begin, so hordes of visitors crammed into all accommodations during the festivities.

Sikin and Aurelio agreed that their first priority should be to determine when and how to make their appearance at the Palazzo Da Ponte.

In need of advice, the following morning both friends waited in vain for a familiar face to show up at the German warehouse. Not surprisingly, none of Sikin's comrades worked there anymore. Going upstairs to visit the manager of the establishment he knocked at the office door several times without receiving an answer. Suddenly a coarse hand behind him grabbed his shoulder.

"Boss! What in the world are you doing here?"

"Paolo! What if I ask you the same question?"

"Don't tell me this young fellow is the result of your mission!"

"Yes, he is!" Sikin introduced Aurelio.

"My God, Sikin. You did it, by golly! What a handsome young man he is! Has he met his mother yet?" Asked the former thug.

"Not yet. We weren't sure that showing up unannounced would be the best way for them to meet. Besides, we have no way of knowing whether his mother is at home. We would hate to water down her greatest moment in case she is absent. We thought about asking Carlo to carry a message to Mariu explaining our concerns before we make a hasty decision. I hoped I might find news of him here."

"Come into my office!" Paolo insisted.

"To *your* office?"

Paolo grinned. "Please come in and sit down!"

The comfortable room had three large windows facing the Rialto and the Grand Canal presenting a spectacular view of Venetian life in and around the water.

Aurelio and Sikin sat on an attractive leather sofa facing the Asian table that Paolo used as a desk. The piece was exquisitely hand carved along its wide borders and massive legs with images depicting life in a Chinese village. Miniature models of junks and other Asian trading vessels adorned the highly polished top. A large, detailed map of the city of Venice and the Grand Canal lined the wall behind his chair.

As the loud noises of working stevedores emerged from the docks underneath, and the sweet smell of the Adriatic wafted through the homelike room through a series of windows and openings, Paolo sank his undersized body into a heavily cushioned chair that stood behind the magnificent table.

"Your furniture certainly betrays the hedonistic frailties of a successful businessman!" Sikin said jokingly.

"Not at all!" Paolo replied. "I have developed piles from sitting on hard surfaces all the time, and unless I swing from a tree or squat on the floor, the pain can be awfully excruciating." He winked at his own jest. Then the new enterpreneur began to relate the events that followed their arrival from Genoa.

"Let me begin by saying that the previous owners of this venture, two Germanic brothers and a Sicilian partner drove their workers like slaves. The bloodiest of battles ensued when one of the siblings embezzled a large sum of money from the outsider. The scandal eventually led to the sale of the business.

Since money became so plentiful upon my return, I haggled with the avaricious brothers until they offered me their entire shipping operation at a bargain price. Now I run it with the help of two formerly disgruntled employees who are teaching me its idiosyncracies while I pay them decent salaries for a change.

As you can see, I'm doing exceedingly well. Actually, I don't need to work but I have nothing else to do with my life. It's a novelty to make a clean living. And do you remember the Da Ponte's maid, my former flame?" Paolo beamed. "We are seriously considering marrying next summer. So, my friend, if you want to know what goes on at the Palazzo Da Ponte, all you need to do is ask your former associate, and he'll be glad to provide the answers. And this time believe it or not, the information is for free. Furthermore, your lady friends regard me as the only person in town capable of making repairs of equal or better quality than most competent workers. They consider me more honest and reliable than anyone else around, to the point where I am allowed to enter their property even without permission."

"You? Entering their house without consent?" Sikin asked facetiously. "They must be out of their minds!"

Paolo feigned insult. "Haven't you noticed a complete transformation in my character? Can't you see I am a different person? Why don't you let *me* take your letter to Signorina Mariu? This time I promise to keep its content intact instead of steaming the envelope. Come on, Sikin, if you relied on little Paolo before, why don't you take a chance on him again?"

Sikin laughed heartily.

"All right, if I've asked Aurelio to believe the impossible, perhaps this is my turn to teach by example. You can go ahead and take the letter anytime. But I'd like to hear some news about Naguib and the others before you go."

"My pleasure, boss! Naguib decided to return the ship to its rightful owner in person. He also delivered a letter written by

Caramello exorcising the merchant from all curses.

After delivering the vessel, he went back to his family in Northern Africa, where he is known to be the richest Moor in town. According to rumors, they all live in an older but sumptuous palace owned by an Indian maharani before a religious fanatic murdered him.

In fact, a merchant friend of mine recently brought a message from Naguib asking about you and the mission. The black giant left Venice fully convinced you'd be bringing the boy back to his mother safe and sound. Perhaps you should pass him the good news!"

"Most definitely, Naguib was too good a man for me to ignore. Now, why don't you tell us about Carlo?"

"I will, but only after listening to your story."

Sikin began the narrative by bringing up his spiritual and physical renewal at the monastery, calling Paolo's attention to the devotion, affection, and support offered by Friar Giovanni. Curiously enough, the little man demonstrated more interest in the mystical aspects of his experiences than in any other event. Occasionally interrupted by Aurelio, Sikin described every detail leading to their encounter in Catalonia as well as their return trip home. Then, he asked again about Carlo.

"As you already know, Carlo promised to conquer the racing world someday," Paolo said. "He refuses to become involved in anything besides his one and only aim, which I'm sure he also uses to avoid accepting responsibilities. The man is already too old to compete for the top, and he's beginning to notice. His only "superfluous" pastime is, as he puts it, 'socializing with a different lady every night.' In short, Carlo is taking pleasure in a hedonistic, empty lifestyle while abandoning everything meaningful."

"Don't you think that perhaps he was too young to handle sudden wealth?" Sikin asked.

"Come on, Sikin, not every young person is like him." Aurelio interrupted.

"Thou shall not say, 'from that cup I'll never drink,'" Sikin answered ceremoniously.

"Don't you think I know about the aberrations of wealth?" Aurelio remarked bitterly. "Why in God's name did I end up in an orphanage to begin with?"

"I must say he was the straightest of the bunch," Paolo continued. "But the fact that money made him so vulnerable and light headed makes me wonder if he would have been better off without it."

"How about Renato?" Sikin inquired.

"Well, he finally found his niche in the French countryside, where he learned to value solitude for the first time in his life. As he said in his last message, 'I'm learning to grow wine grapes in a country where its citizens couldn't care less about my gypsy background.'"

"Renato wanted to settle down and have a family someday. He comes back occasionally to visit old cronies like me, and according to plans he is acquiring a large stretch of fertile land north of the Camargue, with the intention of harvesting a wide variety of grapes. Although he is lonely, I wonder if Renato would be any happier anywhere else.

Caramello remained in town. He started a business dedicated to repair structures affected by the waters of the lagoon. Being a contortionist, the man has no trouble crawling into cavities and fissures to repair walls and foundations.

He doesn't need to work, but he loves to use his physical abilities, and his new occupation gives him an opportunity to do so in a clean and lawful way.

"Whatever happened to Leif?" Sikin asked.

"He was tried and executed for torturing and murdering hundreds of Venetian citizens. And you know something, boss? From the very day he got caught, I always felt that Leif wanted to end his life, but could not gather enough courage to do it on his own. Those who witnessed his execution say that as the man was walking toward the scaffold, he rudely told an accompanying priest to go to hell. To the amazement of the watching populace, Leif then removed the black hood from his head and tossed it into the bloodthirsty crowd.

Uncovered, but incredibly at ease, the condemned man

placed his neck comfortably inside the groove of a blood-stained wooden block, and faked the bailiff's dark voice, shouting a loud order to kill, which the executioner in black instantly obeyed.

Even before he had a chance to wipe the blood from his polished ax, thousands of festive spectators were already yelling profanities and abominations at the decapitated body.

They just couldn't wait for Leif's head to roll down into the waiting basket to placate their appetite for revenge. I just wished Naguib had seen it."

To change the ghastly subject, Sikin asked Paolo about Gabriel Lombardo's fate.

"After we left him dangling from the tree across from the government building, Lombardo, still wrapped in the canvas, swung from the branch for hours.

"While being brought down by a soldier, the scoundrel never stopped screaming profanities at the crowd underneath. As you can imagine, they responded in kind by yelling at him all kinds of obscenities and accusations.

During the investigation," Paolo continued, "evidence of fraud and larceny was also discovered. After a huge scandal, his inner circle of 'friends,' incriminated him even more, and while many citizens reveled over his fate, the miserable creature was tried, found guilty of instigating a murder and of crimes against the republic, so he was condemned to spend the rest of his life in a dungeon doing hard labor."

"He should have been executed like Leif," Aurelio said bitterly.

"To make the situation even spookier," Paolo continued, "the night following the trial, a raging fire scorched his mansion to the ground. No one ever knew how it started, or who set it up. Gossip has it that one of his oldest and most disgruntled servants did it as an act of revenge."

"Let's talk about Stella and her mother, since it is perhaps a less depressing subject?" Sikin said.

"Mariu found them decent occupations at the filature in Sicily, and within a month following our arrival in Venice, the two ladies moved South to begin a new life. We haven't heard from them since, although we assume things are going well for both."

"Now tell us about Aurelio's mother."

"Oh no, my friend! You will have to find that out on your own. Otherwise it will be unfair to her."

"Are you going to leave us wondering?" Demanded Sikin.

"You can call it that if you want, but keep in mind this whole set-up is supposed to become a pleasant surprise for everyone, especially her, and I for one wouldn't want to spoil it."

At last Aurelio, tired of the inaction, asked Sikin to make up his mind, or he would go meet Tiblina on his own.

That same evening, inside their room at the inn, the friends faced each other across a table and drafted to Mariu Da Ponte the following note:

Dearest Mariu,

Please accept our warmest greetings and sincere apologies for not contacting you earlier. Nevertheless, allow me the privilege to be the bearer of the most wonderful of news…

Aurelio and I are in Venice at the present time. We are deeply concerned about his mother's unexpected impact of meeting her only son, and in this spirit we seek your advice as to when and how we should make our appearance. Although he is eager to the point of restlessness, Aurelio feels, above all else, a deep sense of responsibility for his mother's well being.

After arriving from a tiresome and lengthy journey, we have virtually nothing left to wear except for shabby garments that are either torn at the seams or filled with holes around the seats and knees. Therefore, tomorrow morning we shall be procuring decent-looking attire to wear at such a wonderful occasion. The last impression we want to convey is one of vulgar and filthy beggars! We've been in La Serenissima less than two days, but Aurelio, as you can imagine, refuses to wait much longer.

The bearer of this letter, who happens to be "devotedly attached to you and the family," refuses to disclose anything pertaining to Tiblina, for he doesn't want to spoil what otherwise could become, according to him, the carnival's most incredible event. Therefore, my faithful and dearest friend, don't waste your patience asking questions about us either. His head is hard as a cobblestone.

Thanks for handling the finances during my absence. We are in good health and wonderful spirits.

Sincerely,
Sikin and Aurelio.

Paolo showed up the following morning to deliver the note, and that same evening he returned with Mariu's answer.

Sikin hastily unsealed the envelope with Aurelio leaning over his shoulder.

To my dearest nephew Aurelio and beloved brother Sikin,
Your letter was yet another revelation that miracles in fact do occur! Not in my wildest of fantasies have I imagined such a momentous event ever becoming reality.

As you already know, Tiblina is one of life's most prodigious survivors, therefore she is in excellent health, always looking forward to finding her beloved son sometime, somewhere.

It has been our family's tradition for many generations to mark the beginning of the carnival season with a masquerade party at our home, to which relatives and good friends are always invited. There is singing and dancing to the music of instruments. Some of our guests are fascinating people, and their conversations are most engaging. Those preferring a quieter and more subdued atmosphere usually join partners of equal manners at various games of cards. Magicians and puppeteers add color to the evening, as food from our seas and wines from Toscana sustain our cheerful spirits throughout the night.

In light of this, allow me to present you and Aurelio with the following idea: Come early to the gathering dressed as a Plague Doctor and Aurelio as Il Capitano. By then I should be able to discern who is who among our mystery guests, which shall remain as such until halfway into the night.

313

We will be sharing this joyful occasion with the many friends, relatives, and supporters Tiblina has known for years. What a unique opportunity to partake in such a marvelous event!

Try to gather patience, and take plenty of time to become as creative as you can. Then relax, and allow Our Lady of Fortune handle the rest!

If our mutual friend Paolo does not bring a negative reply within a day, I will assume that my invitation has been accepted.

Please be here not later than sunset the day after tomorrow.

Looking forward to the warmest of hugs,
Mariu.

The following day, Aurelio and Sikin visited dozens of novelty shops in pursuit of masks, hats, and other articles suited to the occasion. The waters were crowded with local revelers and visitors alike. There wasn't a vessel or gondola available for hire, and the narrow streets of Venice were heavily packed with busy pedestrians wearing costumes and masks from the sublime to the ridiculous in anticipation of the coming festivities. The scenario gave Aurelio the impression that no one in town worked for a living. Sikin had to reassure him that the whole city came to a complete stop only during that week, except for eager shopkeepers who would rather make extra profits than celebrate with the crowds.

Entering a garment shop dedicated to the making of traditional costumes, they asked to see the ones Mariu had recommended. Fortunately, they still had one "Captain" outfit left in their small storage room, but it needed a few alterations to fit Aurelio.

Due in part to its hideous appearance, the shopkeeper couldn't sell enough of the "Plague Doctor" costumes to dwindle their stock, so the store had enough inventory to cover another carnival and perhaps another plague.

While they waited for the tailor to finish Aurelio's alteration, the boy made some very funny remarks about the ghastly looking outfit his friend was trying.

"You look more like a famished vulture than a Doctor, in fact, if I was dying, your presence not only will hasten my departure but make of it a delight."

"Don't make fun of it! You might not believe it, but this ugly thing has a curious historical meaning. The costume represents the most terrifying scourge ever to affect Europe. The deadly disease, known as the black plague, struck at different times during the last century, and it lasted throughout the beginning of ours."

Sikin explained that most doctors attending the sick wore the same black linen tunic he had on including the broadly winged hat, the obnoxious looking mask with spectacles, and the elongated beak the likes of a vulture's bill.

"Plague doctors also carried a black staff to remove the cursed items of clothing from the bodies of the sick and the dying for further incineration." Sikin continued, "this process took place without ever touching the patient, since in this fashion they supposedly protected themselves from contracting the disease.

The poor victims died either from the dreadful affliction, or, like you said, Aurelio, from the horror of witnessing someone like me enter their room dramatizing death and wearing this hideous outfit.

"Yours is perhaps the most popular among the traditional costumes," Sikin said pointing at the captain's hat Aurelio held, "which explains why they only had one left. You see women are encouraged to believe that underneath the tunic, there is a very handsome and vibrant Spanish gentleman, which of course is only an attitude.

Also part of an old heritage, the mask portrays a boastful nobleman who brags about his romantic encounters and daring escapades. It dates back to Roman times, since it actually originated from the mercenaries occupying Italy in those days."

"I remember seeing Spaniards dressed in such costumes during our Sunday outings in Barcelona." Aurelio said. "They certainly stuck out like black moles!

Since you're fluent in Spanish besides Catalan you must

315

speak only that language at the party in order to make your presence even more mysterious. As a matter of fact, why don't you fake being a Spanish linguist traveling to Asia as well?"

Interrupting their conversation, the old tailor showed up with Aurelio's multicolored tunic adorned with gold buttons, which would accompany a large feathered hat three times the size of his foot and a sheathed sword so massive it had to be tied to the knee to keep it from wobbling during walking or dancing.

Two days later, the Palazzo Da Ponte was already showing its shine and glitter in anticipation of the evening's celebration. The skies were unusually starry but a bit misty and it wasn't as cold and humid as Venice is during that time of the year.

Inside the mansion, uniformed maids, bustled to and fro, making sure every detail was covered for what was expected to be a long, joyful evening full of surprises and entertainment.

Wearing the most unusual and imaginative outfits one could muster, guests began to reach the palazzo by land and sea. The elitists came elegantly dressed, their faces concealed by graceful masks and their costumes ornamented in silver, gold, and precious stones, revealing their pretentious desires to boast about their wealth and social status. Some even brought their own codegas; servants with lamps who accompanied people through the streets of Venice after dark, in case the party lasted well into the night.

Among the genuine fun-seekers, one could see figures disguised as demons, peasant girls, butchers, lackeys, lawyers with papers, buffoons on stilts and more, while the traditionalists wore costumes such as "The Turk With a Pipe", "Buranello", "Tracagnan," and so on. No one else had dressed as a "Plague Doctor" except for Sikin, who felt like an outcast wearing such an awful disguise, but he trusted Mariu must have had good reason for asking him to do so. Only one other Spanish Captain showed up besides Aurelio.

Uninvited neighbors, pedestrians, and small groups of onlookers, stood in front of the palazzo to admire and scrutinize the endless parade of guests, which included many of the city's upper crust.

At the mansion's foyer, the hostess, accompanied by uniformed servants, welcomed the participants one by one. With the exception of the maids, Mariu was the only one in the house wearing an evening dress and no mask. No two costumes were alike except for the two Captains.

With guests laughing and chattering inside a building filled to capacity, no one dared say a word in his own voice if he or she wanted to remain incognito, they either wrote their thoughts on specially designed pieces of paper or used false voices when they talked.

The noise level was such that the music of lutes and other medieval instruments could not be heard even if the listener stood in front of the players, and from the outside, the onlookers sensed that the building was either vibrating or desperately gasping for air.

As the clamor continued in ascending overtones, maids kept serving glasses upon glasses of luscious vino Toscano, as if the crowd needed to reach an even more frenetic mood.

Only someone accustomed to such melee could possibly feel at ease. The ambiance was so fabulous for a party of that nature that unless a guest paid close attention to every detail, the presence of two silent and intimidated visitors would have gone unnoticed. They were, of course, Sikin and Aurelio who, not knowing what to do, how to act, and worst of all, what to expect, stood in a corner merely as spectators. Sikin realized Aurelio's heart must have been pounding relentlessly with anxiety, while Sikin strained his senses trying to figure out behind which mask his timeless flame was hiding.

Mariu, who knew exactly who Doctor dea Peste was, came close enough to hug him, kiss the vulture's elongated beak, and whisper in his ear, "everything is coming out as planned, Sikin, I am ecstatic to see you again!"

Bothered by his long beak and ugly looks, Sikin didn't know how to respond, so he simply squeezed her hand for a moment until one of the maids offered another glass of the delicious red wine, whose amazing effects he had perhaps underestimated.

As the consumption of liquor dwindled and the guests felt

more comfortable with one another, the noise began to level off. Some got together to play cards while others sat around the exquisitely inlaid parquet floor in anticipation of what would soon become a dancing stage.

After losing count of how many glasses the young man had had, Sikin noticed Aurelio had begun to feel the effects of a transformation that allowed him to put aside his repressed, disciplined self, and project instead the character of precisely the Spanish Captain he was portraying so well.

"After all, this is supposed to be a joyful occasion for everyone," Sikin told him, "so why not join the jubilant crowd and pursue a great time?"

Since Aurelio only spoke Spanish to the guests, everyone's attention turned toward the mysterious person wearing the Captain's outfit. He soon gained the notoriety of a young linguist for the mere reason that no one within Mariu's social circle spoke the language. In no time the fascinating Spanish traveler acquired such a celebrity status that most of the young ladies couldn't wait to meet the mysterious gentleman so "beautifully attired in such a lively outfit" and listen to his exciting stories.

Also attending the party, were the staunch supporters Tiblina used to call "effeminate and spoiled," as well as their influential cardinal friend who came disguised as a Pope wearing a mask with the face of a child. Only an idiot would have mistaken the false Pope's real identity, since the cardinal's only aim in life was, is, and always would be, to be anointed Pope.

Well into the masquerade, Mariu introduced Aurelio and Sikin to a woman dressed as Pulcinella, who asked the Spanish Captain to show her his techniques in dancing to the music of Cordoba and Granada.

The young man, unaware of the existence of such dances, didn't know how to respond to that kind of request. By accepting, he would be making a fool of himself, and by declining he would be most rude to the lady. But playing the role of a dashing captain, Aurelio decided to escort Pulcinella to the dance floor and fake dancing to the music that preceded what Ivan would know as flamenco.

In an attempt to save Aurelio from certain embarrassment, Sikin stepped between the young man and the mysterious woman at the edge of the stage. He told the lady, that he was the captain's professor of foreign dance in Barcelona, and the one who had taught him the major steps in the fine art of exotic dancing. In view of this, he requested that he should be the first one to dance with her. Aurelio bowed out with a grateful sigh.

Sliding his arm gently around her waist, Sikin led Pulcinella to the stage just in time for the musicians to begin playing a tune with strong Moorish overtones.

Mariu, whose carefully planned scheme had begun to unfold, invited the abandoned Aurelio to join her in the exotic dance. In spite of his awkwardness, the young man managed to follow Sikin's steps well enough to make everyone believe in his Spanish ancestry and dancing expertise.

After a couple of pieces, the music changed to more familiar versions of local folk tunes. Sikin began to wonder about the familiar fragrance enshrouding his partner, a perfume that smelled like the one offered by Curzio Da Ponte to Tiblina back in the days of the Taklamakan.

The unforgettable scent brought a cold sweat to the hands, and a chill rolled down his spine. Feeling her soft and delicate hands, he delighted in the gracefulness and elegance of her movements. The warmth he felt every time their bodies came close to one another unsettled Sikin to the point where he desperately wanted to lift off her mask and discover if she had, in fact, changed into a completely different person.

How could she be the same gritty barbarian he had learned to love so dearly? Did she still have the same innocent and provocative smile? How about that indomitable spirit Sikin so much admired, and her eyes' memorable expression of sweetness, so evident the night they kissed each other farewell?

Curious, and at the same time apprehensive about a possible disappointment, Sikin's mind could not adjust to the fact that an abyss of time had passed between Tiblina then and Tiblina at that moment, since by then she had aged over fifteen years.

What if she had become a middle-aged spinster with gray

hair, wrinkles, and a bitter disposition?

His most exciting, yet most painful memory came tumbling back as he relived the scene at Master Han's mansion the evening he felt the ardent touch of her lips as she begged him to stay.

Would they feel the same passion for each other this time?

At that moment, there was nothing more meaningful and urgent to him than unveiling the woman behind the mask.

Conversely, Pulcinella had begun to detect something odd about her ugly partner's demeanor. Sikin knew what she must have been thinking. Why his hands were so sweaty and his body so stiff? And why had Mariu introduced her to such a horrible-looking creature that hasn't said one word except to mumble incomprehensibly?

Therefore he was not surprised when she chose the next music break to excuse herself, leaving his heart pounding in his chest, overcome with regret at his lack of nerve for not saying who he was.

The music stopped, and three magicians appeared. One was as tall as two Aurelios, another as obese as the basilica's bell, and the third a midget who didn't measure over two feet in height. Following the obese man's introduction, the group began to perform exciting magic tricks that were almost impossible for the audience to uncover.

Subsequent to their act, six buffoons wearing tight colorful outfits appeared. One did nothing but face contortions and funny grimaces, while the other five entertained the audience with all kinds of unusual acrobatics. Immediately following the buffoon act, children wearing masks and costumes entered the ballroom offering flowers to those guests wearing male outfits.

After finding himself holding a bouquet of roses, Sikin presented them gallantly to Pulcinella without saying a word, then as quickly withdrew.

At the end of the intermission and on the opposite side of the room, Mariu asked Aurelio for another dance so they could talk. For starters, she inquired who would be the lucky lady to receive his flowers, to which he responded by pulling a small bunch from a pocket and offering it to her.

Flattered, Mariu pointed out that she had something very important to say.

"First of all," she began, "I will feel extremely disappointed if you ever consider yourself an intruder in our lives. Your mother needs you perhaps as much as you need her, and I'm willing to do everything in my power to see you grow in the midst of our family just as if you were of my own blood. Deep in my heart I know how much this would have meant to my beloved father. Therefore, Aurelio, in his memory I urge you to consider yourself as much a part my life as your mother's.

Aurelio, whose concealed eyes, were by then blurred with tears, took her hands under his mask and stamped on them a kiss.

Perceiving how upset and confused the young man was, she asked him to find Sikin and bring him to the rear of the room.

Doing exactly as he was told, Aurelio went after his older friend, who he found standing in the rear porch, overlooking the canal lonely and tormented. Moments later, Mariu climbed on to a makeshift platform, and after requesting everyone's attention, she began addressing the audience in a slightly broken voice.

"My dearest guests, this evening is a special occasion for all members and friends of the Da Ponte family, and for my beloved sister Tiblina in particular.

As most of you know, there are three mystery guests sharing with us this memorable evening, and I believe the time has come for me to introduce the first one of the three."

"Three?" Sikin whispered to Aurelio as the two eyed one another in puzzlement.

"The man you are about to meet has played a momentous role in my life during the last few months," Mariu continued. "He is a distinctive gentleman of impeccable character and noble attributes, a wonderful man I've learned to love, trust, and respect. This special person, ladies and gentlemen, has asked me to become his wife."

After loud "oohs" and "ahhhs" expressed by the surprised audience, Mariu gestured for silence…

321

"My future husband arrived from Genoa in pursuit of suitable investing opportunities in the silk trade. After meeting on several occasions, we discovered that in addition to common economic interests, we also shared an emotional and physical attraction for each other.

We met for the first time at the silk operation formerly owned by our family in Sicily. While there, we also enjoyed lots of free time together thus having the opportunity to appreciate each other's company for quite some time.

Besides being involved in a lucrative business, we are also delighting in a wonderful relationship.

Therefore, it is my sincere pleasure to present to you my business partner and husband to be. Ladies and gentlemen, please welcome Signore Dino de la Francesca!"

Sikin burst out laughing and clapped delightedly.

After a lengthy round of applause, Mariu announced, "May I please ask Il Capitano sitting on the chair by the window to remove his mask and come forward?"

The crowd cheered Dino as he made his way to the stage.

Sikin couldn't conceal his amazement on seeing his almost-forgotten friend from the Genoa Merchant Guild kiss Mariu.

After bowing to the wild audience, Dino added some words of humor regarding their meeting and relationship. He also mentioned the formation of a new partnership to repurchase the filature in Sicily and their plans to make the factory more efficient and competitive in the silk markets of Europe.

Saying he considered himself a very fortunate man, Dino confessed to admiring Mariu for everything she was and was not, adding that he felt more than ready to settle down and start a family with her. He also praised her social skills and love of life, stressing that he looked forward to developing new and meaningful relationships among the members of Mariu's family and her many friends.

Sikin, who couldn't wait much longer to reach the stage and greet his friend, slowly began to sneak forward, when Aurelio, with the speed of lightning, grabbed his tunic and told him to keep his sudden bravery under control and allow Mariu to run her own show.

"And now, ladies and gentlemen!" Mariu said, her voice quavering. "Allow me to introduce you to a most amazing man, a great family friend, and a loyal confidant." She beckoned to the "Plague Doctor," who slowly walked forward. "Once a stranger to our household, I came to love and appreciate this person like a brother."

"However, ladies and gentlemen," Mariu interrupted, raising her hand. "I'd like to take this opportunity to extend him an invitation to stay with us for as long as he wishes. My beloved friend is committed to returning to another land soon, a far away country much more advanced and sophisticated than our beloved Serenissima."

At this, everyone in the audience began to boo and whistle at the plague doctor for such an affront.

"I know he considers it a great misfortune not being able to stay with us forever,"

The audience switched from boos and whistles to applause and greetings.

"The main reason he feels this way is not just on account of his love and admiration for our noble city, but also because in it's midst, and with us tonight, the love of his life silently awaits him. And love, my dear friends, is the only human quality that transcends time and distance."

The onlooking guests hooted wildly.

"This friend, of whom I am so proud and to whom I owe so much, has gone beyond the unyielding laws of universal order to fulfill his commitment and devotion to the woman he adores.

And now, without further delay, I'd like to ask my brother Sikin, the second mystery guest, to remove his ugly mask, stop looking like a vulture, and reveal himself to the audience.

Ladies and gentlemen, it is my sincere pleasure to introduce the one and only ruling monarch of my sister's heart."

As the audience exploded in a round of enthusiastic shouting and applause, Sikin removed his hideous mask and searched the crowd for Tiblina, who, still masked, ran up to the stage and fell into her lover's arms.

Sikin tenderly lifted Pulcinella's mask and kissed Tiblina, who looked to him more beautiful than ever.

The audience gasped and murmured their joyous approval.

"And now, dear friends," Mariu said. "My last mystery guest promises to leave you speechless and awed by demonstrating once again how far-fetched expectations and impossible dreams can magically transform themselves into realities right before our incredulous eyes."

Mariu walked dramatically toward the back of the room until, halting in front of Aurelio, she swiftly pulled his mask off, grabbed his hand, and led him back to the stage where Dino, Sikin, and Tiblina awaited in suspense.

There she turned Aurelio's face towards his mother and said, "My dear sister, this is your beloved son!"

With a cry of anguished elation, Tiblina disentangled herself from Sikin's arms and stared for a moment at her son before crushing him to her, her tears flowing free.

Soon dozens of weeping, jubilant guests began to push their ways toward the front in an attempt to share with the new celebrities such a wonderful moment of rapture and delight.

Using the euphoric pandemonium to his advantage, Sikin quietly squeezed through the crowd toward the rear of the salon to watch from a distance the love of his life for the last time.

Then he rushed to the front door, hopefully unnoticed, and without bidding farewell or showing due courtesy to anyone, he ran from the house.

He could never deprive Tiblina of her immense happiness by bringing up his approaching departure, their relationship's new dimension, or the many other complex issues he would rather avoid altogether, he reasoned. He convinced himself that this was their opportunity to share, and that he should not infringe by standing in its midst.

Lastly, he didn't have the guts to face Aurelio whenever the inevitable farewell arrived.

Feeling like a coward, tired of breathing the same salty air, weary of playing his role, and enwrapped in terrible sorrow, the former American teenager trudged heavily and in silence toward the inn. It was a perfect evening for a stroll, the sounds of merriment echoing everywhere, but for Sikin, every step hurt all the way to the heart.

Caught in his own quagmire a deeply frustrated Sikin changed clothes and went to bed, wishing that some mystical power perhaps from his ancestors would take him back where he belonged. He didn't have the desire or the courage to induce his own teleportation anymore. Feeling impotent before adversity, he covered his head with the blanket in a desperate attempt to fall asleep.

Shortly thereafter, someone was already knocking at his door, prompting him to get up and answer the call.

It must be Paolo chasing the gossip and news of the party, he thought. *I'm sure he wants first hand information, just like in the old days. A horse can't change his colors.*

Well, what's the difference? I might not be here tomorrow anyway, so let him start digging.

With his mind still at full steam, Sikin opened the door.

To his amazement the caller wasn't Paolo. It was Tiblina, accompanied by Aurelio and a codega, angrily asking Sikin for permission to enter.

"After all the nice comments Mariu made about you," Tiblina said in now-perfect unaccented Italian. "The greatest of the great! Master of Wisdom! The glorious hero of the Da Ponte family! Then guess what? He escapes like a thief in the dark, leaving everyone behind, including Aurelio and me worrying about his sanity and wondering how he could be so rude to our family and guests."

She took a breath and continued her tirade.

"I've heard humiliating questions; 'If Sikin loved you so much, why did he run away?' 'Is he shy, or is he running away from the law?' Even the midget wondered, 'what was the name of the sophisticated country he came from?' I can't believe you were capable of doing us such a thing!"

"Oh, my love, I am so sorry. There is absolutely no excuse for my behavior." Sikin said remorsefuly, deeply embarrassed, his self-esteem bruised, and his fame for good judgment shattered.

After gathering more stamina, Tiblina continued her diatribe,

"Aurelio, who has seen in you the image of the father he never had and a reflection of the hero he dreams to become someday, gathered enough courage to step in and defend you!

He stood up on a chair, and after silencing the crowd with comments like 'I am the only person here, who knows the truth,' 'I know why he left unannounced' and 'Please listen to me,' my son finally gained control of the group. Then he explained remarkably well and with a reassuring smile, that in order for you to stay in Venice another day, you had to establish contact with some sort of entity and ask permission to stay longer. He said you followed this kind of ritual nightly and with religious dedication, and that you did it always before midnight. He added on your behalf that this time was no different except you had forgotten because of the great time you were having at the party. He also stressed that you, his living hero and role model, have never neglected a responsibility, much less run away from friends.

After finishing his little speech, Aurelio asked the guests for patience and understanding, promising to visit the spot where your contact usually takes place and then bring you back to the party safe and sound."

Tiblina stamped her elegant foot.

"The incredible part of this whole episode was seeing how many guests were gullible enough to believe Aurelio's story. In fact one of them offered his personal codega to accompany us to the mysterious spot and bring you back."

"So get dressed, and let's go!" Tiblina by now was trying to conceal a smile that unrestrained would have changed into a loud laughter.

On their way back, Sikin used all the kind words left in his repertoire to placate Tiblina's frustration and disappointment. He also asked for Aurelio's help to bring sense to his mother. Finally, since he wasn't making any progress with words, Sikin decided to offer something more substantial.

"Tell me what I must do to bring our relationship back to the way it was before. Ask me for riches. Ask me for the fulfillment of a dream. Ask for my own life if it pleases you. Ask me for anything in the world, for anything in my power, and I'll make it happen!"

"Aurelio, what kind of atonement do you think would be appropriate?" Asked his mother.

"There is only one thing in the world I'd like to see you do," the young man replied.

"Well, say it! For goodness sake, speak!"

"Staying with us longer will be compensation enough, at least from my point of view. How about you, Mother? What do you think he should do to deserve forgiveness?"

Tiblina paused ominously. "I don't think he needs to go beyond that," she finally said, "and I'll be more than satisfied if he accepts."

"Well, Sikin. What do you say to that?" His young friend asked.

Sikin sighed with relief and contentment.

"If that's all you want, I shall definitely stay longer, perhaps another year or so, if you don't mind. But then I must go back home for sure."

"All right, then." Aurelio said following his mother's nod of approval.

Shortly past midnight, the three made their appearance back at the palazzo, where the music had mellowed, and conversation became subdued.

As they entered the mansion, no one seemed to pay much attention to the fact that they were coming back together.

Sikin felt greatly relieved. He had imagined everyone jumping all over him, asking questions and cracking jokes about his unexpected disappearance, but everyone was busy drinking and eating, talking, laughing, singing and dancing, napping, or doing whatever suited their fancies.

Leaving Tiblina and Aurelio behind, Sikin took the opportunity to apologize to Mariu in private for his immature behavior, blaming his indiscretions on a state of confusion resulting from a combination of recent events and vin santo.

"What are you talking about?" She replied. "We all assumed

you'd stepped out for a breath of fresh air. As a matter of fact, I thought it was quite considerate to leave Tiblina and Aurelio alone for a while. Why are you making such a big fuss about something so unimportant?"

Puzzled, Sikin described Tiblina's displeasure and mentioned how grateful he felt towards Aurelio for explaining to the guests the reason for his misconduct. He also told Mariu of his commitment to stay longer in order to make up for his actions.

Mariu couldn't wait any longer to explode in laughter, prompting Sikin to realize that he had become the victim of a trick carried out by mother and son to prevent him from leaving. But instead of being upset by their shady tactics, Sikin felt relieved the whole episode was nothing but a scam. In fact, he began to laugh at himself, realizing he couldn't feel any happier.

"And now, my dear brother," Mariu continued, "when will you bring your things from that hostel? Oh, Sikin! We'll be so thrilled to share our home with you! What do you say to that?"

"The truth is that I'd love to," Sikin said hesitantly. "I know Aurelio is a welcome addition to the clan, but my case is different. If Tiblina and I become too involved, she will suffer in the end, and so will I."

"Sikin," Mariu said impatiently, "I think is about time you start living in the *present*. Don't be so concerned about what might happen afterwards. After all, your future is now! Stop planning your life around avoiding suffering. Sometimes is better to risk pain and enjoy a relationship, than avoid love and joy because you could suffer later. Tiblina and you are sufficiently mature to understand that everything in life has a beginning and an end, and when the latter comes around you have to accept it gracefully. In the meantime, why not enjoy each other's company? Don't you see that the future is the source of all worries? Always try to remember the words of St. John of the Cross, 'If a man wishes to be sure of the road he treads on, he must close his eyes and walk in the dark.'"

Mariu fixed him with a compassionate gaze. "What's your alternative? Go back to your land, avoid complications, and live the rest of your life burdened by regrets? You've already lost her once. For God's sake, enjoy the precious moment! She deserves it and so do you. Now stop wasting time and go tell her how much you want her, as I am sure she will respond in kind."

She held up a finger. "One more thing. I'd like to see you become a father and brother to Aurelio; even if is only for a limited time. You exert a tremendous influence on the boy, who is at a vulnerable age, and needs to identify with a role model. That model, my friend, is you! Offer your sincere friendship, and let him copy your irreproachable values. Become the mirror to his future.

This time you must listen to your heart, Sikin. Take this marvelous opportunity to bring your spirit to life. Don't you see? Tiblina, my friend, is the life of your spirit."

"Perhaps you are right," Sikin replied after a moment of reflection. "It all sounds so wonderful!"

"You are most welcome to use the large room on the upper floor. It has a beautiful view of the Grand Canal. And think about, Sikin; why not stay forever?" Her face lit up in a trademark smile.

The party was far from over for Sikin, Dino, Mariu, Aurelio, and Tiblina. The musicians were long gone, the servants had already cleaned up, the street in front was empty, and the only ones left inside were the five of them, who didn't care in the least how late it was. Other than an occasional passerby carrying a lamp or a handful of drunks singing loudly and clinging to each other, the only perceptible sound came from the basilica's bells marking the passage of the hours.

***

Four months following Carnival, after setting up a second home in Sicily, Dino and Mariu became husband and wife. Both liked the excitement of commerce and the creation of wealth perhaps as much as they liked each other. Sometimes with Dino and sometimes on her own, Mariu made a point to visit Venice at least every two months.

In spite of difficulties arising from the distance, Tiblina and her loyal sister remained as inseparable as always, with even more to share than when they lived under the same roof.

Tiblina, Sikin, and Aurelio remained at the Palazzo along with the servants. Tiblina dedicated most of her days to taking care of the orphanage, while Sikin, unable to find a meaningful occupation that would only last a year or so, assisted her with the children as well as maintaining the building.

Aurelio attended an institution where he learned literature, arts, and government. The young man decided to choose bureaucracy and politics as his future career in order to bring about, as he said, "justice to those without a voice."

He vowed to prove that a politician doesn't have to be crooked to survive their competitive and ruthless environment, unlike his grandfather, who had ruined hundreds of lives.

The young man absorbed Sikin's experiences and teachings like a sponge. The two became so close that Sikin took care to make sure that Aurelio's thoughts and values were primarily his own, and not exact replicas of his or someone else's.

The young man adored his new family and vice versa.

Without much to do or clean at the mansion anymore since their "slave driver" stayed in Sicily most of the time, the faithful household maids have acquired the dubious habit of pampering and spoiling Aurelio, who unlike a fool has eagerly adapted to the lifestyle of a prince, thus enjoying the sweet life as much as he could.

Sikin warned that so much pampering would have a negative effect on Aurelio's character and personality. Tiblina on the other hand believed that her son was different, and thus immune to such concerns.

Sikin and Paolo continued to see each other often. Married to the head servant of the Da Ponte's mansion made it easier for them to share conversation, which was usually fueled by gossip and stories from the grapevine.

One day, after discovering that his former boss was in Venice, Naguib decided to cross the sea and bring his whole family to visit the city, his old friends, and the man who made him wealthy and free.

Sikin and Tiblina finally attained their life's dream of living for each other one day at a time, willfully avoiding conversations and thoughts about their future.

They loved to take the family gondola out during late afternoon, to cruise the busy, colorful canals in pursuit of spectacular sunsets and starry nights. They also spent time visiting friends in the nearby islands.

One year and four months following the masquerade party, Sikin's inevitable departure finally became a reality. Just as the law of gravity brings down the rock that has been thrown aloft, just as birds migrate before the approaching winter and the sun rises and sets without fail, the inexorable qualities of time ultimately triumph over all existing matter. Sikin, too had to follow his destiny and return to the land of his future. Therefore, one quiet summer evening, shortly before sunset, just like the rock, the birds, and the sun, Sikin quietly returned to the time and place where it all started.

THE END

Epilogue

To make his exhortations readily available to the public, Ivan McKinley decided to write and publish his memoirs instead of challenging live audiences. As a result, his teleportation experiences were thought provoking and fun to read, but no one ever believed their authenticity. Alas, instead of passing wisdom and enlightment to future generations as intended by the Druid priest, Ivan McKinley became one of the most celebrated novelists of the times.

Faced with humankind's reluctance to learn from the lessons of history and disenchanted with his plan, the ancient cleric finally withdrew Ivan's teleportation privileges.

A final note: Not intended to compete against Ivan's previously published works, this novel, also a compilation of his diaries, makes a final appeal to its readers to listen to the voices of the past and to the wisdom of the ages.

Aknowledgements

Carol Gaskin, editor and friend from Editorial Alchemy for her expertise and support.

The following authors and books:
"Coleridge Poems"
Editor: William Sharp.
Prefatory notice: Joseph Skipsey.
Published by The Walter Scott Publishing Co. Ltd. 1884
Registered in England, No. 04017216 VAT Number 763 0857 17

"The Travels of Marco Polo, the Venetian"
Editor: Ernest Rhys
Introduction: John Masefield
Publisher: J.M. Dent and Sons, Ltd. in London
                E.P. Dutton & Co. in New York
First Edition: 1908
Reprinted: 1911, 1914, 1918, and 1921
For details about Asia and the Silk Road during the Middle Ages, the Celestial City of Kinsay, the lifestyle of Kublai Khan, the description of his palaces, etc.

"The Interpretation of Dreams"
Author: Prof. Sigmund Freud, LL.D.
Authorized translation of third edition with introduction by A.A. Brill, Ph.B., M.D.
Published by: George Allen & Unwin, Ltd. in London
The Mac Millan Co. in New York
Published April 1913 and re-printed May 1913 and November 1913. Revised edition: December 1915, reprinted December 1916. Printed in Great Britain by Turnbull & Spears.
For data regarding the anthropological notion of dreams and conceptualization during the early nineteenth century

"Memoirs of an Arabian Princess"
Authored by Emily Ruete
Translated by Lionel Strachey
Published by Doubleday, Page & Co. in 1907
Copyright 1907 by Doubleday, Page, and Co.,
Published September 1907.
For offering a general idea of the rituals and traditions in an Arab wedding

Other data sources:
Encyclopaedia Britannica
The National Geographic
Encarta Encyclopaedia
Catholic Encyclopaedia
Literature from the Parc Naturel Regional de Camargue
Miscellaneous resources